CAREER GAME

LOUISE BAGSHAWE, NOW WRITING AS ...

LOUISE MENSCH

CAREER GAME

headline
review

First published in Great Britain in 2015 by
HEADLINE REVIEW
An imprint of HEADLINE PUBLISHING GROUP

1

Cataloguing in Publication Data is available from the British Library

ISBN 978 0 7553 5900 4 (Hardback)
ISBN 978 0 7553 5901 1 (Trade Paperback)

Typeset in Meridien by Avon DataSet Ltd,
Bidford-on-Avon, Warwickshire

Printed and bound in Great Britain by Clays Ltd, St Ives plc

MIX
Paper from
responsible sources
FSC® C104740
FSC
www.fsc.org

Headline's policy is to use papers that are natural, renewable and
recyclable products and made from wood grown in well-managed
forests and other controlled sources. The logging and manufacturing
processes are expected to conform to the environmental regulations
of the country of origin.

HEADLINE PUBLISHING GROUP
An Hachette UK Company
Carmelite House
50 Victoria Embankment
London EC4Y 0DZ

www.headline.co.uk
www.hachette.co.uk

To Michael Sissons and Fiona Petheram –
thanks for a wonderful adventure.

Chapter One

'Ladies and gentlemen – please welcome to the Rock 'n' Roll Hall of Fame, the one, the only, the legend – Rowena Krebs!'

The packed hall burst into thunderous applause. Coloured spotlights swept the stage, back and forth, as piped music played, a real blast from the past, 'Tender Trap', an Atomic Mass number one hit. The audience shot to their feet – rock stars, pop idols, mega-producers, record company moguls, and big-shot managers: anybody who was anybody was at the annual Hall of Fame ceremony.

This was for all time. For the immortals.

If you made it to Cleveland, music called you a king.

Or a queen.

Rowena Krebs swept on to the stage. She was a goddess: statuesque, beautiful, blonde hair piled regally on top of her head. There weren't many forty-two-year-olds who could pull off cream chiffon and diamonds, but Rowena floated in a long, lean gown of buttermilk fabric that clung to her slim frame, setting off her natural tan and her toned back and arms. There was that eternal confidence and poise, reflecting the drive that had seen her become the first woman ever to run a global record label. She had dominated a man's world for the past twenty years.

Rowena Krebs was missing nothing tonight but an actual crown.

1

A collar of diamonds fit for a Russian empress glittered around her long neck. Under the lights they sparkled wildly, her own personal firework display, flashing reds, greens and blues in their explosion of light. On her left hand was her engagement ring, a huge five-carat rock from super-producer Michael Krebs, twenty years her elder and the subject of vicious rumours since the day they'd first met.

Krebs could be a son of a bitch, and jealous rivals whispered that his wife wasn't much better. He'd been inducted in the Hall of Fame years ago, of course, alongside Dr Dre and Mutt Lange, as one of the most successful rock producers in the history of music. Now Rowena was going to score another Krebs triumph. They were music's ultimate power couple, and this was their night.

TV monitors zoomed in on Rowena's husband. Michael Krebs sat there basking in the applause, his eyes fixed on his wife. Krebs was bald and thickset, the muscles in his chest and arms clearly visible through the tuxedo he hated having to wear. Even at sixty, he was strictly a T-shirt and jeans guy. Decades of weight-lifting had given him a firm military bearing, and the dark eyes fringed with heavy black lashes were still hypnotically sexy. That cruel stare was now focused on Rowena, full of desire. Krebs was staring at his wife as though he could hardly wait to get her back in their penthouse suite and rip that elegant dress right off her. Several women in the audience groaned a little under their breath as the camera shot caught the expression on his face; there were sidelong glances at husbands.

It was a famously obsessive love affair. Lust and possession were written all over Michael's face, and the TV monitors showed it.

The applause and whistling reached a towering crescendo. Rowena smiled at the audience – and the cameras. Then she lifted one hand for silence.

She was just an executive – but she had the presence of a star.

'Thank you. Thank you all so much.'

More cheering.

'This is an incredible honour. Mostly, it'll just stop Michael lording it over me at home quite so much.'

The audience laughed. Cameras shot to Krebs, who shook his head slightly. More laughter.

'But I have to thank him – he's been key to my career. As has everybody at Musica Records. My close friend, the legendary manager Barbara Lincoln. Atomic Mass, who started everything for me in that pub in Sheffield. It's so good to see them still touring today. Most of all, though, I want to remember Joshua Oberstein. When I started in business, men didn't mentor women. He changed all of that. Josh was like a father to me. I hope that all of us here tonight remember to pull at least one other person up the ladder behind us.'

She raised her golden statuette to the heavens.

'You took a chance, Josh, and I love you. This is for you.'

A huge picture of the old man's face filled the screens beside her, and the sound of applause swelled to take over the hall once again. Everybody here remembered the legendary mogul, and respect for Rowena doubled throughout the room.

Closing music started to swell up at the podium, but Rowena Krebs wasn't quite done. She leaned closer to the mike.

'Oh, and Topaz Rossi,' she said. 'Thanks for making it interesting.'

Topaz Rossi's apartment stretched the entire twentieth floor of the building, and she liked to take advantage.

She was up early. It was her habit to make a steaming mug of fragrant cinnamon coffee and take it out to the balcony to watch the sun rise. This morning the weather was perfect. The city was peaceful at this hour, and Topaz's balcony was a garden in the sky; as dawn light filtered through the leaves and flowers that surrounded her, she sipped from her bone-china mug, savouring the rich taste, carving out a little space for herself before the chaos of the day and the city took over.

Below her, Central Park spread out like a green carpet, fringed on every side by skyscrapers, museums, and high-rise buildings. Sunshine glinted on the windscreens of the cars crawling like ants towards Manhattan, the centre of the universe.

To Topaz Rossi, New York was still the most exciting city on earth. And she was on top of it in more ways than one. Literally, in her sky garden. And metaphorically, as she ruled the roost at American Magazines, where as publisher-in-chief she was finally at the apex of the country's biggest stable of monthly glossies; everything from fashion to finance was covered in the slickly designed titles that Topaz Rossi's team pumped out each month. She was the undisputed heavyweight champ in the industry.

Topaz Rossi had only ever had two rivals. One, Rowena Gordon, now Krebs, was once again her best friend – even if she lived thousands of miles away on the laid-back Californian coast. The other, who had briefly defeated her, was Joe Goldstein, now her husband.

Years ago, Joe had left magazines to head into television, and last year he had agreed to take over the moribund National American Broadcasting Network, or NAB. So now the Goldsteins were two major powers in Manhattan media – and with two kids into the bargain, Topaz felt she deserved her rooftop oasis, and the private, peaceful ritual that set her up for the morning.

No lie, it cost a ton. But it was worth every red cent.

New York City was renowned for many things, but 'space' and 'quiet' were not amongst them. If you wanted 'country,' you could get it every summer in the Hamptons, *if* you had the kind of life that would allow you to be two and a half hours' drive from the action.

Topaz Rossi and Joe Goldstein wanted the high life: the great views, the sprawling layout, and – most importantly for the

Italian-American girl from the back streets of the Bronx who'd somehow managed to get herself a Rhodes Scholarship to Oxford University – something green, private and leafy, a quiet backyard where they could go to decompress.

Hence the extra half-mil and nine months' worth of planting. Every inch was used, from the railings to the walls, and on a summer morning like today, Topaz Rossi, high-heeled killer queen, was just a girl in a Mediterranean bower.

The cinnamon-scented coffee was delicious. She lay back on her sunlounger and enjoyed the view.

Her roof garden was designed in 'rooms', outdoor spaces so you could shift your mood: verdant moss in one corner with a reflecting pool and Zen stones, a gravel garden for Joe to contemplate in, while Topaz's side of the terrace concentrated on her Sicilian heritage. Rosemary thickly scented the air in pots under a pair of silver-leaved olive trees, and lemon blossoms grew against dark glossy leaves behind her, while hardy climbing roses scaled the high walls.

Topaz contemplated the green expanse of Central Park below her, basking in the warm morning. Soon she would pull on her running gear and walk back through the apartment, very quietly, so as not to wake her husband. The kids, asleep in their bedrooms, wouldn't hear her now if she stomped like an elephant; they'd probably crashed to bed late again, even though it was a school day. Joe was another matter.

Topaz loved this time. She finished her drink slowly, staring up at the white fluffy clouds. Soon she'd be hitting the running trail, up to Central Park's boating lake and around it, through the trees, pounding her way over the horse-riding paths. It was perfect, a little slice of the country – well, almost – in the midst of town, better than other city parks, bigger, more splendid; Manhattan knew what it was doing. The space was designed to shield the concrete walls of the city from view wherever possible. Before 9 a.m., dogs could be walked off the lead; her run involved dodging greyhounds and spaniels and enthusiastic mutts, waving at the community of early risers who were getting it done, like her, before the day kicked off. And there were runners and walkers everywhere, shirtless men out on the lawns pressing their bodies to the ground, or hauling themselves up from branches, making time for fitness. The city was full of life, and the biggest achievers regarded taking care of their bodies as an investment; from 5 till 7.30, runners were everywhere you looked, along the sea walls and the Hudson River, down amongst the docks, racing round the East River and through the parks. Central Park, her local, was at the very hub.

Topaz jotted some notes on a pad, setting herself up for the day. The summer issues were arriving, and later she needed to co-ordinate, to knock her editors' heads together. As chief executive, everything depended on her. Fashion, housing, financials . . . American Magazines covered the gamut, and Topaz was hands-on over content. She had edited half these magazines at some point in her brilliant career, and finally she was the top dog in the company. Top bitch? Some would say so. No doubt about that. But this was New York, and you didn't make it here without riling a few people.

Like Topaz cared. *My way or the highway.*

She drained her coffee, the scent of cinnamon mixing with the lemon blossoms and her kitchen herbs. Still feeling a little tired, she sprang to her feet. Time to get going – exhaustion was no excuse. The answer to that was action. *Just Do It?* Best slogan ever.

She padded inside to her enormous walk-in closet and pulled on her running gear. The body reflected in the mirror showed off her good habits, and she smiled. Topaz was still curvy, still firm; her ass jutted out from lean, strong thighs and a cinched-in, worked-out waist. Even after three kids her breasts were high and full, surgically lifted but all hers, and pretty much perfect. She ran her ass off and lifted weights, and it showed.

That sexy figure still collected whistles on the street.

She thought about Joe, smiling. Her husband was just as fine. He boxed four times a week and took mixed martial arts; once out of his sweats or karate robes, he switched to his perfect Savile Row suits and ties, a complement to his chestnut-brown hair and dark eyes. There were few accessories; typically just a thick platinum Rolex and the air of confidence that came with success.

It would be another good, busy day in the office. Topaz laced up her sneakers and prepared to take charge of her morning.

The limousine was waiting at the kerb. Krebs shook a few more hands, received congratulations. Then he went to find Rowena. She was standing in a group of rock stars, most of them younger than her, all the men looking at her with longing in their eyes, that mix of desire and fear he was so used to seeing. The girls – there was that twenty-year-old bassist from Crater, this year's rock sensation – were simply gazing at her with moonstruck adoration.

Rowena Krebs was one of the world's truly powerful women. No guitar, no mike; she wasn't a rock star or pop singer. Instead, as president of Musica Records, she bought and sold them. And they loved her for it.

'Time to roll.' Krebs strode over, breaking up the group. He placed his hand on the small of Rowena's back, splaying two fingers over the keyhole shape in her gown, stroking her bare skin. He felt the immediate, electric reaction to his touch; she straightened, as though shocked; shivers ran through her skin. She was superbly, helplessly responsive, and it excited him. The younger men scattered; the dominant male was marking his turf.

'Thanks for taking the time, Rowena.'

'Congratulations, Rowena.'

'It was such an honour to meet you.'

'Damn it, I'm going to boast about this all year.'

'Sign to Musica,' Rowena told them lightly, pressing herself back against Krebs's fingers. 'Then we can talk every day.' She turned to face Michael, her admirers forgotten. 'Car's ready?'

He nodded. 'This way.'

'Hey, what's the rush?' Jefé, a million-selling rapper whose record was crouched like a tiger at the top of the charts, held up one hand, thick with knuckle-duster rings of solid gold, obviously unwilling to let Rowena go. He looked sullenly at Michael Krebs, challenging him. The older man was a legendary producer, sure, but he'd been out of the game for years now, sitting on the goddamned beach in Malibu or whatever. What right did he have to hang on to a babe as fine as this one? Rowena Krebs was the ultimate trophy wife. This woman was class.

He scowled. 'Getting an early night? Let the lady stay. If your plane leaves, I can always buy you guys some fresh tickets.' He grinned, displaying white teeth filled with solid gold. 'First class.'

'That's nice of you.' Krebs looked the younger man right in the face. 'But we head out tomorrow, and our plane leaves when I say it leaves. We're on a private jet.'

The other guys in the group snickered, and the rapper flushed a dark red. Goddamn, that was some kind of a burn. He inclined his head to Krebs in reluctant admiration.

'Good night,' Rowena said. She followed her man out without a backwards glance.

'That's ballin', man,' one of Jefé's hangers-on said to him. 'They're legends. And that ass is smoking hot.'

'Meh.' He shrugged, masking his jealousy. 'She'll get tired of the old man soon. And you know, both of them are dinosaurs. That's what "legend" means, right?' He stared back at the huge ballroom, waving dismissively at the black-tie crowd, the jewels, the spotlights. 'That's what happens here. You come and get buried.' He grabbed a flute of champagne from a passing waitress. 'It's our time now.' There were sycophantic hoots of agreement. 'Krebs and the Ice Queen are finished.'

* * *

The hotel suite had been meticulously prepared. There was more champagne, unopened, in a silver bucket, and dozens of red roses, artful designer arrangements of peony and iris, clouds of scented daffodils and narcissi filled the room. Half the record industry was paying tribute to Rowena Krebs. Nobody wanted to be forgotten. Other gifts were scattered around – baskets of scents from Floris, Charbonnel and Walker chocolates, Americans paying tribute to Rowena's British roots.

'All very sweet,' she commented as Krebs shut the door behind them, pressing the 'Do Not Disturb' button and sliding the old-fashioned chain on to its latch. 'Do we have to find out who they're from?'

'The concierge can catalogue them. And send the flowers to a local hospital.'

'That'll take him forever.' Rowena took in the profusion of blooms, ribbons, cut-crystal vases.

'I tipped him five hundred bucks.'

She laughed. 'Then I guess it's fine.'

There was a stab of fresh desire. Michael took charge, always. Whatever they needed, he had already thought of it.

He came up to her, eyes sweeping over her gown. It was the same predatory look he'd given her at the Hall of Fame, but now, the TV lights gone and the audience vanished, Rowena could see it too. She breathed in sharply.

Krebs moved closer, crowding her, standing over her, his lips inches from her face. Her breath came faster, her body warming, opening. She was wet and excited. She had seen this look from him before, a thousand times. She knew what came next.

'Nice dress,' he said shortly. 'Take it off.'

Rowena reached up behind her back, her fingers struggling with the hook and eye. Krebs didn't help her. The gown, her haute couture confection of buttery chiffon, slithered down her body to pool on the floor. She was there before him, her small, sweet breasts in a strapless bra, her panties a scrap of coffee-coloured lace, bare, toned legs tapering down to Manolo Blahnik heels.

Krebs felt himself harden further. Rowena was luscious, delicious. And his. He reached behind her back, loosened her bra, threw it away. Her little apple breasts were warm, welcoming in his hands, the nipples sharp with wanting against the roughness of his palms.

'Hair,' he said thickly.

She whimpered and raised her arms, pulling the pins from her long blonde hair, allowing it to tumble endlessly down her back. It reached almost halfway down; she never shortened it, never gave in to fashion. He played with her breasts, constantly, mercilessly, still fully dressed, as she struggled to control herself, rubbing her thighs together.

'All these kudos. Great. Wouldn't do for you to get an attitude. Right?'

'Right,' she managed, soaking wet for him, so hot she could hardly stand. Krebs yanked her panties down around her thighs, cupping her, trailing one finger backwards and forwards over the slit of her pussy, teasing. 'Oh God, Michael, please . . .'

'Please?' He grinned, moving closer, taking her in his arms, nude against the fabric of his suit. 'Is that what you said? I didn't hear you right.' His hand was under her ass now, caressing her, warming her. 'Say it again.'

'I need you . . . God, please, baby . . .'

He slid one finger inside her, caressing the heat and warmth of her belly. She was his, completely his. Still hot and helpless for him every night, every time he reached for her. Krebs wanted to laugh with pure triumph, draw it out, *really* make her suffer with wanting, the way she liked to, the way they both liked. But he was too hot for her to wait. He scooped her into his arms, her slim body nothing against his muscled frame, and carried her over to the bed.

There was a huge mirror opposite them, covering the whole of one wall. Krebs ripped off his jacket, his shirt, unzipped the front of his pants, and pinned Rowena's hands over her head, pushing her legs apart. She gasped in pleasure, turning her head to see her husband moving over her.

'It's like they knew we were coming,' Krebs said, and bent his head to her, grinning, holding her tight as he took her.

Joe Goldstein was hung-over. The night before had been heavy: the cast and crew of NAB's biggest hit series, *Summerside*, were celebrating the record-breaking viewing figures for the series finale. The network's board of directors wanted him to schmooze with the guys, all of them, in the faint hope that the showrunners would come up with a spin-off. The end of *Summerside* meant the end of five years of top ratings and advertising dollars, even in this incredibly fractured world. And that scared NAB.

Dan Patrice and Jordan Ballot were hardly geniuses in the world of the one-hour drama. But they owned the modern police procedural, and it was all because of the megawatt sex appeal of one woman.

Summerside's cranky, gorgeous star, brunette bombshell Maria Gonzales, had decided she'd just about had enough, and her legions of fans were going with her. Desperate to hang on to some of her magic, Goldstein's bosses ordered him to stay up, show up, and smile. If Maria wouldn't do another *Summerside*, better get her for something else.

Joe hated this crap. The executive suite wasn't meant for ego-stroking. The network's dependence on Gonzales had aggravated him for the last two seasons of *Summerside*, but nobody wanted to rock the boat. As the new chief exec, Joe was meant to improve NAB's financials and leave the programming directors in charge of their content. Only they were failing. NAB's old, tired schedule just stunk, and last night's party didn't mask the stench of desperation around the place.

Joe's head thumped. He looked at his watch. The kids were

late for school. They'd already missed the bus. Damn it, where the hell was Topaz? Running again? OK, so it was his morning to make breakfast, but Topaz should have known, should have realised. After all, she knew he had to go to the *Summerside* wrap party last night. How was he going to be fit to make breakfast?

'Get up,' he barked towards the kids' rooms, and winced at the pain pounding through his skull.

'Whatever,' came the reply behind the left-hand door.

'Rona, what the hell.' Enraged, Goldstein strode into his daughter's room, turned up the lights, and pulled the covers off her. 'Get dressed in the next five minutes or I swear you're grounded this weekend. I don't want another meeting with the principal.'

'Fascist,' she said, but she swung her long legs out of bed. He could hear the sound of his son showering in the en-suite bathroom behind her wall.

They'd be ready shortly, dozy and ill-prepared. Joe grabbed his cell phone and called the garage, telling them to have his car ready. Because of these two entitled, lazy teenage jerks, he was going to be late to the office, that is, if *he* wanted to shower.

'Better get a muffin from the fridge. That's your breakfast. I don't have time.'

'Dad,' David said. 'That's not breakfast.'

Rona emerged from her room in jeans and a dark shirt, her still-wet hair in a ponytail, her dark eyes sleepy.

'Get up earlier, then. Don't stay up on school nights playing World of Bullshit.'

Goldstein slammed the door to his bathroom while the kids sniggered. He was furious with himself and them, with Topaz, with Maria Gonzales, with the company, with the whole goddamned world.

Just another day in paradise.

Chapter Two

American Magazines' head office took up the whole of the thirtieth floor. They were sited on Sixth Avenue, just south of NewsCorp, in a flashy building designed in the 1990s by some prize-winning architect. Half the windows were mirrored in triangular panes, so wherever you stood on the street, reflecting light flashed in a harlequin pattern, moving with the sun and your eyes. The building thrust into the air like a glass volcano, always burning, always sparking. Like Topaz Rossi herself.

She got there early, whenever possible. The day went a lot better when you bought yourself just a little time to think.

And today, Topaz needed to think.

The circulation figures for last month were in. And they were not good. More importantly, American was losing where it really counted: advertising dollars. That was the secret of success in her business. You could have the hottest fashion spreads in the world, or the slickest architecture, and still not make it. Readers, like men, could scent desperation. They wanted magazines heavy with glossy adverts, magazines that smelled like success, with more to read, more to love.

'Good morning, Karl.'

'Good morning, Ms Rossi.' The guard at reception was just starting his shift and was still a little tired, but the sight of Topaz Rossi always perked him up.

'Anybody in yet?'

'Not to the executive suite. No, ma'am.'

'That's OK. You and me, we got things covered.'

He chuckled. 'Yes, ma'am.'

She was a great boss. Kept a list of all the guards in her office, her secretary told him once. The receptionists too, and the folks on the switchboard. She memorised names, and she took time for a connection with all of them.

American Magazines ran a tight ship. Nobody leaked under Topaz. The little guys didn't want to, and the bigger guys didn't dare.

It would please her that she was first in. Hyper-competitive, that chick. A real type-A New Yorker. And once you were the boss, who was left to compete with?

'Have a great day,' Topaz said. She waved her pass, walked through the electric gates that swished open to admit her, and headed left, to the executive elevators.

There was a coffee machine in Topaz's office and a little fridge, and she fussed around, fixing herself a cup. The rich, warm scent filled the room. Topaz was buzzed from her run, her breakfast. Even the bad figures; she liked having a problem to solve. Behind her kidney-shaped desk, a huge window looked over the avenue and into Midtown, framing the rush-hour traffic crawling below, the news tickers on the side of the building opposite. American Magazines was in media central, and you could watch camera crews filming on the street half the time. Topaz enjoyed the location: right next to a subway station, so you could zip anywhere you wanted in the city. She had never been a limousine kind of girl. What, sit in gridlock and waste time?

Her computer hummed and the company's figures scrolled on her screen. Topaz sipped her coffee, ignoring the view behind her and the rising sun flooding Manhattan with light. She couldn't be distracted. The figures were even worse than their public circulation sheets had announced. They were truly bad.

What the hell was going on?

Tapping her fingers, she pulled up graphs and laid them over each other. *Economic Monthly. Lotus. American Girl. Newsbreak. Home and Hearth. Rock Life. Travelista.* There were some duds and some spikes: *American Girl* had been dropping readers like flies for the last four months. Joanna Watson, the new editor they'd hired from Canada, just wasn't working out. Every issue was a disaster. Topaz resolved to fire her. Today. She'd only hesitated because her rule was to give any manager at least six months; things often got worse before they got better. But Joanna wasn't clicking, and the drops in circulation were too big to ignore on their flagship title.

Topaz was going with her instinct. This was the worst part of her job – the worst part of any executive's job. Still had to be done, though. She owed it to Ms Watson to see her face to face, and not hand the bad news off to the head of Human Resources. That was the coward's way out.

Better get it out of the way, fast.

She put *American Girl* and Joanna Watson out of her mind, and moved on.

Travelista was good. Susan Lewis had taken over there. For some reason the little travel title was ahead of the game. It was gaining readers, and advertisers had increased bookings. Of course, Topaz couldn't get too excited. Susan was starting from a low base after all.

Home and Hearth, *Newsbreak*, and *Economic Monthly* were a puzzle, though. These titles had had no major changes, and yet their numbers were sinking at alarming rates. She had the same team, so what could explain this cross-title stiffing?

There's an answer, Topaz told herself. You just haven't found it yet.

A door opened in the outer office.

'Brad?'

'Yes, Ms Rossi?'

Her secretary appeared in the doorway, immaculately dressed as always in a Brooks Brothers suit. Brad was young and handsome and unfazed by people's assumptions about executive assistants. Topaz had liked him when she'd met him on a business trip to LA, where he was a junior concierge at a hotel she was staying in, and had hired him on the spot. Manhattan seemed like a great change of scene, and Brad Wilkins was sick of overpaid actors and stressed-out agents. He took the job in a second.

'I'm hungry.'

'Yes, ma'am. You're always hungry.'

She grinned. 'I run a lot. Can you rustle me up a bowl of salted cashew nuts and walnuts?'

'Right away.'

'And schedule a meeting with Joanna Watson, first thing.'

'I'll see when she's got a gap in her appointments.'

'I don't care about her appointments. Tell her assistant to cancel her first one and send her up here. Immediately afterwards, I want to see Lucy Klein, her deputy.'

'Certainly,' Brad said. 'Would you like me to give her assistant a heads-up to have her car ready to go?'

Topaz smiled. Brad was no dummy. He was studying for the bar at nights, and then she'd lose him to business affairs as a lawyer. Frankly she hoped he flunked. She'd never had a better secretary.

'Yes. As you correctly guessed, I'm firing her. Confidential, of course. As soon as she's left her office to come and see me, have security change the password on her corporate email account, her computer, and so forth, and cancel her security pass.'

'Yes, ma'am.' Brad suppressed a wince. Topaz Rossi didn't mess around. The chance that the disgruntled editor would resort to sabotage was small, but it existed. So Topaz made sure it didn't happen. 'I'll go get your snacks.'

His boss wasn't listening. Her eyes were fixed on her screen, trying to see a pattern, trying to figure out something she wasn't used to.

Failure. On her watch.

Joe Goldstein sat at the head of the table and tried to get a hold of his temper. He'd left two messages on Topaz's cell already. She'd ignored both of them. Why did that woman never look at her cell?

David and Rona were late again, bitching at *him* for not getting them up. He would hear it from Dr Raynor, the principal at Pointer Academy. Probably another letter from the disciplinary committee. His twins were close to getting chucked out of that school, despite the hundreds of thousands he'd donated to their fund-raisers. You couldn't buy discipline, it turned out. His head thudded from the hangover, only partly muffled by Advil and coffee. His mouth felt like a garbage can. Fuck. He was too old for this, too old to be partying like a goddamned teenager because a bunch of tired old farts wanted him to suck up to some creative geniuses in love with themselves and their stupid projects.

'Did you stay till the party was over, Joe? Tell me you didn't leave early,' Harvey Bostock said.

Goldstein swallowed a sigh.

'Yes, I stayed until the end of the evening.'

He looked around the room. NAB's board of directors was staring back at him. Harvey Bostock, the chairman, all-powerful at the company. Jack Travis, the dotcom entrepreneur, thirty-eight and sharp, already a billionaire, who owned a big slice of the network. Emma Sanderson, a Harvard grad and PR guru, appointed to the board for PR purposes following a class-action lawsuit for sexism under his predecessor. Personally Goldstein thought Emma was worse than useless. Lilah Evans, on the other hand, the other woman at the table, was a tough cookie. Sixty-seven, she wore thick glasses and a permanent steely smile, and

Joe respected her. Lilah had been a super-agent back in the seventies, and still had a great sense of people and ideas. Lou Conrad and Steve Byers were both in their fifties, both honchos from other networks, and the closest the board came to understanding how things worked in TV now. But neither of them had commissioned a show in years – or made one for decades for that matter.

Joe Goldstein had a large salary and stock options here, but those stock options had taken a bath with the end of the party last night. And that was what worried Harvey – Maria Gonzales was their major bankable star.

'That's good. It's important you be *seen* as the host. That you *personally* backed the show,' Emma Sanderson said fatuously. 'It's all about PR, Joe. These people demand respect; you have to be seen to give it to them. If we want a shot at another Maria Gonzales vehicle.'

'That's exactly right,' Bostock said.

'No. It's bullshit,' Joe said.

'Excuse me?' Emma demanded.

'Sure,' Joe replied. She scowled, and he saw Lilah Evans smother a smile. 'You didn't hire me to yes you to death. You hired me to turn around a failing TV station. That's what I've been doing the last few years.'

'But this year, ratings are dropping. In case you hadn't noticed,' Jack said sarcastically. 'In which case, sorry to be the bearer of bad news.'

'Ratings are dropping because this board isn't listening to me. You poached me from NBC but you aren't giving me the tools to do the job.' Goldstein crunched his fingertips against his throbbing temples. 'That's because you're afraid, all of you. I told you we needed to branch out. Cut the dead programming. I wanted to end *Summerside* last season.'

'It's been our lifeblood this quarter,' Lou Conrad said.

'Sure. Because we have nothing else. The best creatives in LA don't bring us new work. They see this network as clinging on to reliable hits well past their sell-by date. Hot producers don't think we'll give anything new a chance. Why pitch to NAB when *Summerside* hogs the prime-time line-up two nights a week, and we put *Alien Dad* and *Lucky Dip* in the other two slots? It's NBC, HBO, the other places that get the original hits. *House of Cards* went straight to Netflix, for God's sake. You people are so afraid of losing what you have that you'll never get close to owning anything new. When a show has run for five years, it's done, OK? *Summerside* was done. The great ratings masked the fact that we had no new shows. Nothing big. Nothing fresh.'

Sceptical faces looked back at him.

'Like you said, there's nothing great in the pipeline,' Lilah remarked. 'If you get something hot, we could consider dropping a prime-time show. Until then, we need Maria Gonzales back on this network.'

Goldstein thought for a moment – just a moment. He and Topaz were a power couple, but they lived for the creative energy. They focused on stories – hers in print, his on screen. And they lived large. There was the huge house, the private schools, the place in the Hamptons, right on the beach – an acre of oceanfront. They had the best of everything as a couple in terms of assets, but not too much in the bank. He needed this stupid job.

'That's not how I work.' He lifted his head, stared at everybody in the room. 'You guys can run this network into the ground if you want. But you can't use my name to do it. I have a reputation. I'm not pinning it to a strategy of do nothing.'

There was a sharp intake of breath.

'Give me free rein or I quit.' He turned to Jack, the youngest man in the room. 'You're big on the internet. You know what they call NAB, right?'

Travis nodded, reluctantly.

'Why don't you tell our colleagues here. And it's not National American Broadcasting.'

Travis cleared his throat. 'Numbing American Boredom.'

Goldstein had to smile. But he was the only one in the room who did.

'I want to clear house and have a free budget. I want to go out and get the biggest talent. And I need to do it entirely on my own terms.'

There was silence. He spread his hands, relaxed.

'Or go get yourselves your third CEO in four years, and see how Wall Street likes *that*.'

Goldstein breathed in. He was perfectly calm. He had made his decision. Nobody messed him around. Ever.

Admiration registered in Travis's eyes. He saw Emma scowling in dislike, but the others ignored her; she was a makeweight.

'Joe,' Bostock said, 'we hear you. You want to make massive changes to this company. It would be wrong to decide that without discussion. Can you give us a few minutes here?'

'Sure.' Goldstein glanced at his Rolex. 'There's a Starbucks across the street. I'm going for an iced coffee. You guys chat amongst yourselves. I'll be back in twenty.'

The coffee shop was ideal. There was free Wi-Fi, the early morning rush had disappeared, and nobody in there knew who he was. Goldstein often snuck in to check mail on his phone, get a bran muffin or just sit and think.

He called his wife. Shit. There was more at stake here than Joe cared to admit. Sure, if NAB dicked him around, he would quit, but it was hard to see how they would make the payments on their high-rolling life without his salary. He'd also signed a non-compete clause, so there was no TV position waiting in the wings somewhere else. It would probably mean firing staff, and selling the beach house, which Topaz loved even though they hardly got to use it. It had been out of their price range really, and Joe had taken a risk. Pushing all his chips to the centre of the pile. Topaz had encouraged him – a place for when they retired.

'We'll live here spring through fall.' She'd gestured around at the sand in front of them. 'An acre right on the beach, Joe, when do you get that?'

He'd kind of agreed. Like his wife, he found the ocean very soothing.

'It's going to be brutal in the winter. And wouldn't we miss the city?'

'We'll keep a two-bedroom apartment someplace nice, for theatre and so forth. And we'll spend the winters in Florida like all the old New Yorkers.' She kissed him on the cheek. 'We'll be snowbirds. How about that? You like the picture?'

He smiled at the thought. Yeah, he liked it a lot. They bought the house.

Well, if his whiny kids got chucked out of Pointer Academy, they were always zoned for a great public school. And Topaz would support his decision . . . right?

Goldstein hoped so. She'd been buried in work lately, as had he. That wasn't right, but it was the reality.

'Topaz Rossi's office.'

'Can I speak with her, please?'

'Hey, hi, Mr Goldstein.'

'What's up, Brad?'

'Not too much. Can I get her to call you back? She's in with somebody right now.'

'This is kind of important. Can you interrupt the meeting?'

There was a pause. 'Sir, is it a health matter, anything like that?'

Goldstein felt a surge of unaccustomed anger at Brad. He wasn't used to having his orders questioned. Not by assistants. Not by his *wife's* assistant.

'No. Now put her on the phone.'

'I'm so sorry, I can't. She's having a meeting that I can't interrupt. I will get the message to her as soon as—'

Joe's knuckles whitened on the cell. 'What fucking meeting?'

'I can't tell you, Mr Goldstein, I apologise. It's company business. She'll tell you herself if—'

'Of course it's company business. She runs the company,' he said, and hung up.

The coffee was cooling in his hand. Joe breathed in, trying to calm down. Nothing fazed him more than disrespect. Than having to make appointments to speak to his own spouse.

His phone buzzed. But it wasn't Topaz.

A text message from Maria Gonzales.

Mr Goldstein – sir. Or can I call you Joe? I had sooo much fun last night. Just wanted to thank you.

Goldstein sighed. How did this *actress* have his cell phone number? The producers must have handed it over. He resented that. Maria Gonzales was a huge star, but to Joe she was just another talent, and he thought her overrated. It was the shapely ass, the almond-shaped eyes, and the huge natural breasts that had made her so big. Full marks for maximising her natural assets, but *Summerside* wasn't great drama, and it wasn't where he wanted NAB to be.

Reluctantly he texted back.

Hey, Maria! Please call me Joe. Glad you had a good time. It was great to see you.

That was a brush-off, polite as he could make it. Surely that would be it. He toyed with the bran muffin, and ate half of it because he was bored. Five minutes more and he would walk back and hear his fate. Their fate.

I should never have let it get to this, he thought.

He was angry all around, but mostly with himself. How was it he'd made so much dough yet was still in a position where these fuckers had something on him?

If NAB went for it, if they gave him real control of the network, he would do something about the family finances. Get secure. One of the housekeepers could go. He and Topaz would start cooking again themselves. No more resort holidays and six-figure bids on items in charity auctions. They would save, pay off the summer house. Perhaps he should downsize the apartment, too; the building's monthly charges would have paid his parents' mortgage eight times over, and that was just for the maintenance. He had art, they could sell that. Look for a town house, a small one maybe – the twins would graduate eventually, at least he hoped so, and go to college. In a house, they wouldn't have to pay thousands a month for their share of the doormen and roof maintenance.

His phone buzzed.

I never really saw anything of you, did I? Last night showed that was a mistake. There must be lots of stuff we can talk about.

Goldstein hesitated. He did not want to rehire Maria Gonzales. No way. He wanted to move the network on. But she *was* an insanely big star. He imagined the panic of the people in the building opposite if they could see these texts, see her *asking* him for a meeting. Everything they'd wanted from that stupid party last night.

Network execs would love to talk to you about that, he replied.

I don't want them, I want you. That's OK, right? I'm bored of suits.

Goldstein smiled. Flattering.

I'm wearing a suit right now, he joked back. This was unexpectedly enjoyable.

Not your kind of suit. That looked good. Suit is an attitude. You don't have it.

His phone buzzed again. His timer. He switched it off and stood, ready to head across the road for the meeting. What they said in there would determine how he replied to Maria.

The screen lit up with another text bubble.

Well? Joe? Can we meet?

Well nothing, Goldstein thought. You'll wait. And you'll like it. At the end of the day, Maria was just another star.

He switched the phone off, slipped it back in his pocket and returned to the office.

* * *

'I hope we've come to a decision,' Goldstein said.

'Yes.' Bostock spoke for the board. 'A compromise.'

His heart sank, but he didn't allow his face to flicker. 'I don't do compromise.'

'I told you,' Emma said loudly.

'Quiet, please,' Jack interrupted. 'Hear us out, Joe.'

'Very well,' Goldstein said. He looked at Harvey.

'OK, Joe. You've got carte blanche. Clear the schedule. Re-spend the budget. But that's taking a risk with everything our shareholders depend on. We can't allow this company to take a huge bath on our watch. Everybody here has a reputation.'

But not a good one, Joe thought.

'I'm listening,' he said.

'So here's our deal. Develop anything you want, clear anything you want. But offer this board one tried and true bedrock star we can appeal to advertisers with. That sound fair?'

'One warhorse while I look for new blood?' Goldstein smiled. 'Reasonable. I can live with it.'

'And Maria Gonzales is the one the board wants.'

'She's solid gold,' Emma said loudly. 'She gets more press than anyone on the planet.'

'Can you deliver Maria in something new?' Jack asked. 'We don't care what you think of her acting chops. We want *ratings*.'

Which aren't just about stars, Joe thought, but he nodded. It was a small price to pay. 'Yes. I can deliver Maria Gonzales.'

Could he? Texts in the café were one thing. Reeling Maria in was quite another. She was out of contract, and she had a hot-shot agent. He'd be wanting *big* money.

'Come back to us in a month with a new two-year contract for Maria,' Bostock said. 'Then you can clear the rest of the schedule and run it your way. We'll sign that memo as soon as her deal's done.'

In that case, Maria's deal was getting done at lightning speed.

Goldstein ran over their exchanges in his head. She wanted to work with him – and he wanted to make it happen.

Piece of cake.

'That's fair,' he said. 'See you next week.'

'I said a month.'

'It won't take me a month. She'll be signed by next week. And if you guys will excuse me, I have meetings to go to.'

He stood up and walked out of the room. Behind him he could hear the excited chatter of the board. He flicked his phone back on: texts from Maria and voicemail from Topaz.

They could both wait. Especially his wife.

Joe Goldstein was busy.

Chapter Three

'Barbara Lincoln on the phone,' Krebs's assistant said.

'Finally.' Krebs looked out of his office window down the Sunset Strip. The billboards for new TV shows grinned at him, all huge Photoshopped faces, shiny white teeth. The posters came and went, but Hollywood remained the same. Down the road was the Whisky a Go Go club, a heavy metal haven back in the day, still loved for its nostalgia value, still played by the old rock acts at times. Wide roads, boutique hotels, and the Hollywood Hills rising up behind his small suite.

The music business had shifted west sometime back in the nineties, and Rowena and Michael Krebs had gone with it. Rowena hadn't objected. Her brief engagement to movie executive John Metcalf had once crashed and burned out here, a long time ago, but Rowena had still had a good time. For a Scotswoman turned New Yorker, the promise of endless sun was enticing. The idea of swimming pools in January thrilled her. Besides, if the music business was here now, so was a new life. And Rowena Krebs loved adventure. Like a shark swimming forward, she needed to keep moving.

Michael was willing, too. His sons from his first marriage, to Debbie, had scattered to college. It was good to get away from New York, start a new life, a fresh page. He and Rowena had married privately, in the garden of their new house; an interfaith ceremony with a liberal rabbi, under the chuppah in the sunlight. Rowena had sobbed and looked radiant. None of her family was there; they wouldn't approve, and she had broken away from them long ago. Her best friend, Barbara Lincoln, manager of Atomic Mass, her superstar act, was her maid of honour; they looked awesome together walking to that wedding canopy, the lean blonde and the black Amazon, two of the most stylish, powerful women in music, giggling like a couple of teenagers.

He loved marriage to Rowena. It was strange to Krebs to be so in love. The sexual thrill of their affair was the most intense he had ever known. And more than that, she was brilliant, ambitious, driven. He *liked* her . . . and he wanted her. And she was desperately in love with him. When she cut him off and ended it, getting engaged to another man, he was consumed with rage. At the time, he couldn't explain it. Hadn't he told himself it was just sex; what his wife didn't know wouldn't hurt her?

But it wasn't. And the torrid heat of Rowena's love for him tormented him night and day. He contrasted it with Deborah's endless criticisms, her coldness in bed, her bargaining for sex, doling it out like some kind of a favour. They were parents first, lovers a distant second, and friends . . . rarely. Sometimes, just sometimes, Krebs admitted that his liking for Rowena was a little more than he let on. Maybe he was in love with her.

But he hadn't been ready to rock the boat. How could he? The perfect house, the neat marriage, his sons' feelings. A loveless marriage perhaps, but it ticked on. And Rowena Gordon was a comet, blazing through the skies. Making waves. Making enemies. Not the normal successful man's wife. She reminded him of him. That was why he warmed so totally to her.

That, and the explosive orgasms they had together. It was impossible to resist the girl's wild heat and responsiveness to him. When he saw her with her fiancé, a single glance told Krebs that compared to him, this was tame, this was nothing.

And he wanted her back. He pestered her. Campaigned for

her. When she broke down and he took her, shoved up against the wall of a stadium in Spain, down one of those deserted, endless corridors, risking discovery, she melted harder than ever. And she dumped the fiancé and moved back to New York.

Then came magnate Conrad Miles' attempted corporate take-over of Musica and her use of the classic 'Pac-Man defence', engineered with her rival Topaz Rossi, the magazine mogul. Rowena was victorious, the first woman to run a global record label. It was a triumph.

One problem, though: she never took Michael back as her lover.

Krebs recalled her voice still, all these years down the line, as he protested that he loved Debbie, that this was all he could give.

'So be with her. I don't want this life any more.'

And she'd meant it. They were friends – kind of. She took his calls. She signed his bands. He produced Musica records. At industry events, he saw her, alone, beautiful, married to her work.

Nothing could shake her. And when old Josh Oberstein, her mentor, the chairman of Musica, told him that one day Rowena would just leave town and he would never see her again, Krebs finally understood.

That day, he asked Debbie for a divorce.

He turned up at Rowena's door after a run, as though to say hi, as though for coffee. Delivering himself to her, finally. Krebs took Rowena, and then Rowena, the love of his life, took him.

Michael Krebs was not an emotional man. Emotion was alien to one who always wanted control. But when he saw Rowena, so happy, Barbara carrying the train of her Gucci evening gown, walking towards him as he waited there under the chuppah, something he had never done before, a tribute to his dormant faith, he couldn't help but wonder at the strength of the emotions that overtook him.

They lived in her place for a couple of years while the kids grew out of school, and once that was done, when Musica made noises about moving to LA, Krebs was only too ready. He set up Mirror, Mirror studios, his state-of-the-art facility, in a new building on the Malibu coast; a magnet for musicians, who could now swap their dreary climates for glorious sun, LA strip bars and surfing in their downtime. Business was brisk, and Krebs's Grammy count climbed. He and Rowena remodelled the house they'd bought in the Hollywood Hills, perfectly placed to see the city spread out before them, a web of glittering lights, the playground of the movie business.

And it was amazing what happened to Michael Krebs in that second, happy marriage. What a transformation takes place when a loner finally meets true love.

Michael Krebs, control freak, was bathed in Rowena's love, sunk in it. He told his friends it was like warm rain on his face. That the fortress of his heart was suddenly breached by joy, by finding a woman who truly loved him for himself, liked him just as he was. She didn't react to his masculinity by berating or critising him. Instead, she got turned on. For a little while Krebs resisted, but slowly he started to enjoy life. Fully. Not just his career, or his kids. Everything.

He got involved with their house build, crafting their mansion on its smallish lot perfectly. It was an architectural marvel, and he'd loved it ever since. There was the garden, a verdant oasis bordered with hedges of climbing roses and bougainvillea, planted with lavender and green lawns, where Rowena reclined in a striped deckchair imported from England, hidden from prying eyes. When the children arrived, it was big enough for a climbing frame, a swing, a tree house, an apple tree and some secret spaces. Their rooftop swimming pool, always heated, gloriously light, was surrounded by a deck for loungers and parties. Krebs had a library, a modern gym and a mini studio for hearing mixes; and Rowena loved their family room, the home cinema with reclining seats and surround sound, and the small modern kitchen where she never made anything. That was fine: Krebs hired a cook. The kids' bedroom was fun too, rigged with a climbing wall and soft floors, picture books and a whiteboard with crayons. As they got older, it became a sleek teenage den, and Joshua was moved to his own small place at the top of the house, with an Xbox and a gaming computer.

Their careers carried on. Krebs bought modern art, sculpture; when the bands got less interesting, he simply stopped recording them. These days he was lucky to find one great album a year. He was more or less done. Other producers rented his studio. With Rowena, there was great sex, travel when she could, and enough fun that he let himself relax. As he aged, the weights he used got heavier, he swam harder: physical activity that kept his body strong and almost – *almost* – staved off the boredom.

But not quite. The Hall of Fame had been enjoyable. A private man, a power broker, Krebs enjoyed the adulation. It was even better to see Rowena inducted. He was proud of his wife, his friend, his protégée, of how far she'd come, staying at the top longer than anyone had dreamed of.

And yet back in LA, it all felt flat. God, he didn't want to face it. Another morning listening to master tapes that excited him as much as a tin of baked beans. Christ. He was getting old.

'Put her through,' he said.

It was always good to talk to Barbara Lincoln. She took no crap and offered no sympathy.

'Michael. How's half of music's power couple?'

'Bored out of my brain,' he said.

'I hear you. Rowena talk to you about Europe yet?'

'What about it?'

A pause. 'Have you seen the ticket sales on Lumosand Kassius?'

Musica's two biggest acts. 'No. You know me, I live in the studio.'

'Yes, I get it. Well, they're stiffing.'

He grinned. Ms Lincoln never used two words where one would do.

'Don't sit on the fence, Barbara. Tell me what you really think.'

'Seriously. Word of mouth on both records is horrible, and the ticket sales are just dying on the vine. Those stadiums won't be a quarter full. They both want to fire their managers. But Rowena's on the hook for tour support and she's going to take one hell of a bath.'

Krebs rolled his eyes. 'Her A and R guys suck.'

'This is going to be a legendary bad quarter. I don't even know if it's Rowena's fault. Nobody buys music any more. We're OK . . .'

'I know you are.' Atomic Mass hadn't put out a record in five years, but they could still sell stadiums out in minutes, every year. 'It's great to be a legend, huh?'

'You should know. But nostalgia tours are all the rage. The new U2 is still U2.'

Krebs sighed. 'Goddamned depressing.'

'I think Rowena's going to need some support. I hear rumblings that the shareholders aren't happy. OK, not rumblings. They're pissed. I know Deutsche Group holds fifteen per cent and there's a UK pension fund with another five. It's going to be rough at the shareholder meeting next month.'

Krebs nodded. A surge of adrenalin rushed through him. 'That's soon.'

'I only just found out.'

'And you called me?'

'You can see it a little clearer than she can. You know Rowena, always loyal to her acts.'

'You're a good woman, for a Limey. I'll have Rowena call you, OK?'

'OK.'

Krebs hung up. For Barbara to call, it must be bad. Rowena was in trouble.

'Can you get hold of my wife?' he called out to his assistant, Ellen.

'Yes, sir. Right away. But one second, Mr Krebs . . . I have Mr Krebs on the line for you.'

'Huh?'

'Mr Martin Krebs,' Ellen said.

'Oh.' Krebs beamed. Martin, his eldest boy. They didn't talk as much as he'd like – typical father–son stuff; typical divorce stuff too, he guessed. But he'd been a good weekend father after that divorce, stuck around, gone to every parent conference and college trip. Debbie had remarried almost instantly: her childhood sweetheart from the cold climes of Minneapolis. There was no good way to get divorced, Krebs didn't kid himself, but they were all civil, and his three elder sons were college graduates now, either married or dating. He was secretly hoping to be a grandfather soon.

Martin was the most successful of them all; he was a tenured professor at the University of Brandeis, having sold his architectural practice after winning national awards for his ecological apartment buildings. And all before the age of forty. Krebs was very proud of him.

'I'll call Rowena later. Let me take this one. Hold everything else and shut my door, please.'

Ellen smiled and did it.

'Marty?' Krebs said. He jumped to his feet, pacing with the handset across the room. 'So good to hear from you, man.'

'It's good to hear you too, Dad,' his son said.

'When you coming out here? I want to meet that new girl you've been dating. Emily, right?'

'Amelia. Close enough.'

'I promise I won't freak her out if you bring her. You two can even share a room.'

Marty laughed at the old joke, which Krebs had been cracking ever since his son hit twenty.

'Good to know. But I'm afraid that Amelia and I won't be travelling anywhere for a bit. You'll have to come to us.'

There was something in Martin's tone. Something dark.

Krebs sat down again, heavily. A feeling of great dread washed across him.

'Don't talk like that, dude, you'll make me think you're sick,' he said lightly.

'I am kind of sick. I moved back to New York; I'm on a leave of absence from the university. They've been great.'

'So you're close to Mom,' Krebs said, stupidly. He knew he'd only said it so he could go a minute more without hearing what his son had to tell him.

'Yes. But I've actually got a sublet. Amelia's hanging out with me. She can finish her dissertation. I just felt it was going to be better if we had our own place, better for me, so I can handle things.'

Krebs couldn't bring himself to ask. The moment hung in the air.

'The apartment's also close to Sloane-Kettering,' his eldest son said. 'Dad, I've got liver cancer.'

Topaz looked at the woman sitting opposite her, and her voice was ice cold.

'There's really nothing to discuss.'

'Oh Topaz, you're so wrong,' Joanna Watson said in a sing-song voice. She tilted her head, the chic Louise Brooks bob swinging as she did so. She wore an incredibly expensive Tom Ford haute couture day dress and a string of pearls the size of marbles, with a lustre that said they'd been hand-dived for somewhere in the South Seas. She was perfectly made up, too, and her nails were scarlet and sharply filed, like talons.

Topaz was starting to dislike her immensely. She kicked herself for making the hire. Joanna had had a hot reputation in Ottawa, and the magazine she'd edited there, *Flashy*, a cult jewellery hit, was still selling, unlike *American Girl*.

Should have done more research, Topaz chided herself. Getting lazy in my old age. Probably somebody else was the engine of that growth. Topaz had just swooped in and poached the editor.

'When you hired me, you offered me creative control.'

'Yes, and I gave it to you. With disastrous results.'

'I'm proud of the stories we've done. It hasn't even been six months.'

Topaz inclined her head slightly. 'Yes, I realise that, and normally I would give an editor a chance to work through. But I'm afraid your sales drop-off is just too steep.'

'I'll bring a lawsuit.'

'You're most welcome to try,' Topaz said. 'See if you get hired again by any magazine house anywhere.'

'You messed me around. You took me from a successful magazine to this dumpy dinosaur of a property and didn't even give me time to bed in . . .'

'*American Girl* was a flagship women's title. Still is, even after your butchery,' Topaz snarled. How dare this overdone tart insult her magazine, her staffers? She stood up. 'Get out of my office. No goddamned press release about mutual agreement. You're being dismissed.'

'For what?'

'Underperformance,' Topaz said brutally. 'I have a clause in the contract that lets me sack you for any reason I choose under a six-month window. How can you talk about *American Girl* that way?'

Joanna preened, tossing her head like a petulant teenager, sending her dark bob flying. Her heavily made-up eyes narrowed at Topaz Rossi, regarding the older woman with open loathing. 'It's overblown, like you. Living in the past. You need thinner girls, and you don't airbrush as much as the competition does. *That's* what sells these days, not these chubby chicks you kept featuring. I just needed time to reach that new, sophisticated audience.'

Watson was twenty-eight, with flawless skin. She gazed at Topaz with naked contempt. 'I know lots of people, lady, powerful people, *rich* people. I'm *from* money. That's what our market should be: aspirational, glossy. You don't understand that, because you're just some nouveau riche bum with a cute ass.'

Topaz actually laughed. 'Was that your brave speech, Joanna? You rehearse that to make you seem like a rebel? Hilarious. You're from money? I know. I hired you *despite* that. What makes you think I give a flying fuck about your relations?'

Watson's father ran an investment bank north of the border; he was known to be a runner for Canada's ambassador to the UN. Watson Snr wasn't a billionaire, but there was plenty of money swimming around.

'People like me *buy* people like you,' Joanna threatened.

'No, honey. Women like me aren't for sale.'

Topaz got to her feet, walked to her desk and buzzed for security. Within seconds, two burly guards had appeared at her door, Brad hovering behind them.

'Joanna Watson is leaving the building right now,' she said.

'I can find my own way out.' Joanna tossed her bob. 'You haven't heard the last of me, Topaz.'

'Maybe not, but that's why I own a pair of headphones,' Topaz snapped. 'Drowns out all the whining and crazies on my commute.'

'I'm glad to be quitting this stupid company. Nobody wants to work with a loser like you.'

'You're not quitting. You're fired.' Topaz turned to the guards. 'I fired Joanna Watson about two minutes ago. Get rid of her, please, gentlemen.'

'Ma'am, I'm going to have to ask you to leave,' the taller of the security guards said.

'I'm taking my pass and going back to my office. I'm going to collect my things.'

'Your pass doesn't work, Joanna. It's been cancelled. Like your email, and your access to our computers. Your assistant – your *ex*-assistant – is boxing up all your personal effects. A messenger will deliver them to your apartment building within the hour. You have a doorman there, right?'

Joanna stared. 'Topaz Rossi, you are a total bitch.'

'Too late for flattery,' Topaz said. 'Now get out.'

Returning to her desk, Topaz could see messages from Joe flashing on her phone. She called him back, got his voicemail. That was kind of a relief. Too much to deal with right now. She didn't leave a message. Her husband was mad, Topaz knew that. And Joanna was enough drama for one morning.

'Ms Rossi. Lucy Klein is here.'

The deputy editor. She'd be producing this month's issue while Topaz figured out what to do. That gave her about two weeks to source a really dynamite talent to edit the flagship magazine. She couldn't afford any more mistakes.

'Great. Send her in.'

She *would* take care of Joe Goldstein – just a little later.

'Actually, hold on one second. I have a call to make first.'

'Sure thing,' Brad said briskly, closing her glass door.

Topaz walked back around her desk and spun her Eames chair so that it faced the window. She poured herself a third cup of coffee, reached for her phone, and dialled a number from memory.

'Rowena Krebs's office,' a voice said.

'Wow.' Sunlight streamed in through the windows and danced around Rowena's desk. She lifted her phone from the cradle and swung herself over to her buttery leather couch, flinging herself back against its cushions. 'Look who it is. Topaz Rossi, queen of New York.'

'And Hall of Famer Rowena Krebs. You're queen of the world, no?'

'No.' Rowena grimaced. 'Nice statue and all, but my releases this summer are going to stink out the joint like a New Jersey fish market.'

'That sucks. I'm sorry.'

'How are things in print?'

'Better than music – just barely.'

'Hey, some music is selling great. Rap, teen pop. We have some stuff on our urban label.' Rowena sighed heavily, extending her long, lean legs encased in tight denim and cowboy boots. 'It just doesn't make up for the numbers we used to move.'

'Internet pirates?'

'That's kind of happened already. What you see now is just a lack of the good stuff.' Rowena breathed deep. 'I need another Atomic Mass. And I don't have one.'

'Maybe you should start going to clubs again,' Topaz suggested. 'Listen to acts yourself. You were always so good at that kind of thing. Talent-spotting, A and R.'

Rowena sat bolt upright. 'Goddamn, maybe I will.'

That thought was exciting. Her life was too corporate these days. She wore jeans and dangly earrings, but she was a suit now, no doubt about it. 'I want to see some good bands again. I miss all of that.'

'What are your kids listening to?'

'Urban. That's where all the excitement is these days. Maybe some Metallica, some Muse, Black Keys. They don't care for the pop acts. At least I raised them right.'

'Mine are gaming freaks. And Rona's already on Facebook.'

'How is my goddaughter? And when are you going to start using her real name? Rowena. Say it loud and proud. Rowena.'

Topaz laughed. 'Rona will do. It was bad enough I had them baptised. I'm letting Joe use the Jewish nickname.'

'Fair enough. I miss you.' Rowena hadn't seen her best friend in ages, and she suddenly felt very guilty. 'Work swallows us all whole. Why don't you bring everyone here for the weekend?

The kids can amuse each other, we'll pack them all off to Universal and the four of us can hang out and do bad stuff.'

'I would love to, but I just had to fire an editor.' Topaz hesitated. 'And Joe and me are in kind of a rough patch right now. It's not a great time.'

'Joe and you? No way.' They were the closest couple Rowena knew, apart from herself and Michael. 'Can't be true. Tell me all.'

'Got a meeting waiting at the door. Why don't you fly up to New York?'

'I might just do that,' Rowena said, anxious for her friend. 'I'll call you later, OK?'

'Sounds good.'

Topaz hung up, and despite the afterglow of friendship, Rowena felt a dark cloud of anxiety gather on the fringes of her mind.

Trouble in paradise. No doubt about it.

Chapter Four

Maria Gonzales lay on the massage table, relaxing.

Warm, flat stones had been placed on the small of her back and strategically up her spine. Her tanned skin glistened with rosemary oil, and her raven-black hair was scooped up on her neck, secured with ivory combs.

The Victrix ran the most exclusive spa in Manhattan, and Maria was enjoying the services of two of its best therapists. She was feeling sexy, worked out from her personal training session this morning, followed by a light breakfast of solid protein, egg whites and bacon, that kept her famous booty high and tight but her waist wasp-tiny. Yesterday's manicurist and dental appointments meant her nails were sharp and her teeth gleaming white. The soothing hands rubbed her, the warm stones opened her muscles. Soft Japanese-style music played in the room. She shifted languorously and thought about Joe Goldstein.

Hmmm. That vision made Maria even warmer than the stones did. Joe Goldstein was *so* hot. That sexy somewhat-older-male type, with the brains and the muscles and so much *power*. Maria was used to men drooling over her, flirting with her, begging her for dates. Joe had looked blankly past her, almost as if she were some kind of annoyance. She couldn't even *deal* with how sexy that was.

He wasn't gay. There was the marriage to Topaz Rossi, the

feared magazine editor, but she was old and a harpy, that was the word on the street. Well, you didn't get to that position without it. They had twins, and anyway, Maria could just tell that Joe was straight. He was an alpha male of the old-fashioned kind. All testosterone. She'd googled him, looked him up on Wikipedia. Yep, the new network chief at NAB was smoking hot. And exactly the kind of boyfriend she needed.

Already Maria was regretting her decision to wind *Summerside* up. She was mega-famous, but that could fade in the blink of an eye. Maria liked to think she was realistic. She could be sexy for *ages*, if she worked at it, but every year would mean a little less so, and she wasn't so great at managing money. There were millions in her account, but millions more had been spent already. That wasn't good, not at all. A boyfriend with smarts would be a great thing for her. And Joe Goldstein had power over her future. She could go someplace else, get a new series, of course – if she wanted to do a *Summerside* clone all over again.

But, paradoxically, Maria loved that Mr Goldstein wanted to make better decisions for the network. He wanted fresh blood; her spies at NAB told her that.

What if she, Maria, could be that fresh blood?

It was about being different – and she thought she had it in her.

Joe Goldstein could get her a real part, she knew. He could make her money. Maria wanted Joe Goldstein. No two ways about it. She hadn't slept with anyone in four months – what the hell was the point? Diffident little fanboys and stupid-ass basketball players looking to pick up their own celebrity. Maria hated that attitude. She knew she had a great pair of tits. Maybe she wasn't a Harvard grad, but she had brains.

She wanted a *quality* man. She wanted to develop her career, go out on a high.

Go back to being poor? Never.

Bad things happened when you were poor.

Real bad things. The kind Maria Gonzales had spent a lifetime forgetting.

When Maria retired, she had a vision of her ideal self – a Hamptons housewife in the summer and a New York hostess in the fall. Winter on Miami Beach or resorts in the Caribbean.

Anything would be better than the life she'd come from.

Gritting her teeth, Maria shifted under the masseuse, bringing those skilled thumbs exactly to the point where she wanted them.

Despite herself, her thoughts were drifting back.

No amount of money, beauty or fame could drive those memories out. She hated herself for remembering them right now. That whiny, crying girl she'd once been, the victim, the hurt one. Beaten at home. Hurt in ways she didn't want to think about. And then when she got bigger, trying so hard to make them all love her, her gangster half-brothers and her drunk father. Schooling hadn't helped. Maria's bright, quick brain, the one the sisters at their local church-run primary school had loved, got her into trouble at home. *Sassing. Smart mouth. Nagging little puta. Runt, skinny, always whining . . .*

Tears prickled in her eyes. She shut them, determined not to let her father win.

The memory surfaced as she lay there being rubbed and pampered, her face down on the massage table's head cradle. At least nobody could see her teary eyes.

Maria saw herself again. When she was innocent, a lifetime ago. There she was, a little girl, maybe eleven, laboriously writing out her creative story with a cheap plastic pen. It was called 'A Load of Old Rubbish', her idea of a joke; that was what Papa called everything she did, so why not make him laugh? It was her story of garbage coming alive, the broken toys, dolls and teddy bears she saw on the garbage pile outside of town, where the orphans went foraging for food. The toys would come to life secretly at night, because of a magical birthday wish a child made, and go on a great adventure northwards. They would cross the border, sneak over the Rio Grande, into America . . .

Maria remembered that story so well. She would never forget it. The sheets of extra paper the nuns gave her. Working it all out, planning in her head. The little book had five chapters and it took her all that autumn to write. It was her project in writing class, and her teacher, Sister Fatima, wrote on the front page of her story how wonderful Maria's brain was. She got a prize, an anthology of poems bound in red leather, the title stamped in gold on the cover and the crimson spine.

It was glorious, the most precious thing Maria had ever owned.

'Papa! I won the prize!' she shouted when she got home that day. She walked a mile to and from school, morning and evening. 'Look!' She thrust forward her book.

'What is that?' her father, Carlos, demanded.

'Poems,' Maria said. 'For my writing. Because I'm a writer. It's my prize.' She glowed.

Carlos stared. 'They didn't give you any money, did they?'

She shook her head.

'Of course not. The Church is all take, all the time. This is stupid.' He waved his hand angrily at the book.

'Will you read my story, Papa?' she said, holding out her own chapters.

'I don't have time.'

'I *want* you to read it,' Maria persisted. She usually gave up, but this time her face was bright with effort. If her mother was alive, *she* would have read it. Her father *had* to see that Maria was not a stupid *puta*; that she was smart and she was getting prizes.

'Maybe later,' Carlos grunted, and swigged out of the whiskey bottle.

Maria stood there.

'*Later*,' her father barked, and swept her papers on to the floor, all of them, her story, forty sheets' worth.

'Papa! You'll get it dirty!' Little Maria, bending over, picking them up, while her eldest half-brother, Chico, laughed in a corner. Her brothers were already on the streets, with guns, working shitty jobs for the drug lords; they were dumb-ass soldiers, not trusted to handle the product. 'I'll show it to you later, OK?'

Carlos drank some more and fixed his eyes on the soccer game playing on their crackling TV.

Over the next few days, Maria pestered her father, telling him how good her story was.

'I called it "A Load of Old Rubbish". Do you like that, Papa? It's a joke. Can you read it today?'

She would leave the stack of paper neatly on his bedside table, or on the shelf where he kept his clothes. Carlos Gonzales would yell at her to leave him alone.

'You *should* read it. It won a *prize*,' Maria shouted, after a week had passed. 'You're not *busy*. You could just read one chapter—'

'God damn you to hell! Leave me alone!' Carlos roared suddenly, leaping up, anger turning his skin purple. Maria yelped and stumbled back, clutching her story to her. 'Give it to me! Right now!'

And he ripped it out of her hands, and, right in front of her, tore her story to little pieces.

And when Maria cried, and ran to the bathroom to throw up from her pain, her father stumbled in and slapped her to shut up, then sobbed and said she'd made him do it, and then tried to glue the pages back together with water and flour. While she watched, weeping, he got drunker, threatened to hit her again, and then threw the whole thing in the fire.

The next night, Maria heard her father talking to the *jefe*, the local gangster her half-brothers worked for.

'Yes, she's going to be pretty,' the *jefe* said.

'She's skinny, she's nothing, always books and running away to school. My house is filthy, for pigs. She never helps. Her mother was a bitch, the same way.'

'She got what she deserved, Carlos. Long time ago.'

'Fuck that bitch. Not like my Anna.' Her half-brothers' mom, who'd died of cancer. Her father had told her that her own mom, Lucita, had died of cancer too. Long ago. Before Maria could remember. 'Anna was a saint,' her father said hoarsely, morose in his cups. 'I had no problems when it was Anna and *mi hijos*.'

'They are growing up to be loyal soldiers. The cartel is pleased. They are thinking of taking Chico to the operation in Colombia.'

'That is dangerous,' said her father, but without real protest. 'Will there be extra pay?'

'Something for the *familia, sí*. We look after our own, Carlos, you know that. We would like to do something about the Maria problem . . .'

'I'm not marrying again. I like the whores at the bar.'

'She doesn't need a mother, she's full grown.'

'Eleven,' her father said uncertainly, not wanting to contradict the *jefe*. '*Señor* . . . maybe a little while longer.'

'You have misremembered her birthday, I think. She is twelve.'

Not for another eight months. Maria lay still on her bed, straining to hear, to breathe very quietly.

'Oh, yes . . . you are right, *señor*. *Gracias. Gracias.*' Maria could hear money being handed over. 'What do you have in mind?'

'Soon she will be a teenager, and the streets are not safe for girls. She could be raped. Taken to a brothel. You do not want that.'

Now there was silence. She waited for her father to say something, to defend her, but no, nothing. The men were . . . *trading*. Maria understood that clearly, even at eleven years old. They were trading her.

'Your family is very fortunate. Señor Alonso was down at the school this morning. Chico told him you had some trouble with the girl yesterday. Some nonsense about a book.'

'Yes. Caterwauling like a little fool. I can't even read. Why is she bothering me?'

'She thinks she is better than you. This is the trouble with too much learning, it ruins a pretty girl. The women are not like they were in Anna's day.'

'Her mother was a faithless whore.'

'So you shot her,' the *jefe* said soothingly. 'No harm done. She is dead. The girl is not to blame.'

'Women are no good to me.' A swig, a swallow. 'Anna left me, and Lucita was a whore, and Maria is stuck-up. For all I know she is some other man's kid anyway. Most likely I'm raising Lucita's bastard, like a fool.'

Little Maria stuffed her hands into her mouth, anxious that her father might hear her ragged breathing.

'Chico thought she might appeal to Señor Alonso. He is prepared to take her off your hands. She will live with him in the compound in Tijuana. They will find a judge to marry them.'

'But he's old . . .'

'Fifty or sixty, who knows? Yet a teenage girl will prefer an older man who can take care of her. Alonso wants a virgin. She *is* a virgin?'

'No man ever touched her!' Carlos slurred. 'She is innocent as the Madonna!'

'Excellent. It will be an honourable marriage then. Girls her age get sold to dealers. Trafficked. Good price on them.' The threat was clear, and Maria shuddered, horrified. She was fighting tears, fighting terror, fighting darkness. *Papa killed Mama. Papa would sell me. He* is *selling me.*

'She will live a life of luxury few can dream of. Horses, swimming pools, they have everything there. Señor Alonso is a big captain. He wants a quiet, obedient, pretty girl to mother his children. She will mix with the big wives, even the wives of the leaders. She can read and write, that is good. These are women of society. When she is a little older and has some children of her own, they will dine at restaurants and go shopping.'

'Maria is a lucky girl,' Carlos said, and he sounded jealous.

She was lucky? Being traded for an old man to rape? And she was meant to be thankful. Her mother was dead, and the man who had killed her mom hated her. He was drunk, a loser. He couldn't read, so he destroyed her little book.

They were still talking, but her father switched the TV on now, in the background, so she couldn't hear any more. Maria, tears flowing, lowered her face to her bare mattress – no pillow for her; their scrubby little house was one of the few round here with light and water, and she was lucky to have her own mattress in the attic.

A sense of exhaustion settled on her. She decided to sleep. Tomorrow was a big day. She opened her curtains wide, despite the grimy glow of the street lamps. She wanted the morning light to wake her, wake her before anyone else.

She closed her eyes and prayed to the Virgin, and then, like a miracle, sleep came.

In the morning, Maria dressed in her school uniform, a free one donated by the rich American gringos with their charity. She took a backpack and filled it with more clothes, sweaters and rough jeans and socks and her hardest sneakers. She packed a toothbrush, water, toilet roll, soap, and she worked fast. Her brothers were snoring, still half-drunk, and would be for hours.

Methodically Maria went through the house and took all the money she could find. She hid it about herself in different places, cut a slit in the waistband of her jeans. She took a hat of Chico's, a Red Sox baseball cap, old and weathered. Then she left the house. It was still early. Maria's family lived in a shanty area on the edge of Irapuato, the golden city for tourists, full of fine churches and good hotels. She knew where she was going, that was simple. To America. She would not take trains. No. She was going to hide. Until she was far away, where they would never find her.

There was a long walk, two miles maybe, up the hill. Fear growing with every step. Her father waking. Her brothers. But they would not look for her. She would be at school. Her clock started when somebody wanted money, to go to the liquor store, or buy some more food. But she was smart, she'd left the money in their wallets, Chico and Papa's. They would only discover the theft if they noticed her things missing, or needed more money.

And why would they notice anything to do with her? She was invisible.

Maria knew what she was looking for. A gringo. A tourist. An American with a car. Or a bus she could take, not for Mexicans, not one the police would check, the police in the pay of the cartel her brothers served. Maria was smart, very smart, like a street kid had to be.

Like the broken dolls and teddy bears in the story she had written, Maria was getting away.

The dolls and the bears had escaped in the end, and gone to America with a gringo girl called Maria, like her. That was a name the Anglos used too. Story Maria found them when they made sure they fell down in front of a museum entrance. She hid them away in her pockets and then they climbed into her momma's suitcase and they flew, they flew, all the way to Hollywood . . .

'How's the pressure for you, ma'am?' the masseuse asked soothingly.

Maria jerked. *How's the pressure?* That was funny.

Intense. The pressure she was under was always intense.

'It's great, thank you,' she muttered.

But it was no good. She was so lost in the fear and the hope and the heartbreak. That unloved little girl, running. That girl who was about to learn what it meant to be abused, and alone, with no family . . .

Fuck that, she thought firmly. My father will not get me. Señor Alonso will not get me. None of them will. The men. I beat them all.

That skinny, helpless victim, that was a long time ago. Maria

Gonzales was a new woman now. A superstar. Rich. Famous. And she craved the security that a man like Joe Goldstein could bring. If he was unwilling . . .

But he wouldn't be.

Men like him were her prey. It was everyone for herself in this world, *sí*? She'd learned that the hard way. And after all, Goldstein was no baby, and Topaz Rossi was no saint. Wasn't she having an affair with Joe when married to her first husband?

Maria had chosen her target, done her research. After that first, blundering escape, and the rapes, and the abuse, she never did anything again without the perfect goddamned plan.

Forcibly she pulled herself out of her memories. The masseuse was wiping her down with a warm washcloth. Time to wake up, Maria, time to get going.

Yes. It was the right moment to make a career change – *and* a personal one.

Maria's future was under threat. But she was also at the height of her beauty. Wasn't this the perfect moment for her transition?

A fling with Joe would test her theory out. Maria shifted, bringing the warm cloth's rubbing to a new, delicious point, just above the swell of her pretty ass. It was so great that she could be reasonable about it all. Topaz Rossi didn't worry Maria. Well preserved, maybe, but she was Joe's age, and that never worked out, did it? Men were biologically programmed. Maybe they wouldn't divorce, but Joe would recommend somebody better for Maria after she'd banged the hell out of him for a few months. He'd introduce her to a better husband.

She sighed, sure of her sexual power. Whatever. Who was she kidding? The fantasy was Maria Goldstein. Topaz hadn't even taken the guy's name, and rumour had it she was never around anyway. It was one of those hotshot convenience marriages now. Maria felt no scruples. After all, she was hardly going to *rape* Joe. If he didn't want her, then he'd let it go, right?

Men were all pigs. They used you, they abused you. Years of

rape and exploitation had taught Maria that. She didn't talk about it. She just dealt with it. Her own way.

Using the bastards right back.

Love? She didn't believe in it. Nobody ever showed it to her. But Maria did believe in security, in status, in position. She knew what it was like to claw your way up to the light. She would never be that little girl again, with her pathetic scribbled story, hoping and trusting in men.

Trust yourself, baby.

She smirked and glanced at the clock. Another ten minutes and this blissful massage would be over. She would dress carefully and the limo would swing by to pick her up. Maybe she would sign a few autographs in front of the hotel today. She was in *such* a good mood. Her interview with Goldstein was in his office, and she'd already made him promise there would be no interruptions.

Joe Goldstein just wouldn't know what had hit him.

Topaz and Joe sat together in their living room, nestled on a couch. He had an arm round his wife, but his thoughts were racing.

Why couldn't they handle this? Every day started with a fight. It sucked. This morning they were screaming at each other over the latest email from the school principal.

This lateness is disrespectful to fellow students, educators, and our school community. The disciplinary committee has decided to offer a final warning. If either Rona or David is late for the rest of the semester they will be asked to leave the school. Attendance at class is not optional at Pointer Academy, nor is the completion and attainment scores of assigned homework duties.

'You know, you really could have got them up. I mean, you run every day.'

'We have a schedule,' Topaz said angrily. 'It was *your* day.'

Joe removed his arm. He was furious.

'But you knew I had a party. I had to stay.'

'If you were going to be hung-over, Joe, you could have asked me, OK? And I'd gladly have swapped. I have work to do as well.'

'Mine is a little bit more important. It pays the bills.'

Topaz coloured scarlet. 'I make plenty of goddamned money. That's an obnoxious thing to say.'

He flushed too. 'OK, it is, I'm sorry. I know you work. It's just that the station isn't doing so great just now. I figured you could accommodate me.'

'If you ever bothered to ask, you'd know that *my* work—'

His head was thumping. 'Whatever. I'm sorry I brought it up. You're right, it was my day on the calendar. We run our lives by the calendar, and it was my day.'

'What's that supposed to mean?'

'Damn, I don't know. I guess just once I'm wishing for an ordinary life.'

She tensed. 'You mean an ordinary *wife*.'

'It's not that I don't love you. You know I do. But it kills me to reach out and have your goddamn pretty-boy secretary refuse to put me through.'

'Wow, go fuck yourself,' snapped Topaz. 'Brad is a clever young guy on the fast track. It's always bothered you that my secretary's a man.'

'He sees more of you than I do.'

'*And* treats me with more respect.'

'Maybe you want that kind of deferential guy, Topaz. I'm not that way. If I call you, it's not to share weather updates, OK? I have a reason.'

She breathed in deeply. 'Brad told me what happened. He asked you if it was life or death; you said no.'

'No. Just *our* life, I guess.'

'Well for your information, I couldn't take the call because I was firing somebody. I should have done it way back, but there it is. I couldn't interrupt that to sympathise with you.'

The contemptuous way she said *sympathise* set his teeth on edge. He wasn't being fair, and he knew it, but she was hardly helping, was she?

He put his arm back around her shoulder. Topaz received it stiffly, but didn't move away.

'We should have sex tonight.'

Topaz choked back a sob. She missed Joe on top of her, inside her, handling her so well. But she couldn't stand to be overridden. And she couldn't make love when he was acting like this.

'I think we need counselling first.'

There. The words were out. She'd said them.

Joe moved back. 'What the hell? Are you serious?'

'You know. Therapy . . .'

'Therapy? We don't do that bullshit, you and I. Never have. Tell some stranger our problems?' He passed a hand through his hair. 'We need to have sex, eat some dinners, get a plan for disciplining the kids. Be a family.'

'That would be nice.' Topaz swallowed hard. 'But Joe, it's your attitude. You have to work through it for me to be comfortable.'

Joe couldn't believe it. She was threatening him now?

'You won't have sex till we go to therapy?'

Topaz said nothing.

Joe stood up. 'Well, that sounds a lot like blackmail to me, honey. I don't do *therapy*. Not now, not ever. So where does that leave us?'

He walked to the door and took his coat from the closet.

'I have a meeting,' he said, and walked out.

Joe's office was sterile and spare, but right now it felt like a place of refuge. There were two small couches in the corner, because at times you needed to host bigger meetings than you'd planned;

a bank of TV screens showing NAB and all their broadcast rivals; and Joe's medium-sized antique English desk, which kept him grounded. There was nothing but a small laptop on it, which he used to work out ideas and deals. Ninety per cent of the station's game plan was in his head.

Industry magazines littered the coffee table. He picked up *Daily Variety* and flicked through it idly, trying to calm down. The best way to deal with Topaz Rossi was to forget her. Otherwise, anger would consume him.

His marriage sucked right now. But his career was improving. *Focus on that.*

He had to fix this dying network, and he'd finally bought the right to do so.

That was exhilarating. If a little scary.

'Mr Goldstein.' His secretary, Shawna, was buzzing him. 'Your nine thirty is here.'

Joe glanced at his watch: she was bang on time. That was refreshing. He was used to spoiled starlets standing him and everybody else up. If Maria Gonzales was polite enough not to keep him waiting, it was a start.

'Show her in.'

The door opened and Joe stood up. He looked the young woman up and down, taking her in. Maria was better dressed than she had been for the party. No make-up, or very little. Instead of an elaborate updo, her hair snaked loose down her back. She had a healthy glow, and when she smiled, her teeth gleamed white. He determinedly kept his gaze on her face, so as not to stare at those famous breasts, encased in a snug mohair sweater, though not one so tight as to be tacky. In fact, you might almost call the outfit demure. Beneath the sweater was a fitted tweed pencil skirt that hit at the knee, some kind of smooth hose and small heels. It showed off her wasp waist and jutting ass, that hourglass figure that was straight out of the 1940s. And that was what this felt like: a forties vixen in his office, ready to peel off a pair of kid gloves and start sassing him till he took her in his arms, over his knee, or maybe both.

He felt himself stirring. Felt a pang of guilt. But Maria was hard to look away from, that was for damned sure.

'Thank you for making the time to see me, Mr Goldstein,' she said, walking forward. 'I appreciate it.'

'Thanks for coming in,' he said firmly. 'Take a seat. Can I get you something to drink?'

'Coffee would be lovely. If it's not too much trouble.'

He buzzed Shawna. 'Two coffees, please. How do you like yours?'

'Just plain is good. Thanks. Whatever's going.'

The undemanding attitude was so pleasant. *Topaz used to be like this.*

'Two black coffees,' Joe said brusquely, hanging up. 'So, here's the deal, Maria. We would love to work with you again.'

'Oh, the *channel* would, sure.' She waved a tiny hand. 'My agent fields offers all day long. I know you know that, Mr Goldstein. I don't mean to boast, it's just how it is.'

'I bet. And it's Joe. Mr Goldstein is my dad.'

'Thank you,' Maria replied, beaming up at him as though he had just given her an Oscar. 'Anyway, for *me*, the question is do *you* want to work with me. I don't mean to be arrogant, Mr Goldstein – Joe.' She smiled warmly at him, sweet as melted caramel. 'But I can go anyplace. Networks will do anything to poach me. So you see, it's not really a question of money for me. It's about working with you personally.' She was purring a little now. 'And closely. If we do a project together, you'll need to be there with me. Supervising. Getting involved on a creative level.' She paused for dramatic effect.

'Like I say, Joe, working together needs to be more than a catchphrase. If you want me to re-sign with NAB, that is.'

Joe shrugged. 'But Maria, I'm not a showrunner. I *hire* showrunners. That's what running a network means.'

'Yes,' she said softly. 'You're the boss. I get it. But you can keep a tight leash, get involved in the shows you programme. You see, I admire what you're doing *sooo* much. How you're clearing house. It's risky. It's a new direction for NAB.'

As Shawna walked in with a tray of coffee, Goldstein took a second to register what she'd said. Then he blinked in surprise.

'You know about that?'

Stupid comment. But she'd taken him aback.

'I'm a big star. I have my spies round here. Shall I be mother?' Maria said lightly, and leaned forward for the coffee pot as soon as Shawna turned around. Those breasts were peeping out at him. *Goddamn.*

'Thank you.' He gritted his teeth. 'My wife, Topaz, loves serving the coffee as well.'

Wow. Obvious. Where the hell had that come from? He blushed.

'Powerful women like to show their girlie side once in a while.' Maria nodded. 'But all anybody sees is my girlie side. I'd like to display something different.'

'You would?' Joe asked mechanically. He found it very hard to take his eyes off her ass as she stood up, apparently for a better coffee-pouring angle. She was displaying *that* very well indeed.

But she was still talking. *Focus, Joe.*

'You see, everybody will assume that you made another show with me just to keep the suits happy. I know you say you're a suit, but you're a *rebel* suit. And if you want to surprise the critics, Mr Gold—'

'Joe.'

'Sorry. I just *respect* you so much. Anyway, if you want to surprise the critics, you'll make a good show with me. I mean an *interesting* show. Not another dumb cop drama. Something different.'

'Such as what?' he asked, his mouth dry.

'Hey, that's why they pay you the big bucks. But if you cast me against type in something interesting, you could get creative renewal *and* a bankable star. You could have your cake,' Maria licked her lips and bit into a cookie, 'and eat it.'

Joe shivered. Maria knew what she was doing, right? Surely she did. This was nuclear-grade flirting.

The question is, do you *know what you're doing?*

But the voice of his conscience was getting ever fainter. Joe made an effort, and stared into her sexy dark eyes.

'Maria,' he said thickly. 'You're not a great actress.'

'Ouch.' Those dark eyes widened.

'I don't bullshit people. Nobody's going to cast you as Miss Moneypenny in a minimiser bra. The network will want to see that body. Still.'

'I understand. But you see, I also have a sense of humour. I can be funny. We can get girls to like me, as well as the dudes. I want to make something feminist.'

Joe choked on his coffee. 'Feminist?'

'Yeah. And fun. Like, you know, a modern version of *Xena, Warrior Princess*. Empowering, amusing, a little bit cult classic. With me on horseback. *Game of Thrones* won't know what's hit them.' Maria laughed. 'But if we rate it PG-13, I'll make a *fortune* on reruns – and so will you.'

Goldstein shook his head to clear it.

'Wow,' he laughed.

He could see the ad teasers in his mind already. The girls would laugh. The men would laugh and get turned on. And the kids would love it.

'What do you do when you want to be more than just a great body?' Maria said, pressing her advantage home. 'You know, in the nineties, Arnold Schwarzenegger's answer was to do *Twins*, with Danny de Vito. Conan the Barbarian in a comedy! He made a *ton* of money on that.'

'Yes, he did.' Schwarzenegger's move was the stuff of Hollywood legend, but you didn't expect movie stars to be up on business deals. The bombshell evidently had a brain. 'When you finish being a sexpot, you'll make one hell of a producer,' Joe said, without thinking.

Maria lifted one carefully arched brow.

Joe shook his head, horrified. *Holy fucking shit! I said that out loud!*

'I'm so sorry, Maria, I didn't mean that.' With great self-control, he bit back a gasp of dismay. 'It just slipped out. I wasn't thinking. I never refer to our actors in those terms. I apologise completely.'

Instant lawsuit, if she felt like it.

Maria stood up and offered him one hand.

Wow. Thank God. He could breathe again.

He didn't know if he should bend and kiss her hand like a Frenchman, or pump it like a jock, so he just took it and held it for a second.

Unmistakably, she traced one little finger up and down his palm. He blushed scarlet.

'Now, Joe. You would only have to apologise if you *didn't* think I was a sexpot.' She grinned. 'Relax. I'm glad you like what you see. You're in charge here. I guess I'll see you tomorrow, and we can work up some good ideas. How's that?'

Tam Watson looked up from his Kindle and sighed.

The Miami Beach mansion he and his wife kept as a vacation home wasn't as peaceable as usual.

And there was only one reason. Joanna was home. Tail between her legs.

She was stomping around the deck of their oceanfront infinity pool, sighing loudly, taking up her copy of *American Girl* and flinging it back down on the lounger.

Damn it. I thought this was over when she left college, the financier thought.

He was ill-equipped to deal with women's stuff. Joanna was his only daughter; her brother was sensible and already working in the M&A division of his company. Vaguely he looked around for his wife. But Miriam was out shopping, or brunching, or some other goddamned thing.

'Joanna, please. I'm trying to concentrate.'

'I'm sorry, Daddy, I just can't get over that *bitch* Topaz Rossi. She's made me into a laughing stock. She fired me.'

'It just didn't work out. Sweetie, you're not a laughing stock. You can do something else,' Tam said placidly.

'Like what?'

'Your mother practises philanthropy. Why don't you join her on some of those charity boards or whatnot? Save the Trees.'

Joanna blinked. 'Save the Trees?'

'Or the Whales. Rainforests, that's it. They're still cutting down the rainforests.' Tam searched around. 'Or you could start collecting art. Plenty to do.'

'I want a career, Daddy.'

So go start a company then, her father didn't say. He almost thought of offering to make her a vice president of public relations at his firm, but decided against it. Buying a huge stake in the Canadian magazine and making her editor had seemed like a masterstroke. But it had ended in her abandoning the project.

'More trouble than they're worth.' Tam attempted levity. 'I did that so you don't have to.'

'Daddy. She *scorned* you. She said that you can't influence her. If you let Topaz Rossi push me around like that, you're letting her push *you* around. Can't you buy her stupid company and fire her?'

Tam shook his head. 'Magazines are a dying business, honey. American isn't bad, but Rossi's numbers are falling all round. I wouldn't want a print house. Not unless it was at a knock-down price and I could spin the assets right off.'

'Do that,' she wheedled.

Tam yawned. 'Look, Joanna. This isn't for me. You should go pitch the deal to somebody else.'

Joanna stamped her Jimmy Choos in frustration. 'Like who? Daddy, if it's a horrible deal, then you have to do it, because who else will? You can't let her do that to me!'

'Given the several hundred million bucks it would cost me to buy American Magazines, yes, Jo, I can.' Wearily Tam Watson picked up his Kindle again. 'It's true you need somebody motivated by more than money.' He laughed. 'Hey, you should try Conrad Miles.'

'Conrad Miles? The billionaire?'

'Yeah. He has a few billion. Fifty-plus at last count.'

Joanna had stopped whining. 'Why would Conrad Miles want American Magazines?'

'He wouldn't, but like you, he hates Topaz Rossi. And Rowena Krebs.'

'Who?'

'She's the president of Musica Records, another dying company.' Tam yawned. 'Really, honey, I'm on vacation. Can we drop it?'

'Sure. Just tell me about Topaz Rossi and Rowena Krebs and Conrad Miles,' Joanna said eagerly.

'If I do, will you go away?'

'I swear, Daddy! Tell me!'

The stamping foot was back. He hadn't liked it when she was fourteen. 'Look, it's legendary in my world that Conrad Miles tried to buy Musica and American back in the early nineties, and Topaz and Rowena – who'd been well-known rivals in business – got together and utilised a poison pill, some unattractive stock in the business. The bid fell apart, and for a while it looked as though Conrad would lose control of his own company. In the end he re-formed it, but a lot of his class A stock got diluted to other shareholders. It's a famous story, because it's about the only time Conrad Miles has ever been beaten. And knowing how much he hates being laughed at, I'd say he still remembers it.'

'You said Musica Records was weak too?'

'Spotify, pirates, and kids preferring Xbox – music has sucked as a business since about 1991.'

'So maybe he could buy them both and break them up. Kick the girls out?'

'He might like that . . .'

'Daddy, can you help me get in touch with him?'

That did it. Tam Watson sat up straight. 'Joanna, here's what I'll do. I'll assign a Watson Industries analyst to put together a paper for you on the financial breakdown of the two companies, and I will ask a friend of mine at Goldman Sachs to get an email from you to Conrad Miles. If he likes the idea, he will see you. I don't approach Miles directly. I don't play in that league. If you want to, knock yourself out. But I'd like you to take the jet back to New York, return to that lovely penthouse your mother and I bought you seven years ago, and let us vacation in peace. You're twenty-eight. Honey, you need to enjoy your trust fund, find a husband or a boyfriend, or both.'

'Dad!'

'Seriously, Joanna. I love you, but I can't deal with this. I'll get you that analyst. And if Conrad Miles isn't interested, don't badger him. Don't annoy him. Whatever you do, don't mess with him. At this point, he's one of the most powerful men in the business world.'

Tam put his shades back on and returned to his Kindle. He missed the glint that had settled into Joanna's eye.

'Thanks, Dad. I'm leaving. Love to Mom. Tell that analyst to email me the report.'

'You'll have it by the time you land,' her father said, relieved. 'Fly safe.'

But he only heard the door slam behind her.

Joanna Watson was already gone.

Chapter Five

'My God, Michael. I . . . I don't know what to say.'

Rowena moved forward and gave her husband a hug, taking him in her arms. She nestled her head against his muscled shoulder, feeling his heart beat.

They were sitting together on the couch in their living room. Kids in bed, sipping iced water after dinner, looking out at the lights of Los Angeles spread below their perch in the Hollywood Hills.

Krebs kissed the top of her head. He didn't say anything either. This must be absolutely brutal for him, and Rowena couldn't do anything to make it better.

He'd come home as normal, but a little subdued; she'd hung out with the kids, made them all dinner for once – home-made pasta puttanesca, a simple recipe Topaz had taught her. Then the young teens had sloped off and he'd turned to her as she stacked the dishwasher.

'Leave that. Janet can do it in the morning.'

Rowena straightened with surprise, spider-sense tingling. Unlike her messy self, Michael Krebs was a neat freak. It was part of his love of order and control. But they survived, mostly because she had a great housekeeper.

'Something's happened?'

He nodded. 'Come through and sit with me and I'll tell you everything.'

Rowena nodded. Fear pulsed through her. What if it was something bad? Really bad?

He started by telling her about Barbara's call.

'She has a good nose, sweetheart. You should take control of this situation.'

Rowena nodded, worried, glad that Barbara called. 'I will. Thanks.'

'Wait. There's more.'

Rowena's stomach flipped over. 'You're not sick, Michael, are you?'

He was her world, her everything. For a moment, time hung suspended in the air.

'No. But Marty's got cancer. Liver cancer.'

And there it was, the moment that changed their world.

'I've talked with Debbie. She's trying to stay strong. I'm flying up to see him, but not right now. She says he needs space to come to terms with it.'

'What does he say?'

Krebs sighed. 'Debbie tells me not to do it, I can't overrule her. I just can't. She was the main custodial parent.'

'But he's long since been an adult.'

'Please.' Her husband's tone was sharp. 'Don't interfere. This one isn't your fight.'

Rowena wanted to open her mouth and argue, but thought better of it. He was right, anyway. If Josh or Ruth were sick, she wouldn't want any other woman sticking her nose in.

'Do you want to tell the kids?'

'No.' Krebs was decisive. 'They've never been that close to Marty. If it looks . . . if it looks like the worst, we'll let them know.'

'But you'll be travelling to see him . . .'

'I'll tell them something. Not everything. Not how serious it is.'

Rowena sat there feeling helpless. She knew it was nothing to how Michael must feel. And she could not be part of it.

'So what do you want me to do?'

He patted her hand. 'You know, I've thought about this all day.'

'I can imagine.'

'It won't help Marty if I fall apart. We need to get on with our lives, protect our kids – that's where you can really help – and act normally. I will be there whenever Marty needs me. But I have to work, and so do you. We need to carry on. I want you to plan a trip to Europe, hit your acts on tour, see if you can spike the trouble Barbara talked about.'

It made sense business-wise, she knew. 'But if I go to Europe, how do you get to see Marty?'

'Try and arrange it soon. When you come back, I'll head to New York. That should give him the space he needs.'

'OK.'

He kissed her. 'And do me a major favour. I'll tell you any major developments, but can you *not* keep asking me about Marty? I want . . . I want you, us, to be the same. Like I can flirt with you, fuck you . . .'

She shifted a little, licked at the base of his chin. 'You can always do that.'

'I feel that if my life with you and the kids is as normal as possible, I have a better shot at keeping it together. And being more useful for my son. Does that make sense?'

Rowena lifted her glass of water. 'Sweetheart, it makes perfect sense. You want a rock to lean on. I can be that.'

'Focus on Musica.' He ran a hand down her corn-silk hair.

She nodded. 'I will. Starting tomorrow. Now put that water down and come to bed.'

Rowena stood up and let the cashmere robe slither from her shoulders on to the deck.

She stepped out of the jewelled flip-flops that Michael had bought her on a holiday to Capri. Rowena had loved walking the island's winding streets, hiking up to the ruins of the villa of Augustus Caesar, perched atop a barren rock fit only for goats and lemon trees. The flip-flops, impossibly expensive, were one souvenir that had stayed with her for years, as had the gold-and-beige Missoni bikini that clung to her slender frame now. Her skin was only a pale gold; even in LA, Rowena Krebs didn't tan much, her pale Scottish skin religiously protected by the best sunscreen money could buy. Her dermatologist marvelled at her face. She didn't smoke, didn't drink, and only now and again needed a pinch of Botox on her forehead to smooth things out.

Really, her doctor said, it was happiness. That was what kept her looking younger than any filler possibly could.

But today, in the slightly chilly morning air in the Hills, there was a light frown on that pretty face. The numbers worried her. There were always slumps. But three of her tent-pole records were dying on the vine, and the company was on the hook for tens of millions in tour support. Normally there were a few bright spots, even in a shitty year, but her young A&R bloods were coming up horribly dry. Radio hated their baby acts. The internet sensations got no traction, the rappers had no swing. Two years ago, her boys and girls had delivered Musica a mammoth year and eight Grammys; now it was a desert.

Rowena swung her toned arms over her head, shivering slightly in the early-morning breeze, and dived into the warmth of her pool, plunging forward, water sluicing over her back, long legs kicking into a crawl. The temperature was perfection, like a warm bath. They spent a fortune on heating it, but Rowena didn't care. It meant that every time she wanted to swim, she could. Early morning. Late night. She loved doing thirty laps before breakfast; it was a hell of a way to exercise, the pool's infinity edge making her feel she was swimming into the sky, off the edge of the world. The Scot in her, a daughter of landed gentry with their own Highland castle, remembered too many icy summers miserable with cold, running through grey-stone halls her father said were too expensive to heat. She'd promised herself she would embrace the golden skies of California, and her life here was true to that: swimming most days, reading in the garden, hiking through the canyons, splashing around on the beach. Her stair-climber and weight bench were housed in a glass-walled gym directly under the pool, facing out towards the city at the edge of the garden; Michael had designed the place for maximum light.

Rowena swam smoothly, quickly, breathing hard, becoming one with the water. She was an excellent swimmer and raced through the workout. The exercise concentrated her mind, let her forget the pressures of work and everything crowding in on her. By the time she stepped out of the pool, warm water sluicing down her tired, toned thighs, breathing heavily, she was calmer, and ready to work.

She swapped the cashmere robe for a towelling one and headed inside. The kids were already up and grabbing breakfast; their school bus would arrive in a few minutes.

'Hey, Mom,' Josh grunted through a mouthful of porridge.

Rowena smiled at him. She fussed about the kids eating correctly when they were studying for SATs. She wanted them to go to good colleges.

She and Topaz had met at Oxford University all those years ago. It seemed like another lifetime. Best friends, and then bitter rivals, until at last they'd come together again. And she still felt shame when she realised she'd broken their bond over a worthless man.

But the cut and thrust of student politics had prepared her, in its way, for big business; even the strangeness of her particular business. And she wanted her kids to have a good experience too.

Michael wasn't so bothered about college, having attended,

and pretty much failed at, the University of Chicago. He was already pushing both kids to start a business, found a radio station, do something concrete with their young lives.

Rowena wasn't worried. Her children would make it. They had ambition, and they were chafing against Mom and Dad. And she didn't mind that one bit.

'Get going,' she said firmly, and walked into her bedroom. She'd laid her clothes out the night before: tailored black drainpipe slacks, a satin T-shirt and chic black flats. Along with her favourite black Prada jacket and a spiked metal leather cuff, this was Rowena Krebs's grown-up twist on the hard-rock look – she enjoyed it, that little rebel kick that allowed her to feel outrageous at forty-two, still kicking ass, surprising everybody. And it was her go-to look when there was a fight to be had. Which there certainly was today.

She showered, conditioned her long hair, then nuked it dry with the top-of-the-range salon hairdryer she'd bribed her stylist to sell her. Best investment of the year. Getting that long mane ready to go in record time saved her hours of productivity over the course of a month alone. She made up fast – hardcore sun protection, BB cream over the top of it, clear lip gloss, copper-gold shadow above her green eyes and a sweep of bronzer on the cheeks – and was out of the door in less than twenty minutes.

The garage was built into the bottom of the house, directly facing the driveway, with room for his-and-hers rides: Michael's white Lexus SUV and Rowena's racing-green Aston Martin. She loved the car, a little James Bond tribute; no flashy Lamborghinis or Maseratis in their house.

She pulled into traffic and was soon barrelling down Sunset Boulevard. The radio on the walnut dashboard was playing Anatomy, another Musica act. 'So High' was their big song of last year. It was impossible for Rowena to get away from her twenty years of music history. And she didn't want to. But nor did she want to *be* history.

Michael had given her permission – even ordered her – to put her career front and central right now.

I can do that, she thought.

By the time the car was parked in the CEO's slot, front and centre under the Musica Tower in the middle of Hollywood, she had already got a battle plan in her mind.

Barbara didn't have to worry.

Rowena was about to make some goddamned *noise*.

Topaz kept it together, even though it was tough. Joe was distant, but the kids needed her. She knew that. And yet she didn't have enough to give.

What would a perfect wife have done? Stayed home, cancelled work? Driven the twins to family therapy?

Maybe. Only unfortunately there wasn't time for her to play at being a hausfrau. Magazines didn't stop for anybody. The deadlines kept coming, rushing at you like trams. By the time one monthly hit the stands, you were already three quarters done with the next. Selling that ad space, negotiating those slots, dealing with supermodels, testy photographers, egotistical politicians . . . stealing exclusives from the other houses, funding that insider investigation that had already cost your organisation a million dollars and twelve full months for an explosive security story the government might never let you publish . . .

A full slate of magazines. A full slate of problems.

And hers had just got much worse.

'We have to get through this,' she said to Joe, after a disastrous supper. The kids had refused to eat her pasta, calling it under-cooked. Joe manfully swallowed his, despite having to chew it into submission. She wanted to cry; this was her one attempt at womanliness, and it wasn't working.

Maybe because her mind was elsewhere. On *American Girl*, to be precise. The meat sauce was burned and the pasta hard, but Topaz thought she had the germ of an idea.

'It doesn't look good,' she murmured doubtfully to her husband. 'Maybe we just can it and call for Chinese?'

'On a school night? Fried brains from MSG is the last thing they need.' Joe scowled. 'I don't approve of them ordering in from Seamless, you know that. We eat dinner as a family, right? Home cooking.'

'Groan cooking,' Topaz said. It was a weak attempt at a joke. Joe didn't smile.

'Mom, this is gross,' Rona said. Her hair was a virulent shade of dark blue and her nails matched. Topaz vaguely remembered it being pink last week. 'I can't eat it.'

'Me neither,' David said. 'Like, you know, I can make myself some ramen noodles, so it's all good.'

'What would be good is you eating what you're given,' Joe snarled. 'Protein might help you to think.'

'I think fine, thank you.'

'Your grades say otherwise. So does your discipline. How do you think Mom and I feel about getting another nasty letter from the school? Not that I blame them.'

Rona forked her burnt sauce. 'This is inedible.'

'Let's just get pizza,' Topaz said, defeated.

'The hell we will. Eat. Not one more word.' Joe shook his head. 'You two kids are just so goddamned entitled.'

'Whose fault is that?' his daughter asked nastily.

'Don't speak to your father like that,' Topaz snapped. She had a hateful vision of her own mother backing her father up when he abused her, shouted at her, ignored her in favour of her brothers.

'Hey, honey, she's right. It is our fault. You never have to work for anything, why would you work at it?' Joe said. 'You two kids have no hunger. No ambition. You're such a disappointment.'

David's face clouded. 'What kind of thing is that to say to your own kids?'

'Don't be stupid. Dad loves you, so do I, you both know that,' Topaz swooped in. 'Your actions are disappointing, is what he meant to say.'

'I can speak for myself,' Joe said, furious at being undermined. 'Your mother and I will come up with some suitable sanctions for last week's behaviour. Eat that pasta and get upstairs. Neither of us wants to see you again tonight.'

Topaz bit her lip, hard. The kids both looked as if they wanted to cry, tight with rage and sorrow. She actually heard Rona sniff, saw her thin shoulders shake. They both forced down several mouthfuls of the disgusting meal she'd put in front of them. Topaz was withered with shame and frustration, wanting to say it was OK, to call for a stupid pizza, even to make them a peanut butter sandwich. And let them both know how loved, how totally loved, they were. But her husband's face was a mirror of rage, and she found herself afraid to cross him. Afraid for the kids, and afraid for the two of them.

David stood up from the table, taking his half-full plate with him. His sister joined him. They scraped the food silently into the garbage, and stomped out of the room, slamming the door behind them.

'Better be on time tomorrow,' Joe shouted. Then he turned to his wife. 'Excuses. Why the hell do you always give them excuses? Options? Just have some discipline, for God's sake.'

'Joe, they're teenagers. And they're not you. Or me.'

'I understand that. I figured that out long ago,' Goldstein said bitterly. As a young man, he'd fought and struggled to get on. Picked out the bullies in the playground, scored with the girls, made sure he had fine grades. But David and Rona weren't that way. They were ticking along, with their Facebook accounts and late-night parties and gaming addictions. They made OK grades. They skipped phys ed and had incompletes to make up each summer. Already he was writing the Ivy League off; their transcripts wouldn't cut it. All that money, all those tutors, wasted.

'You're going to push them away.'

'They're doing that themselves. And David's right, it's our fault. We let them do it.' He scowled at her. 'I don't suppose you're interested in a real punishment this time?'

'Like what? Flogging?'

'Be serious,' he said.

'They're not five. What do you want to confiscate?' Topaz tried to think, to come up with something. 'We can turn off the internet altogether. For a week. No iPhones, no YouTube, no Xbox or whatever.'

Joe shook his head. 'I need email.'

'Really.' Topaz wanted to be creative, to support Joe, but not to scream at her children. It sucked being young; it was great, but it sucked too, no doubt about that. And they were heaping pressure on those slim shoulders, on kids who were bored, bright and alienated, and doing just a horrible job. 'I can get a tech in here tomorrow for a new wireless network, one only we have the password to. They won't be able to jump on.'

'Except David will go out and buy a dongle.'

'He might.' Topaz softened at the thought of her son's ingenuity. Maybe he wasn't conventionally pushy, like her and her husband, but he was cunning and clever enough when it came to the things he really wanted. 'That would be funny.'

As Joe's brows knitted together, she knew she'd said the wrong thing. But resentment was flaring up in her now. An urge to pick up the jug of iced water and dump it all over his crisply cut suit. She was in a work crisis of epic proportions. Did he have to make things worse? Did he have to do it *right now*?

'It wouldn't be funny. And we can't deal with this by banning World of Warcraft. Here's what I propose. We tell the kids that they're almost out at Pointer Academy. It's not just the letters from the disciplinary committee. We tell them that if their grades and attendance don't improve dramatically, we're not paying for private school.'

Topaz gasped. 'What? No. You're not serious.'

'I'm totally serious. They don't want to learn, fine. But they're not fucking about on my dime. There's a pretty good public school down the block. I've been worrying about them having to move there. Maybe that's wrong. Maybe it's exactly what they deserve.'

'I went to public school, and it wasn't pretty.'

'It got you to Oxford.'

'Yeah. It did. But I've been hauling ass ever since to give our kids advantages. So they don't have to struggle like I did.'

'And they haven't paid the blindest bit of notice. They're going to be trust-fund brats.'

'Jesus, Joe.' She was horrified. 'They're coming up for their SATs. College depends on this year. You don't chuck a kid into the system at a time like this.'

Blood rushed to his face. Suddenly she saw him not as her partner, her friend, her forceful, aggravating, deeply sexy husband. She saw him as a *problem*. And she hated it.

'I can't be worrying about this shit now,' she said blankly. 'So stop it, OK?'

'Stop what? I'm serious. You think I'm a bully.'

'You are.'

'What?'

'Right now, you are.'

He made a guttural sound in his throat. 'Topaz, you need to *listen* to me.'

'I'm not deaf. I heard you. The answer is no. I hope that's clear enough for you.'

He paused. 'Give our kids the advantage of needing something in life, Topaz. Give them that. Give them the chance to work for it. Like we had to. We've tied a golden rope around their ankles. They can't walk, they can't run.'

'Very poetic.' The guilt, the exhaustion, the rage was stealing up on her. 'I don't need you to be doing this to me today,

73

Joe Goldstein. We can talk about some scheme like this after SATs.'

'There'll still be a chance for them to work it out. You need to back me.'

'I don't agree with you and I don't back you. Please just come to bed.' She reached out to him. 'We shouldn't fight. We should go have some sex.'

This last was said with a deep effort of will. Joe right now was not an appealing lay. He was blustering, bullying, shouting, not the man she loved. Not the man she'd married.

'I don't feel like sex with you,' he said flatly. 'You need to be different – *we* need to be different – for that to happen. You said so yourself.'

She breathed in. This wasn't how it was meant to be. He pursued her, loved her, ravished her, however much she might try and resist. For a second she felt old, haggard and undesired.

'Joe, we haven't had sex in nearly two weeks. Does it ever occur to you that you're not the only person in the room? That maybe other people have needs? God, I produce magazines. I read agony aunt columns every day. I print advice about love and my own damned man treats me like I'm some kind of a leper.'

He sighed, and the fight seemed to wash out of him. 'Fine. Come to bed. We'll have sex.'

'Don't do me any favours.' Tears sprang to her eyes, her body disgracing her, letting her down. She turned aside, grabbing plates, cups, pulling open the dishwasher. Anything to get away from Joe. She didn't want him to see. And she didn't want pity sex.

'No. You're right. We're married. We need to make love.'

She couldn't help herself. Her body heaved with a sob. 'Stop talking like that. All family and duty and shit. This isn't duty, like paying your taxes. It's about two people and romance and desire. Which we don't have.'

Joe came up behind her. He put his hands on her shoulders, patting them.

'I'm not a two-year-old. I don't want your comfort and I don't need a charity fuck. Trust me, Joe. I find you totally undesirable right now,' Topaz snarled. 'I *don't* respect you and I couldn't get wet for you standing in a shower.'

'Perfect,' he said heavily. 'Then we're agreed. I'm going to a hotel for a couple of days.'

The shock of that washed over her like cold water, cutting through the heat of her rage with a long finger of sheer ice. Fear gripped her heart. She felt like she could hardly breathe.

But her pride kept her upright.

'Do whatever the hell you want,' she said. 'As if I care.'

She stayed frozen at the sink, waiting for him to say something, to apologise, say this was stupid, even touch her again. Reach out. Heal it.

But instead, there was near silence in the room, the sound of his footfalls, the swish of a coat. And the door opening, and quietly, respectably, closing behind him again.

Conrad Miles pulled on the reins of his horse, turning it a little to the left. It was a fine Arabian stallion, one of the best in his stable. Leander, his trainer called it, but Miles didn't bother treating horses like dogs. He had them trained to follow commands, and that was exactly what they did. Leander had been sired by a three-time Kentucky Derby winner, and his flanks were pure muscle under the rich chocolate coat; a noble horse, a mount fit for a billionaire.

Miles enjoyed riding. He hated being old. The horse's power gave him the illusion of youth, the same vitality in body as he had in his mind. Riding was one exercise that pleased him; straining against weights just to keep upright, tortuous yoga stretches, none of those he enjoyed. But it was no matter. Stand still at seventy-eight, even for a month, and you let that old man squat in your body. And once he was in, you never got him out.

Miles would rather die of a heart attack, quickly and mercifully, than suffer away in his bed, a shadow of himself, afraid of nurses he could not report on or control. He thought about this more often than he should. The only way to fight it was to live and live large.

'Sir.' His executive assistant was at the edge of the training ring, waving at him. 'Excuse me, sir.'

He trotted the magnificent beast over to her, looking down on her. Physically as well as mentally. 'Matilda. Yes?'

'I beg your pardon, Mr Miles. But it's time for you to stop riding. You asked me to fetch you at two.'

'So I did.'

He handed the reins to one of his grooms, and another reached up silently to take his free hand and swing him down to the ground. Seventeen hands tall, Leander was a big beast. Miles didn't look back at him. He wasn't the type to pet noses.

'Is the meeting room ready?'

'Yes, sir. All your advisers are gathered.'

His faltering heart was pumping nicely now. The ride, and now the deals. Better than exercise, business kept him young. Miles flew all around the world managing his media empire. And he kept buying, building, attacking. That was the way to stay alive. Retirement? A death sentence.

Conrad Miles would die in the saddle. Literally or figuratively, no matter to him.

'Then let's get going.'

There was a golf cart waiting for him, with a silent driver. Conrad Miles paid well, but preferred not to converse with his staff. He despised the pressure of fake friendships, remembering the names of people he didn't care about. Rather than pretend civility, he dealt instead with bonuses and fat wages. And his staff were happy with that.

Waiting up at the main house, out here on the golden San Diego coast, were some of the world's most important investment bankers and stock analysts, and the chief executives of his various divisions. It was part of Conrad Miles's power that they came to him. He was in the middle of nowhere here. But business was wherever he said it should be.

Within minutes he had been ferried to the front portico of his mansion, an enormous, sprawling white house of gleaming limestone, the triple-height entrance hall flanked by thick Grecian columns. A butler was waiting to assist him from the cart and lead the way towards one of the lesser drawing rooms, his French salon, decorated exclusively with Parisian antiques from the belle époque. The walls were a robin's-egg blue and the curtains washed golden silk; the rug on the floor took its aquamarine and mint tones from Imperial China, and the couches and chairs had been painstakingly sourced from various chateaux and *grandes maisons*. Even the antique humidor on the walnut table was worth over a hundred thousand dollars.

And amid all this sumptuousness sat his allies, employees and lieutenants. Eager to go to work for him. Eager to get it done, to be players, to be *noticed*.

So far, so boringly normal.

But Conrad Miles had spotted something different. Some*one* different. He smiled slightly. He loved to be surprised.

There was one incongruous note among the jackets and ties. Wearing a pretty little Chanel skirt suit in pale pink tweed was Joanna Watson, the Canadian girl, simpering and bowing her head as he appeared, like a new debutante admitted to court, curtseying before the king.

Which, in a way, she was.

Her father was on the very fringes of his world – that of the mega-rich. Not that Conrad Miles took much notice of minnows like Tam Watson. But he did, definitely, like the idea that Joanna had run by him. And not just on purely financial grounds.

Her email had a solid analysis of American Magazines and Musica Records attached. It also had clippings about Rowena Krebs and Topaz Rossi. They hadn't made a ton of money – they were common or garden multi-millionaires – but it enraged him to see all the accolades, the awards, the honours. And Joanna Watson was proposing that Conrad change their happy ending to a horror show.

> *Mr Miles,*
>
> *Back then they called Topaz and Rowena the Career Girls. The only two to beat you at your own game. But this Career Game isn't over until you stop playing, is it? If you bought them both, you could form a media division. I would love to help you run American Magazines, because Topaz Rossi is a dinosaur who's bitter and retrograde and doesn't belong in the world of fashion. I hope you find the attached company analysis interesting and I would love the chance to present this idea to you and your advisers in person.*
>
> *Sincerely,*
>
> *Joanna Watson*

It was so stupid, it was brilliant. But in a way, he couldn't mock her. She was absolutely right. He'd forgotten about those two arrogant bitches, and he would love to set the record straight. Plus, young Miss Watson had been careful to add an attractive-looking headshot. Meeting her would be fun. Settling that particular score would be more fun. In fact, Miles was slightly annoyed that he'd forgotten about Topaz and Rowena. He should have taken care of this himself, long ago.

Credit to the artless Ms Watson for reminding him.

Yep. That was why Joanna had made it as far as this room. Would she have what it took to stay?

The men had also all sprung to their feet, as if the President had just entered the room. Miles waved them back to the antique couches, and the bone-china cups they had just been sipping from.

'Good afternoon, lady and gentlemen,' Miles began. He might be old, but they all paid him extremely close attention. 'Thanks for showing up. We're here today to discuss Miles Industries' two new acquisition targets.'

They nodded, glued to his every word. Only Joanna Watson knew exactly what he was going to say next.

'American Magazines and Musica Records.'

Chapter Six

'Everybody here?'

'Hi, Rowena. George here.'

'Pierre logged in.'

'Heinrich,' barked the head of her German operations.

'Paolo,' said the Italian chief.

'Helga,' said the younger woman who ran Sweden and Norway for her.

There was nobody from Spain. Rowena always noticed that, when she travelled back to the continent to get the Europeans together. She missed Frederico, but the Spanish laws on pirating were so lax, their record industry had been killed off for good. She couldn't employ a staff where no records got sold. The French affiliate took care of the few thousands of downloads that trundled through Spanish smartphones. There were no record stores there for CDs any more.

'Great. Thanks to those of you who've stayed late for this.' It was odd, running a conference call for one of the great American record companies, and not having a Yank on the phone. But these days she regarded herself as half and half. You couldn't live here this long, be married to an American and mother two more without feeling just a little bit native. Certainly Rowena was well known for firing staffers who sneered at the stupid American public, thinking they would ingratiate themselves with the Limey boss. 'But as the therapists say, we need to talk.'

'Rowena, I hope you're not blaming us for the Lumos fiasco,' George Turner said quickly. He was thirty-five and running their UK affiliate, the biggest Musica satellite east of LA. Lumos was British, and one of the acts whose tour was stiffing horribly right now. 'We were kept away from the album by management. And they were too big to piss off.'

'I'm not blaming anyone. Maybe some A and R guys. We're low on replacement acts. You guys need to find me some good scouts, OK? That end of things is your job. But on these three, we took a chance that was justified by prior sales, and I don't know exactly why we've had three stiffs in a row.'

There were grunts.

'Too much deference to managers.'

More grunts. They all felt embarrassed.

'I'm going to start taking care of that today. However. The company's in a situation where we have no fucking hits, and we need some. What I need all of you to do is go through the catalogue and find which of our staples are working in your territories. Especially anything where we control the publishing.' That was the right to play the record, to license it. Bands didn't give that up so easily these days, but catalogue was another matter: legendary seventies bands, eighties pop acts, sixties soul singers – Musica controlled many of these songs. 'Then I want all of you to get marketing involved. License. Attach our biggest hits to whatever you can – commercials, movies, hit TV shows. Give them the rights for nothing, almost nothing, and put out compilations, greatest hits, remixes, I don't give a goddamn. Think that stupid Elvis record.'

'Less conversation and more action?' asked Pierre.

'Yes. *Précisément*,' answered Rowena. 'The song, and our strategy. Call producers, splice in dead singers for duets, whatever you have to. I want to see a ceaseless stream of income and numbers in weekly countdowns. Covers – covers work too.

If you've got big bands, match them with unlikely covers, OK? Like a *Saturday Night Live* thing. Imagine Metallica playing Michael Jackson, Adele doing NWA. Understood? I don't care where or how you get it. Just get it.'

There was a moment of silence. 'Rowena, it's not as easy as all that,' Paolo objected.

'It really is. We need to work our catalogue in ways that make the other companies jealous. And you know, that's why you guys run the place.'

'Making a record takes time,' Pierre observed.

'About two or three weeks. If you've got good producers and a hungry band. All our superstars made their debut records that way, don't you recall?' Rowena was warming up now. God, it pissed her off when executives made excuses. 'You need to channel some of that and be hungry yourselves right now, or this is not going to work. Trust me. People will get *fired*. Costs will have to be cut. I might even decide I need to merge territories.'

Now she had their full attention.

'What we will do here is buy time. In a very creative, net-driven, cost-effective way. We want to call in chips from our best producers, guys that can work fast. At the same time, we need to find and generate press for a truly exciting new act. But let me remind you what I mean by exciting. There need to be songs. Amazing songs. Songs you love without seeing the singer. Songs that radio programmers love. Are you fucking *getting* this? I want one new hit act per territory by the end of the quarter, as well as catalogue to see us through the summer.'

'It might work,' said Helga, an expert in the northern niche business. Rowena liked the fact that she wasn't a defeatist.

'It might. Get me Abba. Or at least A-Teens, Helga. Understood?' She laughed. 'I'll try, boss lady.'

'And the tours,' George said. 'We're fucking bleeding in London. Half of that mess is accounted to us now.'

'I'm taking care of the tours. Musica is cutting its losses,'

Rowena said. 'It's going to mean coming over your way, meeting the bands. And laying down the hammer.'

'And you can do that? These are powerful people.' Heinrich shuddered audibly. Big acts meant big egos, and the managers who guarded them were usually assholes of the first order. At least from the record company's point of view.

'You know what Michael taught me when we first got together? You're exactly as powerful as your last hit record. No more. And acts come and go, but Musica is forever.'

Rowena was glad they couldn't see the look of doubt that crossed her face in the sun-filled room. She hoped that was still true.

'I'll be on a plane tomorrow. Taking care of my end. Now you take care of yours.'

The kids had made the bus on time and sauntered off to school none the wiser. Topaz hadn't said anything. Mostly because she was numb with shock, not knowing what the hell she ought to say. Maybe she could get Joe to come back. Today sometime. And she wouldn't have to say anything.

And maybe she didn't want him to. She had no idea, she just couldn't figure it out.

Feeling sick with anxiety, she dressed automatically and forced herself out of the door on a run, though her brain was fixated on Joe and there was nothing she could do about it. She felt as though she was running through tar, but she made it round the Central Park reservoir for the allotted length of time, and back to her building, panting and sweating, knowing at least she'd done that for herself.

The day's routine was a crutch. Run finished, there was a brief window to shower and dry her hair. Next, the clothes she'd laid out the night before: a warm sweater dress from Missoni and a pair of flats, a stylish version of comfort dressing. She put on her make-up automatically, the no-fail combination of tinted moisturiser, a sweep of rose blush on her high cheekbones, and see-through peony-pink lip gloss laid over a cheap drugstore red stain. She swept mascara on just her upper lashes; waterproof was the way to go. Chief executives couldn't afford smudges, and jilted wives couldn't deal with tear stains.

And then she was done. The car was waiting to pick her up outside. She hadn't had time for breakfast, and she was starving. There was a small Ziploc container in the fridge for emergencies that she replenished every Sunday: hard-boiled eggs, salt and pepper, a bag of walnuts, cashews and raisins, some sharp green grapes and half a bar of dark chocolate with sea salt. Usually Rona would snaffle it all by Thursday, but today Topaz thanked God it was still there.

Her heart might be breaking, but her body didn't care. And it was always hungry. She was Italian, and Italians couldn't think on an empty stomach.

She had to arrive in that office with a plan that would blow her bosses away. Otherwise, it wouldn't just be Joanna Watson who got the sack. This was Manhattan, where you could fall as fast as you rose. Topaz didn't want to be the next big name at American Magazines packing her life into a cardboard box.

In a way, it was a blessing. The threat to her career was the one thing that could keep her mind off Joe Goldstein.

At least for now.

'So, Joe, I heard you have some great concepts,' Maria Gonzales said. She was wearing another knockout dress, this time in navy cotton, strictly designed by Victoria Beckham in some kind of curvy forces-pin-up style.

Goldstein was trying not to stare.

The dress was a lethal weapon. On paper, it was demure – cap sleeves, a pencil skirt, square neckline, hem sitting delicately below the knee. But it wasn't on paper. It was on Maria Gonzales. And his heart rate was speeding up.

Her breasts were modestly covered, but they still entered the room half a foot ahead of her. This time, though, his Achilles heel was her world-beating ass, snug in its tightly cut dark-blue sheath. He was letting Maria lead the conversation. It saved him from having to speak. He needed a second to get his voice back under control.

'I have to say, Ollie and I are so excited about this,' Maria added.

'We really are,' said Ollie Greene, her big-shot agent. He was well known for his epically insincere smiles, and Goldstein didn't trust him an inch. 'Maria tells me you really want to pursue this option, and we are most *definitely* interested in considering what you're putting on the table here – providing you can match our price.'

He gave Joe a full-wattage beam. And there it was: the Hollywood version of 'fuck you'. *Interested in considering. If you can match our price.* Translation: get lost, jerk, she's a free agent and we are *so* out of here.

'That's awesome, because I think it's just amazing when we all get super-together on, like, the same page,' Joe said, mocking him.

Greene's face coloured. 'We're out of contract.'

'One your client wants to re-enter. What I propose is to give her three years' worth of total security, some creative input—'

'Creative *control*.'

'Creative input. I will retain control. And we will be paying her at the same rate plus an extra five per cent a year.'

Greene's eyes boggled. 'You're joking.'

Maria examined her long nails, as if this discussion was about someone else. But she shot Joe secret little encouraging looks from under her endless lashes, forcing him to suppress a smile.

'That's more than the rate of inflation,' he said, deadpan. 'And it's a great deal for Maria.'

* * *

Behind her smiles, Maria's eyes darted from one man to the other. Her agent, that poisonous little queen, reminded her of Tommaso, the sadistic pimp who had first tricked her out in New Mexico. There were no guns in this office, no punches or belts to abuse her, but still, Maria was just a dollar sign to Ollie Green.

But it was weird. She was starting to *like* Joe Goldstein.

Today should put a stop to all that shit. *See! He wants to underpay me. To help his network.* Joe was just another john, like all of them, eyes trailing her ass, tongue hanging out. Maybe he was a little more intriguing, because at least he was fighting that instinct – he hadn't hit on her yet. And he could crack a joke. And he wasn't humiliating her, either . . .

Snap out of it, Maria! You're not one of those dumb broads who's ready to throw a goddamn party just because a man doesn't actually spit in my face.

The men were still talking. Not to her. About her.

Maria leaned back in her seat.

Another flashback. That bus ride to the airport, sneaking on to the Holiday Inn shuttle. Then more buses, in and out of border towns. The teenage boys, *lupos*, who robbed her, and would have raped her, except that a police car came round the corner. They ran away, and Maria ran too. Her water bottle was finished, and when she stopped running, started walking, she saw a gas station, with signs all in English. *America. She'd made it.* She stumbled towards it, her lips white with thirst. There was water there! They would have a bathroom, with taps. But her head swam, and she blacked out by the side of the road.

When she woke up, she didn't know where she was. It was dark. She was bumping up and down. She couldn't speak, her lips were so dry. A man thrust a water bottle into her mouth and she drank, deeply, quickly, without even breathing. He yanked it away.

'*Por favor* . . .' she croaked, begging.

'This is better. You'll get sick on water.' She understood the words, a little bit. In school Sister Fatima said *Ingles* was the most important language. All the good jobs, you needed it. To be a hotel maid, you needed it. 'Try this.'

Maria drank something else. It was a plastic bottle. Warm, old liquid. Very sweet. It was the most delicious thing she had ever tasted. She drank the entire thing.

'Gatorade,' he said, in that warm, rich Southern accent she never forgot. He was fat, and he smelled; he had a beard. To this day, she hated all men with beards. It was in her contract never to work with an actor who had one. 'Got those salts and shit. Electrolytes. You need it. Y'all are dehydrated real bad, *mamacita*.'

Stubby fingers pushed the sweaty fringe of hair away from her face.

'Wetback, right? Runnin' away. That's cool. You ain't legal, though. They catch you, they'll take you back. I can help you with that.' He leered at her. 'Help you if you're nice to me. You want to be nice, don't you, honey?'

Maria closed her eyes.

She thought she knew what was coming.

But she was a child. She didn't know. No child could.

Everything was a blur after the first rape. The grubby little doctor who wouldn't look at her as he dispensed pills. The shack house bordello; more rapes. She escaped after a week. Made it to another town. Lived off garbage till some man found her. Another rape. But Maria was tough. She was determined to survive. Homeless and hungry, she just kept moving, stealing food, learning the lingo, reading from scraps of paper, scraps of magazines. Staying away from the police. Getting to know bus routes real good. She was a nomad. By the time she was thirteen, she'd hitch-hiked almost to California, but there were still plenty of gangs around, barrio gangs that wanted to catch her and sell her.

A year of loneliness, violence and assaults, and Maria Gonzales was cracking up.

That was when she had the best idea of all.

Jefé, you were right, Maria sometimes thought. One man versus many men. One rapist versus many rapists. The street gangs that operated here were as evil as anything back home. They traded women, and girls like her. And she had it good, compared to the Mexicanos they trafficked across the border. When the gangs caught the *pullos*, as they called them – the 'little chickens' – they tortured the men for ransom and fucked and sold the women. It was quite the market, here in America.

She needed a protector. And she needed to get out of this life.

And Maria Gonzales knew exactly what to do.

She would go to a pimp. She would find the right one. The little bastard, the sly one, the guy who didn't drink. Tommaso.

Tommaso could get her out. For money . . .

That was a long time ago, Maria, a lifetime away. You are a big star now. Things are different.

The two men were talking still. With an effort, she pulled herself back into the room. She was older now. Better. Stronger.

And like always, she had a plan.

'I tell you what, Joe Goldstein. When you're ready to have a serious conversation, call my office and we'll see if we can fit you in.' Greene got to his feet. 'Come on, Maria, we're leaving.' He gave Joe a contemptuous look.

'Hold on, sugar,' Maria said, purring slightly. 'I don't think my friend Joe means to insult me.'

Greene spun around and just as quickly sat down. 'Well, since you're in a forgiving mood, I guess we can hear him out,' he said, as though he had a choice.

Joe looked straight at Maria. 'You see, other stations will pay you more. And give you creative control. Which you'll cede to Ollie here. And his agency has other clients they want to place – writers, producers, minor stars. They'll cobble together a nice safe vehicle for you. And your star will keep falling.'

'But I'll have control,' Maria said.

'Why should you? What the hell do you know about showrunning?' Joe said bluntly. 'You're an actress. Your version of control would ruin anything you touched. More lines for the star, no awkward plots, nothing that makes you look bad . . . in short, boring. And short-term gain is long-term pain.'

'Like a doughnut,' Maria said, nodding. 'A moment on the lips, a lifetime on the hips.'

Goldstein thought she was taking the mickey, as Topaz would say, a phrase she'd picked up studying in England, long ago. For a second, the vision of his wife, his love, his best friend, flashed painfully through his mind. It hurt him almost physically. But then he thought of her dismissive, angry, hysterical, telling him how she couldn't get wet for him in the shower. And sexy young Maria was right here, batting those impressive eyelashes his way. Looking like she was ready to put up statues to him.

'Maria needs guidance,' he told Greene, 'not sucking up. And her salary isn't material. What matters is a breakthrough hit that will let audiences see her in a new way. I need budget for that, and spending every cent of it on a headline pay hike will do nothing for Maria, for hiring the best writers and producers, for getting them to take a chance on a girl whose image you've sold out to brand merchants and commercial makers. See, I think she can be more than that, without losing any ground. I think she can be funny and sexy and even smart. And unlike you, I'm giving her credit for being intelligent enough to see that there's no way she should have creative control. When I say she's going to get input, I don't mean fake Hollywood input.' He shifted his eyes away from Ollie and held that beautiful gaze. 'Maria, I give you my word that we will choose something great together. And you will star in it for the next three years.'

'No way,' Greene said immediately. 'Forget it.'

'Done,' said Maria. 'Joe's right. I *shouldn't* have control. And I do want a career.'

Ollie Greene went a dirty shade of plum.

'Joe Goldstein is on the other side of the table, Maria! I have successfully steered your career and I need you to come with me right now. My clients don't treat me like this.'

'You're a hundred per cent correct, Ollie.' She smiled sweetly. 'A client shouldn't treat you this way. So you're fired.'

A surge of pleasure ripped through Goldstein, the joy of defeating an opponent right to his face. He hadn't had that moment in too long. He was ecstatic.

Right now, Maria was his favourite person in the world.

'Thanks for coming, Ollie. My assistant will show you out,' he said calmly.

Greene shot to his feet, visibly shaking with anger, and stormed out of the office.

'That was beautiful. You're beautiful,' Joe said.

Maria laughed. 'I thought it was against your religion to pay me a compliment.'

'No way. You're smarter than they give you credit for.' He paused. 'Although you really shouldn't undermine your representation. He's right, you know. I am technically the enemy.'

'We'll see about that. Anyway, it was him that undermined me. We had this discussion, see, in private. I told him what I wanted – to work with you. And he laughed at me. Said we could do better. Wouldn't listen.' She shrugged. 'What's the point of creative control if my own agent won't give it to me? I should have canned him long ago.'

Maria's honesty was disarming, almost as dangerous as those big eyes. Joe couldn't help himself.

'Let me buy you lunch. Anywhere you want.'

There. He'd said it. Too late to back out now.

Maria smiled. 'How about a hotel? Any place good nearby?'

A hotel? He blinked, but chose not to hear the message. 'Fine.'

'And I want you to open up to me. Like a real friend. You owe me that.'

He did. 'It's a deal.'

Chapter Seven

Topaz was miserable. She shivered against the unseasonably cold day. Joe's phone was off; she had left three messages already. On the third, she'd told him to go fuck himself.

But her vast office seethed with activity. The board of directors was heading to see her. The conference room was being prepared. And this was not a positive development. She'd heard from one of her allies, Christa Mercer, a former senior publisher at *The New Yorker* and a new recruit to the board, that the chairman had even asked the non-execs to turn up.

That spelled trouble. And Topaz Rossi had to be ready for it.

Broken heart was bad enough. Broken brain would be fatal.

She forced herself to get down to work.

'Your coffee, ma'am.' A junior assistant had appeared with a tray. Fragrant cinnamon coffee and a raisin Danish. Perfect. She needed the carbs.

'Thanks,' Topaz said. She grabbed a mug and inhaled the caffeine in unladylike gulps. Her desk was a mess; six months' worth of magazines from all over the stable were spread across it, and she had been staring at the layouts, the ad choices, reading the articles. Acting like an editor, not a chief exec. For years, magazines had been her life, and this was bittersweet; she hated failing, but even looking at the spreads was pumping the adrenalin through her body.

What was great. What was dull. What was standard, just phoning it in. And the occasional book that was so poor she thought they should cut it altogether.

'Brad.' She pressed the button for her assistant.

'Yes, Ms Rossi?'

'Get me six or seven iPads. Have them loaded with our magazines, OK? I don't want to waste time downloading.'

'I understand. Yes, ma'am.'

Digital. It was supposed to be their saviour. Riding to the rescue of print. But things hadn't worked out that way. People didn't subscribe on tablets. They were just falling away from reading altogether. Glossy pictures, once the preserve of a fat printed monthly, were available for free on Instagram. News came from Twitter. Fashion spread through Tumblr. Kids weren't reading anything other than blogs. She was in the information business, and information was everywhere; *coals to Newcastle*, they called it back in England.

'It's all black. And I'm just here selling slightly better coals,' she said aloud.

'Say again?'

Topaz turned. A woman had appeared in the doorway. Christa Mercer, sixty and elegant in her Dolce & Gabanna power suit, black with gold buttons. She'd probably had it since the eighties, Topaz realised, and it had turned full circle and become chic again. She wore her steel-grey hair long, tied in a braid around her head, like a Viking queen with a crowned helmet.

'This stuff. We have ice in a world of Eskimos.' Topaz gestured. 'And I'm here trying to carve it into prettier shapes.'

'I agree. But the board will be looking at relative performance.'

Topaz sighed. *How well are* you *doing?* That was the question for her. They weren't going to care what was happening to the industry. Only to American Magazines. They were behind the competition. And that hurt.

'I have a plan.'

'You'll need one. They're out for blood.' The older woman gave a small smile. 'I felt I should warn you.'

'Received. Understood.'

'I'm heading over there. See you shortly.'

Topaz nodded. She still wasn't sure exactly what she would say. But she had to come up with something, and she had to do it soon.

The production office of the Festhalle was tiny in comparison to the vast arena out front. On stage, Lumos were grinding out their emotive prog rock. A vast web of lasers, red, green and blue, spun through the darkness, framing the five band members as they threw shapes and flirted with the audience; huge projector screens beamed their faces to the half-empty space.

Frankfurt was cheering, but not enough of them. Not nearly enough.

Rowena had made her way through front of house, picking her way in the darkened arena, all-access laminated pass swinging from her neck. She wanted to see for herself how bad it was. Her head turned right and left, picking out the empty seats on the balconies, the rows of unused space; the old road-crew trick, pulling curtains over blank sections, was all about her.

The lasers looked great. So did the screens. She sighed deeply. Musica was paying for all of it.

Rick Wilson, the band's manager, was a legendary asshole. He'd tried to prevent her from coming tonight. She'd had to get her pass from the German promoter. And she was mad about it.

'You can't come in here.' A burly security guard, six foot four of pure muscle, was trying to bar her way.

'Yes I can.' Rowena lifted the laminate. 'All access.'

'I can read. You still can't come in. Rick don't want to see you.'

'Like I give a shit? Out of my way, son.'

The bouncer laughed. 'You and whose army, baby?'

'I can use this.' Rowena held up her right hand; it was long, elegant, and very slender.

'You gonna show me some kung fu with that hand?' he laughed. 'Ooh, I'm scared.'

'No. I'm gonna use it to cancel a cheque tomorrow morning. The cheque that gets you guys to Spain. The cheque that pays your personal wages.' She smiled sweetly. 'So tell me, *baby*, now are you scared?'

He scowled.

'Get the hell out of the way.'

Reluctantly he moved. Rowena strode through into the cramped production office. A wardrobe girl lounged idly against a wall; Rick Wilson was sitting on a crate, laughing, toying with a groupie. Her black hair fell loosely around her shoulders; he had her T-shirt pushed halfway up and was fondling the naked breasts underneath.

'Evening,' Rowena said loudly.

Wilson jumped out of his skin. 'Fuck's sake!' he hissed, in a loud cockney accent. 'Fuck off, Krebs! Where the hell is Jordan? He's supposed to be keeping you out. We're not interested in what a bunch of Yankee suits have to say.'

'I'm Scottish.'

'And I'm the Loch Ness monster.' Insultingly, he jiggled the girl's tits in his hands, leering at Rowena. 'This is what girls should be doing at showtime. So unless you want to put out like the *Fräulein*, get the hell out of here.'

The groupie giggled and arched her back. Rowena lifted her phone and took a photograph. The camera flashed in the room.

'*Ach!*' shrieked the girl, tugging her shirt down.

'*Geh weg,*' said Rowena shortly. '*Hab etwas Selbstachtung.*'

The girl started to cry. She got up and blundered from the room.

'Nice going,' Rick said. But he was eyeing Rowena's phone warily. 'You can't fucking do that.'

'I can. And I just did.' She twisted the phone. 'My pictures are set to go automatically into the cloud. How would you like me to post that online in an essay about sexism in music? This isn't the eighties and you don't manage Mötley Crüe. Your emotive teenage fan base will fire you faster than you can say "dinosaur asshole who's losing my company three million bucks with this embarrassingly shit record and tour".'

'Blackmail,' he said, but without much conviction. 'Now we know what this is really about. You just don't want to support the band. To give our record time to *grow*.'

'To grow a record you need songs. But you don't have any.'

He shrugged. 'Fans will find us again on this tour.'

Rowena perched on a flight case.

'Rick, you are a dire manager. The worst kind. You got lucky with one great act that you happened to know and you rode their coat-tails to get here. You are dependent on this band. As a result, you don't want to be fired. Because who else do you have? And being afraid leads you to make mistakes.'

'Like what?' he sneered.

'Like not telling them their songs were rubbish when they gave you the demos. Like hoping a producer could fix it in the mix. They never can. Like ensuring the same level of tour support from us by not being honest and telling us you had a stiff and you needed more time. You *placate*. Like that bimbo. And what good does it do you? You've got empty halls and a disastrous tour. It's clinging to the band like a bad smell. They see the vacant seats each night; they're embarrassed. It makes the record stiffing even worse. By the end of this tour they'll have figured out you should never have let them release a stinker like this album.'

He sighed. 'What the fuck, Rowena. I can't write the songs for them.'

'No, you moron. We can. We have access to some of the world's best songwriters. They can do it in collaboration or alone. This is the death of every big band, thinking they're immortal, that they can release "Yankee Doodle" and it will be OK. It won't.'

'What do you want? You're a pain in the fucking arse.'

'I'm not wanting. I'm telling. You're going to sign this piece of paper with me tonight. It's a contract renegotiation.'

'Fuck off.'

'It cuts your tour support,' Rowena said. 'We're going to merge big tours. You and Kassius. They're stinking the place out as well. You have a similar fan base. Emo girls and disaffected boys. Together, you *will* sell out. You will perform only the current single and the next single from this record on tour. The rest of your set is strictly crowd-pleasing. Greatest hits. You will finish by covering "Jackrabbit" – Kassius's third biggest hit. They will finish covering "Monkey" – that's yours. The fans will want to hear your top two from the bands themselves.'

A strange mix of emotions was crossing Rick Wilson's face. Pugnacity, anxiety, and hope. As well as sheepishness. They both knew she was right.

'And if I agree?'

'You *will* agree. Don't fuck me about when I'm saving your career. I'm even going to let you tell the band this was your idea. Try talking to them like they're grown-ups. And from now on, if my record company doesn't get to hear the tracks at every stage from demo to release, we won't pay a dime to recording costs.'

'OK.' He ran stubby fingers through dishwater-blonde hair. 'What about the fucking album, though? Radio are being assholes.'

'You mean they'll only play hits? That's what they do. We're going to perform some emergency surgery on this record. I'm giving the five least shitty tracks to my best producers, including Michael. And I have hit songwriters on call. We are going to remix them into something you can hum. Adding bridges, adding entire sections. Plan on marching Seth into the studio whenever the fuck I tell you to. He'll be recording on the road.'

Seth was their lead singer. 'He won't like that,' Wilson said.

'I never met a musician yet who didn't know what happens when the fans drift away,' Rowena told him. 'They're like you. Panicking. Maybe not showing it. Give him the straw. Watch him clutch it. Those five tracks will be the singles. *I* will tell you the order of release.'

Wilson leaned back with an admiring smile. He couldn't help himself. 'You really are a hard bitch, Rowena Krebs.'

'It's done. Kassius already signed.' She opened her Prada backpack and passed over some papers.

Wilson moved to take them. He grabbed a pen from a desk and scribbled his signature.

'Nice doing business with you,' Rowena said.

She retrieved the contract, folded it neatly, and tucked it back into her backpack. Then she turned on her heel and walked away.

The Senator Suite at the Jumeirah suited her very well. The hotel was impersonal and efficient, exactly what you wanted in a business stay. Rowena Krebs travelled light. She didn't use the most expensive places, and she never booked space on a private jet; she flew business class rather than first, and had saved Musica a fortune that way. For a business titan, a Hall of Famer, that was slumming it.

She nonetheless appreciated the luxury. Part of Rowena was forever that twenty-one-year old girl, disowned by her parents, out of Oxford and desperate to get a job, any job, in the record business. To make it against the odds, doing what she loved.

She'd got there. And how.

Now she was sprawling out on her king-size bed. The lounge had an overstuffed couch and the bathroom was bigger than her old flat in London. Fruit, Swiss chocolates, and plates of fine cured meats and Bavarian cheeses were everywhere; she had these delivered, along with bowls of salted nuts, rather than eat a large meal. Tomorrow morning she would do a light workout in the hotel gym, swim in the pool, perhaps. Frankfurt would be her base; the Euro heads would fly in to meet her tomorrow.

And now she had something to show them.

Rowena felt a surge of adrenalin. This was awesome. This was exciting. Just like when she was young, on the up, and dealing with Topaz Rossi, her enemy, who wanted to take her down.

Fixing problems. Breaking acts. Putting the company back together again.

She was flowing.

Musica, on top, was her legacy. And tonight she was thinking about the gig.

She wanted to go out on a high. With the crowd chanting for an encore, the world wanting a part of what she was.

She couldn't leave her company like this. No, she was going to smack heads together, cobble up those hits, patch her three big records and get the acts back to health. Each album must sell at least two million copies this summer.

And finally she wanted to hear and see the new baby acts the scouts had been tasked to find. Meet the future of music.

And at that point, she told herself as she picked up the phone, it would be time for a major life change.

'Michael Krebs's office.'

'It's Rowena. Put me through, would you, Ellen?'

'Yes, ma'am. One second.'

Her stomach creased a little with excitement. Wow. Twenty years and he could still do this to her.

'Rowena,' Michael said.

'Are you alone?'

'I am now.'

'Me too.'

'I would hope so. Thinking about me?'

'No,' she lied.

'You know what happens to you when you don't tell the truth.' Michael was grinning; she could hear that predatory smile in his voice. Arrogant. Sure of himself. Sure of her. 'I should put you on your knees and make you suck me.'

Rowena gasped.

'Remind you where you came from. Sometimes I think you forget that.'

She groaned. 'You're torturing me.'

'One more day. You just think about it.'

'You know I will.'

'I love imagining you at gigs. Reminds me of when I had you under the stage, under the drum riser. With the band playing, and your wrists lashed to the ceiling.'

'Oh God, Michael . . .'

'Let's move on,' he said, and she squirmed with frustration and desire and laughter all mixed up together. He never let her get away with a goddamned thing. 'How was the jerk-off today?'

'Found him with a groupie. Fondling her tits right in front of me.' Rowena laughed. 'He thought he could psych me out by bouncing them up and down. Even asked me if I wanted to play along. I'd rather walk a mile over broken glass, the gross pig. Still pasty and fat. About as attractive as ten pounds of garbage.'

'Like I said. Jerk. I know that kind of manager. Only pussy he can get, he borrows from his band. Like everything else.'

'He wasn't too happy when I snapped a photo of them. Got a great shot of him pawing at her boobs, mouth open and drooling.'

Krebs laughed. 'Attagirl. Then what?'

'I told him he was a shit manager and his band stink and he was going to do what the fuck I told him.'

'This is good. Did he cry?'

'A little bit. He blustered and caved. The hall was pitiful, freaking empty. I was embarrassed for all of them, the suckers.'

'He caved? You're merging the tours?' Her husband's tone changed to one of pure pride. 'That's a great result.'

'We'll be full. Moreover, I have a plan for fixing the records, too.' She explained. 'What do you think?'

'With good songwriters, new bridges . . .' He was thinking about it. 'I like it. It's new thinking. Remixing doesn't work; you're talking about new songwriting. The fans will dig it. Though how are you going to get the new tracks to them if they already bought the album?'

'That's next week's problem. I have an idea on that.' She breathed out. 'I can't wait to come home.'

His voice softened. 'Me neither. I love you.'

'You don't mind it when I talk business? With what you're going through?'

Krebs jumped down her throat. 'Mind? This is the only way I can stay sane. I told you, I need you to distract me.'

'I'm here if you want to talk about it.'

'Yeah.' He was suddenly distant, reserved. Rowena's stomach crunched with anxiety. She couldn't help her husband. On this matter, he was on his own.

'I love you.' She pressed her manicured fingers to her temples. 'Baby, I was thinking.'

'Not another kid. I want to concentrate on the ones I've got.'

She laughed. 'No way. Two's enough for us. Especially since you have five. I was thinking, though. Once this is all fixed . . . I feel like I'm done here.'

There was a moment's pause.

'Done done?'

'Yes.' She was going to say it, going to change her life again. 'I want to quit Musica. I want to retire.'

'You're only forty-two.'

'I know. And you're only sixty. You quit.'

'Because it wasn't great, like it used to be. And I hate things that aren't great. And I have enough money.' Krebs sighed. 'But I tell you, sweetie, I'm goddamned bored. Worried about my kid, and bored. It's a hell of a combination.'

'Then we can be bored together. Maybe I can take some of that boredom out of you.'

'We can't stay in bed *all* day.'

'Unproven,' Rowena grinned. 'Anyway, I never had a gap year. Maybe it's time to take a year off, swim a lot, eat peaches, and figure out something else to do.'

'A *gap* year? Is this your mid-life crisis? Because if it is, I'll happily buy you another car. A cherry-red Maserati? Or a blue Bugatti?'

'I don't do crises. It's like you said, it's just not great any more. I can fix this, but then I've *fixed* it. I'm not breaking a great band . . .'

'It's easier to break great bands than make successes out of poor ones. You get executive points for doing the latter. Because Lumos stink, and so do Kassius. I'd have dropped them.'

'I can't drop them, because I own the masters.' Rowena breathed out. 'You may be right, sweetheart, but I'm actually a music fan. I want to work with great bands. Want to hear that rush, see the young girls scream. I don't want to just cobble stuff together on a balance sheet. I might as well be selling soap powder to Unilever.'

'You love music,' he said softly. 'See, that's your problem.'

'Like you. Which is why you quit.'

'Every generation has its moment in the sun,' Krebs said. 'Fine, I agree with you. Get to the fall, then exit stage left.'

'I'm so glad you're with me,' Rowena said, and there were soft tears in her eyes now. Something was ending, something very wonderful and precious to her. The career girl was about to quit. And she had no idea how to follow any direction but up.

'Don't worry,' Krebs said, reading her mind. 'I'll find you something to do, baby.'

'I bet you will,' Rowena replied, forcing herself to sound cheerful. 'Good night. Call you tomorrow, sugar.'

But as she hung up, great salty tears were already falling steadily down her cheeks.

For the first time in her life, Rowena Krebs had no idea of her future.

And she hated it.

Chapter Eight

'We really believe something radical needs to happen.' Ernesto Joaquinez, a silver-haired corporate raider, looked down his nose towards Topaz. 'Or we will have to explore our options.'

'The shareholders were very disappointed with the last dividend.' Lionel Test, one of the board members, nodded at her. 'I need not remind you, Topaz, that this isn't some internet bubble company where value depends on smoke and mirrors. There are hard facts. Numbers. And ours are dropping. We're losing readers. Advertising revenue. Sales.'

'We're steady in overall market share,' Topaz replied. 'Because of depth in the field, and because titles in other markets are taking hits too.'

'That won't continue if these numbers carry on sliding,' Joaquinez replied.

'Gentlemen – and Christa.' Topaz laid her hands flat on the table, to make her point. The enormous diamond on her engagement ring glinted back at her, and she had to suppress a wash of emotion. This was no time for tears. 'I am not trying to dismiss, or argue away, your concerns. Yes, there are too many bad numbers and bad months. Even the best businesses go through rough patches occasionally. It is my job to fix those numbers. What I want from you is a maximum of two months to go into our magazines, take stock, see what's working, and make changes.

After that, we should see both rising circulation *and* falling costs.'

'Are you willing to bet your job on that?' Ernesto asked bluntly.

There it was. Somebody had said it.

'Topaz Rossi has been a legendary CEO of American Magazines,' said Christa. 'She has charted this company's rise in market share to the very top of the pile. She beat Condé Nast, for God's sake. She is an iconic businesswoman.'

Lionel looked around the table at the other board members, and Topaz felt her back stiffen. She knew an ambush when she saw one. There was absolutely no doubt that the board had come here with an agenda.

To fire her.

'Nobody disputes your record,' Ernesto said. 'But record doesn't pay the bills. We have shareholders to report to. And we feel that your leadership is out of ideas.'

'We will offer you a very generous package,' Lionel Test said. 'We would like a smooth transition.'

'A package to *retire*? Forget it.' Rage flooded her. 'Three bad months and you want to pull the plug?' This was like a replay of her conversation with Joanna Watson, but she was no greenhorn trust-fund brat. 'That's not how this goes. I have a contract. And it was drawn up by one of the best lawyers in the business.'

The men around the table glanced at each other. They knew she was right. Topaz thanked God she had gone to Imelda Consuelas; the provisions in her mega-deal were iron-clad.

'American Magazines can hire good lawyers too. You'd be humiliated.'

Topaz smirked. 'Nothing humiliates *me*, gentlemen. I would give so many interviews you would be begging for an early meeting to tender your own resignations, every damn one of you. I can also spin this out for six months, preventing you finding a new CEO; with disastrous results.'

'Nobody can stop you being fired in the end. CEOs don't have jobs for life. Even ones with fancy lawyers,' Ernesto snapped.

'I agree. Nor do I wish to work without the full support of my board. Here's what we're going to do.' Topaz smiled slightly; she couldn't help it. The adrenalin was pumping through her veins. Do or die, kill or be killed. She had grown far too comfortable in the corporate life. This fight suited her. There was no more sadness. Just strength. And determination. Staring her enemies down.

Even Christa was not arguing her case any more. Hell, *Wall Street* had it right; she loved that film. *If you want a friend, get a dog.*

But Topaz Rossi wasn't looking for friends.

She wanted her crown. Her kingdom. And she would kick the ass of anyone who tried to take it from her.

'You'll give me three months to turn our books around. I'm going to resume an editor-in-chief role. In fact, next month's *American Girl* will be guest-edited by me. If you don't see an improvement of twenty-five per cent in circulation figures on that title, we will announce my retirement one month later. I will write the press release myself. All my remaining stock vests upon my retirement, as you know, so it's very much in my interest to get our numbers up.' She smiled. 'Now is everybody with me?'

Christa was the first to speak. 'This is eminently fair. It's also good business. I'm sure you've all reviewed Topaz's contract; she is absolutely right, as you know.'

'It sounds like blackmail,' Test hissed.

'Please don't let's use intemperate language,' retorted Christa, like a teacher telling a pupil off. 'Topaz is entitled to a chance both legally and morally.'

'This is a business. Not a church,' said Ernesto.

One of the other board members, Roger Symonds, spoke up. 'Having listened carefully, I vote with Christa. The matter is hardly material. We cannot hire a new CEO in three months anyway.'

'Feel free to look around,' Topaz said. 'But do it privately. If I find you have interviewed anyone, even informally, I will sue you into the Stone Age. Are we clear?'

Test nodded, reluctantly.

'Do we need a vote?' Christa demanded. 'No? Very well then. Three months it is.'

Topaz got to her feet and stormed out of the conference room without a goodbye. Fuck these assholes. She was about to show them what a real print woman could do.

Joe Goldstein looked at Maria. His resolve was weakening fast.

She was standing by the side of her rooftop pool house. God, this was living; her apartment put even his to shame. She had a duplex on the Upper East Side, but instead of a wrap-around terrace, there was a full roof garden, complete with indoor swimming pool housed inside a conservatory. Even on this chilly spring day it was blissfully warm. The heated water lapped against the marble sides of the pool with a little current, sending shadows dappling against the walls. It was so relaxing.

As were the two glasses of champagne he'd agreed to drink with her. It had been a pleasant lunch at a hotel restaurant, during which Maria admired him as though he were a rock star. She came out with details of small deals he'd done, quite some time ago, deals even he had forgotten about. In that breathy voice, she did a little comedy for him. She told him about her business, her endorsements, her commercials, spinning things out.

And Joe opened up. He couldn't help it. A private man, he was suddenly dazzled by this funny young thing in front of him, willing to put her career in his hands. Willing to fire her agent. Willing to back him.

Maria was paying attention.

Not like Topaz. No, Maria Gonzales wasn't too busy for him, or focused on some crisis. She didn't worry unduly about her own future. No moaning. No gripes. No nagging. She was an optimist. Maybe not so bright, but full of common sense.

And definitely flirting with him.

Joe couldn't ignore that any longer. It had started at lunch, so that he didn't know where to look. Her fingers brushing his as she reached for her champagne flute. That was OK, but then the giggling, the sly looks from under those long lashes. Holding his gaze a fraction too long. Her leg brushing against his, the pointed toe of her high heels pressing into his pants.

He'd struggled a little, but then there was an inward shrug. Ah, what the hell. If she wanted to play, who was he to say no?

'Powerful men like you are used to dealing with girls like me,' she'd said, laughing easily.

Joe stiffened. She made herself sound like a reward, like a toy. Like a slave girl handed to Caesar as some sort of booty. Goddamn. He hadn't had sex in a week, maybe more, and she was throwing herself at him, with that soft skin and those limpid eyes and those ferocious, unstoppable curves.

He couldn't deny it. He would just love to see what those curves looked like naked, in real life.

'You're an accomplished woman. Not some little girl,' he said. 'And I'm glad to work with you.'

Maria pouted. 'Not more of that. Let's get the check.'

He'd pulled out his black Amex and signed for it. She'd smiled. 'Player, huh?'

You didn't get a black Amex unless you charged over $75,000 a month. Platinum was for suckers. And Maria had noticed.

Joe didn't respond. It was time to go back to the office, but he was enjoying himself too much. Hadn't had this much fun in years. Or that was what it felt like.

'I want a coffee,' she said suddenly.

'Oh. I can get them to bring one.'

'No, not here. Too stuffy. Would you mind coming back to my place? I meet a lot of business types there. I love working from home. Not to sound all diva-ish, but limos are such a pain in the traffic.'

'Stars' privilege – we come to you.'

'We can bust some more producer choices and ideas, or we can talk writers, or talent . . .'

Goldstein looked at his phone. His PA would be expecting him back any time now.

'Come on, Joe. They report to you, not the other way round. Remember that. You run the company.'

Seductive words. She was challenging his manhood, he knew that, but all the same, it was highly effective. He picked up his cell. 'Shawna? It's me. I'm taking Maria downtown, we're going to talk showrunners.'

'Wow,' his assistant said, deeply impressed. 'Yes, sir. That's great. But you have the guys from *Chicago Ambulance* due here in an hour, don't forget.'

'You'll have to ring them and reschedule. Give them my profound apologies. Try to find a slot tomorrow.'

'Yes, Mr Goldstein.'

'I'm going to block off three hours and head back after that. Meanwhile, get me a list of the showrunners from all the top-rated shows that finished last season, in each network, and their contacts, OK? And email it through to me. Maria and I will review them.'

'Yes, sir. Absolutely.' Shawna sounded like she wanted to say more but was thinking better of it. This was making him look amazing; he had the network's meal ticket wrapped around his little finger. 'I'll cancel this afternoon's appointments till four.'

'Great.' He hung up and smiled down at Maria. 'Let's go grab that coffee.'

Her apartment was predictably palatial, but what Joe loved about it was that it showed the star off as a real cook. Maria Gonzales didn't seem the type to get her hands dirty, but that wasn't the case – her home was lived in, used. She had a chef's kitchen, and had baked the day before; she offered him some home-made biscotti with his fresh-brewed espresso. God, they were so good: crunchy and not too sweet, with a little hint of almonds.

Topaz never cooked much any more and when she did, it was a disaster. Joe was impressed.

As she stirred a brown crystal sugar stick around his thick black brew, Maria smiled across the mug at him.

'I don't have much family. My aunt and cousin live in Beverly Hills; I support them both. José has a coke habit, though, so I don't give him any money. He really resents me. Says he's going to make it big, but never turns up to acting school.'

Maria explained how when she became a star, she had found detectives to trace her mother's family. Turned out her grandparents were dead, but Lucita's sister was living in poverty in Bogotá, divorced, with a baby. DNA tests confirmed it. Her name was Selena, and Maria had indulged in lonely fantasies about nestling under the wing of her blood relative. But Selena was sullen, backward, seemingly uninterested in the niece she'd never known. When they'd met, Maria discovered that Selena had been married young, before Lucita, and had lost contact. Then she was dumped while pregnant, and had fallen into a life of theft and prostitution.

By the time Maria's lawyers arrived with plane tickets and a change of clothing, Selena was an addict and José a young thug. Nonetheless, she bought a house and kept them in it, helping Selena to get clean and encouraging José to study, forcing suburban life on them. It was out in the suburbs, in Pasadena, near a good Catholic school. There was a swimming pool in the garden and a lawn with a hedge.

Neither aunt nor cousin showed any motivation to get any more from life. Maria was disappointed, but she bore the fresh rejection of her love cheerfully.

'So why do you tolerate it? You could kick him out.'

'My mother died when I was very little.' Maria's eyes narrowed, warning him not to ask more. 'She would want her sister taken care of, so I do that. I'm glad I can.'

'And boyfriends?' asked Joe.

Maria blushed.

Lucky bastards, he thought. Imagine being able to fondle all *that* just as much as you liked.

'Only one or two since college. I was career-focused. They didn't like it when I got big. Peter hit me; that was his way of keeping control. Leopold decided I was too low-rent to actually marry. He told me the night he proposed to his fiancée that he would set me up in an apartment. It was like *Pretty Woman*, but without the happy ending. No turning the car around. No climbing the ladder up to the apartment. Did you know that was the original ending? He leaves, and she gets down to work.'

'Didn't make it through the screenings, huh?'

'No. The test audiences hated it. Some of them cried. Boom, time for a last-minute rewrite and happily ever after.' Maria's face hardened, but only for a moment; Joe glimpsed a deep anger there, a bitterness. 'You need to realise there ain't nobody coming, not in real life. If you want a knight on a white charger, better saddle up, girls, 'cause you're all there is.'

Then she caught him staring and gave herself a little shake; her breasts bounced delightfully and he was completely distracted. She smiled at him warmly.

'But what about the guys in the gossip mags? The male model, the dancer . . . what was his name, Ramirez . . .'

'You're answering your own question, Mr Goldstein,' she said innocently. 'Gay as the morning is long. Suitable chaperones. After all, male stars have had beards for years, why not us straight women? I don't want to be single, and I don't want any complicated romances. Hasn't worked out so well thus far.'

He leaned in towards her. 'And what *do* you want?'

'Some guy that *likes* me, as well as wants to bang me. Some guy with a good heart, you know? Who likes marriage. Not a player. A smart man I could look up to. And not some scrub who wants me for my money, either. Absolutely no actors, rock stars, or politicians.'

Joe laughed aloud. 'No politicians? Really?'

Maria extended her long, lean legs. 'Can you image a lifetime of good behaviour? Of never being able to say "fuck you" or push ahead in the queue at Dunkin' Donuts? Not for me, man. I wouldn't be the First Lady for a million dollars. Straight up.'

Joe was still chuckling. 'That gets my vote.'

'I'm still hopeful of meeting somebody cool. Being rich as a woman is different from men. It actually narrows your dating pool.'

'First-world problems,' Joe grinned.

'Bitching of the rich and famous. I know, I'm sorry. I feel blessed.'

'But don't you want kids? What about that biological clock?'

'Mine has a snooze alarm. I really respect mothers, but I just know I'm not cut out for it. Unhappy childhood. Don't think I can be that unselfish.' Maria tossed back her mane of raven hair, letting her breasts jiggle a little as she moved. 'My cousin will have some kids and I'm sure I'll be funding college. I'm hoping for a great guy who doesn't need that from me.' Her smile was dazzling enough for sunglasses. 'Maybe because he's divorced and has his own, you know? That would be perfect.'

Joe felt his throat go dry. He should make his excuses. But he didn't move.

'There aren't that many men your age who are already divorced with kids.'

Maria stood up and walked languorously across the room. He watched the globes of her ass shift under her dress.

'I prefer older men. You know, at this time of day I like to swim. There's a pool upstairs. Come join me? I keep trunks and suits for guests. You'll be quite decent.'

'I'd better not.' It was hard to swallow.

113

'Then can we chat while I take a dip?'

He wanted to say no, but nothing came out.

'This way,' Maria said. 'It won't take me a minute to change.'

And now here they were. He was perched on the side of a chaise longue on the deck of her swimming pool, feeling ridiculous in his suit. And excited. And totally aroused.

Maria wasn't in the water yet. She was sitting on the edge of the pool, wrapped in a thick white towelling robe, dangling her feet in the lapping water. He could see shapely manicured toes painted a girlish pink. Her skin was that sexy tan. There was no way to see what was under the robe. And right now he was desperate to know.

'So you haven't told me about your family. I know you have teenage twins: David and Rona?'

'Yes.' He wondered what he would tell them tonight, when he called. 'They're great kids. Things are a little tough there just now, though.'

She made a face. Her mouth pouted and he wanted to kiss it. 'I'm sorry, how come?'

'You know. Maybe you don't. Very privileged kids can sometimes not value what's done for them. I guess I find that hard, because I struggled myself. I don't want to be angry at them, but I don't want to let them fail, either.' For a second, his focus shifted off that dynamite body, that pretty, adoring face. This was the most he'd opened up in years. Joe didn't do therapy; he was all action, no talk. Even in saying the words, he felt something crack in him, break right open.

'What does your wife say?'

He flashed on Topaz, making excuses for the kids, undermining him, and his mood hardened.

'She takes a different view.'

'She didn't back you up?' Maria said, pitching her question at just the right level. Not overtly sympathetic shock, nothing so obvious; more a detatched curiosity, with a tiny hint of surprise.

'No. She didn't.' The next words were a lot easier. 'In fact, we're separated just now.'

Were they? He'd walked out. They hadn't talked. He was going to have to tell his children, but he had no desire to go back to Topaz at the moment, not until she could stop being all about herself and be there for him.

'Will you get back together?'

'I . . . I guess we'll have to wait and see.' The answer was *yes, of course we will*, or *sure, this will blow over*, but that wasn't what he said.

Maria stood up. 'Well, the point is that right now you're separated.' She walked over to a table made of white metal faux-wicker, kicked off her jewelled flip-flops, and slipped out of the robe, laying it neatly over the table.

Joe's mouth dropped open.

She was amazing. Like a cartoon, like a body that had been built by science. Not on a screen, but in front of him. The bikini was tiny, a Missoni nothing in green-gold triangles that barely covered a third of each large, full, youthful breast, tits that had never nursed children – probably enhanced, but like he gave a shit – and a tiny string that tied around a narrow waist, knotted at her left hip, suggesting he could just tug it right off her, strip her for his pleasure. Her stomach was flat, the abs worked into hard lines; of course stars spent hours with personal trainers, and it showed. Her ass – damn, that was the main event, of course, and he licked dry lips as she turned around, showing him the back view. It jutted out, high, round, tight, muscled, full of the juicy DNA of youth; her legs were improbably slim but nicely curved, with great calves.

'I'll just do a couple of laps,' she said carelessly.

Joe didn't answer. He wanted her too much to say a word. Insane.

And then she dived, her golden Hispanic skin arching down

115

into the water. His view of her ass disappeared; he wanted to protest. The shape of her was under the water, like an otter, sleek, legs moving powerfully; she was a good swimmer, not messing around, determined. She reached the other end of the pool before coming up for air. Her hair was slick around her face. Joe wanted to see what that tiny bikini would look like soaking wet.

'Maria . . .'

But she had already turned and dived under again, swimming back to him. Joe shifted miserably in his seat. He had to get out of here. It was like trying to break hypnosis or something. Damn it, man. You can handle some big-breasted young girl. Who the fuck is in charge here?

Maria arrived at the shallow end and planted her feet on the floor. Water sluiced in rivulets down her huge breasts and Joe barely suppressed a moan. That little triangle was stuck to the V of her pussy.

'Maria.' The voice that emerged was surprisingly steady. 'I'd love to talk business with you, but not like this. I have to go.'

'Something came up?' she purred. And shot a sly glance directly at his crotch.

'You're very attractive. I don't mean that in a disrespectful way. I've had a lot of fun. But this is making it hard to concentrate. Besides, a good workout doesn't need somebody watching, unless it's a personal trainer.' He got to his feet. 'We can brainstorm another time.'

'But I don't want you to concentrate.' Maria stepped mercilessly out of the pool, grasping both sides of the rail, moving that practically nude golden body near to him. 'I want you to go to bed with me.'

He gasped. 'What?'

'We're both grown-ups. I know you heard me.'

'I can't,' he muttered. 'I'm married.'

'You're separated. Separated people often date other people.'

'I . . . it just happened. Only just.'

'You're still separated. It's OK, really. And nobody has to know. Not yet,' she added, staking her claim.

He barely heard the qualification. Half an inch closer and those nuclear-missile tits would be touching his shirt.

'I'm your boss. It would be unethical. I could be fired. You would get a bad reputation . . .'

'Sweetie, you're not my boss. I'm a free agent. I don't even have a contract with NAB as a freelancer, not any more. Not till we come up with something new.'

She had a point.

Joe could barely move.

'You know you want to,' she said. And before he could reply, she hiked up the bikini top, not taking it off completely, just letting it sit on the top slopes of her tits, framing them. He groaned aloud with desire. Her nipples were pale pink, and pointing due north. The shape of those puppies was even better without the tease of the bikini. There were faint, sexy little tan lines on them. It was a porn star's body, without the wear.

His hands came up and cupped them. Immediately. He was only human. She was divine.

And a surge of maleness rocked straight through him, surprising him with its ferocity. Tease him? Taunt him? He would make her pay for that. His thumbs started to glide very lightly over the tips of her nipples, barely touching them, testing their responsiveness. She moaned and arched her back. Her legs parted a little, so she was straddling the ground near him. But Joe didn't reach down, didn't untie the little knot, slip a finger into that pussy that wanted him so badly.

'Step back,' he said, squeezing her breasts once.

Maria's eyes flicked open in confusion. 'What?'

'I have to go back to the office when we're done. I don't want you getting me wet. It's going to be the other way around.'

She gasped. Moved back. She was blushing, hot. He could see

she had never been spoken to this way. 'Good girl. Now strip. Take that off. Do it slowly.'

Maria was trembling. Her fingers reached to the knot at her side. She tugged, fumbled. Joe just stood there, arms folded, watching her. Not saying a word. Not helping.

Finally she got the knot loose and looked up at him. He held her gaze, steady. Enjoying himself. Making her perform. The bikini bottom slipped, obediently, slithering slowly away from her. She was clean-shaven, golden all over. Like a teenage boy's wet dream.

There were two pairs of high heels at the edge of the pool area; he imagined her slipping them off and preparing to swim the day before. He pointed. 'Put on the red ones.'

They were high, fuck-me stilettos. Maria did as she was told, whimpering with need. Joe's blood was thundering. He wanted to watch her lead him through the place like a stripper, the heels shortening her stride and lifting her ass up and out.

She did it. Her body looked even hotter. He struggled for control. He had to get her into a bedroom.

'Turn around. Show me that ass,' he ordered. 'Oh yeah. That is world-class. Now walk into the bedroom. I'm going to follow and watch your ass swing. Make sure you sway your hips. Really strut. Every step, I want to see that thing grinding.'

Maria moaned, but she obeyed. Walking in front of him, swinging those ass cheeks back and forth with just a little bounce. His hands made fists. Clutching for control. Thankfully, the bedroom wasn't far; she turned a corner, entered a corridor and there it was. Sumptuous but overdone, a garish fantasy of pink and gold, not that he gave a shit. There was a bed in it. No mirror, which was too bad. He would have her buy one.

'Walk over to the bed but don't get on it. Stand facing it.'

'What are you going to do?'

'You'll find out.'

She moved the two steps and stood still, quivering with desire.

Behind her, he loosened his belt, unzipped his trousers, tugged his boxers halfway down his thighs. That was it, though; he was going to take her half dressed, let her feel her nakedness against his shirt, his cufflinks, his shoes. 'Bend forward.'

Half sobbing, she did so. He reached around and caught those glorious tits in both hands, caressing them, teasing her.

Maria grunted and moaned again. He thrust a thigh against her pussy. She was wet; not just the water droplets still on her skin, but that perfect, hot, welcoming young slickness. There in her red heels, that spectacular ass just imploring him to have her. There was no question. He was past thought, past regret, past morals. He thrust into her, feeling himself go deep, grindingly deep, taking her relentlessly, slamming into her, all that pent-up need and desire and frustration mercifully released, and he could feel her body arching and responding, her knees buckling with pleasure but his hands on her hips holding her still. She was fresh, new, hot. Full of desire for him. Nothing fake.

She was thrashing wildly; he felt her pussy clutch at him, starting to spasm, and he angled himself hard, lifting her up, thrusting against the deep walls of her, hitting that tender, melting little spot. She cried out, shrieking, screaming, her legs shaking uncontrollably, coming for him, and he exploded instantly, matching her, triumphant, feeling so strong and good and powerful, so much of a *man* . . .

And then it was over, and she was panting and crying out, and he slipped from her numbly, a wash of pleasant exhaustion crashing up his body like a wave on a shore. He was breathing hard too, his heart plunging back to earth, getting its rhythm.

And Joe Goldstein tried to concentrate on that, and not on his overwhelming sense of dismay.

David came down to dinner and looked at the table. It was wrong. There were only three places set.

Mom was serving up chicken salad and hot French bread; it

seemed to be store-bought. She was busying herself putting ice in the water glasses, grabbing coasters, talking to Rona. His sister was eyeing the food suspiciously; if it wasn't ramen noodles, she didn't really like it.

But there was no place for his father. And he realised with a shock that he hadn't seen him that morning, either.

'Where's Dad?'

'Oh.' Topaz hesitated. 'He's got meetings late.'

'What kind of meetings?' Rona asked, chewing on a piece of bread.

'I think there's some worry about the network's big star being out of contract. Dad wants to bring in new shows, and they're resisting. He doesn't want to run NAB if they won't let him call the shots.' His mother swallowed. 'It's a difficult time for him,' she said. David thought she sounded horribly choked.

He pulled up a chair and sat down.

'Doesn't want to run NAB? But we need the money!' Rona said.

'We could do without it,' David snapped.

'Not and keep our lives how we're used to.'

'You can live without the Bose headphones and the Four Seasons Costa Rica,' David said.

Rona sat up. 'I love Costa Rica! And you're glued to those headphones, are you kidding me!'

'We could have just as good a time in a Holiday Inn in Puerto Rico.'

'I doubt that.' Rona forked a large helping of salad on to her plate. 'David, you're just doing your social justice shtick again. It sounds good, but you still leave your room a filthy mess for Natasha to clean up.'

That was true. He winced inwardly. But his eye caught Mom, eating, her shoulders untensed now. Why? Because him and Rona squabbling got them off a difficult topic?

He debated it. Mom was stressed; should he add to that?

I have to know, he thought. Secrets just make it worse.

'Mom, I don't want to upset you, but is Dad really not here because of meetings? He normally makes sure to come home anyway.'

She deflated, like a balloon.

'David, why do you have to be so smart? It's worrying. I'm sure I'm raising a lawyer, God help me.'

'Why?' Rona looked up, her brown eyes alarmed now. 'What's happened? Mom?'

'Dad does have meetings,' Topaz defended herself. 'But your brother is correct. We had an argument and he . . . He's taken time out to spend in a hotel.'

'Did you make him?' David asked.

His mother shook her head. Her eyes reddened, and she made a great show of standing up and clearing her plate. David felt like a worm.

'I could text Dad and ask him to come home,' he offered.

'Your father can make his own decisions. What I want you to do is clear the table, then make sure your homework's done so I don't have to chase you in the morning.'

'We have to talk about this!' Rona said.

'When Dad comes home, we will, no doubt. Just finish your food and clear up, Rony. OK?'

David ate a few mouthfuls of salad and bread. It tasted like ashes, but he wanted to show his mother that he'd be fine. What the fuck had happened, and why did adults have to act like kids?

He thought about going back to his room and ringing his father anyway, but the set of Mom's back told him not to.

Fine, David Goldstein thought. Though if his father didn't show his face tomorrow night, there was going to be hell to pay. No excuse for walking out. For not talking to them.

But despite the internal bravado, he was scared. And he knew it.

Chapter Nine

The private jet touched down at Teterboro smoothly enough, and within minutes Michael Krebs was in the back of a limo, heading uptown into the city. It was expensive even reserving a seat on a charter, but Krebs couldn't wait.

Martin needed him.

Finally the phone call, the casual message that maybe 'Dad, you could come up here. You know, if you wanted.' That voicemail was barely minutes old when Krebs was already on his way to Van Nuys airport. There was always some plane ready to go, some favour he could call in. The comfort in these things was an easily ignorable luxury – the speed and simplicity was not.

Rowena was due back home shortly. Meanwhile, he'd left the nanny in charge. Josh and Ruth were big enough to handle it. And Martin was his child too.

As he leaned his head against the dark leather of the interior, Krebs didn't notice the routes and highways slipping past him, his old stomping ground of New York. His thoughts were full of Martin. As a baby, lifted into the air by a nurse, his mother gasping in the bed behind them, Krebs's eyes transfixed on his firstborn; so small, so wet, slimy and angry, but holding his father's entire life in the circumference of that miniature fist. How his heart thumped with love and terror as that delicate, squirmy bundle was placed in his arms, rooting blindly for something he could never give him. And then all the rest of it. Scenes from a life. Laughter at the bris. Little Marty on Dad's shoulders at the zoo. Throwing a tantrum when he brought Pete home from the hospital, because Marty wanted a camel, not a little brother. His first school softball match. His kid, the truly terrible skier. With the great grades, and no interest at all in rock 'n' roll. And the heartache Michael had caused them all when he finally left, called it quits with Debbie. The stand-up rows, the awkward visits, the family therapy, and then, slowly, things getting better. He and Marty bonded after college, when the boy was pursuing academia. A million miles from Krebs's own life, but that was fine. In fact, it was a relief. His kids were strong and independent. And once they were grown, he loved them all exactly the same, though the little kids, his second family, with Rowena, they took up his attention and time; they lived at home, they had play dates, school, all that stuff, and it was hard work and exhausting but like a second lease of life . . .

Life.

Up to now. Now Marty's life was under threat. And Krebs felt his world cracking. It was a bad time, the wrong time. Rowena was being attacked. Marty was just finding his feet in the university, just coming into his own. Thinking about marriage. Krebs couldn't process exactly where he stood in all this. Marty's childhood was a world away, an age away, and yet instantly present. And he couldn't reach out to Rowena about it. The guilt he felt there would never completely leave him. For this one, he was on his own. It put pressure on her, on him, that couldn't be helped. Michael was here for his firstborn. And he hoped the stress gnawing away at him could somehow be resolved.

He was insanely restless, his thoughts racing. There was a *Wall Street Journal* folded in the back seat of the limo, and he opened it unseeingly, pretending to read as the roads and cars slipped past him.

* * *

'So this is home,' Marty said. 'And here's Amelia.'

'Great to meet you,' she said, offering Krebs her hand and a smile.

The young woman was dark-haired and pretty, with hazel eyes and some light freckles around her nose. She held herself confidently, and her face had all the sexy fullness of youth. Her cheeks were slightly red, maybe from walking up the stairs. They were two flights up here. He wondered how long Marty could manage that.

'Hey. Nice to see you at last,' Krebs said. He managed to suppress the emotion in his throat, with an effort. Then he went over and hugged his son, not like the man he'd become, but like the little boy he once was, with a grazed knee, maybe.

Marty was sick. The bear in Krebs rose up against it, wanting to protect his cub. He was unrecognisably thin. His hair was half gone already, and his skin was sallow. The clothes were hanging off him. He looked fifty years old. Michael folded him close, trying to hold him, to warm him up.

'How long have you been on the chemo?'

'Three weeks this session.'

'Dude. Time to shave this off.' Krebs ruffled his son's hair, what was left of it. 'Go full Kojak. Like your old man.'

'I'm hanging on to it for now.' Marty flushed slightly. 'Illusion of normality.'

Krebs looked around. The apartment was neatly kept, and he felt a rush of gratitude to Amelia for that. There was a lot to be said for the fact that Marty didn't need to worry about this part of it – that she was taking care of his day-to-day, doing his chores, feeding him. But it was also tiny, and cramped, and the small window in the sitting room was dingy.

'I'm going to get you another place,' he said. 'This afternoon.'

'Dad.' Marty grinned. 'Don't throw your money around.'

'That's exactly what I'm going to do. I'm going to throw my money around.' Krebs gave his son a grim smile. 'It's the only thing I can do. You understand?'

125

'Would you like some coffee, Michael?' Amelia asked.

'I would freaking love some coffee. Thank you.'

She moved into the kitchenette. It was only steps away from where he was standing, a little alcove in the centre of the room. There was a shower, a double bed behind a screen, and then the living room with a small wall-mounted TV. A classic walk-up studio.

'Marty, look. I know you think you don't need it—'

'I really don't.'

'I disagree. Maybe you don't need it right now. But you are going to soon. When you get weaker and you can't walk up lots of flights of steps. Also, Amelia. Do you work?'

'I'm finishing my dissertation at Columbia, and I do occasional work around that to help with the bills. Rent's expensive.' She shrugged. 'Even here.'

'What type of work?'

'I'm registered as a childminder and I also walk dogs with an agency. It pays pretty well,' she added. 'You have no idea how many rich New Yorkers buy dogs to coop them up inside all day.'

'She's often out first thing in the morning and last thing at night,' Marty agreed. 'But it's fine, I can't sleep for crap anyway. There's no schedules any more.'

'So you guys will do this as a favour to me,' Krebs said. 'Maybe you *don't* need it, but it will make me feel a lot better. I'm going to rent you a ground-level apartment somewhere close by, with proper amenities in the building. Amelia, let me know what you earn each month and I will double that. I want you to be able to work on your dissertation. Marty can help, it'll take his mind off things. The two of you need to have minimal additional stress in your lives right now.'

'But Dad.' Marty bit his lip. 'I've always wanted to live within my means as an adult, not within *your* means.'

'Right. And I have respected that. You have a trust fund – I know you haven't touched it.'

'That's for my kids.'

Krebs didn't argue. 'It can be; it's your money, not mine. The point is that this situation is temporary. They're going to get the cancer in remission, shrink it down.'

'You think so?'

'I'm certain of it. These are the world's best. Stage two? They laugh at stage two.'

He grinned at Marty, a gallows humour he didn't feel. 'But kid, one thing that will help is you relaxing, not physically stressing yourself, eating right, and not worrying about Amelia schlepping round town with a Great Dane. Besides, whether you need that or not, *I* need it. I need to feel I can do something valuable here. Mom's round all the time?'

Marty shrugged. 'She comes and cooks. Maybe once a week, to give Amelia a break.'

'That's fantastic.'

'You're not . . .'

'I'm not jealous,' Krebs said. Of course he was, just a little bit; his ex had no more children, the boys were her world. She could give all her time to Marty, when he needed her. And Krebs couldn't do that. He had Rowena and the kids to think about. His heart tightened with stress, and he felt a surge of resentment. Just once, why couldn't that be her problem . . . why couldn't he just stay here, with his child, the boy who really needed him?

Something was wrong. Rowena could feel it.

She was three weeks back in LA. The kids were aceing it at school; Michael was handling the pain of Marty well. He seemed more intent at work; he had a project in mind, he said, and he was starting to plan and scheme around it. He wasn't ready to tell Rowena the details yet. But she knew it was a great idea from the way he fucked her.

Maybe a shrink would say it was Michael Krebs's way of holding on to his life force in the face of death. Who the hell knew. But instead of depression and sadness assaulting her husband's libido, the opposite had happened. Michael caressed Rowena as though they were both twenty-one again, as though he could plunge into her and forget his fears. Their already great sex life had taken another turn into the sensational. He would summon her to his office across town, and when she got there, he'd lock his door and fling her over his desk on her belly without a word, hiking up her skirt and fucking her; he pulled her into the sea when they were walking the dogs in Malibu, tugged her bikini down, and took her right in the water, making her gasp quietly as other couples paced oblivious on the beach; there were morning sessions when he came to the pool to watch her swim before the kids got up, evening ones where he made excruciatingly slow love to her right on their own bed, tormenting her with his lips, his tongue and his fingers until she was pleading with him to come inside her. Such a frenzy of desire turned Rowena on so much she could hardly stand it. She thought about her husband all the time these days, often catching herself staring into space, fantasising about what he would do with her that night, or what she wanted to do to him.

Rowena's omnipresent need to have sex with Krebs just increased. Her man didn't make polite, boring, respectful married love. He banged her like he was the forty-year-old super-producer she'd first met as a wet-behind-the ears junior record executive, the man who'd once held her career in his hands; the forbidden fruit, the most dominant, dangerous male she'd ever known.

Once her idol, her mentor, her hopeless love.

Now her soulmate, her husband.

How many times had she wept for joy at odd moments, overcome by the fact that they were really together? That the dream had come true for her, that Michael Krebs had woken up, claimed her as his own?

But Michael was stripping away all softness when he came to her bed, and she loved it. Rowena had never been big on 'lovemaking'; timid, polite, obliging, deferential love. Boys like that had turned her off at college, and Michael Krebs, so alien, so different – American, Jewish, a player – was like an explosion in her world, under her skin. Their connection was pure eroticism, on the highest plane. And they liked each other immensely. There was more for her right away: infatuation, then love. And in the end her passion won his heart, broke through that tightly guarded, secret, vulnerable chink at the centre of his psyche; the man who was so feared, so respected, so in control, needed love as much as she did.

Once romance was really there, and marriage came next, Rowena feared their lust would die out. It was meant to, right? That was what you read. Two years of marriage, and that sick, squirmy feeling died right off. And if by some miracle not time, then children would surely kill it. No doubt at all. Yet she'd passed through both, and despite quarrels, rows, and exhaustion, her desire for him had never waned. They remained deeply in love, and the sex was never humdrum. Never a chore. That tepid 'best friend' shit never materialised. They were equals, mostly; even though she would never reach his levels of wealth and reputation, she was still good, damned good, and she had the ability to hear great rock and make inspired decisions, even if only Krebs could create it.

Love – that came a million ways. When he cooked at night. When she left him a note telling him how much she adored him. When they snuck kisses while feeding the kids breakfast, and were showered with Cheerios if they got caught. But sex, sex was different. Krebs never deferred to Rowena, never let her slide, take him for granted. And she exulted in thinking of ways to surprise him, challenge him, tease him, make him explode.

It was, to be honest, a pretty great goddamned marriage. But her man was taking things to a whole new level. And Rowena loved it. She read sex with Krebs like a gypsy read tea leaves: something major, some big play, was happening in his world at work, and that success was being worked out, in superb, blindingly orgasmic ways, on her body.

She thanked God for it and him. Because something else wasn't right here. Something wasn't on point.

'God! Look at this!' Barbara Lincoln had said to her, a fortnight ago.

They were standing together in the warm twilight outside Milan's Prada stadium, listening to the sound of Kassius's latest smash, 'Battery', pumping into the air, the coloured floodlights sweeping the sky, lasers spinning in a web. The place was completely sold out, but they were still looking at crowds of kids outside the stadium walls, some of them begging for tickets, others sitting smoking joints, dancing up and down, celebrating a gig they could only hear.

'There must be a thousand people out here!'

'Two thou at least.'

'You're right. Fuck.'

Barbara tucked her pass into her jacket, just in case. Rowena let hers swing. She felt all-powerful. Who the hell was going to fuck with her?

'Let's get inside,' she suggested. 'Backstage is this way.'

They walked a couple of hundred yards round the outside of the stadium. Barbara wore tailored black slacks and a gorgeous white shirt that set off her smooth espresso skin, and some of the lads lounging about on the crowd barriers whistled at her.

'Those boys must be about nineteen,' Rowena joked. 'They reckon you're twenty-five, looking like that.'

Barbara smirked. 'What did I tell you, honey? Black don't crack.'

They laughed aloud. God, it felt so good, Rowena thought. When it *worked*. When she was here with her friend. When the gig was sold out, with fans scrambling to get in. When the song they were swaying to outside now had eighty thousand hands in the air. When she walked past the security guards with yet another all-access pass, and they melted away from her like snow in the sun, saluting her like a queen. Even the surliest roadie was no trouble to Rowena now. It was osmosis; the success of her masterplan had somehow filtered down through the ranks.

Things had changed. And the steely beauty, the icy suit from LA, she was the one who had changed them. These men knew the difference between half-sold gigs and standing-room ones. The adrenalin was back. The entire vibe was different. Hotter. The stench of despair was gone, and their bands – two bands, two road crews – were no longer acting pissed.

'Evening, Ms Gordon,' a burly guard said.

Rowena looked up. He was Idris Evans, so it said on his laminate. The man who'd tried to bar her way in Frankfurt. Now bowing slightly, as though she were the Empress of Japan.

'Hi, Idris. Call me Rowena.' She never held grudges, particularly with juniors, workmen, any blue-collar types. 'And this is my friend, the legendary Barbara Lincoln. She manages Atomic Mass.'

His eyes widened. 'Oh. Wow. Nice to meet you.'

'I need to get out front. Side of stage.'

'This way,' he said immediately, and they walked together down a rabbit warren of grey concrete passageways, past the white production signs taped to the walls, through curtains rigged up across the corridors, the usual ants' nest of a backstage, more complicated now because there were two acts headlining. But Rowena recognised the maze: VIP guests here, another barrier for the lesser passes – local record companies, girls the bands were thinking about banging – and even further back, a meet-and-greet pen for contest winners, fan club members, and anybody who'd made friends with a roadie in a local trattoria the night before. There were production offices, catering halls, a wardrobe section, dressing rooms with extra guards – that was the inner sanctum, no fucker got in there – and the stadium's own hospitality area where the promoter could show off. Flight cases lined the walls, men and a few women strode around trying to look busy. Showtime was downtime for most, though; the hard work was done hours ago, the stage assembled, the lights rigged, fans processed. As soon as the last note sounded, these guys would descend like a swarm of black-clad ants, stripping everything down, packing it up, boxing it, loading it into lorries to travel to another country with precision timing Napoleon would have envied.

It was a world that most fans never saw. One that many dreamed of. And one Rowena Krebs absolutely loved.

She felt her pulse quicken as they turned out of the grey corridors, closer to the stage. Everything was louder. The lights were brighter. They were there. She was looking up maybe thirty feet of industrial scaffolding, with ramps and stairs at either side.

'Where are the punters?' she shouted.

Idris grinned. That was what the crew called those super-duper VIPs with extra sauce, the ones that got to stand in a little pen at the side of the stage and watch all the action as the band saw it. The bane of a sound man's life. The techs hated them too, but they were a fact of life. Some TV star, another musician, a cousin, a school friend; the big connections got you up there and you just stood around in the way.

'Nosebleed pen is stage left.'

'We'll head stage right.'

He nodded and wordlessly offered them both a small packet. Rowena didn't need to ask; earplugs were standard protection onstage. Unless you wanted to be deaf in five years. Not great for a record executive.

They walked up the ramp. Even with shouting, no way to make yourself heard now. A roadie started to block them, saw Rowena, and melted away. She lifted a hand to Idris and stood just back from the on-stage mixing desk; the bassist, moving to wave at fans on this side, clocked her and gave her a thumbs-up, grinning and tossing his long hair like any eighties metalhead.

'Battery' was finishing. Rowena looked through the web of red and green lasers at the crowd. This was more fucking like it, this was what they needed. Eighty thousand kids, as far as the eye could see, jumping up and down, screaming, pounding the song. A song that would have been a goddamned stiff had she not performed emergency surgery. Remixed, with an extra verse, brand-new vocals, and a rapper guesting over the top, the dull track had suddenly become a global, viral hit.

The co-headlining tour was selling out. Europe was fixed. Lumos were thrilled. Album sales were heading to the millions, and Rowena added the new mix to the record and emailed all the fans who'd already bought it with the extra track, plus a bonus live recording of the song. That was customer service, punk-rock style. And with some emergency surgery, Dr Krebs had brought this summer back to life.

Barbara grabbed her arm and grinned. There was no point in speaking. Rowena knew her best friend felt the same. In the darkness, with the band pounding and the wall of sound rising, with the lasers spinning and the fans screaming . . .

It was sacred. It was magic. It was *home*.

After the show they went backstage, to shake hands with both bands, receive the managers' grateful thanks, and touch base with the Italian record company. Paolo Gametti, Musica Italy's president, had flown in from Rome; he was lean and young in his well-cut suit, maybe thirty-five, and distinctly impressed.

'I guess I didn't expect this,' he told Rowena, as they sat on a couch in hospitality. 'Italy is totally sold out. "Battery" is all over the radio.'

'Great. Our next push is for Lumos. The remix of "Science" comes out on Monday. I want you to get some RAI TV spots lined up.'

He nodded. 'Off the shows in Rome and here, I think we can

manage that. What's the trick this time? Extra verse? Rap cut?'

Rowena shook her head. 'Michael listened and suggested a harmony. We just cut some backing singers weaving melodics up and down around the vocal. Now it sounds like *Pitch Perfect* or some a capella Bee Gees shit. We also looped George's lead vocals on one verse so it sounds like a round.'

'A round?' Paolo asked.

'Don't know how to say it in Italian. It's an English folk form where one line harmonises the next if you start the song at different times. Barbara, let's do "London's Burning" for him.'

'Will I fuck,' said Barbara, snorting with laughter.

'The idea is the song will go viral. Kids will work out it's a round and start remixes. A week after we drop "Science" with harmonies, we're going to email fans a bonus track of it as a round.'

Barbara raised an eyebrow. 'Damn, that's some clever stuff. You think of that?'

'I asked Michael if we could make it work, and he said yes. By the end of the tour, this should be a two-million-selling record. I'm sticking with that goal.'

Paolo blew the air from his cheeks. He was impressed.

'How's the catalogue marketing coming along?' Rowena asked.

'We managed to get tie-ins on four campaigns so far. Big units shifting in Italy. Our catalogue will be selling piecemeal, but it *will* be selling. A pasta brand, a beer, Al Italia and a coffee machine. I'm surprised; being honest, Rowena, I was not sure this would work.'

'That's why they pay me,' she said. 'And market share?'

'In Italy, we look to finish top three. If these two singles take off as you say, then maybe even number two in the quarter. Only behind Universal.'

'Rowena.' It was Adam, Lumos's drummer, hovering by the couch like a schoolboy waiting for an interview with the head-mistress. Rowena got to her feet and shook his hand warmly. She made talent come to her; record company execs who sucked up to artists were all too common, in her view. That way you couldn't tell them when they were fucking up, and you lied to the act. Sooner or later every record company dropped every band. Hollow protestations of love and friendship she left to Hollywood and its sleazy agents.

'Good show tonight. Make sure you work the crowd.'

'OK,' he said eagerly.

'How are the rest of the band? Changed?'

'Why?'

'There was a crowd of kids outside the stadium who couldn't get tickets. Couple of thousand.'

'Really? Wow, that's great. I mean, not that they couldn't get tickets. That they wanted to. You know.' He was stumbling, blushing, trying not to be gauche.

'Why don't you go ask the boys if they can take some security and a couple of instruments, set up behind the crowd barriers and play a short impromptu set. Maybe five songs. As a gift for waiting.'

'Wow. Yes!' Paolo's eyes lit up. 'Insane. Please do it.'

'Paolo, you can translate that the band wanted to give this gift to the fans in Milan. Make sure they play the single.'

'I . . . It does sound amazing, but Luke's kind of smoking a reefer,' Adam said.

'Do you want it, or don't you? Make up your goddamned minds. I pushed this record incredibly hard. I need you to be on it. To *work*. Do you remember what life was like two years ago? When you couldn't get booked in the Camden Falcon?'

'Yeah,' he said, pushing a hand through his hair.

'Well if you want to go back, you're doing it the right way. Forget two years, try two months. Remember the ticket sales?'

'OK. I'll get them.'

Rowena called a roadie across. 'Go get Rick Wilson. Now.'

Barbara leaned back against the smooth leather of the backstage couch, admiring her friend. 'You should have been a manager.'

'I am. Of the company.'

'You're wasted there, man. This is some slick stuff. I should know.'

Wilson appeared. He'd cut his hair and looked like he'd had a shower within the past week. He glanced at Barbara warily. A much bigger manager appearing at his show was not exactly cause for joy.

'Adam told me what you want to do.'

'You tell the roadies to start setting up, right now,' Rowena said. 'I don't want the crowd to leave. That will give time for them to gather and spread the word. Four songs and an encore. Paolo, you call the press office. Get them talking to local TV, radio, national press. Get HuffPost Italy out here. Get BuzzFeed. And get the band's videographer too; we want it for YouTube. Get sound to record it; it can be a free fan track down the road, or an extra, or we'll hide the file as an Easter egg on the website. Understand?'

Rick looked like he wanted to argue the toss, but Rowena simply raised a brow.

'Yeah, OK. Guess I got it.'

'Put the mike stands up first, that should be something they understand.' She stood up. 'Good gig, lads. I'm off. Got a plane home tomorrow.'

'You don't want to stay for the free jam?' Rick Wilson asked.

'Paolo will send me the file. You'll thank me tomorrow when they're all over the news.'

He deflated. 'Yeah. Probably. Uh, you know, thanks for the advice last time. Things are quite a bit better.'

'Advice?' Rowena grinned. 'That's one way to put it.'

'*Bitch*,' he muttered under his breath, but she was well past caring.

'You coming?' she asked Barbara.

'I'll stay. Talk to Paolo,' her friend replied, to Rick Wilson's obvious discomfiture.

'Take excellent care of Barbara,' Rowena ordered. 'Talk soon, OK? Good night.'

Rowena's return to LA was triumphant. The trade magazines noticed her turnaround. *Billboard* had already run five or six pieces on her campaign, as word leaked out about her strategy. First it was the co-headline tour, then the catalogue marketing. By the time she dropped major remixes of Musica's three big album stiffs – and turned them into hits – every other record company in town finally figured out what Rowena Krebs was doing.

Hall of Famer's Frankenstein Act, read one *Billboard* headline, next to a flattering picture of Rowena with Lumos at an award ceremony. *We know what you did this summer – Rowena Krebs has single-handedly raised Musica's first two quarters from the dead, adding volume to album sales and the stock price. Looks like the 42-year-old legend's still got it – and she's not going anywhere soon.*

Yeah, well, Rowena thought. You guys are wrong about that one. I can't wait to get out of here . . .

And yet. Although her phone kept ringing, other record execs congratulating her, joking with her, something was wrong. Rowena could sense it. Call it female intuition, whatever the hell you wanted. This, right now, should be her triumphant swansong. Michael's great mood, the insane sex, the blissful weather, and the bouquets from her industry . . .

Why can't I figure this out? she thought.

She spun in her chair and decided. There was one person who could see things clearly. One girl who didn't give a shit about music, and who knew the corporate world as well as she did.

Her former rival. Her closest friend.

Topaz Rossi.

Chapter Ten

Topaz looked at her kids. Her eyes weren't red any more; she'd made sure to do her weeping in the hour before they came home.

Joe was back. But not how she wanted him.

'What do you think we should tell them?' he asked her.

Topaz looked blank. 'What do you mean, tell them? Aren't you coming back home tonight?'

'We're separated,' Joe replied, and his eyes slid away from her.

Topaz gasped. 'What? You went to a hotel for a night. That doesn't equal separated.'

'It does in my mind,' he muttered.

'Joe – one fight. We're married. We love each other.' Topaz swayed on her feet, dizzy from a headrush. Was this happening? Really?

'Yeah, well. You haven't been showing me that love.'

'The hell I haven't. All of a sudden you want a geisha, not a wife.' Her Italian anger was boiling up in her again. 'Don't lay your mid-life crisis on me and the kids. Just grow up.'

'You see? This is what I'm talking about. No support, no respect. How can you think this is what I want from our marriage? Are you going to back me up about pulling the twins out of Pointer Academy if their grades don't improve?'

'No way. I'm not.' Topaz was seeing red. 'And I don't want to hear that again. They have SATs. Whatever kind of disciplinarian schtick you want to get into, don't waste my time with it right now. I'm not interested in having our kids hate us for the rest of their lives because Daddy threw a hissy fit.'

'My God,' Goldstein snapped. 'You're unbelievable. I have enough stress in the office right now without dealing with this shit.'

'You? *You* have stress in the office? Why don't you ask about my job?'

'Topaz, you've been running American Magazines for fifteen years. I just got hired a season ago at NAB. Whatever's happening at American is pretty much your fault. You're always trying to blame other people. It's getting old.'

Her fists clenched. 'You loser, Joe Goldstein. To think I actually wanted you home.'

'Well we won't make that mistake again. We're *separated*. I guess I should stay here and tell the kids with you.'

Tears sprang to her eyes. She wanted to sob, to plead, to fling herself at Joe's legs and beg him to stay forever.

But pride wouldn't let her. Rage wouldn't let her.

She turned aside sharply so he wouldn't see the tears, and forced out her words in an ice-cold voice.

'You can stay till they get back, and we'll tell them together. After that, leave immediately. I don't want you here.'

Then she went to her home office and shut the door. Whatever crying she needed to do, she would do it in private.

Telling the children was brutal. As bad a life moment as Topaz Rossi had ever experienced.

'Dad and I have some bad news,' she said. 'We're separating. Dad has moved out.'

'What?' Rona laughed. Then her face fell. 'Uh, *what*?'

David protested. 'That is some bullshit, Mom. You threw him out?'

'It's entirely his decision. Your father left, and we are separated.'

Topaz bit her lip and looked at Joe, hating him.

'I thought Mom and I needed a break,' he said. 'We both still love you . . .'

'Please don't give us the standard bullshit,' David challenged him, his handsome young face dark with emotion. 'What the hell happened? You guys love each other.'

'We have some major disagreements right now,' Joe replied.

'So go to counselling!' Rona squealed. 'You don't just *bail*! We're supposed to be the teenage brats in this family!'

Her father's face clouded. 'Not funny, Rona.'

'What's the issue exactly?' David asked, folding his arms in a way that reminded Topaz so much of Joe her heart collapsed on itself. She started breathing raggedly. She felt dizzy again.

'Is it us?' Rona asked, and started to cry. 'I'm sorry we were late for school before, Dad.'

'No!' Topaz said, immediately, before Joe could open his mouth. She shot him a look that could have melted lead in its fury. 'You two have nothing, zero, to do with this.'

'Why can't you be honest and say you're getting a divorce. This is some kind of crap meant to ease us into it,' David blustered.

'It's what it is. A separation. I will tell you both right away if it's going any further,' Joe insisted.

'We both love you and we have agreed that Dad can see you at weekends, and for one night's dinner in the week.'

'Holy shit.' Rona sat down heavily at the table. 'Holy fucking shit.'

'Don't swear like that,' Joe said.

She looked at him with fury. 'You've lost the right to tell me anything, *Joe*.'

'Rona! Don't call your father that.'

Topaz was flooded with emotion. Loss. Anger. But mostly protectiveness. For her children, and even for Joe. She hated the way the kids were looking at him now. As though they would never forgive him.

'Weekends and a dinner? I want to know who started this,' David said. 'Dad, was it you?'

'No.' Topaz forced herself to speak with calm authority. 'It was a mutual decision. Although your father chose to leave, I wanted him to. If you want to blame anyone, it's both of us. We believe this to be the best course right now.'

'Blame you both. That sounds good, you goddamned losers,' Rona said. She jumped to her feet and stormed out of the kitchen. A second later, without commentary, David followed.

Topaz mentally probed herself. She was alive, functioning. The pain of their children's anger hit her in the gut. It hung around the room like a physical chill.

'I don't know. Maybe I shouldn't leave it like this. I could stay the night,' Joe said.

'Too late now. You can't toy with them.' Topaz found she no longer wanted to cry. The passion had drained through her. She was empty. 'Get the fuck out and don't contact me till Friday afternoon. I'll let you know when you can come by to pick them up on Saturday.'

'Topaz. Look, please—'

'I said get out.' She stood and looked at him, and the ferocity of her anger made Joe stumble back. Without a word, he took his coat, left the apartment.

There was chilli and rice in the fridge. Topaz heated a couple of bowls in the microwave and laid them on the table. Then she buzzed their intercom system and called the kids for supper.

No reply.

No surprise.

On autopilot, she prepared a bowl for herself and took out a bottle of water. Then she went to her bedroom – their bedroom. The en-suite bathroom was full of his stuff. The whole place was full of his stuff.

She opened the medicine cabinet and reached for her Valium bottle. Mostly used just to steady her nerves on flights to

LA or Europe – Topaz detested flying. But right now, she needed a sedative more desperately than for any in-flight turbulence. Fingers shaking, she opened the pill bottle and popped one out.

There was work tomorrow. No time off. No compassionate leave. The next issue of *American Girl* was fast approaching deadline.

I have *got* to get some sleep, Topaz told herself. If more drugs were needed, no problem. She'd get medication.

Numbly, she ate her meal, choking down every mouthful. She swallowed a vitamin capsule. She took off her clothes and made sure they went in the laundry basket, not on the floor. No falling apart. No breaking down.

She didn't have time for crazy.

She cleaned her teeth mechanically and got into the shower, washing and conditioning her hair, then stepped out, pulled on a bathrobe and picked up a wide-toothed comb. If she got herself ready now, it was one less thing to do tomorrow morning.

The phone rang as she was sitting there combing through her hair. Her heart leaped.

Joe. He wanted to talk, to work it out . . .

It wasn't Joe. It was an LA number. Rowena Krebs.

She picked up.

'Hi, Rowena,' she said, and started to sob. 'I'm so glad you called. I needed to hear a friendly voice.'

Conrad Miles was delighted. The targets both looked better every morning. And of course, they had that scent about them.

Unfinished business.

'I know, Mr Miles, that my daddy would just *love* to work with you on the financing,' Joanna Watson said.

They were riding in his limousine through the New York traffic. Bestellen, Klaus and Weintraub were his corporate lawyers.

They'd already been working on a package. Best guys for the job. He would likely go with Goldman, at least to lead the bid. Everything needed to be blue-chip.

'He can advise. How's that?' Miles smiled briskly at the young woman. Did she want to play? 'If your information is valuable, you'll get a seat on the board.'

'I want to edit *American Girl*,' Joanna said, and pouted.

'And I want to be twenty-five. It doesn't work that way.' Miles catalogued Joanna. She was definitely pretty, though no knockout. Was she flirting with him? He was used to that, from a certain type of chick: mercenary and unconcerned with her image. Joanna Watson interested him, though, just a little. She was, after all, an heiress. Not in his league, but she had eighty to a hundred coming. The enticing prospect danced before him: sex with a younger woman, dating a younger woman, without looking utterly ridiculous. Because Joanna Watson would not get pegged with a gold-digger tag.

Her daddy had a goldmine all his own.

So if not money, what did Joanna want?

Power.

There were only ever two bribes that bought youth, in Conrad Miles's cynical, hardened view. Money was one. Power was the other. He had both, and made a number of discreet arrangements, trades, you might call them, that both parties entered into with their eyes wide open. He collected women of the utmost discretion. Women who were educated, attractive, and always available to him. Who signed legal contracts with binding gag clauses, and then accepted his handsome payments. An apartment in a major city, usually, and a stipend for five years. After which the apartment became theirs to keep, unless they told a soul. In which case, it was instantly forfeit.

Conrad Miles selected carefully. He only wanted professional, intelligent women who were willing to undergo medical tests. Who acknowledged in writing that this was a contractual arrangement, that they knew he was dating other girls. More than he could ever need. There was no love.

But there was friendship. Miles had thought about it long and hard when setting up his costly, brilliant little scheme. He was not simply looking for hookers; you could get supermodels delivered nightly if you knew the right brokers. Instead, he wanted women who would ease his loneliness, on the rare occasions that it gripped him. Women who could go to classical music concerts with him, talk with him at the theatre, converse with him after a catered dinner in the apartment. Maybe it was the Western version of a geisha: highly trained, a woman to serve, to converse, to pour out the green tea with a delicate hand. And, of course, with a great body, a talented mouth, and an ability to work his old frame into excitement and virility when he felt the need to screw a girl.

This worked great. Conrad Miles was as proud of his sex life as of any deal he'd constructed. It was discreet, it was global, and it was elegant. He had respectable, old-fashioned mistresses. Kept women.

But did he want an actual girlfriend?

Did he want a wife?

It would add a certain something to life. Fewer air miles. Less need for caution. He was tired of game-playing.

'Conrad.' He had given her permission to use his first name. 'Be fair. I brought you this deal.'

'And I'm going to dispose of the assets. Besides, you're a lousy editor. Rossi was right to fire you.'

Joanna Watson gaped at him. He grinned. If she wanted to go further with him, it would be on his terms.

'Better to be seen as your father's daughter, brokering this deal with me. You will supervise editors when you sit on the American Magazines board, in the six months before I break the company up.'

Joanna tossed her hair. 'Well at least grant me one thing.'

Miles smiled inwardly. He liked that use of the word *grant*.

Joanna had processed exactly who was in charge here, and it wasn't her.

'Which is?'

'I want to be the one to fire Topaz Rossi. And I want to do it publicly.'

'A girl after my own heart. Done.' Conrad's eyes swept up and down her attractive dress, the old-fashioned black-seamed stockings. He suspected she had worn them deliberately to remind him of the girls of his youth. It was working.

'After we're done here, can I take you out to dinner? We can get to know each other a little better.'

Joanna Watson tilted her head and smiled brightly at him. 'I thought you'd never ask.'

Rowena didn't hesitate. It was a bad time; she had only just returned from Europe, and already she was on another plane. But her best friend needed scraping off the floor. And this was not something a phone call would take care of.

'It's Topaz,' she told Michael. 'Joe's left her; they just told the children. I'm sorry, darling. I have to go.'

'No problem,' Krebs said. 'I can handle the kids. Plus, of course, I get to bang the housekeeper.'

She laughed. 'Of course. Goes without saying.'

Marianne was fifty-five and twenty pounds overweight, despite walking around their house all day.

'Come back soon, baby,' he said, his voice softening. 'I miss you when you walk out of the room. Let alone take a trip.'

'Are you supposed to say that?' Rowena asked. Tears sprang to her eyes, but she dashed them away.

'Maybe not. Normal service will be resumed when you come home. Make it soon.'

'Couple of days. Love you, honey.'

She booked herself on an evening flight. That way she could make sure she saw the kids before she left.

'Mom, you just got back.' Ruth grimaced. She wasn't flooded with teenage hormones yet, wasn't spiky and rebellious. They were close, and Rowena's heart pinched for her daughter. 'Do you really have to go?'

'I do. You guys have to look after Dad for me.'

'Dad's only interested in Martin,' Joshua muttered.

Rowena frowned. 'Joshua Krebs, I know I didn't hear you say that. Martin's sick. If you were sick, Dad would be focused on you.'

Her son kicked the table. 'I know, but it's like we're not even here. If you leave again . . .'

Rowena felt the wave of guilt crash over her. Kids always knew your sore spots. 'My darlings, Topaz is my best, best friend and she really needs me. Dad and I love you guys more than anything in the world. I'm sorry for all the travelling, but it's temporary. Hang in there. Can you do that for me?'

Ruth blew the air out of her cheeks and rolled her eyes to indicate her martyrdom, but she nodded her dark head.

'It's cool,' she said.

'Come back soon,' Joshua said gruffly. He was fourteen now, too old to get upset. Or at least to let it show.

Rowena went to her closet, where a small suitcase with clothes for warm weather was always there, ready-packed, along with one for cold climates. If you ran a global corporation, you needed to be able to go at short notice. Something nagged at Rowena that this was not quite wise, this trip, right now. That she should be in LA, taking care of business. But it didn't matter: Topaz really needed her.

And she was heading out. Come what may.

As she slipped on her Burberry mac and headed downstairs to her waiting limo, Rowena chewed on that bad feeling like a dog with a bone. How come she couldn't pinpoint it? Her antennae were never wrong.

Never mind. Even with her heart in pieces, Topaz Rossi would be able to help her. She was enough of a career woman to see this clearly, better than Rowena could herself. And she would welcome the distraction. Help her friend find the problem, solve it, and get out with maximum grace.

When they'd worked together, they'd made a great team. All those years back, when they'd fought off the Conrad Miles takeover, maybe the last target companies ever to avoid him. Goddamn, she remembered the adrenalin of those frantic weeks, she and Topaz working desperately to avoid becoming the chief execs with the shortest terms on record. Topaz even gave birth in the middle of it. And Rowena drove her to the hospital. She'd be damned if she would let Joe Goldstein fuck things up now.

'Good morning,' Topaz said.

The editorial staff looked up from the table, where they were arguing loudly over prints and layouts. Two of them squealed.

'Oh my God,' said a young woman. Then she clapped a hand over her mouth.

'That's Rossi,' said a guy in a Dior suit. His brows knitted, realising he'd blurted the words aloud.

'Correct. It's Rossi. Lucy, good to see you.'

'Hello, Topaz.'

'Thanks for steering things so far. We have eight days to deadline?'

'Counting today.'

'I am taking over as editor for this current edition.'

There was a murmur of shock, dissent. Topaz was ready for that.

'I absolutely do not have time to deal with any sort of rebellion,' she said. 'So here's the story; get with the programme or get fired. This magazine is the flagship of our company and it reads like it's being phoned in. Is this understood?'

There were nods.

'Let me have your names. Left to right.' She pointed at Dior guy.

'Martin Weigl, photo editor.'

'Janice Tuffnel, features ed.'

'Iris Lelland, beauty ed.'

'Laura Morgan, sales and marketing.'

'Peter Farrow, contributor – features.'

'Gary Hersh, staff photographer.'

Topaz nodded. 'I used to edit this magazine. It sold five times the number of copies back then. The market was approximately twice the size. So I was still way ahead of your game. You know the problem? You guys are *boring*.'

'That's harsh,' Janice said. 'We're a market leader.'

'Not for much longer, if sales carry on this way. Here.' Topaz strode over to the table and cleared some space with her arm. She dumped down the three last issues of the magazine. 'Models on the cover. Skinny white girls. No stars. Look at the straplines – *Make-Up Resolutions. Happy New You!* Ugh. I'm cringing already. Where's *Your Best Year Yet*? Oh yeah, up there on the right-hand corner. That was January. Here's February – *Viviacious Valentines – Dress to Impress. Spring-Clean Your Wardrobe. Men Spill Their Love Secrets. Top 50 Purses.* Wow, I just threw up. And March? *Hip Hop – Be a Funky Easter Bunny. Madonna at 60 – Still Rocking. Gossip Girls – Why Tattling's so Addictive.*' She looked at the staff with a weary sense of contempt. Carefully she picked up the January issue. 'Pretty thin, huh? Never a good month, though, we all know that.' She chucked it down. 'But February's not much better. Flick through it, where are the pictures? Where's the beef? March? We're thirty pages lighter than this time last year.'

'Surely there's nothing wrong with any of those pieces,' Iris Lelland objected. She was a conventionally pretty petite brunette; she looked to be about twenty-eight. Private school, Topaz thought, summers in the Hamptons, interned at *Vogue*.

'And there's nothing right about them. Nothing big. Nothing new.' Topaz shook her head. 'We cannot afford to tread water. *American Girl* needs to make news. Not pass time.'

Lucy Klein asked the right question. 'So what next?'

'We need to shock. We need to be the news. Give me the features list and the cover shot.'

Martin handed over some stills, biting his lip. 'This is Lena Lewis. She was the hottest thing in New York Fashion Week.'

Topaz looked at the photo. Another run-of-the-mill model, pouting at the camera. 'Too late to change this?'

'We spent twelve grand on the shoot.'

She nodded. 'Show me the original, before retouching.'

Martin Weigl started. 'Why? My retouching is *fabulous*, you won't find better.'

'Don't worry. I'm sure it's amazing.' Topaz waited. He shuffled the pile and passed over another shot.

She clenched her fist. It was everything she'd hoped: still pretty, but sallow skin, bags under the eyes, bloodshot whites, yellowing teeth from cigarettes.

'Run the front cover as a spliced shot and get it to me today. The left half the retouched photo. The right half natural. Not a single line is to be blurred.'

'Oh my God!' Martin shrieked. 'You can't do that! She'll look *horrible*!'

'No she won't,' Topaz told him. 'That's how Lena actually looks. That's how she looked that day.' She turned to Janice Tuffnel. 'You're features?'

'Yes, ma'am.'

'Great. Here's the feature strapline: *Sorry*. I want that word in giant black letters. Underneath, *How Our Industry Sold You Short: Our 50 Biggest Photoshop Fails.* Next you publish fifty shots of models – how we ran them, and the originals. Pick models who signed our standard release. Nobody with a special contract – I don't want to get sued.'

Janice had started to nod. 'This is big on the internet.'

'But magazines don't cop to it. We're going to.' She turned to Lucy. 'We launch the *American Girl* pledge. We label every retouched photo.'

'But that'll be all of them.'

'So be it,' Topaz said. 'Things are going to be different. Next, I want some actual American girls to comment. Headshots inserted. A quote on each picture. Get them out to contributors round the states. One girl per state. Make it a good mix of races and backgrounds. Ages sixteen to twenty-seven.'

'Saying what?' Lucy asked.

'How they feel about the industry smoothing everything. Slimming it. Our lies to them. Two sentences each.'

'Man.' Lucy Klein nodded. 'That story will be massive. And the cover.'

'We need to make news. Whatever features we have, run them, but let's add some twists. I want a star to interview a critic. Romance? Let's get real. Ask some guys what they look for in a woman and print the real answers. Cheerleaders.'

'Cheerleaders?' asked Laura Morgan. 'Isn't that against your new ethos?'

'No, I want you to attack cheerleading. Get a puff-piece interview set up with some NFL girls and then, after you have the pictures, go hard. Ask them why they take slave wages for the season. The NFL makes nine billion a year and these women take home less than a thousand bucks. I want a major piece. I want shots. I want ads. I want statements from each NFL team. And quotes from champion cheerleaders. You should be able to get that done tomorrow. Set up a shoot for Wednesday. Get four reporters on quotes the second the pictures arrive on our computers. Janice, the feature stuff should be written this afternoon so all we need is the quotes.'

'Wow,' Lucy Klein said. She shook her head. 'I . . . I think this is going to be amazing.'

'Good. Let's get going.' Topaz looked around. 'Where's the editor's office?'

'In the corner there.'

Topaz glanced at it. Compared to her own giant executive suite at headquarters, it was tiny. Just a desk and a computer monitor and a couple of chairs. She loved it.

'I'll get set up. Somebody bring me a black coffee,' she said.

For the first time in days, Topaz felt just a tiny chink of happiness. She was back to doing what she was best at. Somewhere that it counted. She could forget Joe here, at least for a few hours, at least if she worked hard enough, smart enough.

Joe Goldstein sat with Maria on his lap. He was leaning back, his ab muscles holding tight as she bounced up and down, sliding her pussy up and down his cock, clenching it, working him. There was absolutely nothing in his mind but the excitement, the pleasure, the sensational feel of her riding him, those big breasts bouncing, her lips open and parted with excitement. The flame of her long black hair cascaded down her back, whipping around. She was hot, no faking, her pale pink nipples sharp with blood and desire.

He was lost in her. Letting her enjoy herself. Fighting his own desire to come. No fucking way: he was hell-bent on making her shake, making her scream his name. Maria's surrender, her conquest. Nothing else would do.

He gritted his teeth and started to thrust back a little. She squirmed in protest, wanting to ride him, to grind it out of him, but Joe wasn't interested; instead, he held her hips, arched his back, lifting her up, angling himself, fucking her, pinning her, not letting her decide anything. Helplessly, she moaned aloud, and her head lolled, her eyes half shut.

'That's it, baby. Give it to me. You know you want to.' He grinned, moving her, lifting her up and down. Bouncing her. She was light in his arms, slippery wet.

'Oh God! Joe!' She gasped and tensed. 'Ah!'

'There you go,' he said mockingly, and she screamed and shuddered and rocked on him, clawing at him, choking out his name. Instantly he let himself go and surged inside her, dizzy with the force of it, his heart hammering inside his chest, panting, gasping for air.

He stayed still for a couple of seconds, then lightly slid her off him. She was bathed in sweat, her skin mottled pink, gasping. Mechanically, he bent over to kiss her.

'Mmm,' Maria said. 'Oh damn, baby, you are so freaking *hot*.'

'Yeah. So are you,' Joe said.

He stood quickly and headed for her guest bathroom, down the hall. He preferred, by far, to wash in there. It was luxurious in an antiseptic, hotel-suite way. He did not have to face the pink and gold towels, her shampoos and perfumes and expensive little jars of face cream, everything that reminded him of where he was, instead of at home.

The sex was great. He was trapped. He chewed on it: his anger at Topaz, his alienation from the kids. Pain washed through him, but it was not as simple as calling it off with Maria, heading home. She would toss her head and storm out of his network, no doubt, but he didn't give a fuck about that. NAB would roll with him, or he would quit.

Would he, though? He told himself that, but he was doing nothing to put himself in that dangerous position. While he was with Maria, she was likely to sign up – and he'd be covered at work.

More to the point, he was definitely weak, and foolish. One afternoon of seduction, and he'd cracked like an egg. After having sex with Maria, how could he walk away?

You're separated. It's OK. Magical words, permission given to him to act on his desires, to sleep with this woman, to have her. Have sex with someone else.

The marble wet room was equipped with all the latest toys:

water and steam, an angled floor, stone-coloured towels behind a glass door, a bench to sit on. He selected the rain setting, and water poured evenly from the ceiling, a relaxing, pattering stream of warm droplets all over him, like a fantasy. He closed his eyes for a second, turning his face upwards. Letting the warmth take everything away.

He needed to stay with Maria. He needed to actually make the lie true. To really be separated. So that it wasn't just a one-afternoon stand, a cheap, angry, total and complete betrayal of his wife. The thought danced around the back of his mind, but he was reluctant to acknowledge it openly.

Instead, he grabbed the shower gel and washed briskly. It was cucumber. Joe preferred plain, unscented soap. Next time, he would bring one with him. There would be a next time, after all. He knew that.

He turned off the water and towel-dried himself fast. Then he moved to the guest bedroom, where his clothes were. After sex was finished, he had no desire to watch Maria dress. The time women took always annoyed him. Besides, he was not keen to be a front-page story. He wanted to leave Maria's building at least twenty minutes before she did.

Within five minutes he was buttoning his cufflinks, solid gold stamped with his initials, hand-cast by Asprey's in London.

'See you in an hour,' he shouted into her bathroom.

Maria was in her own black-lined shower stall, cast in solid basalt. She looked at him over her shoulder.

'Hey, baby. See you then,' she purred.

The water was sluicing over her unforgettable curves, but Goldstein was completely immune. He looked at her ass with an aesthetic appreciation only. It would be fantastic to see that moving on the back of a horse, in skin-tight leathers or a skirt, while Maria cracked jokes. Like a fantasy version of *The Dukes of Hazzard*. The TV mogul in him loved the idea. And today he was going to sign up Maria, and her ass.

Two minutes after waving goodbye, Joe Goldstein was in a cab headed uptown, looking at his phone and checking through meetings.

Today was going to be a busy day in the office. Thank God. He didn't want time to think.

'Now, here's the direction I want you to take,' Topaz said. She had the marketing and sales people gathered around her, crammed into a conference room. 'We should see a large news following from the week of publication onwards. There will be excitement around *American Girl*. I want you to reach out to advertisers and offer them large discounts. Twenty per cent off our nearest rival in circulation. Offer our top ten biggest ad spenders a free page.'

Laura Morgan almost squealed. 'A *free* page? That's unheard of.'

'Everybody shows the love to new advertisers. But older advertisers are our bread and butter. Offer them a single-page ad for a new product, something they want to test out. They can use it for anything they like. They can also use it for community work, or corporate branding, at zero cost to the company.' Topaz grinned. 'Those poor VPs that need to do good works, as part of their brief. They can advertise all that stuff right in *American Girl* and still not blow their budget for the quarter. You guys get it? Get on the phones and work your best relationships. We want this issue to be *fat*. Something that says "major investment".'

'Ms Rossi,' one of the sales team said. 'It's hammered into us to always sell at the best price. What happens when we can't sell to them at a discount rate the next month?'

'This is the rate. We're going for volume. I'm spending money on extra pages in the book. Not on fancy photographers and overpaid stick insects. From now on, *American Girl* is going to court controversy and sex because both of them sell. Everything here is too bland. We have to cut through. My marketing budget is being spent on giving away marketing.'

'There will be a production cost for the new pages,' a man said, with a frown. 'You'll need American Magazines' approval for that.'

'Lucky I'm the CEO, then, isn't it?' Topaz said, and was rewarded by a burst of genuine laughter. 'Get out there, people. Pick up the phones.'

She jumped from her seat, eager to get back to the main building. The sales team followed suit, chattering excitedly. This was so weird, Topaz thought. It was an unfamiliar feeling.

She was actually having *fun*.

'Lucy,' she said.

Lucy Klein skulked over. Topaz had completely steamrollered her, she knew that, but she couldn't worry about some deputy's hurt feelings. This was emergency surgery, CPR on a dying magazine. 'Hold the fort. I'm going back to HQ.'

'Another brilliant idea?' said the deputy editor. She was smiling, but it didn't reach her eyes.

Topaz looked directly into them. 'Yes. I'm full of them just now. Try and learn something. The best of us never stop.'

Why hadn't she done this before? It was how the great work was created, how ideas flowed. She'd already hit on ways to save more than just one magazine. And she wanted to start to create titles too.

As she raced up the stairwell, too impatient to take the elevator, she reached for her phone to call . . .

Joe.

Her hand froze. She'd done that automatically. Gone for her iPhone to call him. Let him know her big idea. How it was going. What ass she was kicking right now.

But he wasn't there. He wasn't around, not in any way that mattered.

She swallowed, hard. She should email him, press for marriage counselling. But maybe Joe should make the first move. This was like dating, like being single again, worrying about how stuff looked, whether she should play hard to get.

Topaz needed a shrink. And she needed to work out. Just get back to running, clear her head. She couldn't fall apart right now. She didn't have that luxury.

Besides, she reminded herself, when she got home tonight, she could ask somebody fresh for help. *Rowena*. Thank God.

It was way too long since she'd had a real friend to talk to.

Chapter Eleven

'Wow. Man, this is just insane.' Rowena looked around her, deeply impressed. 'Your place is gorgeous.'

'Thanks. We spent a lot of time on it.' Topaz bit her lip. 'Joe found it and I decorated, mostly.'

'You both did a great job.' She pushed her case up against the closet wall of the guest bedroom; it had a beautiful view towards the park and the Museum of Natural History. Already she was a little nostalgic for Manhattan, where she'd met Michael, built her own empire.

The door opened, and Rona and David walked in, book bags over their arms.

'Kids, this is Rowena Krebs, you remember her.'

'Sure. Hi,' David said.

'My namesake,' Rona smiled.

'Oh my God.' Rowena leant back against the wall, shocked. 'You're teenagers. I mean, I knew you were teenagers, but actually seeing it is messed up.'

'I know, right?' said Topaz fondly.

'Mom, you're embarrassing me,' said Rona. 'Come on . . .'

'Can we get Seamless web for supper?' David asked.

'Actually, no. I'm making lamb curry. You guys can come down and help yourselves.'

'Cool. Nice to see you, Rowena,' Rona said. She slouched off with her brother, up to their rooms.

'My two are the same age, almost,' Rowena said. 'Don't know why I'm so surprised. It makes me feel old.'

'We are.'

'Hey, speak for yourself. I'm hitting my prime,' Rowena replied. 'Do you have a kettle, or is it all coffee makers and milk frothers?'

'I can make you tea. Still such a goddamned Limey.' Topaz smiled, and it was genuine. It felt good to have Rowena here with her. Life did suck, but there were consolations. Surely she and Joe would patch things up, maybe be better for it.

'Thanks. Black with sugar, if you don't mind. And then let's go somewhere private, and you can tell me what the hell's been going on.'

They settled into the library – Joe's library, but screw him, he wasn't around to object, Topaz thought – and Rowena sipped tea while Topaz drank vanilla decaf coffee and talked. She led her through the fights, the walk-out, the dramatic return to the house. Then she talked about American, and Joanna Watson, her near-death experience in the boardroom . . .

'Yes. God.'

'What?' Topaz asked.

'Don't mind me,' Rowena said. 'I was just – what you said reminded me of something. Why I've been so worried lately. When it should all be going well. Sorry, I didn't mean to interrupt. Carry on.'

Topaz took another gulp of coffee and dabbed a little at her eyes. 'I'm banging on about myself.'

'No. I flew here to listen. It's going to be OK, Topaz, really. Tell me what you're doing at the coalface.'

Topaz filled her in, and Rowena listened in silence, apart from the occasional enthusiastic nod. When her friend was finally done, she shrugged, blushed, and blew the air out of her cheeks.

'And that's it. My tale of woe.' Topaz wrinkled her nose. 'I'm sorry, I know it's serious. I just don't do pathos all that well.'

'It's deadly serious,' Rowena said. 'I get that. But if you can't keep strong, you'll crack. Joking around helps with all that.'

'You're right. I know.' Topaz's fingers curled around the mug. 'So what's the diagnosis?'

Rowena shook out her long hair and thought for a few moments.

'Let's start with Joe. First of all, I'm your friend, not a shrink; this comes with all the usual health warnings. OK?'

'Obviously.'

'There's something else going on. The way you two love each other. Something unsettling him. It could be a mid-life crisis, sure, but that's not going to be all that's bothering him. It sounds like his work is failing too, that maybe there's a crisis there. You, his rock, aren't around. The kids are acting up. He tries to impose order at home. Joe's an alpha male, maybe a bit less of a bulldog than Michael, but he still likes having things his own way. And you stand up to him.'

'So he walks out?'

'I think he snapped. What I can't figure out is why he didn't come back right away. He made his point with you, surely.'

'You think marriage counselling?'

Rowena nodded. 'I wouldn't let this go another week. The kids will visit him this weekend wherever he's staying, and after that, just focus on getting the two of you back together. It's important to have him move home as soon as possible. Even if you guys go to counselling every day.'

Topaz rolled her neck around, trying to get comfortable. 'So I should kind of give in, huh? I should let him yell and snap and insist the kids do everything his way? Rowena, I just . . . I don't know. I'll resent him whenever he comes to bed. It won't be the same.' She started to sob. 'It just will never be the same.'

'No! I don't mean that. I mean that people find each other

161

when they're with each other. He was afraid to be weak; Joe Goldstein doesn't do that. And then with the kids . . . and you . . . it was easier for him to just snap than to be constructive and work it out. Walking is always a nice full stop. He can thrash out his issues by himself. But once you guys get into counselling, it'll all pour out.'

'Joe hates the idea of therapy.'

'But he's going to have to suck it up. A therapist really doesn't do much; they just ask questions and let you talk. And nobody storms out when they've paid five hundred an hour to sit in a counsellor's fancy offices. Joe will understand that bit of it.'

'I guess.' Topaz felt a little brighter. 'But he hasn't called.'

'You're both proud. He did the walking, so he should call you, but don't stand on ceremony. Will he pick up the kids?'

'I doubt it,' Topaz said. 'That will be too painful for him. They're not eight any more, you see. They're mobile enough to go to his rental and come back here without either of us needing to see the other.' She pressed her fingers to her forehead. 'I should call him, but I just *can't*. I have this anger, as well as the sadness. It'll just boil over and I'll scream at him. And it's the stuff I'm doing at work right now. I feel . . . at home. It's a big gamble, and I'm ordering everyone around, but if I just roll over for Joe, I think it'll affect the office. Because I'll know it's bullshit, all the empowerment that *American Girl* writes about. And if *I* don't believe it, I can't sell it to other girls. I won't like myself, and the magazines I supervise will be stale as shit, because I just won't care. You can't fake it. You need to shock staff when you want big changes, impact them with something you believe in yourself.' Topaz shook her head. 'None of that probably makes sense.'

'It makes perfect sense. You shouldn't call Joe and cave. Nor should you grow old waiting for him to get over his pride. Fuck it,' Rowena said. 'I'll do it. Not a phone call, either. I'll go see him at his office and tell him he needs to get his ass into counselling and come home to his family. Then all you have to do is listen when he speaks and not tear him apart out of the gate. Can you do that?'

Topaz nodded. 'Sure. Of course. I love him.'

'And he loves you.'

The tears sat in Topaz's throat like a big lump of undigested bread, like she couldn't physically swallow them down.

'Don't tell me that,' she wept. 'If he loves me, why isn't he here? Why isn't he home?'

Rowena felt her heart clench seeing Topaz like this, hunched into a little ball, sobbing like a child. Topaz and Joe were supposed to be solid, unassailable. It scared her; the thought of being parted from Michael, even for a couple of days. Married people could be like that – bailing on their friends like divorce was a disease, like you could catch it . . .

She stopped herself. Divorce? Don't be insane.

It was twenty years. Joe and Topaz were not about to get divorced. She was here to stop that train leaving the station.

She leaned forward and gave Topaz a giant, enveloping hug.

'Come on, honey, cheer up. We need to go put the curry on. No crying in front of the kids. We can talk business. I could use *your* help there, if you want the truth.'

'Hey.' Topaz pulled herself together. 'Happy to do that. You're right, let's go do this thing.'

They headed back into the kitchen. 'Since when did you start to cook?' Rowena demanded. 'I thought you were as bad as me.'

'Worse. But the thing is, I didn't want to do that whole single-woman-with-pizza deal when the kids are around. Home-cooked meals, that's what my mom thinks I should provide.'

'Your mom is an asshole,' Rowena said. Topaz's parents had cut her off, years ago, for marrying a Jew. They occasionally sent begging letters, and she sent money back. Catholic guilt, though she had no reason. They had yet to see the grandchildren, and it was probably too late to start now.

'Correct,' Topaz replied. 'However, she's an asshole who knows her way around a plate of meatballs. Unlike me. Anyway, I decided to fix my little home-cooked meal the way I fix everything.'

Rowena laughed. 'You threw money at it?'

Topaz made finger guns at her, and Rowena cracked up.

'God, we're such disasters,' she said. 'I'm exactly the same. Can't clean. Can't cook, can't garden, can't change a bloody spark plug.'

'*Can* run a record company.'

'*Can* sell magazines.'

They hi-fived.

'Well, I found this great little gastro-pub in the Village, the Black Sheep. They do the best comfort food. And the owner owes me a favour because two of my magazines gave him amazing reviews and *New York Life* even put him on the cover. I told him I had a goddamned food emergency and he better shape up. The next day he messengers up here five trays of stuff: bolognese sauce, an awesome chilli, enchiladas, a lamb passanda curry, a casserole, a stew and four different types of soup, which are now in the freezer. All top-of-the-line shit I just have to reheat.'

'Get the fuck out of here,' Rowena said. 'My God, I'm so jealous.'

'Not only that. He sent me four tubs of home-made ice cream. This tutti-frutti that'll blow your mind. A rhubarb, a cappuccino and a strawberry-mint.'

'I'm never going home.'

'And boxes of Charbonnel and Walker chocolates for afterwards.'

Rowena spread her hands. 'The power of the press, for God's sake. All I can do for someone is messenger over some obsolete CDs.'

'Bullshit, man, you got concert tickets and rock stars on your side.'

'In Hollywood? Nobody gives a damn.' Rowena grabbed a pan and started filling it with water. 'Seriously, I'm proud of you. Mom of the year. Creative thinking.'

'The way I see it, I can make them breakfast myself. I'm a dab hand at frying up bacon and scrambling eggs.'

'There you go. You probably juice the oranges too.'

'Let's not go crazy,' Topaz chided. 'That sounds like work.'

They stood around in the kitchen, cooking and talking, and Rowena poured them both a large glass of red wine. Just one wouldn't hurt, and it seemed like Topaz could really use it, just a little relaxation till she got used to managing the kids alone. The curry warmed gently in a pan, smelling heavenly. Rowena laid the table and called the kids back in. God, they were good-looking: Rona with her dark hair and blue eyes, and David, more fiery, red-haired like his mother, muscled like his dad.

'Wow, Mom. This sauce tastes delicious.' David forked some more into his mouth. 'You didn't make it, right?'

'Doofus,' Rona said. '*Obviously* she didn't.'

'Oh hey, thanks for the vote of confidence.' Topaz grinned.

'Your mom sourced some home-cooked meals she can make you fast. You have to learn these tricks now for when you're older,' Rowena told them. 'The last thing you want to do at the end of a long day is start cooking.'

'I'm going to be a gourmet cook,' David announced. 'Like Dad.'

He coloured, and looked at Topaz. 'Sorry, Mom.'

'It's fine,' she said brightly. 'Your father's a brilliant cook.'

'I love this,' Rona said. 'But I'm OK just eating sandwiches. I don't really care. Food's all right, I guess. Can't get worked up about it.'

'Attagirl,' Rowena nodded. 'See, that great name they gave you rubbed off.'

'Men like food,' David said. 'Stop laughing, Rona. I mean men *really* like it. And we need to be great cooks, see, because nobody marries young any more. And even then your wife probably won't cook.'

'You've got it all figured out,' Topaz said, but that lump was back in her throat. God, she wished Joe were sitting with them right now to laugh at this.

Her son looked at her wisely, then grabbed his bowl. 'Mom, I'd kind of like to finish in my room if that's OK. Got to get this essay done. And I'm tired from last night.'

'Sure.'

'Me too,' Rona said at once. 'See you tomorrow, Rowena. How long are you staying?'

'Just till the weekend,' Rowena replied. 'Got my own kids back in LA. Can't bunk off too much.'

'I get that. It's good to have you here,' Rona said. 'Look after Mom, OK?'

She picked up her own bowl and retreated.

'Good kids,' Rowena observed. 'Tactful. Which is a miracle, with teenagers.'

'I know. I've been lucky.'

They cleared the table and Rowena fixed a pot of decaf. It was a warm evening, and Topaz led her out to the terrace, where they sat companionably looking out over the park.

'Beautiful,' Rowena sighed. 'Skyscrapers behind you and green in front of you. Amazing.'

They were more relaxed now, from the wine and the food, and the teenagers clearing off. Rowena had a plan for dealing with Joe; tomorrow she would surprise him at his offices, and it would all be sorted.

'It's not the Hollywood Hills. But I could never cope outside the Big Apple,' Topaz said. 'I get hives if I go to New Jersey.' She took a long, deep pull at her coffee mug. She'd only managed half a glass of the red; there was just too much to do tomorrow to deal with a hangover. Besides, she didn't need it. Rowena being here relaxed her enough, made her feel that somebody had her back.

'Tell me about your problem. Not that I really believe you can have one.'

'It started right after the Hall of Fame. Bad numbers were coming in.'

'I know the feeling.'

'Our three biggest acts released stiffs. We were on the hook for millions in tour support, nothing was selling, they were playing to empty halls. The press started to notice. Worse, we didn't have anything coming up through the pipeline. That was the killer, really. The fact that I had no fig leaves around to spare my blushes. It was looking horrible.'

Topaz shuddered, drank more coffee. 'Yes, I get that. Not great. And?'

'So I guess we really are pretty alike. I came up with emergency surgery, a bit like you. And it worked.'

'I don't know that mine's gonna work yet,' Topaz said. Then she smiled. 'OK, I'm pretty sure it will.'

'I forced the bands to merge the tours. That cut costs and sold out the stadiums. The press was a lot better and there were fans lining up to get in. I made them all remix their records from scratch, with great songwriters and producers. Then the albums sold too.'

Topaz shook her head. 'Nice work. Were the acts mad?'

'I really didn't give a damn. They should have made better records if they wanted to be left alone.'

'Tough girl.'

'We have to be. And on top of all that stuff, I had my affiliates work the hell out of their catalogues and threatened to fire everybody if they didn't come up with great new acts. The old records picked up, and we're heading to a great quarter now. The last piece in the jigsaw is getting some good new bands on my roster. Still waiting on that.'

'So what's the problem? I saw your industry press. They love you.'

Rowena nodded. 'Ever since I came back from Europe, something's been off. I can't say what. Michael's happy, things with us are . . .' she wanted to be tactful, 'fine. But I feel that work is not what it should be. And I was hoping you could figure it out for me.' She leaned back on her lounger, relaxing, looking at Central Park. 'It might take another businesswoman. I'm too close to it. Either that, or I'm just paranoid.'

Topaz thought about it for several moments.

'Have you heard from your board?'

'What?'

'Your board of directors. When sales were plunging, they half fired me. I had to claw my way back to three months' grace.'

'Wow,' Rowena said slowly. 'No.'

'I would expect a summit when they realised things were bad. Or at the very least calls, emails once you kicked it into shape. It's strange they didn't ring you.'

There was a nasty pit at the bottom of Rowena's stomach.

'Oh my God,' she said.

'Are the Musica board normally hands-off?'

'No. They love talking to me. They go over our results with a nit-comb every time. I can't *believe* I didn't notice that.' Rowena smacked her forehead. 'How could I have been so dumb?'

'Maybe they're just processing what happened. Or arguing about it. Whether to praise you as a fixer or bawl you out for letting it get that way in the first place.'

'No.' Rowena shook her head. 'No way. Silence is the worst possible thing. They need me distracted, out of the picture.'

'You think they're interviewing to replace you?'

'That's possible. I hope I would have heard, but the executive always thinks they have ears everywhere and sometimes they just don't.' Her slim fingers curled into a fist. 'I'm an idiot.'

'Hey, look. You don't have to stay up here in New York and hold my hand.' Topaz patted her back. 'I'm a big girl. I get that this matters.'

Rowena swallowed. She was feeling panicky. There were plots, schemes on her turf, and she was here in Manhattan. Thousands of miles from the action. Her instincts were screaming at her to turn around and get straight on a plane.

'Not a chance.' She smiled firmly and looked at her friend. 'This is where I need to be. With you.'

Goddamn you, Joe Goldstein. This is all your fault.

'Gentlemen, I think I've heard enough.'

Conrad Miles looked around the room at the twenty or so senior bankers gathered to tell him what he already knew.

'American Magazines and Musica Records are ripe as first targets. Now I want you to put together an aggressive price offering. I've already made overtures to both boards, of course. We should announce our bid publicly. But it's only a first step. I am looking to move into entertainment, hard. What film studio should we buy, what television network? It's the internet age, and old media is undervalued. That's great. That's what I want to get to work on. Like my mother said, never pay retail.'

He thumped the table. 'I don't want any hiccups with these first two purchases. The market mustn't get the idea that Miles Industries will overpay. Ultimately, if my stock doesn't put on five dollars the day of the deal, you guys are doing it wrong.'

'Yes, sir,' said Phil Ramon, leader of the deal team. 'We are coming up with that exact number in the sweet spot. Both companies are bleeding. I like a hundred for Musica and eighty-six for American.'

Miles smiled. 'Real number or opening bid?'

'Real number, Mr Miles. We can open up to three bucks lower.'

'Let's get on this. Ultimately, I want to launch this thing in two weeks' time. We need corporate relations, analysts, whoever else you want on the team sewn up by then. Plus we need lists of everybody we can fire. I want to cut costs to the bone. Austerity.'

'Yes, sir,' Ramon answered confidently. 'It will be done.'

'And every asset we can sell, lease or exploit. Particularly writers and bands. We need some analyst papers on content exploitation.' He grinned. 'The Musica catalogue is very rich in that respect.'

The men in the room made notes, tapping on their iPads or slimline laptops. Everyone nodding and trying to look busy.

But Miles wasn't worried. These were great investment bankers, and this was an old-fashioned corporate raid. He was going after two companies, ripping them to shreds and selling them for less than the sum of their parts.

But the greatest asset to him would be the story – how he, Conrad Miles, fired the two CEOs. Women of substance, honoured in their industries. Rare female leaders. The fall of their companies – simultaneously – was a terrific story. The fact that they were friends even better. Miles loved the human angle, and himself at the heart of it, the Dark Lord striking again. The more the press wrote about Topaz Rossi and Rowena Gordon, the bigger and ballsier his corporate play became. Analysts would refocus their attention on Miles Industries. He would be profiled in *Fortune* magazine once more. There might be books in it, pieces in the *Wall Street Journal* or the *New York Times*. His legend would grow. Power raced through him, an incredible sense of strength and vigour. It was Topaz and Rowena, his attractive quarries, who would serve to make Conrad Miles the biggest man on campus, even at seventy-eight.

Conrad smiled. The hunt, that was what he loved. It was better than Viagra, better than anything.

'OK. Come back to me daily with a progress report. That's it,' he said, and walked out.

'Everybody's ready, Mr Goldstein,' Shawna said.

'Thank you.' He smiled at his assistant, still terribly formal after two years. But Shawna was in her early sixties, and ran a tight office with clockwork precision. He knew better than to mess with her.

'Mr Bostock has asked if he can have a moment before the press conference.'

'Sure.' Goldstein grinned. That was the equivalent of being summoned by the Queen, but he was grateful to Shawna for making it sound like he had a choice.

The board were gathered in a small conference room. They jumped to their feet as Shawna showed him in.

'The man himself. Congratulations.' Harvey Bostock pumped Joe's hand in a clammy grip. 'You delivered.'

'I said I'd have her signed within the week,' Joe remarked coolly.

'Well done,' Steve Byers nodded. 'That was fast.'

'And she fired her agent – right in your office,' Lou Conrad smirked. As a former network head himself, he could appreciate the vignette. 'It was all over town. I wish a star would do that for me, goddamn. Those ten-percenters are jerks, the lot of them.'

'If you don't mind,' Lilah Evans sniffed.

They all laughed. Joe was struck by the deference towards the former super-agent. Even more by the level of relief in the room. He had signed their ratings warhorse. The stock wasn't going to sink. Not right now, anyway. The board was relieved and happy, and every last one of them was beaming away at him, even that humourless bitch Emma Sanderson. Of course, PR was her expertise, if you gave a shit about that sort of thing.

Goldstein did not. But it was a fact of corporate life. Especially in the world of TV.

'We've got everybody that counts out in that press room,' Sanderson gushed. 'You know the story should be a great one. Re-signing Maria Gonzales really shows our commitment to women.'

Joe forced himself not to roll his eyes. Sanderson was NAB's punishment for sexism; a token extra woman stuck on the board to bolster Lilah Evans. Yet despite the Harvard degree, she was six shades of useless. They'd panicked and hired a woman with some expertise in public relations after a public relations disaster. It looked good on paper, but he had to deal with the reality.

'Maria Gonzales mostly appeals to our male audience,' he said mildly.

Bostock smothered a smile.

'But she's female. That's what counts. More females on air,' Emma said earnestly.

'Then I know you'll be thrilled I just green-lit our reality series *Strippers of Vegas Uncovered*,' replied Joe. 'That features twenty-two really prominent female leads.'

'I . . . well . . .'

Joe glanced around the room and saw Jack Travis grinning into his coffee cup.

'Well, the real stories of women in the exotic industry can be a strong voice against exploitation,' Emma said. 'It depends how you present it.'

Goldstein smiled. 'I'm just messing with you, Emma. We aren't that kind of network.'

'Oh. I see.' She scowled at him. 'That's not very supportive.'

'So with this deal, Joe, you will now have a free hand,' Bostock announced. 'That was our guarantee. Just make sure you don't waste Maria's star power.'

'Not a chance.' Goldstein took in his board; all the men were dressed in their sharpest power suits. 'You want to say hi to her?'

'That would be great,' said Jack Travis eagerly. The chance to press the flesh with Hollywood's hottest sexpot was not to be turned down.

'Of course. I'll have them bring her in. Shawna, go fetch Ms Gonzales, please.'

'Yes, sir.'

A second later, Maria was in the room, accompanied by a bowing, smirking press maven, her minder from one of the big PR agencies. Goldstein marvelled. Despite the fact he'd fucked her stupid less than an hour before, he still felt a little twitch at the sight of her now. Her long dark hair was exquisitely styled, falling sleekly down her back almost to her ass. She wore high Christian Louboutin pumps in classic black with that unmistakable red heel, and a bronze Hervé Leger bandage dress that clung sensationally to every curve on her fantastic body. It was otherwise demure, hitting right at the knee and with a three-quarter sleeve that emphasised her toned arms, but nothing could take away from the insane va-va-voom of her wonderful ass and tits, and her tiny waist.

He heard Harvey Bostock involuntarily suck in his breath. Lilah Evans's watery eyes lit up too, with a predatory glare. *She's gay*, he suddenly realised. And he understood the reaction. Maria would make a statue jump to attention.

'Ms Gonzales. Nice to meet you!' Emma said brightly. 'It's wonderful having another woman in a leading position at our network!'

'It's Joe Goldstein's network,' Maria said, smiling at her with dazzling white teeth. The effect was rather like a spectacular peacock butterfly spreading its wings over a small brown moth. 'And I'm just the talent. But I'm glad we could re-negotiate'

'I'm a board member here,' Emma persisted. 'We supervise Joe's work.'

'Oh, well. I was really only attracted by working with Joe. It's day-to-day management that matters to actors,' Maria said, and Steve Byers snorted with amusement.

'Maria. Let me introduce everybody,' said Joe. 'You've met Emma.'

Maria narrowed her eyes a fraction, and Emma looked away, discomfited. Joe was vastly amused, and impressed with her loyalty. He really liked the kid. His feelings were too mixed up to deal with right now, so he stopped trying. 'And this is Harvey Bostock, our chairman. Lilah Evans, once a powerhouse at her own agency and now a powerhouse here. Jack Travis you know from joyhacks.com. There's Steve Harvey and Lou Conrad. Both of them are television executives, recently done with running their own networks.' She was busily shaking hands as he was talking, a brisk, unafraid squeeze, a little extra pressure for the chairman, he saw.

'We're thrilled to have you back on board,' Harvey Bostock said. 'It's wonderful that Joe has persuaded you so soon.'

'He's a real sweet-talker,' Maria laughed.

Goldstein squirmed, just a little. The men in the room were all sending him impressed glances. God, if they had any real idea, they would put a hit on him.

'This is great. I look forward to getting to know all of you, when Joe lets me,' Maria said. 'Shall we go and do this thing? Boss, will you lead the way?'

'Absolutely.' Joe smiled benignly at her. She was making him look so good. Undeniably impressive.

His earlier guilt was washing away. Of course, he still felt bad, but there was no time to think of the family right now. He had a job to do, and Maria Gonzales was helping him do it.

'Ladies, gentlemen, if you'll follow me, there are reserved seats in the front row.'

Goldstein's assistants were holding open the doors. He led Maria out towards the executive suite. Corporate PR had erected banners and cardboard cut-outs of the network logo and Maria in her hottest outfits, with infographics representing her brand, her fame, her viewing figures. A small press corps was sitting on rows of black chairs: TV correspondents for the big entertainment magazines and some of the broadsheets, TV cameras for E! and their own record of the great event. Joe had carefully pulled out a list of Wall Street analysts of the TV business, along with key social media players; BuzzFeed and *HuffPo* were sitting in the second row.

'Good morning. Thanks for coming. Today NAB is proud to announce that we have re-signed Maria Gonzales for an exclusive three-year deal. Although *Summerside* is finished, Maria will be back on your screens in new projects she is developing with our network. Everybody is familiar with our creatively and commercially successful partnership. I'm delighted that this will continue – and that Maria's career will branch out into a new direction. Maria?'

Goldstein stood aside. There she was, and the wolf pack in front of her visibly attempted not to drool down the front of their T-shirts and suits. The handful of female reporters looked unimpressed; their biros were poised menacingly, heads tilted. Maria was a wet dream in the flesh. He felt an unrepentant pride that he had fucked this girl into screams of pleasure. The competitive, male part of him wanted to beat his chest with both fists. Goddamn, what a score. Every man in the room would give his left pinky to have traded places with him this morning . . .

What are you saying? his brain chided him, and as soon as the thought came, it left. Maria was a great piece of ass in a too-tight dress. Maybe he was tricked by the fact that she was acting so likeable, so much fun, but honestly, where was the connection? Maria Gonzales was pure sex for Joe. She wasn't Topaz. Nothing like her. If he tried to move the topic on from the one thing they had in common – his network, her career – where would they be?

He flushed, and hoped nobody could see it.

Didn't matter. Every set of eyes was fixed on the star.

'Joe Goldstein is offering visionary leadership at NAB.' The sound of his own name forced him to pay attention; he too turned his eyes to Maria. 'He was able to discuss my potential in ways few executives ever have. He didn't flatter me and he didn't tell me I was going to be a universal brand like Coca-Cola.'

There was a sudden murmur of real interest among the press pack. Notes were scrawled, Dictaphones lifted higher.

'Joe actually told me I shouldn't have script control, and that if I did I'd ruin good work. He treated me with enough respect to

175

tell me the truth. That gives me confidence in him and this network. Plus, I'd rather be a big fish in a small pond.'

Ouch, Goldstein thought. That stung. Maria looked at him under long black lashes. Was she sending a warning? Saying publicly that the network couldn't survive without her?

'I'm looking forward to the next couple of years. Thank you.'

'Maria. Janet Cossack, *New York Times*. Can you give us an idea of how much the deal is worth financially?'

Goldstein stepped back up to the podium, next to Maria. 'We don't release details of our agreements with artists.'

'Let me put it this way. I didn't ask for anything more than I got last season. I think Joe is truly consulting with me, and that means more to me than money,' Maria said. She smoothed a non-existent wrinkle out of her dress at the hips, and all the men present sighed with desire.

'Maria. Rick Emont, *People* magazine. Can you tell us about your new project?'

'Joe and I have been extensively brainstorming,' Maria purred. 'We have some fantastic ideas. Not ready to tip you guys off just yet, though!'

'OK, thanks for coming.' Goldstein nodded briskly. 'We'll keep you posted.'

He stood to one side like a gentleman, escorting Maria out of the room into the privacy of his office. The board followed him. He felt ten feet tall. The girl was great, she'd really impressed him – and everyone else there.

'Wonderful.' Emma smiled.

'Brilliant. You handle speeches as easily as an acting role,' Jack gushed.

'It's inspiring to think of the great programming we can create here together at NAB,' said Harvey Bostock ponderously.

Joe nodded. 'I don't think we can trespass on Maria's time any longer,' he said. Best to get her out of here: Maria rubbing shoulders with these people was starting to make him nervous.

He'd delivered her to them, got his deal, made his reputation. But now all he wanted to do was get to work. And she was shooting him intense sidelong glances. 'You have a meeting downtown, I think?'

'Oh! Yes. Certainly. Well, nice to meet you all,' Maria said sweetly. She did another round of hand-shaking and was gone, with the PR whisking her away.

'That was beautifully managed,' Emma announced, as though Goldstein gave a damn about her opinions. 'We should see a great uptick in our press mentions tomorrow.'

'We can review it in a week or so.' Goldstein held their gaze; with Maria's weapons-grade ass out of the room, this was easier to do. 'I would like a letter from you this afternoon, Mr Chairman, signed by the board, confirming your backing for my strategy of complete review of all the channel's programming, including our higher-rated prime-time shows. It's time for me to get to work.'

'Done,' Bostock said loudly. 'You should have it by the end of the day.'

'I've taken the liberty of preparing a draft.' Joe gestured to Shawna, who passed a neatly typed document to each board member. 'I'd like it back in an hour.'

Bostock opened his mouth, like he wanted to protest; but then his shoulders slumped, and he nodded. 'Very well.'

'I must get back to work myself. Thank you for coming,' Goldstein said firmly.

Shawna held the door open, and the board members left.

'Is there anything else you need, sir?' Shawna said.

Goldstein exhaled. He was suddenly exhausted. He'd done it: Maria was signed; he finally had complete control. So why did he feel so lousy?

Suddenly, with a great jolt of understanding, he realised that he wanted to speak to Topaz. More than anything. Nobody else could really share this moment with him. His wife had always been his partner in crime, his co-pilot, his wing man, his best friend. Maria Gonzales' perfect tits and ass were nothing in comparison to that. Besides, Topaz Rossi's ass was pretty goddamn fine in its own right. And it didn't come with a side order of awkward guilt.

Maybe he hadn't wanted to see that. I've got a hell of a temper, he admitted to himself. Topaz and he butted heads, but that was normal. He'd just run into more trouble than he believed possible, and he'd taken it out on her. Add into the mix the scent of adoration from a nubile female hot enough to melt steel – it was toxic.

Maria was signed.

It was done.

Time to extricate himself from the whole goddamned mess, and get the fuck back home. Until he fixed that, Goldstein thought, he couldn't exactly work well anyway.

'No thanks, Shawna, I'm good.'

'Yes, sir.' She shut the door. Joe was glad of the privacy. All he wanted to do was reach out to Topaz and fling himself on her mercy.

He picked up his cell, but as he started to dial, the door opened again.

'Excuse me Mr Goldstein, I'm so sorry. Ms Gonzales is here again.' Shawna lowered her voice discreetly. 'She insisted on seeing you. I hope that's OK.'

Goldstein started to sigh, then thought better of it. This was actually great. Better to make a clean break right now, and use the contract signing as an excuse. He smiled.

'Don't worry about it, Shawna. You did the right thing. Show her in.'

Maria practically bounced into the room. She waited until his assistant had shut the door behind them, then flung herself down on the leather couch in the corner of his office, her long legs angled over one of the armrests.

She looked sensational, good enough to eat.

But Joe Goldstein was no longer hungry. At least, not for junk food.

Come on now, he told himself, that's not fair. You knew exactly what you were doing. Maria's not a bad girl. She's smart-sexy, sure, but no dumb brunette. He shouldn't treat her like one now. She deserved to find an interesting guy, one with enough willpower to consider what was above the neck as well as below it. Joe didn't love her, but he respected the chick – even liked her.

But he hadn't broken up with anyone in over twenty years. When you were married, you got out of practice with that shit.

How the hell did he used to do it? Tell a girl they were through, and not leave her heartbroken or outraged? It used to be a lot easier when he was picking up chicks in nightclubs, at ball games. Back in his sexist but undeniably successful single days, when a fling was just that, and the other side didn't expect commitment.

'What's up, honey?' Maria asked. 'You look kinda worried. Something bothering you? I thought that whole thing went perfectly. We're in business now, aren't we?'

'We are. And you did a great job.' Joe stood up. 'I'm not really worried about anything. You were always a star, Maria; now you're going supernova.'

Maria swung her legs back down to the ground. She sat bolt upright with a catlike movement, and her dark eyes narrowed as she focused on him.

Not stupid, Joe thought uneasily.

She knows what's coming.

He had a bad feeling about this.

'It's more about you and me,' he said. The break-up speech wasn't going to get any easier the longer he waited to do it, so he plunged ahead. 'It's been an incredibly stressful time for both of us . . .'

Maria gave him a brief, insincere smile. 'I do hope this isn't going where I think it is,' she said coldly.

'We've done this deal. You showed them what you're worth.

But Maria, you deserve better than me. I can't be the partner you need right now. I'm still married.'

'That's bullshit. We discussed this. I don't fuck around with married men.' Maria tossed her long black hair behind her. 'Please don't insult me by suggesting that. You're separated. And you and I are lovers. Who is getting to you? Did the suits threaten you?'

Joe shook his head. 'Nobody could bully me out of a relationship with you. You're an amazing woman, Maria.'

'So you're giving me the "it's not you, it's me" speech?' Maria jumped to her feet. 'I expected better from you, Joe. I thought you were the one guy who wouldn't look at me as a piece of meat. Who could see something more in me than a good body or dollar signs. But I guess I was wrong. You're just like all the rest of them. In fact, you're worse.'

'That's not fair.'

'Isn't it? At least the other guys didn't treat me like some sort of reverse hooker. You made *me* pay *you* before you dumped me. You got me to fire my agent and sign your stupid contract at less than market value, and once I'd given my life to your goddamn network, you get rid of me within the hour.' Her dark eyes filled with tears. 'It's funny. You tell me I'm a star, but I've never felt so worthless in my life.'

Goldstein was horrified. 'Maria, I swear to you, it was nothing like that. I shouldn't have got involved with you during contract negotiations, I know that. But you were funny, and gorgeous, and I liked you. I was extremely attracted to you.' His throat went dry. 'I *am* extremely attracted to you.'

'Then why the hell are you leaving me?'

'Believe me. In another life, I would cut off my right arm to date you.'

She rubbed the tears away, and Joe's heart sank as he noticed the smears of mascara running down her cheeks. Anybody who saw her right now would know that something had gone on between them. He was racked with pity and fear.

'But we're not in another life. We're in *this* life. And if you liked me at all, you'd give me a chance.'

Goldstein thought hard. Maria was right: dumping her the moment the ink was dry on her deal looked bad. Humiliating bad. Calculating bad. And more to the point, probably *lawsuit* bad.

'I respect you,' he said. 'But the fact is, I still have feelings for my wife. I miss her. We've got more than twenty years together. Right now, I want to go back to her, and that's got nothing to do with you. You're sexy, you're smart, and you make me feel good about myself. That hasn't happened to me in a very long time. But it doesn't wipe out my deeper feelings for Topaz.'

'Most men who leave their wives go through this. Regrets. Anxiety. That's natural. But if you loved her so much, you never would've jumped on me.'

'I don't know what you want me to say.'

'That you'll give me a chance. That you'll give *us* a chance. I want you to commit to dating me for at least a month.' Maria snapped open the clasp of her Birkin bag and withdrew a couple of small, round pads, which she used to dab away the black stains on her cheeks. 'Eye make-up remover. Never leave home without it,' she said lightly, tearfully, in response to Joe's relieved stare. 'Think of it as my personal deal this time. You prove to me that you weren't just fucking me to get ahead, and if you still feel the same way in a month, I'll let you off the hook. You can go running back to wifey, and I won't stand in your way. What do you say, Mr Goldstein?'

Joe was miserable. He was longing for Topaz. But Maria could make life incredibly unpleasant for him. Hell hath no fury like a woman scorned. No goddamned kidding. He was trapped.

Maria Gonzales had him by the balls. Literally.

'One month? That's the deal?'

'Mark it on your calendar,' Maria said, smiling. A real smile this time, full of sex and triumph.

'You know I'm not promising you anything. I don't think this is going to work out. As long as you're going into it with your eyes open.'

'Wide open, baby,' she said. 'But you're dating me. And I don't want it to be a secret.'

Goldstein shook his head. 'Maria, that's crazy.'

'Why is it?'

'Topaz will find out. The company will find out. Hell, we'll be all over the front pages.'

'I want to Topaz to know. If this is real, then you can't be afraid to be seen with me. And as to the network, let me tell you something. *Everything* you do comes out sooner or later. The only way to get ahead is to be public about it. That way, they've got nowhere to go.'

Joe bit his lip.

'If you think Topaz will never discover this, you're dreaming. The same goes for your bosses back there. You've got to announce that we've decided to start dating. You can say it won't affect our professional relationship.'

'Will that be true?'

He was instantly sorry he'd asked the question. Why admit he was worried?

'It will be – *if* you stick to our deal. I'm a Latina, Joe. The only way you fuck with us is with an invitation.' Maria smiled sexily, but Goldstein wasn't laughing. He believed every word. 'And lucky Joe, you've got an invitation.'

There was no trace now of the trembling lips or the tear-filled eyes; she seemed perfectly contented. She walked over towards his desk, her hips swaying, those breasts bouncing, strutting like a beauty queen on the catwalk. It was obvious, sure, but it was highly effective.

'Some men seem to think I look good,' she purred. 'One month in my bed isn't a life sentence in Guantanamo, angel.'

'I guess not,' he said hoarsely.

'Public, then.'

'Public,' Joe agreed.

If she had him by the balls, they weren't exactly objecting. It all made a kind of weird logic. No more blackmail. Say he was separated; that way he wasn't cheating on Topaz. The company would have nothing on him. Neither would Maria. After one month, he could apologise to his wife, grovel, go to therapy, promise whatever she wanted, reconcile. And all he had to do was bang this sensational body for thirty days . . .

Maria was smiling like she'd just won the lottery. Joe couldn't help but be flattered at how much this meant to her. Maria Gonzales could have any guy on the planet. And yet she wanted him.

She lifted those lips to kiss him, offering them up like berries on a plate, soft and red, warm and inviting. She snaked her lean, tanned arms around his neck and crushed those sensational tits into the stiff cotton of his dress shirt . . .

The door opened again, but Joe barely heard it.

'Mr Goldstein, there's somebody here to see you—' Shawna stopped dead. 'Oh my God, I'm sorry, sir. I didn't mean to interrupt . . .'

He broke away from Maria. 'That's OK, Shawna. Topaz and I separated some time ago.' The words, now spoken, flowed easily enough. Joe went for Part Two. 'Maria and I are dating.'

Maria smiled radiantly. 'We just didn't want to tell anybody about it until after the festivities today. I guess that makes you the first to know, Shawna.'

Goldstein felt the wave of his assistant's disapproval. He admired how she was brave enough to let that show in front of the network's big star. But it wasn't going to stop him.

'I guess so, ma'am,' Shawna replied icily. 'Should I show your visitor in, Mr Goldstein, or would you like me to reschedule?'

'Show them in.' In for a penny, in for a pound, like the Brits said. 'Who is it?'

Maria was still draped across him. She hadn't moved an inch.

'In here, please,' Shawna said. 'It's Rowena Krebs, Mr Goldstein. Of Musica Records.'

What? What did you just say?

Rowena Krebs? My wife's best friend?

Joe couldn't help it. He gasped in shock and his heart sank through his boots. But Maria's smile grew even wider, and her grip on his shoulders tightened.

Rowena stormed into the room. It was obvious she'd already taken in their little scene. She ignored Maria completely and turned her green eyes directly on Joe.

'Joseph Goldstein,' she said. 'Exactly what the *fuck* do you think you're doing?'

Chapter Twelve

Joanna Watson slipped from the bed and looked around her.

Goddamn. This place was even more sensational in daylight.

She was standing at the edge of an exquisite Chinese silk carpet that fanned out across the entire suite – or this end of it, at least. The cavernous bedroom had a sumptuousness that shocked even her, a trust-fund brat. It was immediately clear that she was playing in the big league now. Conrad Miles didn't live like your average banker; he lived like a king.

Rooms like this belonged in museums. Or palaces. The Old Masters on his walls would do credit to the Queen of England. There were stateroom-worthy drapes in cloth of gold, chaise longues straight from Versailles, and the most impressive Grecian friezes she'd ever seen outside of the Elgin Marbles. But mixed in with all the world-class heritage was a sizeable slice of Manhattan luxury. Conrad Miles was high-tech. The bed he'd entertained her on had the incredible softness of pure goose down, covered in Egyptian cotton. Between two huge panels of wall-mounted Greek statues, there was a cinema-sized television screen, broken up into multiple channels. Miles got his news from all over the world, and mixed it up with financial updates, stock prices and feeds on his business interests. Discreet control panels offered seven different temperatures in different areas of the room.

There were three separate en-suite bathrooms. One was for him – and Conrad made it very clear that he didn't want her going in there. One was for her, or for the woman of the moment at least. It raised excess to an art form. The softest peach marble, heated to be warm under her feet, mined from the finest quarries in Italy, was complemented by orange-gold beechwood, tumbling glass tiles in all the shades of sunset, and cut glass vases filled with artful bouquets of roses in yellows, pinks and flames. There were hand-stitched Moroccan slippers placed neatly to one side in various sizes, alongside bathrobes ranging from voluminous Turkish towelling to crisp white waffle to what looked like antique kimonos from Japan. She had a choice of a bath big enough to swim in, a beautifully designed wet room, a hot tub, or a personal sauna. And the third bathroom was his-and-hers, unisex, with the emphasis on 'sex'. In simple neutral stone, with the same level of luxury, it was covered in mirrors, and decorated with tasteful, but undeniably erotic, art and statuary. Everything in that one was big enough for two.

Joanna was deeply impressed.

In front of her, large, graceful pre-war windows offered a fabulous view directly over Central Park, taking in the skyline and the wider city beyond. On the other side of the bedroom, secure French doors opened on to a beautifully kept balcony garden, laid with its own lawn, including a croquet pitch. There was a dining table, an arbor, and a miniature orchard of apple, pear, and plum trees thriving at one end of it, while an incredibly realistic artificial stream wound its way to a fountain at the other end.

It was paradise. And this was only Conrad Miles's bedroom.

The guy owned the whole of the building. There were four floors to this apartment alone. Underneath that, he rented other magnificent homes to lesser corporate titans, mostly guys from China and the Middle East. Nobody else could afford it. Joanna was trying to do the sums in her head. It was possible that he made so much income from this place that the mind-blowing home she was standing in actually paid for itself.

And that would be Conrad Miles all over. Money was a game to him. One he kept winning.

Her nipples hardened slightly. She found this unrepentant display of wealth intensely arousing. Miles had amazed her. Sure, he was an old man, but she'd never met a brighter one. His brain turned like a supercomputer, always calculating, always on the attack. There was almost nothing she could tell him that he didn't already know.

That was why her information about Topaz Rossi and American Magazines had been so very useful to Conrad. It was under the radar. Joanna got it – Conrad Miles's real problem was boredom.

What did you give the man who had everything?

Something else to want.

Joanna congratulated herself. Being useful to a man like Conrad Miles was a great career move. Like any good prince, he rewarded his vassals. He collected human assets as well as corporate ones.

She had already received plenty of signs of his favour. There was the million-dollar consulting contract with Miles Industries – Joanna cashed the cheque, but she wasn't stupid enough to start boasting about it. Nevertheless, the shame of being publicly fired was wiped out. Technically speaking, she was now an industry consultant to one of the most powerful businessmen on the planet. Didn't that beat being the editor of *American Girl*?

What else? There was the promise of revenge. She would see Topaz Rossi attacked, humiliated and driven out of her company. Topaz had cut short Joanna's career. Now she could return the favour. The thought was delicious. Conrad was going to put her on the company board. That would make Joanna Watson a player in her own right. She loved it. Destroy her enemies, take their companies. Maybe using somebody else's money, but so what? Didn't that make her a kind of junior Conrad Miles herself?

Conrad thought he was using her. Maybe it was the other way round.

She had to admit, a multi-billionaire backer was *the* hot accessory this season!

'Like what you see?'

Joanna started. She spun around to see Conrad, already fully dressed in a dark bespoke suit and hand-crafted John Lobb shoes, standing behind her, smiling.

Her heart started to race. She felt guilty, as if he could read her mind.

'Of course. It's amazing.'

'Your father's done quite well, hasn't he?'

Miles was patronising her. They both knew it.

Joanna flushed. 'Nothing like this. As you well know.'

He grinned. 'You did well last night.'

Her blush deepened.

'You make it sound like it was some sort of audition,' she said.

Miles looked directly into her eyes. 'Wasn't it?'

'I don't know what you're talking about,' Joanna said weakly. 'Really, Conrad . . .'

'Joanna. I hate having to repeat myself. Let's make this the last time. OK?'

'OK.'

'I don't like playing games. At least, not this kind.' He gave a slight smile. 'You would like me to consider you as a wife.'

She gasped. No man had ever talked to her this way.

'True or false? Warning: the wrong answer right now will have consequences.'

Joanna paused. 'Any woman dating any man has marriage on her mind. Otherwise, why bother?'

Conrad grinned. 'Close enough. Women sometimes try to pretend otherwise, but they're lying.'

'And no man dates a woman without wanting to sleep with her,' said Joanna, getting bolder. 'That's a reasonably old bargain.

I don't know why it's suddenly so unfashionable to admit it.'

'Now we're getting somewhere,' the billionaire said. 'I have a breakfast meeting. Let's continue this at lunch.'

'I'd love to,' Joanna replied, with her first genuine smile of the morning. 'Where shall I meet you?'

'I'll text you, let you know. Ring a bell by the side of the bed to order some breakfast.'

Joanna's eyebrows lifted. 'A bell? Like for servants?'

'Exactly like that.' Conrad grinned. 'You may have noticed I have a taste for the past. And I have the money to indulge it. No need to feel guilty,' he said as he turned and walked towards the door. 'My cook earns as much as some partners and more than most middle managers in the city. That's because he's the best at what he does. Believe me, Joanna, you'll enjoy breakfast.'

And with that, he was gone.

Joanna Watson suppressed a shriek of glee. She raced back to the centre of the room and jumped up on the enormous, beautiful bed, bouncing up and down like an overexcited schoolgirl.

Oh man! It was working! Conrad Miles was thinking about her for a *wife*!

She looked to her left. There was indeed an antique brass bell with a little chain for a handle, one mounted on each side of the bed. Although she didn't feel like eating, she would have some breakfast. Somehow she was pretty sure that Conrad Miles didn't make suggestions. He gave orders. Her host, her lover, wanted to show off his cook and his butler. That was fine with Joanna. But naturally, she would order modestly. After all, a man like Miles was going to want a woman to maintain a pretty perfect figure.

She pulled her borrowed antique kimono tighter around her slender waist, reached over, and carefully rang the bell.

Rowena was wretched. No matter how many times she ran that movie in her head, it always came out with the same ending: Maria Gonzales hugging her best friend's husband and kissing

189

him on the lips, and Joe Goldstein unable to meet Rowena's eyes but definitely able to speak.

'I was going to call Topaz today, Rowena. We separated. You know that. And right now, Maria and I are dating.'

'Joe, you can't be serious.'

'I don't appreciate you talking to my boyfriend like that,' the TV star said. Rowena completely ignored her. Maria might be famous, but to Rowena Krebs she was an ant, dirt, nothing.

'You and Topaz have been married forever. This is a cliché, Joe, a bad one. For God's sake, there are less disastrous ways to have a mid-life crisis. I'll buy you a cherry-red Porsche myself.'

'Lady, I don't know who you are, but I'm guessing you're some kind of friend to Joe's ex-wife. And really, you're just embarrassing yourself. He's with me. Believe your eyes,' Maria snapped.

'My name is Rowena Krebs,' Rowena told her. 'I'm the CEO of Musica Records. And I've been friends with Joe and Topaz since before you could walk. Topaz Rossi is his *wife*, not his ex-wife. They're not divorced. And they're not going to be. So if you want to be Joe's little fuck toy while he works it out of his system, be my guest. But nobody who gets into a battle with Topaz Rossi walks away from it.'

Even as she spoke, Rowena didn't take her eyes off Joe. He hung his head like a dog. But he also didn't move.

Despite her brave words, Rowena was sick to her stomach. She was watching Topaz's heart shatter in slow motion, and her friend didn't even know it was happening. The easy reconciliation Rowena had thought would be the work of an evening had just turned into a life-changing disaster.

'It's sweet of you to be so loyal,' Maria purred. 'But this is the twenty-first century, honey. Marriages occasionally break up. I guess you never got the memo.' She stepped back, relinquishing her grip on Joe for a second, then drew herself up and focused again on Rowena, an actress's dramatic gesture.

'Wait just one second. Did you say Rowena Krebs? Oh, sure, I've heard of you. I adore Atomic Mass. They're like one of my favourite vintage bands. You signed them, right?'

'Yes. And I'm not really interested in your musical taste.'

'But you see, *I'm* pretty interested in your hypocrisy.'

'Maria,' Joe said, warning her. But the girl smiled, and Rowena felt the knot of tension grow in the pit of her stomach. She sensed the axe just before it fell.

'Your maiden name was Rowena Gordon,' Maria said with triumph. 'When you met Michael Krebs, he was married, too. Let me see.' She put one finger to her forehead theatrically. 'Big-league producer. Hall of Fame. About twenty years older than you. And married. Very married. He had kids, didn't he? Left his first wife for you? How long were *they* married? About as long as Joe and Topaz?'

'That's enough,' Goldstein said.

'Oh sweetie, Rowena's a big girl. She can handle it. Am I right?'

'Yes you are,' Rowena replied. She was staring directly at Maria now. Face it, the girl deserved that. She knew how to fight.

'So were you Michael Krebs's little *fuck toy*, Rowena? Because I seem to remember that it turned into a pretty solid marriage of its own. You guys have a couple of kids between you. I don't know how you can be so mad, when I'm only repeating your personal history.' Maria tossed her a smile of triumph.

'Well done. Top marks for the debate team.' Rowena stared at Maria Gonzales, stared her down. 'But do you know what that little victory of yours tells me, Maria? It tells me you've been planning this for a *long* time. You've researched Topaz Rossi. You know about her. Her kids with Joe. Her best friend. Even the biggest Atomic Mass fan in the world isn't going to know about the personal life of their A and R scout. You looked me up, because I'm connected to Joe's wife. And that makes you more dangerous than the average dumb starlet. It also makes you kind

191

of a stalker. Maybe Joe should consider whether he wants to get involved with that.'

Maria's gorgeous olive skin darkened with rage, and Rowena knew she had scored a direct hit. No letting up now.

'And I'll tell you one other big difference between my story and yours,' Rowena continued. 'Yes, it's true I had an affair with Michael. I'm not proud of that. But I really loved him. You *don't* love Joe. You want him, but you don't love him. And Michael and Debbie were having more than just a couple of problems. Debbie had fallen out of love with him some years ago. You're going to find that Topaz Rossi is madly in love with Joe. And guess what else? Joe is madly in love with his wife. I don't know why he can't see it at this moment. But that's the reality.'

'Ma'am, you're delusional. I'm not going anywhere. And I just love how you think that you and your bestie are the only fighters in this city. Now kindly leave this office, before I call security and have you thrown out.'

Rowena turned back to Joe, but he wouldn't look at her. Maybe he *couldn't* look at her. Whatever. She'd never seen him so weak. She was disgusted.

'Don't worry, *Miss* Gonzales. I've got no desire to stay. Somebody has to go and update Joe Goldstein's family, since he doesn't have the balls to do it himself.'

'Rowena, no! I'm going to do it. I want to be the one to talk to the kids—'

'Cry me a river, Joe,' Rowena said, and turned her back on him.

Outside, it was ridiculously warm and sunny. Shouldn't it be raining? Shouldn't there be a goddamned hurricane? Rowena walked a block just to get her breath back, to master the situation. And then she pulled out her phone.

Maybe Joe would man up. And maybe he wouldn't. She couldn't take that chance. Maria Gonzales had him in her pocket.

Rowena had a horrible vision of her forcing Joe to call his wife while she stood there listening, smiling to herself, maybe hearing Topaz cry on the speakerphone. Oh, of course, she'd tell Joe it was all for his own good and she just wanted to be sure they were being upfront, some bullshit like that. When really, she just wanted to win.

Rowena was dreading this.

Time to do it.

She stood at a crosswalk, tapped out Topaz's number.

'Rowena. Hi.'

'Hi, sweetheart.'

There was immediate panic at the other end of the line. Topaz could hear something was wrong right away.

'Rowena! Are you OK? What's happened? Tell me.'

Rowena arched her neck back in agony, gripping the phone. 'Topaz, I'm so, so sorry. Joe is having an affair.'

There was a long pause.

'You're certain?' She sounded choked.

'I went to his office. I saw them together. We talked about it. He says he separated from you, he's with her, and he was going to call you. But she was very in my face. I wanted you to be prepared. I hope I didn't do the wrong thing.'

'No.' Topaz's voice was perfectly calm now, perfectly dead. 'Carry on. Let's get this finished. Tell me what you know.'

'He's been fucking her for a while, I don't know how long, but she's calling herself his girlfriend, and he just stood there and let her. It was pathetic. He couldn't look me in the face. Topaz, the girl is one of his stars at the network. Maria Gonzales.'

'What?' Despite herself, Topaz sounded genuinely shocked. 'Joe is having an affair with Maria Gonzales? *Summerside* Maria Gonzales? The sex symbol?'

'Yes. I'm sorry. And the fact that they didn't deny it makes me assume they're about to go public. You and the kids are going to be surrounded by press. You should prepare for that. I know I'm telling you your business, but sometimes when it affects you directly, you can lose sight of things . . .'

'No shit.' Topaz gave a small laugh. 'I . . . I can't believe this is happening. It's nuts. I knew Joe was angry, but I didn't think he'd screw around on me. How naive can you be? Why did I think I was going to be the one woman in the world who was different? It's what guys do.'

'Not all guys.'

'Well, mine did. And I never saw it coming. Twenty years of agony aunt columns, you'd think I would've absorbed some of that stuff.'

'You should come home from the office. I can pick the kids up from school.'

'That might be a good idea,' Topaz said numbly. 'Maria Gonzales is a superstar. The press will be all over it. I need to get them ready to deal with it.'

'It's nearly spring break, right?'

'Yes. Why? We never go away. Not till the summer. Joe and I could never get the time off work.' For the first time, Rowena heard a sob rising in her friend's voice.

'We are exactly the same. But I have an idea. Topaz, you know I love you, but I can't stay. I have to get back to my family. Back to my job. There's trouble.'

'I know that, honey. You go home. Nobody could've been a better friend.'

'Let me take the twins with me,' Rowena suggested. 'You can tell the principal you're pulling them out of school for the last couple of days, and after you talk to them this afternoon, they can come crash with us in LA. My kids would love to see them. They can all amuse themselves. I'm sure it will be too emotional for David and Rona to deal with their dad. And it's going to be too much pressure on you to have to play the perfect mom in front of them. You've got to handle Joe, *and* pull *American Girl* together. That's just about enough for any woman.'

'Oh God, Rowena, that is a brilliant idea,' Topaz sobbed, and Rowena cursed Joe once again. 'I know my kids. They're going to be devastated. It'll be an incredible relief for them to get to Cali. Could you really do that?'

'Don't be dumb. Piece of cake.' Rowena sounded more cheerful than she felt. She was British, after all, and somebody had to do the stiff-upper-lip thing. Trying to keep it together in front of the kids would be the hardest thing of all for Topaz. At least she could take that burden off her friend's back.

She lifted her arm to hail a cab, and one worked its way out of the traffic towards her immediately, like a grimy yellow angel of mercy.

'I'll head to school now and pick them up. Meet you back at the apartment.'

'Thanks, Rowena,' Topaz said. 'I'll be back in an hour. I have work to do here.'

'Maybe you should can that,' said Rowena, sliding into the cab and closing the door. 'Just come home.'

'No way. I'm not going to let that son of a bitch run my entire life,' Topaz replied. 'Oh look, here's Joe calling on the other line right now.'

'You going to take it?'

'Hell no,' Topaz said. 'He's lost the right to talk to me.'

'Stay strong,' Rowena said, and hung up.

Thank God for fury, she thought. For a little while it would protect Topaz from sorrow.

The private dining room at the Victrix hotel was full to capacity. Manhattan had enough captains of industry and banking titans that a three Michelin star restaurant was always booked out, even though you could easily drop five hundred bucks for lunch, and that was without wine or coffee.

The men and women who lunched here were not the type of people who looked at their bills before slipping their black Amex cards into the leather-bound wallet. If you had to ask, you couldn't afford it.

Joanna had eaten in the Victrix's private room several times before; it was a supremely classy joint. She was unsurprised, but nevertheless gratified, to see that Conrad Miles had secured the most prominent table, in the centre of the room. When she announced whom she was eating with, the maître d' practically bowed before her.

'So, you liked your breakfast?' Miles asked, as soon as she sat down.

Joanna reached forward and ran the tip of her finger across the back of his hand, smiling her most dazzling smile. 'Oh Conrad, it was sensational. Just like you said. I asked for croissants and coffee, and they made the croissants from scratch. I've never tasted anything like it; even in Paris.'

'The President has something similar at the White House,' Miles answered. 'I need to make sure that my guys are better.'

'They get my vote.' Joanna treated her date to an adoring gaze, well aware that the eyes of half the diners in the room were boring into their backs. This was her second meal in public with Conrad, and no doubt it would hit the gossip columns tomorrow. In terms of sheer wealth, the guy was probably the world's most eligible bachelor.

But not for long, if she had anything to do with it.

'And what did you do with your morning?'

'I did a little research on Musica Records,' Joanna said. This was only half a lie. She knew she had to be careful. Miles was so good at reading people, he was like a human polygraph. Knowing that she was on round two of her audition, she had worked out like a demon in her upscale gym, then showered briefly and headed straight to the beauty parlour, the best Manhattan had to offer. It hadn't failed her. Her hair was washed, coloured, and blow-dried into a shimmering cap of glossy raven strands. At the same time, manicurists and pedicurists worked simultaneously on her hands and feet, updating her classic French polish to the palest pink. Nothing too red; nothing too obvious. To win Conrad Miles, a woman who was sexy in the bedroom, and could contort herself into half the positions of the Kama Sutra, had to be ladylike and elegant in a setting like this one.

As the polish dried, Joanna had leaned back in her chair while an expert team of make-up artists applied cosmetics to her reasonably pretty but still fairly ordinary features. Joanna was thrilled with the results. Her eyebrows were thickened, shaped and arched, giving a lift to her face; her lashes wore a delicate coat of chocolate-brown mascara that picked out her hazelnut eyes, and artfully applied foundation and blush smoothed her skin, evened its tone, and gave her cheekbones she didn't really have. They had talked her into wearing nothing else but clear lip gloss, and as a result, her naturally full lips looked wet and aroused, as though she had just licked them. And with this much money dancing in front of her, that might as well be true.

Painful hours in the chair, but they had delivered excellent results. Joanna Watson was no longer ordinary. She looked way more than reasonably pretty right now. She looked stunning. She had carefully selected a Victoria Beckham couture dress in dark green felt, with a matching jacket with three-quarter sleeves and modest Vera Wang platform heels. She wore no jewellery. Perhaps Conrad would be inspired to add to that part himself.

In between all the primping and pressing, Joanna *had* managed to read some stock analysts' reports on Musica Records and its results. It seemed important that Conrad not think of her as just a pretty face, or a good frock. She knew he could get that anywhere.

'Did you indeed?' he grinned. 'I like initiative in a woman. What did you find out?'

'I don't know if you'll like it,' Joanna flirted. 'Should I be straight with you?'

'I *always* like information. It just has to be accurate. Being afraid of facts is like being afraid of your mirror. Whether you look or not, your reflection is still right there waiting.'

Joanna laughed. 'You certainly know how to speak to a woman, Conrad.'

'Do you want to order something?' he asked.

'I'll have whatever you recommend,' Joanna said obediently.

'Very good. We'll have the usual.'

'Yes, sir,' said the waiter, bowing slightly.

'They do a peerless Dover sole with lemon and caper butter,' Conrad said. 'It's one of those simple dishes, like roast chicken, that requires real skill to pull off well.'

'It sounds wonderful,' Joanna said. 'So you wanted to know about Musica Records?'

Conrad lifted his fork. 'Go ahead.'

'The trouble is, Rowena Krebs has been doing exceptionally well lately. The company was in trouble at the beginning of the year, but it looks like she did some fancy footwork with two or three of her big bands, cut some costs, and basically has managed to turn her results around. Their second quarter is going to be huge.'

Joanna smiled smugly. An hour reading industry reports, and she felt like she was ready for Wall Street.

'I know,' he said. 'All the better for me.'

She tilted her head delicately. 'But how can that be? Won't a better performance drive up the stock price?'

'Rowena put a decent enough sticking plaster on a field injury,' Conrad told her. 'She's just too bright for her own good. The Musica board was terrified. They wanted to fire her, then she turns around and pulls this off. How many times do you think she can do that? The fact is, now they all know their stock options depend on one woman. Without Rowena Krebs, Musica will be dead and buried. This quarter couldn't have been better for us. Investors know that once Krebs is out of the picture, Musica is just a second-rate label for old has-beens. As soon as she quits, that stock will sink through the floor. I've already started the process. I've been talking to her board. They sell to me, at the price I feel like giving them, and maybe they all still walk away millionaires. If they mess around with me, I'll just remove Rowena Krebs for them.'

'Sweetheart, she's not going to resign. Music is her life. Ever since college.'

'Sweetheart? That's a little bold, don't you think?'

'Is it?' Joanna flashed another smile as the fish arrived and was quietly set down in front of them. 'I think we're getting along famously. Of course I could go back to Mr Miles, if you prefer.'

He ignored this.

'Rowena Krebs will quit or be fired. I don't really care which. As long as everybody knows that it's me behind it.'

'You really are quite ruthless,' Joanna said.

'Thank you.' He smiled back at her and started to eat his sole. 'This is as much about me showing the Street what I can do as it is about acquiring these two companies.'

'I think I understand,' Joanna replied. 'You like the hunt.' She breathed in deeply, trying to gather her courage. He was insanely powerful. She desperately wanted to be part of that. Now was the moment. 'And you know what? So do I.'

'You can make your pitch like everybody else,' Conrad replied, cruelly. But he was looking at her in a very calculating way, a smile playing on his lips. He wasn't going to make this easy for her. For a second, Joanna Watson wondered if she knew what she was getting into. 'Go ahead,' he said.

Whatever. Talk is cheap, she told herself, and I have very expensive tastes.

'You asked me this morning if I wanted to be your wife. The answer to that is yes. You also told me I did well last night. So I've been thinking. What do you want? I'm a rich woman, Mr Miles.'

'Nothing like as rich as I am.'

'That's a given. And clearly I want more. But I enjoyed last night too. I enjoyed being with you.'

She knew she sounded surprised. But that was OK. It made her seem more honest. Miles had lain back on the bed, propped up on his goose feather pillows, and ordered her to perform for him. She'd twisted this way and that, displaying herself, licking, sucking, stroking, fondling and caressing him until he was rock hard and she was surprisingly wet and aroused. When he took her, he held her slim body firmly, and she had no doubt who was controlling the encounter. His penetration, his thrusts, even though she had schemed to get herself into this position, seemed like a very definite conquest to Joanna, and as she surrendered, she found herself surging towards orgasm. Even if she wasn't screaming the place down, she was gasping, thrashing around beneath him like a newly landed fish on a bank, gulping air as her heart pounded. The look of shock and surprise on her face didn't faze Conrad Miles. He clutched her more firmly, aimed upwards, thrust into her harder, and came strongly inside her, holding her tight as he did so.

'I know you did.'

Joanna blushed again. What she wasn't telling him was that she rarely achieved orgasm with *any* lover, let alone a guy in his seventies. But Conrad Miles was no ordinary man. That much was clear.

'That's what I liked about it. You have some skill, and you take direction well. And you're endearingly obvious in your greed and ambition.' He held up one wrinkled hand. 'Please don't bother denying it. That would spoil the whole effect.'

Joanna took a small sip of water and wondered what the next move was. But the words came out naturally.

'Very well then, Conrad. Two can play this game. *You* must want a wife yourself, or you would never have brought the subject up. And a man like you can only marry a certain sort of woman. One who won't embarrass you. One who knows how

200

the game is played. A woman attractive enough to pass in polite society as your wife, but somebody who won't look completely greedy – even if she is.' She smiled back at him, getting more confident now. 'You have to enjoy her in bed, and if you're going to spend a number of days in her company, you also need a woman who actually enjoys you back. I've proved I can sell myself on all those fronts. And the fact that my father has money is going to make you look even better, isn't it? You wind up with a woman who has funds of her own, that tells other men that I *want* to be with you, despite the age difference. So there we have it. It's a pretty small pool of women, if you want to tick every single one of those boxes.'

'And your point?'

'You may not need me as much as I need you,' Joanna said, 'but it's a close-run thing. Your alternative is to keep seeing whichever high-class call girls you use at the moment, but I imagine at your stage of life that's undignified. I'm a sort of one-stop shop for all your feminine needs.' She laughed, delighted with her own joke.

'Very good. Bravo. You didn't disappoint.' He lifted one eyebrow.

'Do you think we can come to some sort of arrangement?' Joanna dared to ask.

And there it was. On the table. The $64 million question. Joanna could hardly breathe.

'Why, Miss Watson, you're obviously an incurable romantic.' Conrad Miles lifted his water glass to her. 'Yes, I think so.'

Nervously, she picked her own up. 'Maybe we shouldn't toast with water. They say it's bad luck.'

'I'm not superstitious. I make my own luck.' Miles clinked his glass against hers. 'To Mr and Mrs Conrad Miles. How do you like the sound of that?'

Joanna smirked. 'I like it very much indeed.'

* * *

The pre-nup took a matter of days. She had to go through the farce of finding her own lawyer, and then reading her the riot act in case she tried to alter anything. Conrad Miles was going to settle matters his own way. Joanna knew her goal was simply to get him to the altar. If they divorced for any reason, she would receive $1 million for every year in the marriage; unless she committed adultery, in which case she would pay him $1 million for every year. There was a token penalty for Conrad committing adultery: a flat fee of $5 million, no matter how many times he sinned, or how many partners he betrayed her with. Clearly, five million bucks was pocket change to her beloved bridegroom-to-be. The provision was really there, her disgruntled lawyer told her, to provide some level of parity between them, so that the agreement was enforceable.

'If all the really sucky rules go against you,' said Patricia Greenburg, sniffing with disdain, 'a court might throw this out. At five million dollars, he's bought insurance against that happening. It's obvious that a million a year would really hurt you, if you cheated on him at the seven-year itch. But to him the money is nothing.'

And that was everything. Joanna was forced to agree that as they were both so wealthy, they would take from the marriage only what they brought into it. Aside from the $1 million payment, Conrad was free to walk away at any time. But if she stuck around, behaved herself, pleased him enough that he didn't ditch her, then when he died, she'd receive about a third of his estate. That was more money than she could begin to think about. The rest would go to his adult children by a long-forgotten marriage: two indolent playboys living it up in Dubai, and a disdainful academic daughter who went by her mother's maiden name and was living a life of gilded obscurity teaching art history at the University of Vienna. His children were bitter disappointments to Conrad Miles. Joanna Watson didn't intend to be.

'When shall we announce the wedding?' she asked, as they

drove away together after signing the document in her lawyer's office. She had to admire her future husband. He had set things up perfectly, so that she could never relax. She'd have to court him, woo him and satisfy him every day, to stop him leaving her for some other heiress.

'Once we make our move on Topaz and Rowena,' Conrad said. 'The business press really are a bunch of vultures. They love a good soap opera. Anyway, *darling*, just think of it: you'll be getting married, and Topaz Rossi will be getting sacked.'

Joanna clapped her hands. 'That's perfect!'

Topaz Rossi, the snooty, autocratic bitch! She deserved everything that was coming to her. Pre-nup or no pre-nup, Joanna was about to become half of one of the world's richest couples. And she'd organised it all in less than a couple of months.

Don't mess with Joanna Watson. She smiled. And definitely don't mess with Joanna Miles.

Chapter Thirteen

The second the plane touched down, Rowena sensed something was wrong. The familiar welcoming sun of LAX was suddenly blinding. She wondered why she felt this way, and then it hit her: she'd switched her phone on, and it was buzzing constantly in her pocket.

Even for Rowena Krebs, that was a lot of texts and emails.

Resolutely she refrained from unlocking it. Whatever it was could wait. She had one job right now, and that was to get Rona and David through the airport before some low-life bastard took photographs of them and stuck them up on the internet. It had been a pretty goddamned awkward plane ride, with Rona weeping constantly into her lap, and her red-eyed brother staring out of the plane's tiny window for the entire five and a half hours. Jet Blue was the first flight leaving that night, and Rowena had convinced Topaz they should jump on it, economy class or not. It was more important to extract the twins before the news broke.

And she was just in time. Unfortunately, though, the carrier prided itself on showing live domestic television throughout the flight. That was awesome, unless you were trying to protect two teenage kids from the sight of their father standing tall and wearing a thin smile, his arm around the waist of America's number one TV sexpot.

'Maria Gonzales confirmed today that she's found a new boyfriend,

network chief Joseph Goldstein. Mr Goldstein, the widely respected head of Maria's studio NAB, is a lot older than her at forty-six. He's also recently separated from his wife, magazine exec Topaz Rossi, seen here attending the Grammies last year . . .'

The camera switched to a shot of Topaz walking down the red carpet, wearing a sensational satin and chiffon gown in robin's-egg-blue. Joe was standing beside her in a dark suit just like the one he was wearing today, but he looked much happier, the smile genuine. Rowena recognised the glittering necklace Topaz was sporting, a fabulous creation made of white zircons and huge natural pink topazes; it had been created by Cartier at Joe's request, a bank-breaking gift he had produced for her fortieth birthday.

Rona pressed her hand to her mouth to cover a moan of distress, and Rowena reached across to switch channels.

'This was the scene outside Topaz Rossi's luxury apartment building on Central Park West as camera crews waited for a glimpse of the jilted wife. Ms Rossi of course is one of America's most celebrated businesswomen, recipient of a large number of industry awards and a very successful woman in her own right. But Tanya, I don't think anybody could say she is as well known as Maria Gonzales.'

'That's exactly right, Jack, but then again, who is? A lot of men will be calling Mr Goldstein the luckiest guy around. Rumours have surrounded Maria since she dumped her pop star boyfriend Rico Consuelas last year, but in the past we've always had to see snaps of her and her man of the moment outside a nightclub or a restaurant. I think this is the first time she has ever given a press statement on a new love . . .'

'Industry insiders have seen Joe Goldstein at a press conference recently – to announce the fact that he signed Maria Gonzales to a new multi-million-dollar deal after her contract with NAB expired. But it has to be said, there was no word of the steamy soap opera the star and the executive were conducting in real life – when the cameras weren't rolling. Why do you think they've come clean now?'

'Well, word on the street is that a major national tabloid was about

to expose the affair, and the two lovebirds decided that they should be the ones to control this story. Or could it just be a publicity stunt for the ailing network's next Maria Gonzales vehicle . . .'

On and on it went, mercilessly. Desperately Rowena flicked through the channels, looking for something safe – cartoons, for God's sake. She landed on *Sesame Street* and gently lifted the headphones off Rona's ears.

'Sweetheart, don't torture yourself. Your mom wanted you to come out west and get a break. This isn't going to help.'

'I feel like I have to watch it,' Rona said, tears rolling down her face. 'Otherwise I'll be the only person who doesn't know what's going on. I just can't believe my dad would do this shit unless I see it myself . . .'

'I wish I could tell you that was a mistake. But I can't. He has to figure this one out on his own. Seriously, Rona, watch a movie or something. Distract yourself.'

The two of them stared at the tiny screen. At that moment, a younger, prettier Maria Gonzales strolled on to the *Sesame Street* set wearing a white T-shirt and denim dungarees, holding up a large pink letter X that she showed to Cookie Monster.

'The letter of the day is X,' she said, smiling brilliantly. 'What are you excited about today?'

Rona glanced at Rowena and managed to crack a weary smile. 'OK, you've made your point.'

'I think they're showing *Mockingjay* on channel 39. And I guarantee you Maria Gonzales didn't have a part in that.'

'Perfect. Senseless violence is exactly what I need right now.'

'There you go.' Rowena changed the channel again. 'Once we get to my place, you can call your dad and talk to him.'

'No way. I never wanna speak to that son of a bitch again.'

'He's still your dad,' Rowena said.

'To hell with that.' David butted into the conversation without turning his head. He'd been listening to every word. 'He's totally humiliating our family. He just did that to my mom on national television, and he hasn't even spoken to us yet. When he acts like a father, he gets to be a father. Really, I don't want anything to do with him.'

'Your mom will tell him where you are.'

'Maybe, but we still won't talk to him,' Rona said. She replaced her headphones and leaned back against the functional blue leather, her dark eyes fixed on Jennifer Lawrence rising above the post-apocalyptic landscape, an arrow drawn to her bow.

Rowena didn't say anything further. In their place, she'd have felt the same way. And right now, she just wanted to get them to the safety of the Hollywood Hills, where everybody was famous and they could blend right in. Michael was going to pick them up, and her two kids were looking forward to having guests. They'd probably do a better job of listening right now than any professional therapist. Teenagers understood each other when the world of adults felt closed.

Exhausted, she put her head back on the neck rest and almost instantly fell asleep.

But that was then. Now they were landed. And her phone was buzzing like it wanted to break out of her jeans. Maybe they'd found out already, somehow got wind of the fact that she was spiriting the kids to Los Angeles. Of course paparazzi couldn't get past the security gates, unless they already happened to be there travelling. That wasn't the greatest danger. Any clown with a smartphone was a tabloid photographer now. She could find pictures of these heartbroken teenagers on the front page of the *National Enquirer* next to a glossy shot of Maria Gonzales and her famous tits. Was it ridiculous to tell them to put jackets over their heads? Rowena wondered, as she shepherded the two of them down the aisle of the plane, determinedly staring straight ahead.

'Excuse me, ma'am.' A flight attendant touched her gently on the shoulder. 'Rowena Krebs? You were in 14 C?'

'That's right,' Rowena said warily.

'Just take a seat in this empty row, ma'am. We're going to

deplane you, and the young lady and gentleman, separately.'

Rowena gestured to the Goldstein twins that they should sit down. 'What's going on?'

'Nothing to worry about, ma'am. Just a special request from your husband. A courtesy bus will collect you and your party from the back of the plane.'

Minutes later, they were staring at each other inside an empty airport minibus as it trundled sedately towards the other end of the terminals.

'Probably just a precaution,' Rowena said. 'The airline's trying to avoid you guys being swarmed by press.'

'Really?' David shook his head. 'We're nobody.'

'The next couple of days, you guys are part of Maria Gonzales' whole mad publicity circus. Once the news cycle moves on, people will forget about you. That's the point of hanging at my house.'

'I get it,' Rona said. 'David and I are both very grateful, Rowena.'

'Don't be so formal,' Rowena said, attempting a grin. 'I changed your diapers.'

Both twins laughed, and she was glad to hear that sound. It might be quite a while before she heard it again. But there was no time to brood. The bus was pulling up at a nondescript grey metal door.

Michael was waiting for them just inside the terminal building. Rowena felt unreasonably pleased to see him, and longed to fling herself into his arms and kiss the lips off his face. But she couldn't, not with these two next to her. Not the time to be selfish, she thought. She'd have plenty of time for that tonight. Her belly stirred slightly, warming at the sight of him, his strength, his closeness.

But then she noticed the look on his face.

'You managed to organise a private transport? I'm impressed.'

He held up his left hand. 'What's this?'

She laughed. 'I know. It's the hand of power.'

That was Michael's nickname, and he loved it. So did she.

'Good to see you guys,' he said to the twins. 'I wish it was under better circumstances. The car is waiting for you. Come this way. No luggage?'

'I sent the luggage on separately by FedEx. I thought we might want to get through the airport fast.'

'Smart thinking.' He was keeping it light, keeping up the banter, but Rowena could tell something was seriously wrong. She bit her lip, desperate to ask him about it. But better they got out of the airport first.

Michael led them through a set of glass doors. There were no taxis here, no shuttle buses. His white Lexus SUV was parked in what appeared to be some sort of slip road. He pressed his key fob to unlock it, and the twins wordlessly slipped into the back seat.

'Where are we?' Rowena asked.

'Service area.'

'How the hell did you pull that off?'

'Lots of people owe me favours. I rarely call them in. That way, I've got credit when I really need it.'

Rowena stared at her husband, feeling that warm sensation of love once again, her sense of great good fortune at being with this man, the most masculine guy she had ever known. 'Was there a ton of press at the gate?'

'Not really. Maybe one or two. It's not that big a story yet.'

'No way, honey. It's all over the news. It was leading the broadcasts on every cable channel when we flew down here. Got a complete goddamned disaster on my hands with these two kids. We can hide them from the press, but I can't keep them away from what's happened . . .'

'Rowena. I'm not talking about Joe and Topaz. You made a perfect getaway. Nobody knows you took the kids.' They were standing outside the driver's door now. Michael looked down into her eyes. 'You don't know what I'm talking about, do you? You didn't check your phone yet?'

Rowena was starting to feel sick with fear. 'What's happened? Is somebody ill? Is it our kids?'

'No. Nothing like that. But it's bad. Rowena, I'm so sorry. Musica fired you.'

She just stood there, frozen.

'Get in the car,' Michael said gently.

Numbly Rowena walked around and got in the passenger side. She belted herself in and stared directly ahead as Michael put the car in gear and gently spun it around to exit the industrial service area, turning left towards the freeway and the beautiful, polluted city of Los Angeles, their home.

He was driving carefully, working his way out of the airport's ugly labyrinth, and Rowena didn't disturb him with stupid questions. Michael would never play with her emotions on the subject of her career. She had absolutely no doubt that he was telling her the accurate truth. She'd been fired while she was in the air. And from the sounds of it, very publicly indeed.

In the back seat, the twins were talking in low, pained voices. Rowena turned up the radio to give them privacy. She tuned it to Alt Nation, the channel loved by modern moody teenagers trapped in their parents' cars, forced to listen to music for once instead of losing themselves on social media.

Why did they even call it that? she thought. Antisocial media would be so much better. All the kids these days locked in a virtual world of likes and pokes and tweets, instead of hanging out with each other, getting into trouble, picking up a guitar, forcing their way to the front row of a rock gig.

Nobody wanted to be a rock star any more. Or even in the movies. She was a relic, a dinosaur, in her early forties. Today's ambitious teenager didn't play a guitar in front of his bedroom mirror; he sat at his laptop and dreamed of being able to code like Zuckerberg.

Imagine Dragons wailed into the ether as Rowena took her phone from her pocket, flipped it open, and prepared to digest the bad news.

I never realised how big this place is, Topaz thought.

As morning dawned, she was pacing slowly through the rooms of her apartment, one by one. Without Joe, without the kids, it was deathly silent, like a museum. But she wasn't crying. She'd done enough of that.

This *is* like a death, she thought. After somebody died, you had a lot of shit to do. That was by design. The Jews, like Goldstein, her baby, they had the right idea. An immediate funeral, pulling you out of your work life. Forcing you to think quickly. No time for the instant ferocity of grief. You were busy when the pain was freshest, and then afterwards, you were forced to sit Shiva for seven days with your friends and process everything. It was a great system.

But there was nothing in place for the death of a heart. No rituals, no roadmap. They'd cried and hugged and kissed, she and the kids, Rona vomiting in the lavatory just off the kitchen as her son asked her why Dad would ever do such a thing, why this had all happened so fast, if there was anything Topaz hadn't told them. How long had they been unhappy . . . where had this come from . . . questions, endless questions to which Topaz had no goddamned answers. What she wanted to do was throw her hands in the air and say to Joe, '*You* deal with this.'

Only that wasn't an option.

He'd called, but they didn't talk to him. The kids couldn't bear it. But *she* wanted to. She wanted to so desperately. She longed to run upstairs to their bedroom, bury her face in the sheets that no longer smelled of him, sheets she'd eventually been forced to wash and change even though she would've kept them dirty forever just to have that physical reminder of their love. And then grab her phone and hear his voice, break down sobbing, fling herself at his feet, beg him to come back to her, to come home, to love her.

But Rowena stopped her. She put one manicured hand over Topaz's trembling one, and wordlessly shook her head.

'I have to . . .'

'Oh no you don't. Not till you're stronger. Not one word.' Rowena took the handset and pressed the red button. 'Don't answer his calls. Don't call him. Act like he's invisible.'

'But what about the kids? I've got to tell him where they've gone.'

'Get an attorney. Have a lawyer write a letter, messenger it over to NAB headquarters. That's how he gets to communicate with his family. At least for now. OK?'

'OK.'

It was hideous. It was heartbreaking. And it was absolutely the right thing to do.

That didn't make it any easier.

Topaz was gathering up everything that belonged to her husband. Every last thing he had in the world. She'd had cheap plastic crates delivered in bulk from the container store, just like she planned for when the kids went to college.

In went every reminder. Closet first; that was easy. All those Armani suits, Hugo Boss shirts, black woollen socks, and John Lobb shoes. Joe was a man of habit. Topaz didn't bother to fold anything; she wasn't some shop girl. He could spring for the dry-cleaning. Next his computer, his iPad, iPod, and a box of electronics: a fancy thousand-dollar camera he'd hardly used, noise-cancelling Bose headphones, all the usual boys' toys. Then it was photographs. She ran from room to room until her arms grew sore from the weight of all those burnished silver frames, scooping them up, not looking at them. After twenty years, she knew the position of all Joe's pictures better than he did himself. There was that one on the beach at the Hamptons, Joe playing with their long-dead terrier, Bonzo; another one of him with

David on his back, racing together at school sports day, the two of them shrieking with laughter. There were wedding photos – so many wedding photos – but Topaz removed only the ones of Joe standing next to his mom or dad, laughing with his friends, photos without her. That day in Central Park had been one of the happiest of her life. Why the hell should I give it up now? she thought. He stole my life from me. I won't let him take my memories too.

Even a neat freak like Joe Goldstein attracted a hell of a lot of clutter. That was the lesson she was learning, room after painful room. The framed baseball she'd given him, game-used in the '86 World Series, signed by all the remaining Mets. His book of Hebrew poetry, a relic from his bar mitzvah studies. The framed Giles cartoons he'd bought at auction in England. The hand-carved cuckoo clock he'd picked up at Graz in Austria, that summer they'd holidayed by the lake. Topaz swooped on everything she thought would be of value, anything that might give him an excuse to return to this apartment and shatter the peace of his children. Toiletries, shampoo, his striped Victorian washcloth, all those familiar, heartbreaking little things she never wanted to see again. In ten minutes' time, workmen would knock on the door to remove the heavy containers groaning with books, juicers, pots and pans, all the detritus of her husband and best friend. They would spirit it all away and deliver it to the black marble lobby of the NAB network building. If Joe Goldstein didn't accept it there, they were under instructions to tell his assistant that they would take it to a landfill. Topaz really didn't give a damn either way. She wanted as much pain out of her life as possible.

Maybe she couldn't forget Joe. In fact she knew that would never happen. But at the same time, she didn't need to remind herself of him day in, day out.

I run a bunch of women's magazines, she thought, and now I'm living a column!

What to Do When Your Husband Leaves – 10 Practical Steps to Take Now.

De-stress Your Environment – How to Grief-Proof Your Home.

Spring-Clean Your Life – De-Clutter a Cheater.

Colour Therapy – Can a Summery New Look Mend Your Broken Heart?

Topaz laughed aloud. Gallows humour. Rowena was good at that. She missed her already.

The bell rang. She opened the door, shook hands, handed out a bunch of hundreds. There were protestations, thanks, and she showed the guys where to go.

'No worries, ma'am. We'll take care of all of this for you.'

'Thank you,' she said. 'I just want it out the door.'

'I hear you. Done this for many ladies before,' the foreman said. He was around fifty-five, thickset and grizzled on top, running to fat around the middle that was set off by his brawny shoulders and chest. He looked at her with working-class sympathy, and Topaz was both touched and embarrassed at his pity.

'I guess so. You've probably seen it all.'

'You ask me, the guy's a moron,' said one of his crew knowingly. He was late forties, strong like the rest of them, Italian probably, from the Bronx, like her.

'Excuse me?' Topaz replied, blinking with surprise.

'Your guy. This Joseph Goldstein. Maria Gonzales ain't all that.'

'Yes she is, man,' laughed another guy. Then he noticed Topaz and flushed. 'Excuse me, miss.'

'Shut up, shit-for-brains,' snarled the foreman. 'Sorry.'

'That's quite all right,' said Topaz.

But the truth was, she felt a little light-headed. It was everywhere. All over the news. Nobody had been dumped quite so publicly since that ex-First Lady of France, what was her name? Topaz was a punchline. A joke.

The men could read her mood. 'It's true,' said the foreman. 'Maria Gonzales, she looks OK, if you like plastic. She's used goods. Been around the block more times than my furniture truck. Your old man's gonna want to get out of there.'

Topaz lifted one eyebrow. 'You think? She's got one of the most famous bodies in America.'

'Ma'am, pardon my way of speaking, but this is true about all men. After you banged it a couple of times, all the bodies are pretty much the same. We can get used to anything. Even supermodels get dumped. Movie stars. It's all about what happens *after* the sex. Don't get me wrong, you need that too. But if she's boring, or a bitch, there're ain't no T and A in the world gonna put that right. I can head over to the Bada Bing right now and get a lap dance from four women, all of whom are hotter than Maria Gonzales, for fifty bucks.'

'You tell your wife that, Paulie?' one of the other men cackled. 'He's full of it, miss. Last time he went in a strip joint, Reagan was president.'

Topaz laughed again, a genuine laugh this time. 'Hold on a second, guys.' She ran to the kitchen and grabbed her purse, taking out a business card, which she handed to the foreman. 'I appreciated the therapy.'

Paulie's face darkened a little. 'I was only trying to help.'

He didn't like being laughed at. Topaz hurried to reassure him as the crew turned back to their work, grabbing the containers, lifting them and hauling them out into the corridor, ready for the freight elevator.

'No, seriously. I run American Magazines. Specifically, I'm editing *American Girl* right now. It's one of our biggest-selling women's titles. I'd like to do an interview with you every month. "How Men Really Think", by Paulie . . . what's your name?'

'Paulie Cantucci.'

'Completely honest. Give it to them straight. Women spend a lifetime wondering what men really think. And then guys only tell us what they think we want to hear. You can be my secret weapon. Be as shocking as you like. Just tell the absolute truth.'

'I don't know.'

'A thousand dollars an interview, and one of our journalists does the writing. All you have to do is talk, and agree to be taped. And say what you think, even if it's hurtful. Good and bad.'

'Wow.' Now he was all smiles. 'You serious?'

'Yes, sir.'

'That would be kind of fun. Do I have to use my own name?'

'No. But I think you should. If I'm right about this concept, it's going to make you a star.'

Now he was looking right at her. Topaz had his full attention.

'And how often are you right about concepts?'

'As far as magazines go, about ninety-five per cent of the time. I can't speak for the rest of my life. Obviously.' She nodded at the packing crates. 'If we have a deal, I'll call you tonight for your first session. We go to press tomorrow, and I think your interview could be the cherry on the cake.'

'You work fast,' Paulie Cantucci said, impressed. 'OK, miss. I'll be there. Don't go getting offended, now.'

'I won't. That's the point. Talk to you later,' Topaz said.

She went into her office and picked up the phone.

'Jason? Hi, it's Topaz Rossi. Thank you. No, I'm OK. I actually have a quick job for you. You'll understand; I sent all of Joe's stuff back to him in boxes today. That leaves a lot of gaps around the place. And besides that, it's all kind of mournful. What I'm looking for is one of your lightning-fast specials. You know, pretend you were dressing the apartment for a photo shoot, and it had to look amazingly good in twenty-four hours? I'm thinking silk flowers, new rugs, some simple drapes, rearrange our family pictures. There're spaces on the walls where some of his artwork was. You know the deal . . .'

She listened for a few moments.

217

'That's exactly the kind of thing. I knew you'd get it. I'd like a new feel to the place. Something summery, maybe. Cheerful colours. Sunset colours . . . storm panels, perhaps a little bit of pale blue. Beach house . . . exactly. You've got it.'

The sound of the guys closing the door behind them was a welcome relief. Topaz wrapped up.

'Yes, that sounds like a good budget. I don't want to go overboard. Plus, I'd like most of it done by the time I get back tonight. Oh, sure you can. I work late. I have every faith in you . . . Thanks, Jason, you too. Talk later.'

Topaz hung up. A mere $10,000 and her decorator could sanitise her memories, like wiping down the kitchen countertops with disinfectant. She already knew she would barely recognise the place when she staggered back in this evening.

She brushed the tears from her cheeks. This was the way to fight it. This was the way for her not to fall apart. She wouldn't give Maria Gonzales that satisfaction. Nor the pack of press bloodhounds waiting outside her door.

Carefully she washed her face, patted it dry with a muslin cloth, and applied her make up. Today really mattered. More than any award show or white-tie evening. Joe would see it, one way or another, she knew that. So would his mistress. Possibly the kids, too, in California. She had to look the best she'd ever looked in her goddamned life.

Her hair was already blow-dried to smooth perfection. Now it was time to put her best face forward. She reached for a tiny bottle and put steroid drops in her eyes, eliminating all the redness at the cost of just a tiny sting. Crying? Her? Never. Next, she dabbed concealer sparingly over the dark circles under her eyes, then covered her entire face with Laura Mercier tinted moisturiser. She swept Bobby Brown bronzer up on to her cheekbones, and dusted a light hazel shadow over her lids. Her favourite Chanel lipstick, Rouge Argent, looked amazing on her full lips. There was no need for anything else; just a spritz of Dior perfume. Nothing worse than a middle-aged woman trying too hard. Maria Gonzales was no Rhodes scholar, but she was cunning. Topaz wouldn't get sucked into the trap of trying to compete. She was Topaz Rossi, chief executive, pioneer, proud mother of David and Rowena Goldstein. A skin-tight dress would look desperate. So would thick mascara or teetering heels. Instead, she played up the contrast. A fitted, not clinging, Issa dress in pure silk, with a sensational seventies-inspired diamond pattern and rebelliously modest long sleeves. A pair of Kate Spade kitten heels. On top of it all, one of her favourite summer coats: a swinging Prada pea coat in moss-green felt. She picked up her mock croc Mulberry handbag in beige leather with the traditional brasswear. There. She was ready.

She took one long look at her reflection in the hallway mirror. Yeah, not bad; she looked like what she was. A successful businesswoman, going to work.

But there was one thing that bothered her. For a long moment she just stood there, her green eyes sweeping up and down across her reflection. Then she held out her left hand and pulled off her engagement and wedding rings. There was a little side table just under the coat rack; it had a number of small drawers. Topaz pulled one of them open, dropped in the two heavy, sparkling rings, and snapped the drawer shut again.

'Topaz! Topaz!'

'Over here! Give us a smile, baby!'

'Topaz, what do you think of Maria taking your man?'

'Are you filing for divorce?'

The flashbulbs popped. Paparazzi shouted. She'd had her reporters in scrums like this before. Head up, she tilted her face for the perfect angle, maintaining an air of calm serenity. A couple of wolf whistles rose from the back.

'Let the lady through! Let her through!' It was Harold, her driver, a burly Swede from the Bronx, all blonde hair and muscles.

He shoved his way through the throng, spreading out his arms. 'She needs to get to her car!'

'Excuse me, fellas,' Topaz said, loudly and clearly. 'I have to go to work.'

She strode past Harold, ignoring the press pack as her self-appointed bodyguard sprang forward to open the door of her limousine. Carefully Topaz slipped inside, smoothing her skirt elegantly with one hand and swinging her knees in with a graceful, catlike movement. There wasn't going to be a single opportunity for those bastards to take one photograph of her looking anything other than smooth, confident, totally in control.

Harold closed the door firmly behind her. Then he pushed his way round to the front of the car, opened the driver's door and got in. The photographers pulled back just a fraction as he started the engine, but they were still trying to get pictures of her through the side windows. Topaz opened her briefcase and took out the neatly typed agenda for this morning's meeting.

'Thank you, Harold. I needed that. Let's go.'

'Yes, ma'am,' he said, and the limo pulled smoothly away.

By the time she walked through the door of *American Girl*, adrenalin was already pumping around her system.

'Good morning, Topaz,' said Lucy. Her acting deputy editor looked as though she hadn't slept in twenty-four hours. 'I've managed to finish editing the stories. The photographs have come through for your approval as well.'

'Excellent. How's the advertising?'

Lucy shook her head, a smile on her lips. 'It's absolutely sensational. We've never seen anything like it. I don't think we've ever sold this many ads in a single issue before.'

To her surprise, even with all the tension racing through her, Topaz felt a thrill of pleasure.

'That's what I like to hear.'

'In fact, other magazines in the group are calling us, asking what the hell we're doing.'

'Don't tell them anything.' American Magazines encouraged a Chinese wall between the titles. Inter-group rivalry was a very healthy thing. 'I'll be moving on from this magazine soon; it'll be all yours. And after that, the rest of them can follow our lead.'

Lucy swallowed hard, and blushed. 'I've got to be honest with you, Topaz. I didn't think this was going to work. Your ideas were just so different, so crazy. It's not how women's magazines do it. But we're getting the most incredible response from everybody who's seen advance copies of the articles.'

'Tell me you've only shown people one piece at a time,' Topaz said, staring hard at the younger woman. 'We need to create an air of mystery around this launch.'

'Yes, ma'am. You made that very clear.' Lucy laughed. 'I don't think anybody on this staff is going to be messing with you any time soon.'

'Better not, baby,' Topaz said, smiling. 'Bring the final copy and the photo sheets to my desk. I need to get everything approved by ten a.m. Then it's showtime. We go to print. And *American Girl* leads a new revolution.'

'Right away. Is there anything else I can bring you?'

'A pot of hot coffee. And a cigar.'

'A cigar?'

'I'm joking. It just feels like a new birth.' *Who's the daddy?* Topaz thought, and smiled to herself.

The office was a godsend. She was too busy to think about Joe. There wasn't a second. After focusing on the last few articles, cutting them down, inserting headlines and text, she sent them to print and turned her eyes to the photos. They had some fantastic ones: girls with young, fresh skin, all shapes and sizes – black girls, Hispanics, Germanic blondes from Wisconsin, slender Asian-Americans from San Fran; most athletic in build, a couple plus-sized, one with a sexy, Monica Lewinsky look to her. The photo editors crowded around her, commenting on her choices.

She wanted to keep *American Girl* cute; no point in throwing up that earnest senior from Mount Holyoke with her white-girl cornrows and thick dark-rimmed glasses – 'Are you kidding me? It'll haunt her for the rest of her life,' Topaz insisted.

'But shouldn't we show some ugly girls too?' Emmeline, one of the fashion editors, spoke up. 'Since we're doing the diversity thing?'

'No. Pretty sells. This isn't a public service announcement,' Topaz answered firmly. 'Our job here is to show that anybody can achieve pretty. Plus size, ethnicity – none of that matters. Look at this babe in the wheelchair.' She held up a shot of a Paralympic athlete with startling green eyes and blonde hair. 'If the chick isn't pretty, that's not going to shift a beauty product. We can feature her in a story rather than a fashion spread.'

There were murmurs of agreement.

'I think we should go with Isabella here,' said Charlie, the senior photo guy. 'And make the Kesha photo a small insert.'

'You have to be kidding. Kesha's stunning.'

Charlie folded his arms. 'Her boobs are too big for fashion.'

'They're great. I wish I was racked like that.'

Several of the younger women snickered.

'If you want to talk magazine reality, African-American models don't sell. They just do not.' Charlie tossed his head. 'And her body is too curvy. It's against our whole aesthetic. I have experience in these matters. You need to listen.'

Topaz felt her heart hammer in her chest. 'Experience. How long have you been photo editor of *American Girl*?'

'Over three years.'

'And you've done spread after spread featuring the same old rake-thin white girls. No interest, no great photography. Just laughing chicks with perfect teeth wearing overpriced threads our readers could never afford.'

'We're top of the tree. You can't argue with the numbers. When *Vogue* features a black model on the cover, sales drop by—'

'We're here to educate. Not pander to racism.' Topaz stared him down. 'You're fired. Clear your desk.'

His mouth dropped open with shock.

'You can't do that to me, you bitch.'

'Not only can. Did. Get out so I don't have to call security.'

There was an awkward silence as the room held its collective breath. Then Charlie reached forward and brushed all the photos off the table with his arm.

'You're an old lady, Topaz Rossi, and the company's going to dump you just like your husband did,' he said. Then he turned on his heel and stormed from the room.

'Get the Kesha shot. Full page, with Isabella as the insert.' Topaz didn't even look after him. 'Somebody pick these up and put the layout together. Email it to me. We print at ten. Got it?'

They nodded sheepishly.

'Great. Let's move it.'

By eleven it was done. The magazine, their magazine, *American Girl*, was at the printer. Digital files were being loaded up, printed off. Topaz did a short victory lap, walking round the office patting everybody on the back. Then she headed back to her desk.

'Ms Rossi? There's a call from California. It's your kids,' the secretary said, and blushed.

Her buzz faded immediately. She could drown Joe out, but he wasn't going away. Nor was the pain. She could dull it with work, but only for so long. She gritted her teeth, forced a smile.

'Great. Hold everything else.'

She shut her door and slid into her chair, reaching for her headset. 'Guys? How is it?'

Rona was up first. 'It's beautiful here, Mom. They have this amazing pool. And their kids are great.'

The fist in her stomach uncurled a little. 'OK. OK. That's good to hear.'

David's voice came on the line. 'We saw you on TV.'

'Yes. I think you will for a few more days. There were photographers outside our building this morning. There might be some pictures in the paper or on the internet.' Topaz sighed. 'Do your best to stay away from it.'

'We can't pretend it's not happening,' Rona answered.

'True, but you can manage your focus. This is the first crisis of your lives, you two. There are going to be more. How you handle this is a good test.'

'Did you speak to Dad?' David asked.

'No,' Topaz replied.

'Are you getting divorced?' Rona asked. 'Twitter says you're not wearing your wedding ring.'

Goddamned social media. 'That's right. I took it off. It's a mockery when Dad's with another woman. As to divorce, it looks very likely.' Topaz pulled out her mobile; there were seventeen missed calls from Joe Goldstein. 'I know that must be hard to hear. Have you spoken to Dad?'

'No.' David was definite. 'Not a chance.'

'I don't want to,' Rona agreed.

'We must bite the bullet here. We're still a family, even if we get divorced.' When *we get divorced*, sniped the bitchy voice in her head.

'A family? Please, Mom, don't give us that touchy-feely bullshit,' David said.

'But we are. A father and his kids. A mother and her kids. Dad and I are jointly responsible for you two. None of that changes.'

There was an ominous silence.

'Everybody does wrong in this world,' Topaz said gently. 'Dad did. I have. One day you both will. When that day comes, you will remember how harsh you were with your father now. You don't have to approve of his actions but you do have to still love him. Unconditionally, because he would love both of you unconditionally if you went out right now and shot some guy in the head. He would love you no matter what.'

Pain reached up her throat even as she was speaking, threatening to strangle her. It was easier to be angry; boy, so much easier.

'We do love him, Mom,' said Rona tearfully. 'It's just that we're so angry at him right now.'

'And I don't think that's going to change. At least, not quickly. So maybe we better plan on talking to him.' As soon as the words were out of her mouth, Topaz realised she was right. She'd been procrastinating; trying to put off the pain for as long as possible. But that was cowardly. And whatever else she was guilty of, Topaz Rossi was no coward. 'Here's what I'm going to do. I'm going to call your father as soon as I hang up with you guys. He and I need to have a conversation. After that, I think you should speak to him. Say whatever you want, but try to keep it rational. I'm going to have him call David's cell phone in exactly an hour from now.'

'Mom, I really don't want to,' David said.

'I understand that. But you *have* to. I'm not asking you, I'm telling you. Am I making myself clear?'

'Yes, ma'am,' David said.

'We love you, Mom,' Rona said.

'And I love you guys.'

Topaz hung up. Then, without giving herself time to think about it, she picked up her phone and dialled Joe's cell. It had barely got through the first ring when his voice came on the line.

'Topaz? Is that you?'

'Yes, it's me. Who else would it be? We need to talk.'

'Topaz.' His voice was strangled. 'I don't know what to say. I didn't want it to go down like this. I'm really sorry the press have been harassing you—'

'It's not press harassment that's the problem,' Topaz replied. 'It's the fact that you're a cheating bastard who's fucking some cheap actress. And that you were prepared to throw me and our kids away for a big pair of tits.'

'Topaz, Christ! It's not like that!'

'Joe, it's *exactly* like that. We had one quarrel, and you ditched our marriage and found a bimbo within how long exactly? A week? A day? Or did you have her lined up before then? Maybe you guys have been an item for years, for all I know.'

'We haven't. I swear to you.'

Topaz laughed bitterly. 'What do you want, a cookie?'

'I'm sorry about it all.' There was a strange note in Goldstein's voice. 'I don't know what I was doing. We fought and I just fell into it.'

Topaz rolled her eyes.

'Yes, sure, I know just how that can be. You're walking along one day, and you suddenly trip and fall into a strange piece of pussy. What a disaster! The city really should fix those potholes in the sidewalk.'

Goldstein laughed. 'Oh Topaz, you're exactly the same.'

She had tears in her eyes now, and she was glad that Joe wasn't in the room. 'Of *course* I'm the same. It's only been a few days. I haven't changed. Unfortunately, you have.'

'Maybe we should get together and talk about it.'

'What is there to talk about? Have you left Maria?'

Topaz held her breath, and the room seemed to spin around her for an eternity while she waited for his answer.

'No. We're still together.'

'Then that's all there is to it. I guess my lawyers will be in touch.'

'Topaz, wait—'

'You need to talk to the children. They're in California, staying with Michael and Rowena. I want them as far away from the press as possible.'

'Yes, of course. God. That's great. That's so good of Rowena.'

'She's a loyal friend.' *Unlike you*, Topaz thought. 'I've persuaded them to take a call from you on David's cell at midday exactly. Don't be late. Understand their anger, and whatever you do to me, don't hurt our kids any worse than they have to be hurt.

Leave out the emotional blackmail. Don't tell them how they should respond to this. And don't mention Maria.'

'Topaz! You really think I would do that? You know me better.'

'It turns out I don't know you at all.'

'We need to meet. We need to talk this through.'

'No, we really don't. Just make the call. And don't bother me again. It's a big day here. I've got a magazine going to print. I don't need you complicating things. Understand?'

'Topaz, please. Just one meeting—'

She hung up. She was sweating, her heart pounding as though she'd just run three miles on the treadmill. She breathed in and out heavily, trying to regulate her pulse. She forced herself to be calm. The worst of it was over, at least for now.

Her purse was on the floor by her feet. She picked it up, snapped it open, and took out her compact. It was gold-plated, antique, from the 1920s. Joe had seen it in a flea market in Paris and brought it back as a souvenir. For a second, Topaz winced, then she flicked it open and studied her face. Her make-up was holding up pretty well. She took out the soft powder puff and dabbed Chanel ultra-fine around her eyes, across the bridge of her nose, and over her cheeks. As usual, it worked its magic, taking away the trace of tears, the flush of blood, every sign of emotion. No wonder those prim and proper British ladies had been powdering their faces through two world wars. Looking strong, looking respectable: this was the power of beauty when you needed it most.

Like right now. Like today.

When she got home, Topaz promised herself, she would go into the bathroom, lock the door, and cry her eyes out.

But not now. Not today. She had stuff to do.

She got to her feet, strode to her office door, and flung it open wide. 'Emily!' she screamed.

The *American Girl* corporate PR executive came hurrying across the floor. 'Topaz? Can I help you?'

'Yes. Take notes. I want you to book me on some TV shows tomorrow. Let's try and get everywhere we can. *Today*, Fallon, *Good Morning America*, Fox News, Oprah goddamned Winfrey. Anybody you can think of. Call them all. I want to sell the relaunch of *American Girl*.'

Emily Wilkins swallowed hard. She stared at Topaz like she was a madwoman. 'But Topaz, uh, I know *we're* all super-excited about the relaunch of *American Girl*, but you know, I just don't think it's *Today* show material, it's not Kelly and Michael, you understand . . .'

'Of course not. But you know what *is* Kelly and Michael? The breakdown of my goddamned marriage. Tell them all I'll go on and spill the beans about Joe, Maria and my broken heart as long as they let me plug our new issue. Oh yes, and no questions about my kids. That's off limits.'

Emily blinked. 'You'd really do that?'

Topaz smiled. 'I have something to sell. And since Joe valued our privacy so little, why the hell should I hold back?'

The younger woman's face was a picture. 'Wow. Yes, ma'am. I'll get right on it. How many are you prepared to do?'

'Book me on all you can get. Even goddamned BBC America. No exclusives. And I want to do a Spanish network. And *The Huffington Post* – tell them I'll write them an exclusive blog if they front-page it with a screenshot of our cover.'

Emily bounced a little on the balls of her ballet flats. 'Awesome! OK then!'

Have you left Maria?

No.

Fine, Joe Goldstein, Topaz thought. If you want war, you've got it.

Chapter Fourteen

Rowena Rocks Out

Big news in the record industry today as Rowena Krebs leaves Musica Records. The Hall-of-Famer and one half of what was previously music's biggest power couple, along with her husband, legendary producer Michael Krebs, has been summarily dismissed from the sound shop in a firing insiders are describing as 'brutal' and 'humiliating'. The exec was sent a text by Orlando Stonebridge, chairman of the board, but did not receive it as she was in the air, returning from some unannounced 'personal time' in New York City.

Well, look on the bright side, Rowena – there'll be a lot more personal time in your life from now on. Industry types have been quick to point out that Krebs gracelessly took all the credit for the last-quarter success of her various bands and international operations, while chewing underlings out for problems that were, as one not-sorry employee put it, 'her own damned fault'. 'Rowena could be very abrasive,' said a person familiar with the matter. 'Not what you expected from a woman in power. She was vain and a bully. Most people at Musica will be thrilled by this development. Rowena and Michael Krebs were hot stuff – in 1993.'

There it was. The photo of her looked good, at least: standing there in her Hall of Fame gown, statuette in hand, waving like an Oscar winner.

Waving goodbye.

'Put it down,' Krebs said. 'Better yet. Throw it out.'

'Not a chance.' Rowena folded the copy of *Variety* and put it away. 'I'm keeping them all. *Billboard, Hits, The Wall Street Journal,* the *LA Times*. Not only that, I'm going to make a collage of them. Have it framed.'

He grinned. 'Mount it on the wall of your office?'

'You got it, baby. To look at when I come after those assholes.'

'Hey.' Krebs walked over to his wife, put his strong hands on her shoulders, kneaded her back. 'Are you sure you want to? We have a nice payoff coming.'

'They're going to dispute the payoff.' She shook her head. 'Saying I was terminated for cause. They think they can suspend the stock options.'

Krebs shrugged. 'Fine. We'll sue their asses off.'

'Of course. It's still two years in court.'

'We can wait. They can't get away with taking it from you. More to the point, honey, we don't need their goddamn money. You can go swimming every day.'

'I already swim every day.'

'OK, you can swim every day later than six a.m.' He kissed the top of her head. 'You told me you wanted to quit anyway. So who cares?'

Rowena kissed her husband's hand, a flicker of desire running through her just at the closeness of him.

'I know you know the answer to that. Quit is one thing. Fired is another.'

Krebs smiled. 'Yes. But I still thought I'd lay out the option.'

'And sweetheart, we do need the money. You rented that amazing place for Marty. You're paying all the bills there, and there's the cancer nurse . . .'

'It costs what it costs,' he said shortly.

'I totally agree.' Rowena winced. 'As if I wouldn't. We spend whatever we need to on any of your children. But it is a good argument for keeping my payoff.'

Krebs nodded, relaxing again. Marty was a sore spot between them; he couldn't, just couldn't, let Rowena in.

Before he left New York, he'd made good on his promise to his eldest son.

'I need something near the hospital. Ground floor. Garden.' He'd given the agent, Jessie Nevins, his wish list. 'Six months' rental, and I'll pay the full amount in advance. I want to be able to hand my son the keys today.'

'I suppose there's no point in asking you for references?'

He rolled his eyes. 'My cash is the reference. Otherwise, your clients can take a look on Wikipedia. Or in their iTunes.'

She smiled. 'Yes, sir. I'll call you in an hour with a list of places.'

He settled on the first one she took him to: a fully furnished two-bedroom with a little den, the lower half of an old brownstone tucked away on 70th Street, near the river. It was Victorian, with shelves waiting for Marty's books, and a wonderful back yard his son could sit in, a small patch of green with deck chairs and a water feature mounted on the wall.

'It doesn't have a pool,' Jessie said. 'But you can get him a membership to Equinox, just down the street. There's a great kitchen – does your son cook?'

'When he's stronger.' Krebs looked around, relishing the place. It was old-fashioned, academic, exactly what Marty would want. There were ratty antiques, a threadbare Afghan rug, and brass fixtures in the grate. It would have outdoor space in summer, warmth and cosiness in winter. And there was a second bedroom, if he ever got to visit.

'His girlfriend cooks. But I'm going to engage somebody else, a private cancer nurse, and pay her a fortune to also cook and clean. That way, Marty and Amelia don't have to worry about a goddamned thing. Except getting well.'

The older woman looked at him. 'I sure wish I'd had a dad like you back when I was sick.'

Krebs blinked. 'You had cancer?'

'Breast. Twenty-five years ago.' She pressed her hand to his arm. 'Everybody's different, but they can do incredible things these days. I'm constantly amazed.'

He was embarrassed to find tears springing to his eyes at the kindness of strangers. 'Hey. Thanks.' He swallowed, and looked around. 'It comes furnished?'

'Yes. The owner wants to move right back in. She's on sabbatical in England. Oxford University, in fact. Another professor.'

'I might have guessed. It's pretty close to perfect for my kid. What does she want for it?'

'Forty-five hundred a month. It's pricey, maybe we can do a deal . . .'

'No deals.'

Jessie opened her mouth. 'Honey, you could come to an arrangement. Most people don't want to take somebody else's furniture, you know?'

'Your client wants it rented, and Marty's a nice Jewish boy who won't be running around. What *I* want is the keys, within the hour. I will transfer the entire amount and sign the lease. That's the deal – speed.'

She offered him her hand. 'Nice doing business with you, Mr Krebs.'

Marty and Amelia were ensconced in the place that afternoon; he would never forget the look of wonder and joy on his son's pallid, drawn face.

'You guys can light a fire – it's a wood-burning stove, and they had the chimney swept,' Michael said diffidently.

'It's really ours?' Amelia asked. She could hardly bring herself to believe it. 'For how long, Michael? This place is brilliant.'

'Six months. I'll take over the old lease, too. Pay off your landlord.'

'Dad, I should turn this down . . .' Marty was grinning, and Michael's heart leaped to see it. 'But I can't. It's too special.'

'You're two blocks from the cancer centre. And one more thing. I've engaged a nurse, on recommendations. She's going to supervise your meds and vitamins, and she'll cook, which will give Amelia a break. She's also going to double as housekeeper.'

'A nurse? Cleaning?'

'I found one who used to clean houses for a living before she got certified.' Krebs grinned. 'Trust me, I'm paying incredibly well for any indignity. You need to have a solid home base. She even has a nutritionist certificate. She can shop for you guys and buy you whatever cancer-fighting crap you should be eating.' At Amelia's anxious look, he smiled. 'I've organised a household credit card for her. Her name is Svetlana Ayashinka and she will be here at five p.m. I hope that's OK. I'm covering all the bills now, Marty. You two kids concentrate on your lives.'

And I want them to be long and happy, he thought, but didn't say. No way was he going to risk crying in front of his boy.

'Dad. You're the best. Mom is going to love this place.'

There it was, that twinge of jealousy, that eternal regret.

'Invite your brothers, too. Keep family close.'

'I will. Can't wait to show it off.'

Krebs glanced at his watch. 'Marty, if you guys are good, I'm going to head back out to the airport. There are a couple of things I need to do in LA.'

'You have your kids,' Marty said.

'My *other* kids.'

'Dad. It's OK.' His son hugged him, and Krebs felt the effort his weakened muscles were making to hold him close. 'I love you. Really. It's fine. Go on home.'

The memory of that interlude had sustained Krebs all through the long ride home, and while he tried to settle back into his life with Rowena and the children. He hadn't talked it through with his wife; he couldn't. She knew he needed money, though. She was right about that.

He was drawn back to the present. Rowena's anger was enough to fire up the Los Angeles grid.

'I quit, fine. You fire me? I'll destroy you. Every last damned one of you. Then I get Musica back. *Then* I can quit.' Rowena breathed out. 'I'm mostly annoyed because these assholes stepped on my retirement. Now I'm back in the ring, like it or not.'

'And you do like it.'

'Who said that? They're laughing at me. Mocking me.'

'Of course. Jackals hate lionesses. You're a tough boss, it's why you're good. Why you've stayed on top for twenty years. People hate that. Seeing you fall has made their week.'

'Great. I hope they enjoy it.' Her eyes narrowed. 'I'm going swimming.'

'Attagirl,' Krebs said. He understood her perfectly.

As Rowena grabbed her gold-and-beige Missoni bikini, the one he loved so much, and strode upstairs to their rooftop pool, Michael Krebs felt himself harden with desire for her. She wasn't doing this for leisure. She would swim fifty hard, fast laps, her lean legs slicing through the water like every kick was aimed at unseen enemies. And then she would dress, make herself up and head straight to work.

Something intense surged through him. Something he hadn't felt for years. Adrenalin. He breathed in sharply, dizzy with the pleasure of it. This was better than Rowena putting her company back together. This was the real thing. A white-knuckled survival fight.

Idly he went to his own dressing room and pulled out some workout gear: time to lift. The gym was in the basement. It resembled a medieval torture chamber, with machines and pulleys, kettlebells the size of rocks, barbells and free weights. Religiously he did two hundred sit-ups before his first coffee; he lifted daily, bench-pressing hundreds of pounds in weight. The body was a metaphor for control, and Krebs was always in control. His chest, his biceps were huge; his thighs hard as marble. That was great. He could hold his slender wife down with one hand, her wrists gripped helplessly, as she moaned with desire, his right hand teasing her while she writhed beneath him. The desire he saw in Rowena's eyes, her endless lust for him, fuelled him. He was driven by it. He liked to fuck her daily, sometimes more often, even now. It was life, it was youth, it was everything. Sex with her, even fights with her, put the electricity into his world. For a man who had everything, she was a new world to conquer, every day. Krebs loved her. Was obsessed with her. Their relationship had moved full circle. In her early twenties, she had fallen for him, totally, completely. And now he needed her like he needed air and sunlight, and loved her better than both.

He lay down on his bench and started to do chest flies with eighty-pound weights. For a few moments his muscles screamed in protest, then they started to warm up, to produce adrenalin. He concentrated on his form. The bodybuilding cleared his mind, helped him to see the world as though he were reading a map.

This wasn't just Rowena. It was about him. He had four albums in the pipeline with Musica artists and two for Universal. Nothing but initial payments were due. His close association with Rowena meant that these would now be pulled; suits always thought one producer was exchangeable for another, because they didn't understand the world of music, what they sold. To most of them it was just soap powder.

Lift. Pull. His shoulders screamed. He loved it. Push. The sweat trickled down the side of his face.

That was a total of eight million, royalties not included. And when those acts were pulled, others would follow. He would be reduced to taking 'interesting' projects, indie bands, has-beens who wanted a comeback. Even then, without promotion, it didn't get far.

They had a burn rate, him and Rowena. College was paid for, so was school, but there was travel, resort vacations, the ski chalet in Kitzbühel, her pied-à-terre in London, and the country cottage in the Cotswolds. There were staff, drivers, tutors, taxes. Of course they would not want for anything, but neither could they live as they had done. Marty's new place added more to that. The nurse was expensive; so was the rent, and the bills. Not that he resented even a cent of that cash. In fact, seeing those lines on his bank statement was a blessed relief: just the knowledge that he was doing something, anything to help.

But it still cost. And he needed to be able to make all those numbers, and have stuff left over. At this point, he would be tapping the money in his savings accounts.

For the first time in their lives, he and Rowena would be going backwards.

Krebs grunted. Pushed the weights further. There was lactic acid burn now; he desperately wanted to stop. So he did another two reps. Past the pain barrier, that was where you got growth. Always. Just past pain.

The weights dropped. He got to his feet, stretched, and moved to the barbell for curls. If Rowena was fired, so was he. And if she moved for revenge, he needed to do something new.

It sounded great. It sounded like fun.

He thought about his studio, the vast premises atop the Malibu cliffs, with its outbuildings and smoke huts and garden, the stairs cut in the cliff face down to the beach so guitarists and keyboard players could go dip their feet in the ocean, get some inspiration. It was the best small studio in the world, state-of-the-art. His creation. His baby.

He hoisted up the weight, his wrists straight, feeling his biceps fill with blood.

As soon as he got done here, he was going to destroy it.

A smile flickered across his face for the first time in months.

This was going to be fun.

* * *

'So . . . this is where you guys hang out?' David said.

'Yeah. Mostly.' Joshua shrugged. It was clear he was proud of the game room, which was tricked out with beanbag chairs, hard carpet tiles in grey and brown checks. Big speakers, a huge TV monitor hooked up to the Xbox and cable; cushions everywhere, even a little fridge. There was a desk with a gaming computer too. It was very cool.

'And also on the roof. We have a pool on the roof,' Ruth said, blushing. She was looking at Rona with something like awe. Seventeen and in from New York City. Ruth was just a seventh-grader, barely in her first training bra. 'I like to read in the garden too. Mom and Dad set it up really nicely. Oh. I'm sorry.' She blushed scarlet.

David glanced at his twin sister and they exchanged a tiny smile. 'Hey, Ruth, it's OK. You don't have to apologise because your parents are sane.'

'Our parents are sane,' Rona said protectively.

'Our mom.'

'Maybe there's two sides. Maybe . . . maybe Dad's having, like, a nervous breakdown or something. We just don't know,' Rona said.

Joshua shuffled his feet, looking at the floor.

'We don't. You're right.' David Goldstein decided to step out of it. He didn't want to embarrass his young hosts. Besides, it was good to have some other people to worry about right now. They had to feel as awkward as he and Rona did. 'Anyway, I'm glad to be here. I needed a break from the drama.'

'And the sun is amazing,' Rona said. 'I love swimming. Your rooms are, like, *huge*.'

'My mom told us you guys have an awesome apartment,' Joshua Krebs offered.

'It's cool, but even the best places in Manhattan are tiny compared to LA. This is like a palace. What games do you guys have?'

'Skyrim,' Josh said. 'World of Warcraft . . .'

'Thank God,' David said.

'I like Minecraft,' Ruth offered. 'Mostly on my Mac, though. Do you play?' she asked Rona.

The older girl shook her head.

'Me neither, not too much any more. I like reading and swimming. Josh works out a lot, we have a good gym . . .'

'This is going to be awesome,' David said firmly. 'Work on my tan, buff up, meet some hot chicks . . . You know any, dude?'

'Uh . . . I . . .'

'I'm just kidding, man. Unless you like hang out with seniors at your school. I dig older women.'

The boys laughed.

'Do you want me to show you the pool?' Ruth offered Rona.

'Sure. Love to.'

She meant it, too. Maybe they just needed a break from the drama. She loved her mom and her dad, and she was so worried, and it didn't help watching Mom struggle through by herself. This girl was pretty sweet. And although the Krebs kids were younger, they were still fun. It was nice to hang out with somebody with zero agenda.

'OK, cool. Follow me, you guys,' Ruth said. 'Hey, Rona, there's a big mall at the end of Third Street. I hang out there a lot most weekends. Do you like shopping and stuff?'

'Do you surf, dude? I go to this club in Santa Monica on Sundays if you want to come,' Josh said to David.

'I surf the web. That's about it. I'm a total geek, man,' David answered.

Josh Krebs visibly swelled. 'I could give you some lessons, if you want to learn the basics.'

David grinned. Surfing in the sun, why the hell not? He caught Rona's eye again. It was obvious she felt the same. Relief. They couldn't fix Mom and Dad; they had to work things out themselves, or not. For now, this was something. And he was going to take advantage of not having to think.

'Yeah. Sounds awesome. Love to surf, man, why not.'

Joshua nodded. That was pretty great. He was relieved the Goldstein twins weren't going to be assholes, copping an attitude because they were older, from New York City. And hanging out with them would give him and Ruth something else to do besides getting anxious about Dad and Martin. Mom was worried and stressed most of the time too; even Ruth had picked that up. He didn't want to think about all the bullshit that was going on.

Maybe the four of them could be a team. Distracting each other from all that adult pain going on at the margins. It was hard enough managing all the social crap at school without dealing with his parents' stuff on top.

Yeah – this could be good.

Rowena gasped in the water. Her manicured hand reached out, fingers finding the edge of the pool. She grasped the handrail, slipped her body from the water. She was panting, dripping. Quickly she towelled off and almost ran into the house. Twenty minutes later, she was in the car, heading to Michael's office. It took everything she had not to turn the other way, automatically drive to Musica.

'Good morning, Mrs Krebs.' It was Ellen, his assistant. 'Mr Krebs told us to expect you. We've got an office ready for you, right opposite his. Everything's set up already.'

'Thanks so much,' Rowena said. 'That's very kind of you. Do you think I could get a pot of tea? With some sugar?'

'Of course, ma'am. Right away.'

'You're a lifesaver. And please, call me Rowena.'

'OK, Rowena. I'll go and fix you that tea.'

'I'm pretty impressed you've got any, to tell the truth,' Rowena said. 'Kind of unusual, in LA.'

'Don't be. Mr Krebs called ahead. He thinks of everything.'

Rowena felt a rush of affection wash over her. Michael really did think of everything. God, it was amazing how in love with him she still was. For a second, she thought painfully of Topaz. But her best friend would have to deal with it on her own, at least for now. Rowena's hands were full.

She went into the office. It was a far cry from her massive corner suite at Musica. The windows that looked over Sunset Boulevard were just average size, no wall-to-ceiling spectaculars here. But Michael had taken every opportunity to make her feel at home. Her platinum records, her tour posters, everything personal that had graced her former workspace was already there, mounted on the walls. In fact, because this office was half the size, the mementoes and photographs now covered the entire space from floor to ceiling. It gave the room a quirky, funky look. Rowena had to smile as she saw that Michael had even imported her favourite Turkish kilim rug and laid it out on the floor in front of her new desk. There was a brand-new, top-of-the-range Apple super-laptop, incredible sound speakers, and a telephone deck that would have done credit to the United Nations. On top of all this, he had gone to the trouble of filling several Baccarat crystal vases with glorious scented bouquets of white roses and lavender, freesias and iris, even heavily fragranced hyacinths. It looked as though a top-notch interior decorator had gone to work.

Now she had to do such a good job that all his effort was worthwhile.

She sat down in the ergonomic chair in front of her kidney-shaped desk and picked up the phone. The first person she called would have to be Lillian Carpenter, her executive assistant for the last five years.

'Lillian, it's Rowena. How are you doing?'

'Rowena? Rowena! Oh my goodness. I . . . I'm OK. I didn't think you'd call.'

'Of course I was going to call. You're first on my list. Are you hanging in there?'

'Rowena, I'm really sorry about this, but I can't talk to you.'

'What do you mean?'

'I still have my job. In fact, they're going to promote me. But not if I talk to you. That's strictly forbidden. Please understand! They're saying you did bad things.'

'What the hell? What bad things? That's bullshit, Lillian, and you know it.'

Her former assistant's voice grew distant, cold.

'I don't know anything. I've told you, I can't talk to you. It's not fair to keep me on the phone.'

Rowena was reeling. She pressed her fingers to her temple. 'I don't believe this. I treated you well. How much did they offer you?'

'You never promoted me. The new boss is going to. And I intend to co-operate fully with the internal investigation. Goodbye, Rowena. Please don't embarrass us both by calling again.'

Rowena slowly replaced the phone in its cradle. Lillian had made a decision. Fine. It must have been a lot of money. She ignored her own hurt feelings; this was LA, where loyalty was cheaper than a discount café latte. *Think, damn you, think.*

Something was going on at Musica. Something big. A lot bigger than one record executive getting fired. When they started promoting and bribing the assistants, that meant that corporate governance needed certain things to come out about her – true or false.

'Here's your tea, Rowena.' Ellen bustled in with a small tray and set it down on the desk. There was a beautiful porcelain teapot, and an antique silver sugar bowl with matching spoon, but they were stacked next to a large chipped mug with a picture of Blackpool emblazoned across the front of it. 'Michael said this would make you feel right at home. He says you never drink out of fussy little teacups.'

'He's absolutely right.' Rowena laughed aloud. 'Husband of the year. How did I get so lucky?'

'Should I tell him that?'

'Hell, no. Let's make him think he still has work to do. Men like Michael Krebs can't live without a challenge.'

'You got it.' Ellen withdrew and shut the door behind her.

Rowena poured tea into the chipped mug, stirred in a couple of sugars, and took a deep, warming sip. Then she opened her desk drawer and found a yellow legal pad. Grabbing a biro, she wrote down the first things that came into her head.

Fired. After great results. No warning.

On plane. They didn't want me to know about it.

Scorched-earth strategy? Delaying the bonus – threatening my assistant – bribing her. Unknown sources leaking character assassination to the trade magazines. Next up, internal investigation. Lillian wants to be useful.

Reasons for destroying a former employee?

Don't want to pay out settlement due.

She mulled that one over for a few minutes.

No. Bad for business. Legal fees alone will cost more than the settlement. Hiring the next guy becomes tougher, because his lawyer doesn't believe company will honour its exit promises.

OK. Not money. Something else. Former regime needs to be discredited. In whose eyes? Who benefits? What's the play here?

More tea. This was good. It always amazed Rowena how the old-fashioned method – writing things down by hand on a piece of paper – forced you to think straight. It was like some invisible teacher was marking her essay, back in school. Computers didn't do this for her. This was activation of the brain.

Only the board can authorise this. Therefore, they have to have something to do with it. That means a takeover. Somebody doesn't want any trouble with the shareholders, who have to be happy with our last quarter's results. Normally the company would be terrified of losing me. But this guy – whoever it is – wants to make people scared. Really scared. Scared that they might lose their investment, scared that the company will fold. Means making me the bad guy. That way, shareholders are going to be absolutely thrilled that anybody wants to buy their piece-of-junk company. Of course, it's unethical. But like they say in Spinal Tap, money talks and bullshit walks.

So, somebody bribed the Musica board to fall in with their bid. Somebody with a hell of a lot of money. Not a company. No company would take that legal risk.

Rowena finished her tea, and poured another cup. She was on a roll. Sherlock Krebs.

We need to find a big corporate raider with money to burn, the desire to get into music, and a reputation for being a big swinging dick. Whoever did this wants to wipe me off the face of the earth. They want to make an example of me – and buy an undervalued record company at the same time.

One more gulp of tea. Rowena picked up her pen, and bent her head forward again. She'd written so much, she almost had cramp.

So, who the hell fits that picture?

Suddenly she sat bolt upright in her chair.
'Oh my God,' she said aloud. 'It's Conrad Miles.'
The blood rushed to her head, and she felt dizzy. The room started to spin. Her heart was pounding. She leant back in her chair, glad that she was sitting down. Eventually the head rush subsided. I shouldn't be dumb about this, Rowena thought. It

seems like a good guess. But I can't just fall in love with my theory. I have to test it out.

She didn't want to burden Michael at this stage, and Topaz definitely wasn't available.

You're on your own, baby.

She picked up the phone again and dialled another number. Rick Kravitz, an ex-banker who sat on the board of Musica Records. Boring as hell. Made his first million as an accountant. Rick was the kind of worthy, earnest paragon of corporate life that every company wanted to have on board, just as a safe pair of hands. He was greedy, but he had all the cunning of a three-week-old marshmallow.

'Mr Kravitz's office. How may I direct your call?'

'Hello there, this is Rosalina in Orlando Stonebridge's office,' said Rowena, naming the assistant to the chairman of the board. 'Is Mr Kravitz available for Mr Berman?'

'Of course. Hold just one minute, please.'

There was a pause at the end of the line. And then his voice came on. Rowena was surprisingly nervous.

'Peter! Good to hear from you. How are things going? Did they cut your cheque yet?'

'I don't think Conrad Miles is going to cut you that check after all,' Rowena said firmly. She fought to keep the tremor out of her voice. 'Rick, you really should insist you get paid in cash. I had lunch with Conrad yesterday. He knows I can make him a better deal. He wants the company free and clear, no lawsuits involved. So here is what I suggest, for the sake of our long friendship. I give you and all the rest of the backstabbing jerks twenty-four hours to tender your resignation, you write a statement completely exonerating me, and I don't go to the feds with the audio of your last meeting I have sitting on my computer, just waiting to be uploaded to YouTube.'

'Rowena! I don't understand.'

'From what Conrad tells me, you understand very well indeed.

Like I say, I made the guy a better offer. And I took the recording to tidy up any loose ends. Very stupid of you to assume I didn't know what was going on.'

'Our firing you had nothing to do with Conrad Miles's bid. Anything you say to the contrary is just a lie.' His voice was wobbling from the onslaught. Rick Kravitz was not a guy used to confrontation. 'And I still believe that we can make Miles Industries a better deal. Wait till I talk to him, Rowena. He'll come around. He really doesn't like you all that much.'

And there it was. She had her confirmation. That simple.

'Well, let's see. I'll bet he offers me a lot more money than he's giving each of you.'

'Please. You were a great record executive, Rowena, back in the days when your industry actually *meant* something. But those days are long gone. You showed us the way – it's all about catalogue profits now, not new music. Conrad Miles doesn't want an executive. He wants a smooth purchase. I don't believe he'd offer you anything close to fifty million.'

Fifty million.

'Well,' said Rowena, smiling, 'the market price has certainly gone up from thirty pieces of silver, hasn't it, Rick?'

'Not funny. I'm Jewish.'

'So is my husband, and I thought it was pretty funny. But that's not the point. The point is that you're going to be the real joke around that boardroom table. Conrad Miles might not like me, but I think he's going to really hate you.'

'Indeed?' asked Rick, with a supercilious hint to his tone. 'And why is that, Rowena? Go ahead and enlighten me, since it's clear that you're bluffing. I'll bet Conrad didn't offer you anything at all.'

'Close, but no cigar. Not only did he not offer me anything, but I didn't speak to him either. I had no idea who bribed you bastards to break up this company, pay off my assistant, fire me, and tell lies to the press. But I did a little bit of critical thinking. And after

245

that, I decided to go fish – in the shallowest pool there is. Your brain. Really, I should've signed you to a deal, Rick. After all, you sing like a canary.'

'Oh my God,' Rick Kravitz muttered. 'Oh my God.'

'You told me it was Conrad. You told me that he paid each and every one of you fifty million dollars to go ahead and cheat the shareholders out of their value by firing me just when I'm at my most useful to this company. You used to be an honest man, Rick. A dull son of a bitch, but at least an honest one. And now you're just like any other boardroom crook, with your honour up for sale to the highest bidder. Do you need a second beach house in the Hamptons that badly?'

'You're no saint yourself,' Kravitz said lamely.

'Maybe so. But I'm not a thief.'

Rowena hung up on him. She didn't want to hear one more word. All the nerves were gone now. Without pausing, she grabbed the phone and dialled for a third time.

'Dan Zuckman,' said the voice.

'Dan? How big are your balls?'

He laughed. 'Those have to be the dulcet tones of Rowena Krebs. Sad to say, nobody else is going to ask me about my balls at ten o'clock in the morning.'

'Guilty as charged. Anyway, how are they hanging?'

'You're a bad girl. And they're bigger than ever. Ask my wife. I pay her to verify that, with a diamond tennis bracelet every anniversary.'

Now it was Rowena's turn to laugh. 'That's awesome, because I'm going to need one hell of a lawyer. And he's going to have to have balls of steel.'

'You certainly know how to talk dirty to a litigator,' Dan answered. 'Who am I suing? The President of the United States?'

'Almost as bad, and five times as well resourced. How about Conrad Miles?'

There was a long pause at the end of the phone. When her

friend spoke next, all the levity was gone from his voice.

'Rowena, I've been your lawyer for twenty years, and if you did want to sue the President, I would be all over it for you. If you feel you need to litigate against Conrad Miles, I can do that too. But you'll lose. And then I'll lose. All of my client base. That's the way he operates. The guy shows no mercy. I know you got fired from Musica, and that completely sucks. But if you owned every last share of stock, and all the masters that all the acts on your label ever recorded, you still wouldn't have even one per cent of Miles Industries' wealth.'

'So we can't fight him?' Rowena's heart sank. Dan would never give her bad advice. 'Really?'

'We can approach him and try to get a settlement. As your lawyer, that's the best I can advise you to do.'

'But the facts here—'

'Listen to what I'm saying. The facts are irrelevant. Conrad Miles is a *machine*. Save yourself and Michael years of pain and heartache. You'll spend every cent you have, and you'll still lose. The two of you will wind up living off public assistance in the Valley.'

'I beat him once before,' Rowena said. 'I saved Musica back then.'

'Yes. That was amazing. And in case you didn't notice, Conrad Miles was so burned by that experience that he's never lost a deal since.'

'You think it's why he's coming after me now? Unfinished business?'

'My therapist tells me never to ask a question when I already know the answer.'

Rowena said nothing. For the first time since her firing, she felt trapped. At a loss. She had no idea what was going to happen next.

'If you want to come downtown and see me, we can schedule a conference any time. Maybe there's something I can use in a settlement proposal . . .'

'No. You're right. This is personal to him. He doesn't want to settle with me; he wants to punish me. I'm the only woman who's ever beaten him.'

'Well, there was one other, if you want to get technical. Wasn't your friend Topaz part of that?'

The cold fist clutching Rowena's heart tightened its grip a little.

'Yes,' she said. 'Yes, she was.'

Krebs watched Rowena move towards the phone as it rang in the cradle. Outside the apartment, the kids were kicking a soccer ball around their little patch of green.

'Hello?'

Her face clouded slightly, and she swallowed. 'Yes, of course. He's here.' She offered him the phone. 'It's Debbie.'

Even today, his stomach turned over at the thought of the two of them speaking, despite the fact that Debbie was long remarried, very happy away from him. He was annoyed that Rowena had picked up. Why didn't she check the number before jumping on it like that?

'Hi.' His heart was in his mouth. 'What's the news?'

'There's a treatment he might be good for. Experimental. They shoot radio-charged beads right into the liver. It targets cancers when they're scattered.'

'What are the risks?'

'Further liver damage,' his ex-wife said. 'His white blood cells would need to be up significantly from where they are now even to try it.'

'OK. OK. What does his oncologist think?'

'Says it's a finely balanced risk. Insurance won't cover this . . .'

'No problem. You don't even have to ask, you know that.'

'You've been great. The nurse is working out really well. Amelia told me you got one that can cook.'

Krebs cracked a thin smile. Outside, his other two kids were barrelling around in the sunshine like they had all the life force

248

in the world bottled up inside those teenage legs.

'I figured she might as well make herself useful and force-feed him.'

'The plan's working. Marty says he's never eaten so much broccoli or blueberries in his life.'

Krebs laughed. 'I want to come up there again, meet with the doctors.'

Debbie sighed. 'Michael, maybe wait a little while. Get on with your life.'

His hackles rose. 'Marty *is* my life.'

'Yes, but he doesn't need us crowding him. All you're going to do is transmit anxiety if you hover around him. Plan on flying in every six weeks, why not, and calling him on the phone every couple of days. I can ask him to have Dr Rosenthal call you.'

'Please do that, Debbie. I want to speak to whoever's treating him.'

'They're testing for the next round of results on Monday. See what the chemo did for him.'

'OK,' Krebs said. 'Whatever. I'll pay whatever you need for anything he might want.'

'Great. Well, I'm sure his doctor will call tomorrow.'

He wanted to ask how she was, how she was taking this, but she had already hung up.

Krebs cradled the phone to his chest.

'I'll call the kids in for supper,' Rowena said.

'I might sit this one out.'

'But Michael . . . it's curry, that's meant to be your favourite, and—'

'Leave me alone.' He knew he was snapping at her, but he couldn't help it. 'Give me some space.'

'I know it's a lot of money,' Dr Rosenthal said.

'The money's not the issue. You can have whatever it takes. I just want to know what this will do for my son.' Michael's mouth was dry. He had never been this out of control in his life.

'So far, the tumours have proven resistant to our chemo. They've been pegged back a little in some places; they are growing slowly in others.'

Michael felt physical terror. 'God. No.'

'What I want to do is cut them out. They are mostly concentrated in one half of the liver. I could excise that. It's a lot of tissue to lose, but the liver is one of the most resilient organs in the body. That's why alcoholics survive.'

'There's a but here . . .'

'*But* . . . there are a few small tumours on the other side. I need to target them precisely and get rid of them. That way I can have enough healthy tissue when the liver is cut away.'

'Do it. I can get you that money by tomorrow.'

'Good. This operation will require a lot of staff, that's why the cost is so—'

'Unimportant.' Krebs cut her off. 'Doctor, times like this are what money is for.'

'I'm glad you have that attitude. If it works, we may be able to get more insurance companies to cover the treatment. You'd be helping other families, if that means anything to you.'

Krebs nodded. In another life, it would have meant something, but at this minute, he only gave a shit about Martin Krebs. His world had a population of one.

'I'd like to come up and see my son after the operation.'

'You have to arrange that with him, Mr Krebs. I'm only speaking to you now because he gave me permission. You know that.' Dr Rosenthal paused. 'It wouldn't change if you were funding my entire hospital.'

'I'll talk to Marty. Thanks, Doc.'

Krebs clicked the phone shut, feeling more helpless than ever. But that was something he had to deal with.

Debbie was right. Flying up to see Marty could wait another

day. He had to get back into the game. It was time to regain control, for everyone's sake.

Fuck it, he thought. Retirement sucks anyway.

Michael Krebs stood with his builder on a small hillock far back from the cliff face. It was another gorgeous day in Malibu; the mid-morning sun beat down on them, and a light breeze ruffled the tough grasses and sea pinks that dominated the oceanside landscape. He breathed in the salt scent of the air, and occasionally the wind blew refreshing droplets of sea foam into their faces. There were one or two fluffy white clouds scudding across the sky, and seagulls wheeled overhead, screeching now and again, diving into the warm sea to fish.

The studio was enormous. Set on four acres, it was designed in a long, low crescent, so that every room had a glass-walled view right out to sea. The dune garden had been cleverly planted with ultra-low-maintenance shrubs and grasses, in keeping with a clifftop setting. At one end of the garden was a massive swimming pool, Olympic-sized, and heated with the latest solar technology. It was screened from view of the house on three sides by mature cypress trees, specially imported from Italy. A large, marble decking area had been laid around the pool. Loungers and coffee tables were strategically placed, together with movable sunshades to protect all the rockers and rappers who worried about their skin. The far side of the pool faced out to sea, so Michael's overpaid clients could swim to the edge and look directly into a vast, shimmering expanse of water.

That feeling of solitude was very important. Michael got that about musicians, the successful ones whose lives were spent trying to put on an act for millions of other people. When they were creating music, he wanted them to have space.

A great studio was about more than just good recording equipment. It was about the men inside it, the vibe, the musicians who were playing there. Part of the genius of Michael Krebs was that he understood the second half of the equation. Bands could spend six months, sometimes longer, holed up in a recording studio. If you wanted their best work, it was about more than faders and mixers.

'Man.' Karol Adamek had built Michael and Rowena's own house. His crew worked fast and well, they stuck to budget, and for the last decade Michael had used them for every project he had. 'This is incredible. I've never seen anything like it. If I worked here, I'd never leave.'

'That was the general idea.'

'What's that building in the corner of the plot?' Karol pointed to a large structure, two storeys high, constructed in a modernist, beach house vibe. The dove-grey exterior was made of shingle boards and tinted glossy woods that reflected the light cast from the ocean waves.

'That's my fitness centre. The lower floor is full of weight equipment, all the best stuff, plus a showering and changing area. It's mirrored, and the fourth wall faces the water. It's always good to look out at the ocean. Inspiring if you're trying to get healthy. The top floor is cardio. I have commercial-quality treadmills, elliptical machines, rowers, stair climbers, anything you can think of, pretty much. They can run and contemplate the Pacific. Behind that is a yoga studio with mats. Men use it for stretching and Pilates, and sometimes the girl groups or the soul singers want me to import their favourite dance teachers or yoga gurus.'

Karol stared at him. 'That's mind-blowing. Did anybody tell you it might be overkill?'

Michael shook his head. 'It gets better work from the artist. Most producers don't think like an executive should. Record companies and managers love me, even when I'm not behind that mixing desk myself. This place is so nice, even the worst prima donnas want to come here.' He laughed. 'And I'm emergency surgery when a band's schedule is really tight. They can edit a track, work on a remix, and practise choreography all in one space. Anyplace else, your superstar is wasting valuable primping time driving up and down the freeway to LA.'

'So it was worth it?'

'Totally. I recoup my investment twenty times over. We're booked solid. Or at least we were until Rowena got fired. I was due to make three Musica records in a row.'

'That sucks. I'm sorry.'

'Don't be. That's why you're here. They gave me a huge opportunity. I'm done with recording music. It's time for a new generation to take over. My work's not going anywhere; I want to rest on those laurels. And maybe get some new ones.'

And make some real cash, he didn't say. The cheque to the hospital was painfully huge. A quarter of a million dollars for experimental treatment. And who knew how often Marty might need more?

'So you want to develop it. Smart move, man. This site alone is worth . . .' Karol threw his hands in the air. 'I can't even tell you. It's acres of prime Malibu beachfront. And then more acres of grass behind. Great freeway access; you already have the pool and the gym . . . people will line up to buy apartments here. Even in the existing building alone, I can fit twenty two-bedrooms and another ten three-bedrooms. Maybe more, depending on your floor plan. But you need that planning permission. Know any politicians?'

'You should know me better than that.' Michael Krebs smiled. 'I went and got the planning permits last summer. They're valid for another eighteen months. But I'm not interested in just converting the studio. I have comprehensive plans for a range of low-level green-themed apartment buildings. We're going to create more than a single unit. I sold them on creating a fresh Malibu neighbourhood. What do you think about that?'

Karol whistled. 'I think it's a great idea, but Michael, even if I quit every other project we have lined up tomorrow, I don't have nearly enough guys to make this work for you. You need a major public works manager. And a massive bank loan.'

'I know. That's why I need you to go into the community and find me guys who will join us and work on the space. Legal residents, no union. You can use Americans, Mexicans, Lithuanians, I don't give a damn. I will pay a day rate, and offer good breaks and conditions. You know how we do business. But I don't want to be dependent on the banks.' Krebs ran a hand over his bald head. 'Somebody's fucking with Rowena, and that means if I go get a loan, they'll fuck with me too. Here is what I propose. If you can put me together the right crew, and work on this with the right budget, I'll set aside ten per cent of the equity for your workers. They'll share in the profit pool. I'm not going to sell these apartments. I'm going to rent them. All of them. You source materials, no skimping, the best we've got. And I pay for them. One building at a time. Then we start renting out, premium rate. That income, those deposits, pays for the next building. And so forth. You personally? As the project manager, you take one per cent. But this is pay or play. Nobody vests until the entire project is finished, on time or earlier, and under budget.'

There was silence, nothing but the gulls screeching overhead into the wind, and the crashing of the warm ocean waves on to the white sand of Malibu's beaches.

'Will there be enough for a per diem? Food?'

'Yes, but it'll be basic. This only works if guys want to own something at the end of it. Otherwise, I go the conventional route. Banks, big construction firms.' Michael grinned. 'But that would be no fun.'

Karol whistled. 'I never heard of a deal like that.'

'It's for young men, yes. Guys without families and mortgages, guys with ambition, guys who'd like to sacrifice now to get some real money for themselves at the end of it. Ten per cent. Straight up. The crew you hire gets ten per cent in perpetuity. That way, they'll build it fast and well and cheap. They'll have a piece.

A nest egg. Enough to get them off the streets, buy an apartment of their own, maybe. I want a great crew and there's not much upfront cash, so . . .' Krebs shrugged. 'Let's be creative.'

Rowena had made the same pitch to him once, long ago, when she'd asked him to produce her baby act for nothing. He'd done it – waived millions in fees. Atomic Mass were a mega-hit, and made both their fortunes.

'I love it. It's fucking great,' Karol said, after a pause. 'Let me go talk to some people. I'll come back to you tomorrow.'

'Great. But come back with a yes, a crew, and a wrecking ball. We need to get to work.'

Karol took one last look at the recording studio, its curved surface gleaming in the sun. 'You're really not sentimental, are you, Krebs?'

Michael shrugged. 'The music we made is what matters. The studio's just a tool. And I can be very sentimental.' He smiled thinly. 'The sentiment I'm feeling now, for example, is rage.'

Karol extended his hand. 'I hear you, boss. I'm in.'

Chapter Fifteen

'I think you're so brave.' Kim reached over and put her hand gently on Topaz's knee. 'To be able to deal with all of this so publicly, and still do your job in the way you have to.'

Topaz smiled back at her. The presenter was genuinely sympathetic, and it showed. This was good TV, she could already tell.

'Women struggle with balancing their personal lives and their jobs every day, even when nothing's going wrong. Even when it's just your teenager telling you she hates you because you won't let her paint her fingernails black.'

The audience laughed loudly. There was applause.

'We have to stop trying to pretend we're superwomen, and that we are somehow failures if anything bad happens in our lives.' Topaz raised her head and looked directly at the audience, appealing to their sympathetic smiles. 'So much pressure on women today comes from trying to save face. Oh, I'm totally fine that my husband left me. I never wanted that promotion anyway. I can't find a good place for my kids to go to school, maybe it's just better they stay where they are. We need to be able to say "I hate it, I'm upset." And then just go right on with whatever we were doing before.'

There was another huge round of applause, this time including whistles.

'You may have touched a nerve there,' said Kim. 'But I have to ask you, Topaz, don't you think your industry has contributed to this? All those perfect pictures in women's magazines? None of our daughters can be pretty enough, thin enough . . .'

The audience clapped again. Topaz could see the heads of the women tilted towards her, more hostile now, waiting for her answer.

'You know, Kim, you're a hundred per cent right. That's where I think *American Girl* is about to change history. I've taken charge myself. And it's a big risk.' She looked directly at the camera now. 'For the first time, we've got a cover model who hasn't been Photoshopped. In fact, there's no airbrushing in our editorial features at all.'

The audience went wild. They cheered, they clapped, they drummed their feet on the floor.

'Thank you,' Topaz said. 'Thank you so much.'

'Wait a minute,' Kim said. 'This is big news. Let me see if I've got this straight. We're not just talking about some one-off spread where they experiment with natural photos? This is the entire magazine?'

'Yes, ma'am.'

'And so this is a special issue? What about next month? I'm guessing you go back to normal.'

'We do not. From now on, *American Girl* is going to be airbrush-free. If a model has a pimple, the make-up artist uses concealer. After all, that's exactly what our teenagers do. Even pretty girls get spots. And if you're twenty-five? You might have a couple of wrinkles round your eyes. Even on your forehead. Women age, girls get acne, redheads have freckles . . . and we're all beautiful.'

The applause for Topaz was now so loud it took Kim several seconds of waving to calm them down.

'Wow! That really is ground-breaking. Could this be a new direction for the magazine industry?'

'I don't believe in telling other people what to do. But this is our choice. And even our advertisers will find their commercials labelled if they use airbrushing. Consumers need to know.'

'Topaz Rossi, thank you so much. That special issue of *American Girl* hits the news-stands on Monday. And I can't wait to go out and get my copy. Give it up for Topaz!'

The thunderous applause continued even when the camera lights switched off and a tech ran in to unclip Topaz's microphone so she could walk off the set during the commercial break.

'You were absolutely amazing,' Kim whispered. 'You can expect to see that on the news bulletins tomorrow.'

'Thanks for the opportunity,' Topaz said. She left the stage with the whistles and cheers of the audience ringing in her ears.

'That was sensational,' muttered Margaret Laing, American Magazines' vice president of corporate PR, who was following Topaz around from interview to interview. 'Best one yet. I have no idea how you keep this up. You've said something different everywhere we've been!'

'Because I want them to get the message. I want them all to use the interview. They're in the same business I am.' Topaz was suddenly hit with a wave of exhaustion. 'Is the car ready? Going back to the office will seem like a vacation after today.'

'Your driver's waiting for you. I'll take you out there.' Margaret moved forward, nodding and smiling at everyone. She seemed in a good mood, and Topaz's spirits lifted, despite her tiredness. Margaret would get the praise or the blame, depending on how well this little PR jaunt turned out; Topaz herself was just happy that she had aced it. 'This way. But what did you mean, we're all in the same business? They don't sell magazines. I suppose they sometimes do features on style . . .'

'No. The content creation business. Ultimately, we all have to entertain. So I need to give every one of these guys some unique content, something the other show or interview or blog didn't get. American Magazines would never interview a star without an exclusive angle. So I didn't want to be just a walking press release. If everybody gets their own private angle, then they will use it. Otherwise, the piece gets buried. Just out here? Oh great, there he is. Hi, Harold. You look like a giant Swedish angel of mercy.'

Harold laughed aloud. 'And you look like a twenty-five-year-old model. So we're even.'

Margaret started chattering about the audience demographics for the last three TV shows they'd done. Topaz leaned her neck back against the headrest of buttery yellow leather, and closed her eyes.

Don't fall asleep.

She fixated on getting back to work, hearing the buzz from the news-stands. Subscribers would receive their copies tomorrow; on Monday, the first shipments would hit the shelves. Topaz had done all the prep she could. Now it was out of her hands. It was America's young women who would decide.

And the crazy thing about all this? *American Girl* was just one magazine. In the next two months, Topaz was going to have to repeat this circus all over again. Different titles. Different markets. Same challenge.

'Why aren't we moving?' she said sleepily.

'We're stuck in traffic, Ms Rossi,' Harold said. 'Once it starts moving again, we're about four blocks from the office.'

'That's OK. You take Margaret back. I'm going to get out here and walk. It'll be quicker.'

And with that, she grabbed her purse and opened the side door, threading her way through the stationary cars, ignoring the blasts of the horns, turning on to the sidewalk, and striding off with a determined look on her face.

Margaret Laing closed the passenger door behind her. 'Wow. That girl's in one hell of a hurry.'

'Ma'am, you have no idea,' said her driver. And he smiled.

* * *

Joe Goldstein lay back on the bed. Maria's mouth was working overtime. She was sucking him, licking him, moving her lips up and down his cock like a piston pump. That world-class ass was clearly visible down the line of her back, rising like two glorious golden-brown peaks. Porno style, she was jiggling it as she sucked him, letting the soft flesh shake while she gave him head.

She was every man's fantasy. Yet Goldstein was barely maintaining his erection.

'Mmm,' Maria said, breathing out a little between sucks. 'Joe, baby, you're so hot . . .'

Maybe. But not for her.

Desperately he looked away from her, clamping his eyelids shut. That was better, when he couldn't see her. Long ago, in the days before Topaz, when he used to fuck everything that moved, young Joe Goldstein sometimes wound up in bed with a girl who wasn't all that. She might have a flat ass, or flabby thighs, or tits that had looked great in a push-up bra in a nightclub but which sagged and flopped when he got her into a hotel room. Being too much of a gentleman ever to walk out on an aroused female, though, Joe had mastered the art of closing his eyes and fantasising about a girl whose perfect body looked just like Maria's.

Yet now he was actually with Maria, her round, perky ass, her big, firm tits, and her gorgeous cocksucker lips were turning him *off*.

Joe tried to concentrate on the sensation of that welcoming, greedy wetness sliding up and down his shaft, so badly wanting him to come. He hardened just a little more, and heard Maria moan with pleasure. She was working him all right, as much as any hooker. But at this rate they'd be there till morning. Her tongue was relentless, but the feeling was almost painful. It was never like this with Topaz. She only moaned when she meant it; she didn't indulge in theatrics . . .

When Joe wanted head, he just came up behind Topaz, ran his hands down her back, cupped the cheeks of her ass possessively.

And when her breath quickened with lust, he would spin her around, place his hands on her shoulders, and push her firmly down on her knees, right in front of him. No talking. No nothing. Topaz would already be wet and hot; she'd unbutton his fly, tug his boxers down, and start sucking his painfully erect cock, right there, wherever they were. The bedroom, the living room rug, locked into a bathroom at some friends' boring dinner party . . . Topaz blew him everywhere. God, she was so good at it, and he loved to return the favour, teasing her with his fingertip, his tongue, even the palm of his hand, whenever they were somewhere that fucking was impossible . . .

'Oh my God,' Joe cried out. He thrashed around on the bed 'Oh God . . .'

She was licking, sucking, swallowing him. He felt her mouth and tongue around him again, cleaning up, kissing him. No doubt about it, Maria was a great sexpot.

For someone else.

'Baby, that was wonderful.' Joe reached down the bed, sitting up slightly, which moved his cock out of target range. His strong arms lifted her up easily, her weight nothing to his strength. He pulled her close to him, and forced himself to kiss her on the lips.

'I knew it! I knew you'd get there,' Maria purred. 'I know how to treat you right, baby . . .'

'You're just stunning. You're every man's dream.' He kissed her again, on the forehead this time, and swung his legs over the bed, feeling the relief of a convict finally about to walk free of the prison gates. 'I've got to go.'

'What, already?'

'I know. I wish I could stay,' Goldstein lied. 'But we're pursuing a major new acquisition strategy in the office, and I have to write up a deal memo. It's going to take all day.'

Maria pouted. 'Oh well, I guess this is what it's like dating a busy executive. I hope things calm down for you soon, baby. I want to take you to Beverly Hills, to meet my aunt and cousin.'

The very thought of that made Goldstein feel ill. Luckily, he was already making good his escape, halfway towards her guest bathroom, so Maria never saw the wince on his face.

'Let's talk about all that later.'

Before she could reply, he strode into the marble wet room and turned the taps on, drowning out her voice. The hot water was welcome. He grabbed soap, washed himself thoroughly. He wanted to be clean.

Because for the first time in his adult life, sex had left Joe Goldstein feeling dirty.

This wasn't going to end well. That much he knew already. Maria wasn't the forgiving type. But he no longer gave a damn. He'd fucked her. Worse than that, he'd fucked up.

He soaped himself again, rinsed, grabbed a towel. He let the water stay running so she wouldn't come in to accost him. His clothes were in the cupboard, where he'd left them last night, planning this escape the moment he came in. He dressed hastily. Not until he was ready to go did he lean in, push up his shirtsleeves and turn the shower off.

'Joe . . .' Maria's voice floated in from the bedroom. Goldstein emerged from the bathroom, fully dressed, shoes on, jacket and tie.

'Maria, I really have to go. But I promise I'll be in touch.'

'I love you, honey,' she called.

'Have a good day. Call you later.'

Joe let himself out, shutting the door of her apartment behind him, and ran towards the elevators. He punched the button. As he waited, he had to physically stop himself turning around to look at Maria's front door, as though she would emerge half naked, wrapped in a towel, pursuing him on his way out.

Don't be insane. This isn't Fatal Attraction. *Maria's a grown woman. She can have anyone she wants.*

Except me.

When the lift arrived, he stepped inside with a feeling of relief mixed with panic. His path was set. He was dumping Maria. Not one more day, one more night of this total madness. Being with her wasn't alpha male; it was about as beta a move as you could get. He didn't want to date this woman. He didn't even want to fuck her any more. He'd agreed to it out of fear. Fear of facing what he'd done to Topaz.

On a break. Separated. Not cheating. That was all bullshit, of course, the purest bullshit, but Joe had leaped on it to save his self-image. And on top of that, there was Maria's ambition, his board's demands, Maria's guilt-tripping, and Rowena's arrival forcing him into a public defence when he didn't even want to be there.

Calling his wife. Again and again. Wanting to apologise, to explain. As if you could. *I only need a month. Can I get a temporary cheating licence? I swear I'll never do it again.*

When he finally got to speak to her, of course, it was nothing like that. It was brutal. He would rather go ten rounds in a ring with Mike Tyson than suffer the way Topaz had made him hurt. And he would rather pull out his own fingernails with a rusty pair of pliers than do that publicity circus in front of the cameras with Maria again.

As to the conversation with his kids . . . Goldstein couldn't even *think* about that. He didn't have the means to process the pain. Their distance, emotionally, physically. It sounded like David was speaking from the bottom of a deep well. It sounded like Rona was choking back tears, forced to talk to him. They said they were well, staying with the Krebses. They asked him to stay off TV. They said they loved him. And that hurt the most.

Goldstein had hung up, tears streaming down his face. It took an hour to compose himself. And try to think of a way out of this goddamned bear trap.

Not so easy. He'd made a deal. He'd made a promise. To give Maria Gonzales one month of his life. And less than a week into it, he was going to back the fuck out.

The elevator bumped to a halt in the parking garage. His Lexus was parked in one of the guest slots. Gratefully, he climbed in, put it in gear and drove out on to the street. Photographers were waiting. He stared straight ahead, not looking at them, not giving them anything. If the picture was boring enough, they might not use it. Finally he was able to inch through the small knot of men. He'd take 10th Avenue at this time of the morning, better than the West Side highway. Not that it mattered. Any road was good. Any place away from the media, and his ex-girlfriend.

Within minutes he was parking again, this time under NAB's building, in that nice, wide, easy-to-reach CEO slot.

He wondered just how long he would have it.

No. Screw that. I'm good at this job. Great at it. I wouldn't fire a vice president if she had an affair with the chairman of the board. I shouldn't have banged Maria, it was stupid, but it's personal.

Cheered by the thought, Goldstein stepped out of the vehicle and straight into the executive elevator. It was that golden hour of the morning, 6 a.m., at least an hour before even the earliest risers bounced into the office. He was alone. He could do his best thinking.

He walked over to the coffee machine and set it to brew something strong. Topaz was all over the TV herself, all over the radio. Reminding him what he had lost. Reminding him what he'd been dumb enough to risk. God, she was so beautiful, so brave, so strong! Exactly what you'd expect from the woman he fell in love with, so hard, more than twenty years ago. She had a work crisis, she was fixing it, and she was using Maria to sell her new magazine. Balls of steel. Joe loved it. He hoped he got the chance to tell her.

The coffee pot hissed. It was making good smells. He poured himself a large, steaming mug and took it back to his office. Dumping Maria was something he needed to do for himself. He didn't want to be with her, and that was the end of it. There were polite ways to say that, decent ways to tell her. He would try to be respectful. But he wouldn't be bullied into staying with her one more hour.

He drank his coffee and looked out of the window at the sun rising over the Manhattan skyscrapers that clustered around Midtown. Traffic was slowly beginning to build up. The bagel shops were opening. Bankers and junior lawyers were heading into work, showing how macho they were turning up at this hour. Joe relished it. He understood that feeling: ambition and power, money beating up from the sidewalk, the rhythm of the city. Better than sex. Except when it was with Topaz.

That was the problem. His wife. How much longer would they be apart? She'd taken off her wedding ring, he'd seen that on TV. And in the phone call, she'd told him she only wanted to deal with his lawyer. His entire collection of worldly possessions turning up in the office lobby had cemented his fears.

He could walk away from his mistress, but that was no guarantee Topaz would take him back. That fiery Italian temper was bubbling. And if Topaz was sad now – and Joe had no doubt about that – when he came crawling back to her, begging for forgiveness, all that sorrow would mutate into weapons-grade rage.

Couples therapy. Endless fights. Topaz would throw this in his face until they both dropped dead. Maria's body would insert itself between them long after he walked away from it and its temporary pleasures. How long would he be fucking a ghost? Topaz would never trust him again. And in the end, because this was human nature, Joe would get tired of apologising, and their fights would start all over again.

He could go back to his apartment tonight, if Topaz let him. But could he ever go home?

The coffee was getting cold. He drained the rest of the mug and booted up his computer. The trouble with love was it involved somebody else. Was that why men resisted it? You couldn't control the variables. And he hated being out of control.

Work, on the other hand? His career belonged to him.

And it was time to get back to business.

'Topaz! Thank God you're back.' Lucy Klein ran up to her on kitten heels the second Topaz walked through the door.

'What's the problem now?'

'No problem. Quite the opposite. Unless you count the paper mountain of message slips that are piling up on your desk.' Lucy smiled. 'Your assistant is doing her best, but she just can't cope. I've asked the interns to sit in and handle your calls. It's like air traffic control. Rack 'em, pack 'em, and stack 'em.'

Topaz stared down at the younger woman. 'I don't get it.'

'Never mind Maria Gonzales. You're the big star today. This office has never seen anything like it.'

'You mean, like fan mail?' Topaz asked slowly.

'That's *exactly* what I mean. They *loved* you. We're getting calls from all over. You've got high school seniors, moms from the Midwest, college professors – we had somebody call in from Stanford. This idea is going viral. Have you seen your Twitter feed?'

'Twitter? No. I leave that stuff to the kids.'

'Then you seriously need to call your kids. Somebody has posted a thank you message with a thousand-plus retweets. You gained more than a quarter of a million followers today.'

'It's like you're speaking a different language.'

'Really?' Lucy said, eyebrows knitting. 'Do you want me to try to explain?'

'No. I'm kidding. I don't tweet much, but I think I remember my password. I'll post something. Meanwhile, have somebody go through the pile of rejected interns, and call up the first eight on the list. We need every one of these messages to get a personalised response from *American Girl*. And the staffers don't have time.

This is fun, but first thing tomorrow morning you guys start work on the next issue. Is that clear?'

'Yes, ma'am.'

'Eight interns. Got it?'

Lucy hovered uncertainly, but then decided Topaz was serious. 'I'll have somebody make those calls right now.'

'Let's talk to the switchboard. We need to have the fan calls diverted. Today's when we expect to hear from news-stands. I don't want the buyers unable to get through. My assistant, your assistant, that's all they should be dealing with. Understand?'

Lucy nodded, and Topaz softened. She could see the younger woman was trying to learn, take notes. This was probably the most exciting thing that had happened in her professional life. And Topaz didn't blame her; to be honest, even though she was playing it cool, it was pretty goddamned exciting to her too.

This felt big. This felt like a hit. The hit to end all hits. In fact, Topaz Rossi felt as though she was twenty-two years old again.

'Make sure the sales team are at the end of the phones too. And get the tech guys in here. I want to see a complete revamp of the website. Little tasters of every great feature we're running. Button to buy underneath. Buttons to share them on social media, too.'

'Yes. OK. Right away.'

'Start with those interns. I'll be in my office.'

Topaz walked over to her small corner room, passing her assistant's desk as she went. 'Did you catch any of that?'

'Yes, Ms Rossi. All of it.'

'So bring me a list of our twenty biggest news-stand suppliers. I'll work my way down it. Have somebody get the next ten names on the list to whoever is in charge of sales, the ten after that to her deputy, and so on. You with me?'

'Yes, ma'am,' Miriam said.

'Who is the first call?' Topaz asked.

'Lionel Johnson, of Hudson News. Are you ready for him?'

'Let's go.' Topaz walked into the office, sat down at her desk, and cracked her knuckles. 'And bring me a mug of coffee!' she called out through the open door. 'Before I fall asleep on my keyboard!'

She punched the first number in, and smiled as she heard the pick-up. 'Lionel. How's my favourite customer?'

'Topaz, it's because I know you love me so much that you're going to get me an extra thirty per cent capacity by Tuesday morning. I'm getting killed over here. The kids demanded to see – and buy – all of our stock before tomorrow morning. It's almost gone.'

'Lionel, you're a bad boy,' Topaz said. 'You know that's embargoed.'

'Embargo nothing. You've been selling these like they were lifeboats on the *Titanic*. I need more stock.'

'I can send you more. You're my first call. I have a feeling some of the other guys might be wanting the same thing,' Topaz said, the adrenalin high rushing through her system. Maybe she wouldn't need that coffee after all. 'I have to save some of the stock for them. What about United?'

'Fuck United! You think I give a shit about what they want?'

'Until they poach you to run their news-stands and I remind you of this conversation.'

Lionel laughed. '*Mazel tov*, Topaz. This is one of your best moves.'

She glowed. 'Who are you, and what did you do with Lionel? He never gives out compliments.'

'Moment of weakness,' the old-timer growled. 'Don't get used to it. So thirty per cent? We're good?'

'Fifteen, and only because you flirted with me. Otherwise it would've been ten.'

'You're a miser, Topaz. You know that, right?'

'Lionel, if the rest of my calls are like you, I'll have the printing presses run off more stock today. And I'll get it to you the second we can. Distribution will be primed. I promise you that.'

'I'll take your lousy fifteen per cent, but only because I have to.'

'That's normally a great reason. Now get off the phone. I've got other people waiting.'

'Sweet talker,' he said, and hung up.

A young girl in a pencil skirt walked in, eyes full of awe, and placed in front of Topaz a steaming cup of coffee and a neatly typed call sheet.

Topaz mouthed her thanks and took a swallow of the rich cinnamon coffee. It tasted fantastic, like the best thing she'd ever drunk. Excitement rippled through her. She dialled the next number on her list.

'Matilda! It's Topaz. Any interest out there in our new issue?'

'We're dying over here. You need to get me some more of these magazines. I can't keep up with the demand . . .'

'Just one second, Tilly,' said Topaz. She put the call on hold, then dialled an internal number. 'Production? This is Topaz Rossi. I'm authorising you to increase the print run on the current issue of *American Girl* by another fifty per cent. Depending on the response I get in the next couple of hours, I may need to double it.'

'Fifty? That's huge. I can do it, we have enough paper stock ready to go, but we'll have to buy in if you want to double the run. Can you fax me through a written authorisation?'

'Yes. You'll receive it in the next five minutes. Meanwhile, start printing. I need to ship these babies out tomorrow morning.'

'You got it, Ms Rossi. Presses are *rolling*.'

Topaz switched back to her waiting call. 'Tilly, exactly how much interest do you have?'

'Seriously, Topaz, we need to double our order. How quickly can we get them?'

'You're kidding me.' Topaz tapped at the screen before her. 'Hold on a second. Northern Newsagents' orders for *American Girl* have really sunk in the last six months.'

'Yes, but now we need to go back to what we used to order. Everybody's talking about this magazine. It's like you stapled a twenty-dollar bill to the front cover!'

'So you're saying I shouldn't punish you for being such a bad customer?'

'Don't be like that, Topaz. The customer is always right. Besides, you know perfectly well that your title was sucking donkey balls before you came in to fix it.'

'Elegantly put,' Topaz laughed. 'I'll see what I can do.'

By the end of the day, Topaz had spoken to twenty suppliers, all begging for more copy. The print run was doubled. She left junior magazine execs dealing with the smaller chains, and moved down the hall to the sales teams' offices. Phones were ringing off the hook there too. Advertisers who'd taken a chance with their offers and discounts for this issue were calling to say how grateful they were; many more of them were ringing up to get a piece of the action in the next month's issue, paying full price, asking for double-page spreads. The sales team were hastily putting together spreadsheets, calculating just how many advertisements they could cram into a single issue.

'No price gouging,' Topaz said. 'Charge them our regular price. And it's first come, first served. I don't want the next issue to be any heavier than a September *Vogue*.'

She waited, but nobody laughed. The 2014 September *Vogue* had been a record-breaker, with almost five hundred pages of advertising alone.

'Let's put a limit on this. Cut them off at four hundred pages. After that, advertisers can book in for the November issue.'

'You snooze, you lose,' said Brad Whitley, head of sales, joyfully. He could see his year-end bonus growing bigger by the minute.

Topaz looked around. 'It's six thirty. I'm going home. Let's set up a staff meeting at ten thirty tomorrow, sharp. Main conference room. Every employee. If anybody has a meeting that clashes, cancel it. See you then.'

They all pulled out their smartphones and started tapping at them. As Topaz stood up and walked out, one young man started clapping. Soon the whole room was joining in, and then the noise spread to the hallways, to photography, editorial, and now the entire magazine was applauding.

Topaz stopped by the door, lifted one hand, and waved at the staff whose jobs she'd just saved.

'Great work, everybody,' she said. 'See you tomorrow.'

Her apartment was done. Jason had redecorated it exactly as Topaz had instructed him to. All the old, painful traces of Joe had completely disappeared. There were new hangings, wallpapers, cushions scattered everywhere. He'd rearranged the furniture, taking some pieces out, packing others away, inserting a couple of new glass coffee tables. Her photos were artfully grouped, and it was as though Joe Goldstein had never been there among them. The oranges, yellows and reds Topaz had requested were now all over the space, in cushions, rugs, throws, even hand-fired glass beakers. And an old portrait of Joe, presumably now in storage, had cleverly been replaced by a giant replica print – Topaz Rossi on the cover of *Forbes* magazine. She chuckled when she saw it; the guy really was a magician.

Of course, it still hurt. Topaz couldn't wipe away the love of her life with a new coat of paint. But the less she was reminded of Joe, the less she would have to endure the daggers of pain that stabbed her through the heart whenever he so much as entered her mind.

And that was something.

Don't let him mess you up now. Not today. Today was incredible. Topaz Rossi, career girl, all over again.

She picked up the phone to call the kids. David told her that the call with Joe had gone OK, and Topaz didn't have it in her to press for further details. Rona reported how much she loved the pool. They were going out with the Krebs kids to a party that night, some screening of an indie film.

'No drinking, remember. You're not twenty-one yet. And no smoking. Tobacco will kill you. All that tar. And definitely no pot. Marijuana makes you paranoid, I don't care what those California hippies tell you . . .'

'Mom, really. Stop being embarrassing. Pot's practically legal here. It's legal in Colorado . . .'

'Yes, well. You're not in Colorado, young lady.'

'And what were you doing when you were our age?' David demanded.

'When I was your age, I was working nights at the local diner to save some money so I could take up my scholarship to Oxford. See, my parents didn't *want* me to go. And they didn't have any cash anyway. So I guarantee you,' Topaz said triumphantly, 'that I wasn't wasting my allowance on weed.'

There was a moment's silence.

'Well, Mom, that's why you worked so hard. To give us the kind of advantages that you never got.' David and Rona giggled.

'Very slick,' Topaz said. 'I mean it.'

'Sure, Mom, sure.'

She sighed. They were teenage kids; rebellion was almost mandatory. 'If you're going to smoke, at least use e-cigarettes, OK? It's the tar that kills you.'

They hung up, and Topaz felt a little better.

What now? This was the kind of moment she should be sharing with Joe. An amazing day at work, her company rescued, her personal reputation through the roof . . . Tomorrow the sales figures would be in, and they would show a failing magazine taking off like a rocket and blazing a publicity trail behind it that money couldn't buy. Only ambitious, brilliant, driven Joe Goldstein would understand the almost sexual thrill this gave her.

But Joe wasn't here – and Topaz would never get to share this with him. She would never get to share anything with him again.

Despite herself, despite her strong words, sadness began to creep over her, sending its great grey tendrils across her brain like a freezing fog, sucking the joy out of everything. Tears prickled at the back of her eyes.

No. No. I mustn't give into this.

And there *was* somebody else who'd understand.

Topaz went to the fridge, uncorked a chilled bottle of Chablis, and carefully poured herself one small glass. She took it out on to the terrace. It was a warm evening, and the fragrance from her climbing roses and lavender pots filled the air. She settled back into a cushioned lounge chair, took a long, relaxing sip of wine, and called Rowena's cell.

'Rowena? It's Topaz. Do you have five minutes?'

'For you I've got all day.'

'I've been speaking to the kids. Thanks so much again. I'm sorry I haven't talked much with you; it's been insane at the office. We've been putting the new issue to bed.'

'And? Did your strategy work?'

'Oh God, Rowena, it worked so amazingly. We're due to double our print run. The chains can't get enough. We pre-sold huge amounts of advertising. And the buzz about it is so big, I already overshot my sales target for next month, and our buying period isn't even open yet. If I say so myself, it's a goddamned triumph.' Topaz sighed. 'I shouldn't be bothering you with my little back-slapping routine, but I can't call Joe. And I guess without the kids here I just needed to talk to somebody who would understand.'

'Of course you did. Congratulations. That's awesome. You needed this right now.'

'Yes. I needed something, that's for damned sure. Tomorrow I give the team the blueprint for the next issue, and then I'm going to move on and do the same triage on our next sinking title.'

Topaz took another relaxing sip of wine. It was ice cold, and delicious. 'Forgive me for talking about myself first. I was just too excited. How's it going at Musica?'

There was a long sigh at the end of the phone. 'Oh Topaz, I love you, but I wish you hadn't called me.'

The relaxing sensation was immediately cut short. Topaz sat bolt upright on the sunlounger. 'Rowena! What is it? What's happened? Why shouldn't I call you?'

'Because,' Rowena said, 'I think I'm about to ruin your evening.'

The Spotted Pig seemed like a perfect place to meet. Joe Goldstein had chosen it with care. The English-style gastro pub had the best food in the village, if not the whole of the city, but that was a minor consideration. More importantly, stars hung out there all the time, and the restaurant knew how to protect them from rubbernecking. He and Maria would be seated at a private booth, up the stairs and way in the back. It was also small and cramped: less opportunity for her to create a giant scene.

All things considered, Goldstein would much prefer there to be as little screaming, yelling and broken crockery as possible. But he was fully prepared for it. If Maria chose to be childish, that was her lookout.

He got there early. Technically they didn't take reservations, but there was always a list – if you knew the right people. He tipped everybody liberally with hundreds, leading to raised eyebrows, a very happy coat-check girl, and *extremely* attentive service.

Joe was actually starving. While he waited, he ordered a round of chicken livers on toast and a bowl of mixed pickled vegetables. It was insanely good. Today, capitalising on the fact that Maria didn't know she was about to be dumped, and his stock was still high at the network, Goldstein had cancelled five major series, renewed one, and had excellent meetings with three of the

275

showrunners he most admired, guys who would put together something different, something really cutting-edge. TV that kids would watch again. TV you could talk about. He didn't believe the media was dead. Look at *Game of Thrones*, look at *The Daily Show*, look at *House of Cards*. It was never about television. It was always about telling the right story.

For years, NAB had coasted. No longer.

Joe was as excited about work as he was heartbroken about his marriage. Those two things occupied all his attention; he'd hardly given Maria a thought all day.

But now it was time.

She came walking up the narrow stairs, and even in this place, heads turned to look at her. She had selected a classic day dress, scarlet jersey and seamless, with modest three-quarter-length sleeves. The hemline cut off neatly above her knees, and the bodice line was high, a scoop neck that hardly revealed even a hint of cleavage.

None of that did the slightest thing to make her look less sexy. The fabric clung unforgivingly to her curves, but in Maria's case, there was nothing to forgive. Her massive breasts were right in your face. Her slender waist flared out to that uncompromisingly gorgeous ass, the rear end that made her a star. She didn't even need high heels to push it backwards, but she wore them anyway: a gorgeous pair of strappy Manolo Blahnik sandals. Her raven hair fell loose and glossy around her shoulders. She was lightly made up, for her, but it still looked like overkill to Goldstein. Maria was too young to need heavy mascara, or to have to paint roses on the apples of her naturally flushed cheeks.

Still, how she dressed wasn't Joe's problem – not any more.

She strutted across the room to their table and he stood up to greet her, kissing her on the cheek.

The waiter pulled her chair back, and Maria slipped into it. She smiled expectantly at Joe.

'So, honey, how was your day?'

'All pretty routine,' he lied. 'Shall we order?'

'What's good here? Oh, never mind, I'll have a salad with some steak.' Maria didn't even glance at the menu. She batted her eyelids at the waiter. 'Do you think the chef could make that for me?'

'Yes, ma'am. Of course we can. And what about you, Mr Goldstein?'

'I'll have the British fish and chips. Your beer batter is amazing. And the sparkling mineral water.'

'I'll take sparkling too.' Maria handed back her menu and looked at Goldstein. 'Have you spoken to the kids yet, honey?'

'Yes. We connected yesterday. I also managed to reach Topaz.'

'Finally!' Maria said. 'She's been so childish about all this!'

Goldstein breathed in. This wasn't going to get any easier the longer he put it off with small talk.

'Maria, I know this is difficult for you to hear. But reaching my family put things in perspective. You're a wonderful woman, very smart, and very sexy. But I'm in love with Topaz, and I want to go back to her.'

Holy shit. I did it.

For a second Maria Gonzales just sat there, frozen in place.

Then she rallied.

'Joe, this happens all the time when people first talk to their kids after leaving a relationship. They bounce backwards and forwards. But the things that led you to walk out in the first place – those are all still real . . .'

'That might be true. But I'm not going to go backwards and forwards on this. I've thought it through. I like you, Maria, but I don't love you. And I'm never going to love you.'

Now her face grew cold.

'It's barely been any time since we made our agreement. Is this about the TV coverage? The publicity? I have nothing to do with that.'

Untrue, Joe thought, but why fight that battle? It didn't matter.

'It's not about the press. I didn't enjoy that, but that's not my reasoning. I can't be with a woman I don't love, no matter how hot she is.'

'Joe. We've discussed this. I asked you to give me a month. And you made a deal with me . . .'

'Yes, I did. And I'm sorry about that, Maria. It was weak and stupid of me. I never should've promised you anything. Now I have to break that promise.'

'Why? What difference is another few weeks going to make? You're not even giving me a *chance* to make you happy.'

'I understand that. It doesn't change my mind, though.'

'And what about the fact that you went public? That you'll make a laughing stock of me? Doesn't that mean anything to you?'

'My thought on that is you can always say that you dumped me.'

'And will you confirm that?' Maria's dark eyes narrowed with anger. 'Because you are the first person they'll ask.'

Ouch. This was awful. But he couldn't give her nothing at all, no straw to clutch at.

He shook his head. 'The best I can do is *no comment*. I'm going to ask my wife if she'll take me back. I won't humiliate her any further. I won't agree to a fiction that makes it look as if I only went back to her when you were done with me. There's no painless way to say this, so I'm trying to be straight with you, the way I should have been in the first place. I'm ending our relationship to try and get back with my wife. Now, I won't talk about this, but I can't swear Topaz won't. I don't speak for Topaz. Never have.'

'And here we are . . .' the waiter said, bustling forward and laying a modest salad down in front of Maria. 'This is our prime aged Angus beef, which we source locally and hang out to dry for a minimum of thirty—'

'Hey, man,' Goldstein said. 'I apologise, but could you just give us our privacy, please.'

Interrupted in full flow, the waiter hesitated for a second, then nodded brightly. 'Yes, sir. Of course.'

Silently he laid the food down in front of them. Goldstein palmed him another hundred, and made a discreet little scribbling motion, indicating the bill.

'At once, sir,' said the waiter, melting away.

'So you won't even back me up?' Maria spat. 'I don't believe you. You lied to me. You just used me. Is it race, Joe? Was I just your Latina whore?'

'No!' Goldstein was shocked out of his apathy. 'How can you think that? I love my wife. It's got nothing to do with you. Race? Topaz is Italian.'

'How much did you love your wife when I was sucking your cock this morning?'

Incredibly much, Joe thought, but didn't say it.

'I shouldn't have made love to you today. I needed some time to think about how I was going to tell you.'

'And part of your thinking process was getting in one last blow job?'

'Maria. Please. Lower your voice. Eat something. If you make a scene, it'll be all over the papers tomorrow.'

'Maybe I should. Maybe I should get up on this table and scream, tell all these good people what you did to me. Tell them how you say you love your wife, but I had your cock in my mouth about eight hours ago. Maybe we could let them take a vote on just how good a husband that makes you!'

'You're better than this.'

'*You* aren't,' she hissed. 'Make sure you don't leave that part out when you call Topaz and beg her to take you back. Is this about money? Did some lawyer tell you what you'll lose in the divorce? Because I can compensate you for that. I've got more money than both of you put together.'

Goldstein's own anger was starting to build now. He could feel it, the stone in his heart heating steadily, inexorably, melting into lava, burning and bubbling like a volcano set to explode.

'I'm not a whore. And neither are you. Maria, I'm a fully grown adult. I take total responsibility for this fiasco. I embarrassed you. You hit on me, but I encouraged it. I wanted you. You were beautiful, and you made me laugh. You were something I just really needed, and I'm ashamed to say I reached out and took it. The entire thing is my fault.'

'Is this the part where I give you a round of applause?' she asked bitterly. 'Anyway, what makes you think Topaz will take you back? She probably won't touch you. And when she kicks you to the kerb, don't come running back to me. You'll be on your own. You deserve that.'

'You're right. I have no idea if she will take me back. I can only beg her to.' Joe sighed. 'But even if she doesn't, as gorgeous as you are, there's no future for us, Maria. Please hear what I'm saying. No good will come of talking about it.'

He cut into his fish and ate several mouthfuls with some fries, then swallowed a little of his mineral water. His throat was dry with talking. Maria speared a piece of steak like it was Joe's heart, and chewed it viciously. After a moment or two, she spoke.

'Maybe it's your job you should be worried about, rather than your marriage. You signed a star, right? And I signed for a bargain. You fucked me out of my market price. I should sue you. And I should sue NAB.'

Even though Joe had been expecting this, it still wasn't pleasant to hear. 'You know that's not true.'

'Do I hell!' Maria pushed back her chair and stood up dramatically. 'Enjoy your dinner, you son of a bitch! I'm going home to call my lawyer. You'll hear from him in the morning. Sleep tight, Joe.'

'Good night, Maria,' Goldstein said.

As she stormed out of the restaurant, every man in the place watched the retreat of that fabulous ass. After a second, the waiter materialised apologetically, holding the bill.

'Here you go, sir. Would you like me to clear that away for you?'

'Thanks.' Goldstein inserted his black Amex card. 'I'm still working on mine. Oh, and you can add a glass of champagne to my bill.'

The waiter cracked a grin. 'Yes, sir. Right away.'

Joe leaned back against the worn burgundy leather of the banquette. The lava was cooling, hardening again. A sense of freedom washed over him.

God almighty, what a relief.

Somebody put down a sparkling flute of champagne, and he picked it up and sipped at it.

Topaz might not take him back. Maria was a very rich woman, with excellent lawyers, and she intended to make his life a living hell. She could sue over her contract, and his name would be mud in every trade journal on both coasts. This time tomorrow, he might well be divorced, penniless, and fired.

All of that he had just risked across this dinner table.

And Joe Goldstein didn't give a damn.

That was the first and last time in his life he'd let himself be bossed around by a woman. In fact it was the first time in twenty years he'd let himself be bossed around by *anyone*.

Never again.

The champagne tasted wonderful. He'd bought the right to apologise to Topaz. That much he could do right now.

Oblivious of the stares of his fellow diners, he pulled out a cell phone and dialled her number.

It rang once, twice, then went to voicemail in the middle of a ring. That meant she had depressed the receiver. His heart lifted. *She was there.*

'. . . leave a message.'

'Topaz. It's Joe. I wanted to tell you that I just broke up with

281

Maria. I don't love her. I never did love her. I always loved you. And I still do. It was a huge mistake – not a mistake, something very wrong that I did. Please forgive me. At least talk to me. I'll never be happy with any woman other than you.'

He hung up, and ate the rest of his meal. The waiter came back, and Joe signed for a tip and left the restaurant. There were photographers waiting for him on the street.

Word travels fast.

He didn't care. The evening was full of sunshine. He stuck out his hand and hailed a passing cab. As it pulled away from the clicking flashbulbs behind him, he felt light, better than ever. Somehow he knew that today would be his best night's sleep in weeks.

His phone rang. It was Topaz.

Fingers fumbling with excitement, he answered.

'Baby? Did you hear my message?'

'Yes. I heard it. Come home.'

Joy raced through him, surged up his body like a tidal wave. 'Come home? Seriously?'

'You're sleeping downstairs in the guest wing.'

'Yes, ma'am.'

'I'm not saying I'll take you back, Joe. You broke us.'

Tears swamped his eyes. He blinked them back. 'I know. I love you. I know. I'm so sorry. I'll work on it, I'll do anything you want. Anything. Just let me be with you.'

'OK.' She sounded like she was crying too. 'Just get here.'

His house was different. Joe understood; he admired her. How strong she'd been. All his stuff was gone. It looked like a Malibu sunset. He didn't dare crack a joke, nor walk forward and hug her.

Topaz stood at the end of the living room, awkwardly. He moved closer to her.

'Thanks for letting me stay.'

'You have no clothes here,' she said. 'You want to go fetch some?'

He shook his head. 'I never want to leave. When you go to sleep, I'll just strip these off and wash them.'

'OK.'

'Can I sit down?'

She nodded. She fixed herself a glass of iced water, made one for him. 'So this happened tonight? How did she take it?'

'She's suing me, first thing in the morning. Over the contract she signed. I didn't raise her rate.'

'Does she have a case?'

'Probably. I'll fight her. NAB too, if they try to fire me.'

'Better take a good look around,' Topaz said morosely. 'I don't think we'll be able to afford the service charges on this place much longer.'

He blinked. 'Huh? I saw what you did with *American Girl*. The PR tour. The sales. People tell me these things. That's a triumph, Topaz. Your board is going to give you all the time you need.'

'Or not. There's been a little development. Musica fired Rowena.'

'What?'

'Yes. And we found out why. A raider wants to buy the company cheap. Needs to lower the share price. Successful CEOs not wanted. He bribed the board, and she got the can.'

'That's insane. Rowena won't stand for that, she'll sue.'

'You can't sue this guy. He's too big. Nobody will take the case. And he's almost certainly coming after American Magazines, too. I tried calling my own board tonight. It should be a celebration, right? Not one of them would talk to me.'

'Maybe they were all out.'

'Yannis's assistant said – and I quote – "He doesn't want to talk to you, Ms Rossi, in advance of the emergency board meeting tomorrow morning."'

'I . . .' Joe fell silent. He couldn't tell his wife it was OK. That sounded like a firing. No doubt about it. 'Why would the same raider come after you both?'

Topaz lifted her glass of water. 'Want to take an educated guess? Think about it. Cast your mind back. *Way* back.'

'Oh my God,' Goldstein said. 'You are joking.'

'Nothing funny about Conrad Miles.'

He exhaled. 'Christ. But you'll be hired elsewhere?'

'Doubt it. One good issue of a magazine, versus the shitty results for the last few years . . . This will be seen as a Hail Mary pass. Too little and too late.'

'But *American Girl*'s your flagship.'

'Sure. But investors will say, nice stunt with the women's title, how's she going to turn around *Economic Monthly*?'

Goldstein shook his head. 'How do you know for sure? About Miles?'

'Two ways. And this is where it really starts to get funky. Are you ready?'

He smiled grimly. 'Can't get worse.'

'Don't bet on that. Number one, Rowena pumped some accountant on her board by bluffing that she had a meeting, and he gave it all up. Miles, and fifty million dollars in the pocket of each board member.'

'Wow.'

'So I started calling around myself – not the board, some investigative journalists I know. People I trust on the *Post* and the *Wall Street Journal*. Money guys, society columnists. Turns out Conrad Miles is thinking about a second marriage. There have been tête-à-tête dinners in the best places to be seen in this city – and I emphasise *seen*. He doesn't do that with his mistresses.'

'And who's the lucky girl?'

'Joanna Watson.'

Goldstein looked blank.

'Joanna Watson. Ex-editor of *American Girl*. Talentless hack. The one I fired a couple of months ago.'

'Wow.' Goldstein considered this, then laughed. 'Oh my God. Wow.'

'There's no reason a guy like him would want a record company. It's a horrible business. Like print. We're both dinosaurs. Conrad Miles just wants to slay a couple of she-dragons that got the better of him. Joanna probably suggested American Magazines, and he thought it'd be fun to take us both out.'

Goldstein nodded. 'It does sound likely. Oh honey, what a shitty deal.' He took a long drink of water. 'What are you going to do?'

Topaz shrugged. 'Right now? Go to bed. This feels like the longest day of my life, and I'm completely shattered. Even for an Italian,' she smiled weakly, 'this is a lot of emotion. And I never liked roller-coasters.'

'OK,' Goldstein said. 'OK. I know I can't kiss you . . .'

'No. You can't.'

'I love you. More than you'll ever know.'

Topaz shrugged, and started to walk towards the bedroom.

'No,' Goldstein said suddenly. 'No! Topaz, don't go to bed right this second. This is about your career, not me. Let's start fighting back.'

'Fight Conrad Miles? Rowena doesn't know if we can beat him.'

'But you can. *She* can't, not right now. But *you* can.'

Topaz stared at her husband. 'Is this going to involve staying up?'

'At least another two hours, and maybe three.'

'You're serious.'

'Yes, I'm serious. Because tonight is the only chance you've got.'

Chapter Sixteen

'What?' Joanna Miles said. She clenched her fists. 'What?'

Conrad gazed back at her coldly. 'Have you been indiscreet?'

A terrifying accusation. She flicked back her hair, looked up at him. 'I . . . No. Of course not. There's no way she could have known.'

'But she did, didn't she?' Miles's lined face was an ice-cold picture of rage. 'Or perhaps this is all a wild coincidence?'

They were sitting together reading the news on the internet, both of them staring at their phones in the back of the limo. Conrad Miles wore a dark suit and tie; Joanna was dressed in a bespoke gown of oyster-white chiffon with a gunmetal-grey shrug. The car was headed to the Metropolitan Club, where Manhattan's elite were gathered for a private wedding breakfast. Moments ago, a Supreme Court justice had married them on the garden terrace of Conrad's sumptuous apartment – and the releases had already gone out to the press.

It was a headline all over the world.

And intended to be stage one of a triumphant day. Miles Industries had handled everything. First, the small family celebration that would dominate newspapers across the globe. Next – within an hour – the announcement of Miles Industries' board-backed bid for Musica Records, rescued, as they pointed out, from the slack management of Rowena Krebs, its disgraced ex-chief executive.

The third piece of the puzzle was meant to be American Magazines, with Topaz Rossi sacked the very morning Joanna Watson – now Joanna Miles – moved in.

'You're right, it can't be a coincidence.' The bride was desperate to placate her man. She might be wearing an engagement ring the size of a quail's egg, and a tiara that would suit a princess of Monaco, but the pre-nup was rock solid.

If Conrad wanted to ditch her, he could.

'But I didn't say a word – it didn't come from me, Conrad. Darling, this is as important to me as it is to you.'

Miles's fingers curled into a fist. He didn't need to say anything. *Topaz Rossi had cheated him.*

The bride and groom had moved past the endless articles about their nuptials – full of speculation and wrong detail – and on to the smaller pieces in the business sections, and the woman's features. Joanna was staring at a picture of a triumphant-looking Topaz on the front page of the *Huffington Post*, but Conrad was locked into the online report in the *New York Times*.

A Perfect Exit, the headline said.

His heart pulsed with anger. He tried to control himself. High blood pressure was no good, and moreover, there were people that *mattered* waiting in that club. As infuriated as he was, he could not let them see it. Conrad Miles needed to project victory. Especially today, his wedding morning.

If this had come out before he married Joanna, he would have called it off. But she had scraped in under the wire. Now Conrad was committed, for a period of at least a couple of years. Otherwise he would look ridiculous.

Whatever their legal arrangements, power, to some degree, had just shifted to his new wife.

'I understand,' he said coolly. 'It hardly matters. We'll enjoy our celebration, and figure out how to handle things this afternoon.'

'Oh honey, that's wonderful.' Joanna sighed with relief. Skilled make-up artists had made her look really very attractive, and she was perfectly dressed. She was a suitable enough wife, but he should never have trusted her with business.

Conrad tried to focus. It had happened, it was done. Topaz Rossi had spread her wings and fluttered out of his net. He now had to manage the situation. What a rookie error.

Women – it was always women's fault.

He struggled to remain calm as he read.

Topaz Rossi, doyenne of American Magazines for two decades, went out on a high this morning in a surprise resignation that has shocked the business world. Today saw the publication of a relaunched American Girl, *the company's flagship women's title, stuck in the doldrums over the last several years. Rossi had reportedly put her job on the line to corporate bosses, pledging to turn the struggling title around.*

Caught up in the middle of a very public divorce drama involving her husband, NAB chief Joe Goldstein, and the superstar actress Maria Gonzales, many doubted that Ms Rossi would be able to pull off the turnaround. Yet the return to her first love, editing, has delivered stunning results for the company. The relaunched magazine has led to industry speculation that it would revitalise print publishing.

Insiders at the media group say that numbers are spectacular. Ms Rossi has trebled subscribers and more than doubled the next issue's advertising take. Having performed her Lazarus act on American Girl, *many expected her to move on to* Economic Monthly *and other struggling titles in the company's portfolio.*

Instead, Ms Rossi issued a short statement at 9 a.m.:

'Last night, I resigned as CEO of American Magazines. It was clear to me that the new direction of American Girl *was going to be a stunning success in both commercial and cultural terms. I hope that the model our team has delivered can show a healthier way*

forward for the perception of women in fashion.

'While I had initially planned to repeat this exercise with other titles in our group, it seemed to me that after twenty years, such a victorious moment for me personally, and the company I love, was in fact the perfect time to leave. I firmly believe that in business, and in life, women should not be afraid to surprise the world. I look forward to enjoying more time with my family, to other pursuits, and to picking up my copy of American Girl *at a news-stand this morning – if they have any left in stock!'*

Ms Rossi certainly does seem to have achieved her aim of surprising the industry. Whether or not her editorial direction will be continued by a successor remains to be seen – but Topaz Rossi has certainly proved that real beauty works.

Goddamn it to hell! She might have written that herself, the cunning little Italian minx.

The limousine slowed to a halt. Conrad Miles was forced to drag his eyes from the screen.

'We're here, sir, ma'am,' announced the driver.

'Very good,' Miles said. 'Come along, darling. Your public awaits. Head up!'

She smiled at him – his wife, dripping diamonds – as she stepped out into the summer morning, waving at the society photographers his PR had hand-picked to meet them.

'Mr Miles! Mr Miles! How does it feel to be married?'

'Terrific,' he shouted.

'Mrs Miles! Can we see the ring?'

Joanna hung her hand, letting the knuckle-duster sitting there glitter and sparkle in the morning light.

'Excuse us,' Conrad said with a big smile. 'We've got one or two people waiting upstairs.'

The Mayor, the Governor, an ex-President, a minor Belgian princess and her husband, several movie stars and a whole cavalcade of Wall Street's finest . . . He put his game face on and gallantly offered his arm to his polished young wife.

Topaz Rossi thought she could cheat Conrad of his kill today? Slip his net? She had another think coming. He couldn't wait to get all this ceremony over with and get the hell back to the office. He didn't even want to waste time fucking Joanna. She could wait.

Joanna Miles was about to have the shortest honeymoon in history.

'And you've managed to sign agreements?'

Peter Kalow looked at his guest over lunch with a new respect. Kalow was one of the world's biggest venture capitalists, at forty-seven a giant in the tech world. He was also a long-standing friend of Michael and Rowena Krebs. Rowena had given his band a huge break, signing them to a global record deal, and sixteen-year-old Peter, the drummer, had never forgotten it. In fact, he was so interested in the dynamic, beautiful executive that he'd developed, in his spare time, a computer game about hit records. It proved an underground smash, and he quit the band and moved into tech, an area in which he was now an expert. But even with the brilliant investing, Kalow remained in awe of Rowena and her husband. Michael Krebs was a living legend, and sometimes let the eager Kalow join him in the mixing suite to listen quietly as his acts recorded. Money couldn't buy that, and Peter Kalow, rock fan, was a supplicant in their world.

So when Krebs called him in for lunch, Kalow didn't wait. He chartered the jet.

'Yes. I have a crew, a hundred plus. All working for lunch money. And ten per cent of the equity. Build permits have been in place for years. What I want from you is finance for the equipment.'

Kalow looked at the drawings. 'This is incredible. People will be falling over themselves to rent from you.'

'Looking after spoiled rock stars for years had some benefits, it turns out. If I can please them, I know how to please hipster Angelenos, high-fliers with no families, young kids at the most.'

'Not older?'

'They stop renting then. They buy. And if you put too many kid-centred things into the development, you scare the hipsters off. I am constructing a crèche, with outdoor sandpit and shady area, a little library, crafts and a jungle gym. All soft. All good. No screens or baby TV. There's a little kitchen for messy play, and I plan to hire some great nurses and caretakers. Residents can get childcare when they need it, and the kids will want to go.' Krebs laughed. 'We're even reserving space for a tiny vegetable garden, with little plastic rakes and spades.'

'I guess you remember the early years,' Kalow said, deeply impressed. His wife had just given birth to their third; the oldest boy was three and a half, and finding childcare he wanted to visit was an endless struggle.

'Yes. Vaguely. I also want all our child amenities to stop at five. That way renters know there are only cute pre-schoolers around; it's not a magnet for noisy kids splashing in the pool.'

Kalow mused over the plans, the photographs. Krebs wasn't acting like some casual near-retiree, dabbling in real estate. He had the entire thing down, from the parking spaces to the cycle paths, the gym, the huge, cinema-style flat screens in every apartment. It was almost a resort, with everything a young professional techie could want. In one corner of the plot, he had drawn out plans for an office workspace where residents could rent out a desk or a full office, by the month, with internet, faxes, telephone lines. It was called BeachWork, and he loved the concept.

'This is dedicated to our residents. Of course they pay for it, but it keeps the space mixed-use as far as zoning goes. I also formed a BeachWork company. I have offers in for two derelict premises on Venice Beach for the same idea. Developers keep hoping they'll zone that space residential, but they never will.

Business pods will allow me to get the same rent – and keep more deductions.'

'I want in,' Kalow said simply. 'You don't need to go anywhere else. I'll fund the entire development. Whatever you need.'

'I have eleven per cent equity out to the builders. I don't know how much I want to give away for finance.'

Kalow nodded. 'You don't have to give any of it away. I owe you. I'll finance it at one per cent over prime and give you extended payback terms. Anything goes wrong, you can just declare the company bankrupt. I won't pursue you.'

Michael Krebs grinned. A feeling of warm satisfaction spread through him. 'How about you do that, and I also *give* you five per cent. And then on top of that, you take twenty-five per cent of BeachWork – for another fifteen million dollars. If I come up with five houses I can strip, you lend enough for us to buy a further fifteen. I get crews and permits, and we do all this shit at the same time. Move fast. Make things.'

Kalow shrugged, a big smile on his face. 'You know what, I'm kind of sick of websites. They work, they fizzle out, you take one big smash and you're made for life, and then the next big thing comes up . . .'

'But with my way, you have something you can point at,' Krebs said. 'Your risk has a floor. It also has walls and a ceiling.' He shrugged. 'Besides, right now in my life I need cash. I got a sick kid up in New York, and I want to be able to spend that money on him. I'd rather borrow yours.'

Kalow smiled. 'This is amazing. I'm in. Send me an agreement. Let's get to work.'

'All the time I was making music, I barely thought about money. That's why I made so much of it,' Krebs told him. 'But I knew that one day it would be useful.'

'What does Rowena say?'

'Absolutely nothing. I haven't told her. She's got enough to deal with right now.'

'If this works out the way I think it's going to,' Kalow said, 'she can say "fuck Musica Records". We'll buy her a company of her own.'

Rowena was waiting for Michael when he came home. The kids were out at some party, and she was standing in the bedroom, hair wet from the shower, wearing nothing but a brief silk kimono.

As soon as Krebs saw her, his cock stiffened in his pants. It was a long time since he'd seen his wife like this. Decades. Vulnerable, beautiful, feeling anger, feeling trapped.

'Michael, I—'

'That's enough.' He turned around, locked the bedroom door. Then he walked over to her, slowly, standing directly in front of her. There was no sympathy in his gaze. No understanding. Nothing but animal lust.

'I don't know if I can . . .' she said, but her breath was quickening already. Under the light silk of the robe, her nipples hardened, betraying her.

'Let's see. Strip.'

She gasped, and tugged at the tie. The robe slithered slowly from her. When it moved down past her breasts, Michael held it in place with his left hand, so it framed her tits. He rubbed a thumb across her nipples, and they sharpened further, distending with blood. Then he let the robe go. Rowena was hot now, panting. He didn't move to take off his own clothes, not yet. He cupped her tits, bounced them. She moaned. He spun her around by the shoulders, running his hands slowly down her sides, down her waist, cupping her ass.

'Oh Michael . . . God . . .'

'So maybe you can, after all.' He caressed her pussy, the fine silken hair on the front of it, teasing her with the tip of his finger, her body pressed against him, ass pushed back against his erection. 'What a surprise.'

She gasped and bucked, thrashing against him, her slightness gripped in the muscularity of him. Krebs could feel her excitement rising, the hot blood pooling in her belly. He didn't want her to come, not just yet.

'Move on to the bed. Face down. Ass up. I want a good look. Understand?'

'Yes, Michael,' she whimpered. She stumbled to their bed like she could hardly stand up, as he kicked off his shoes and tugged the clothes from his body. Fighting for his own control, he stood behind her, looking at that peach of an ass up in the air, feeling the peaks of it, her thighs. Then he gripped her, thrust himself into her, and fucked her, holding her tight as she gasped and cried out with pleasure.

'Look,' he said, and Rowena turned her head, her face red, gasping, to look at herself in the mirror next to their bed, to see him taking her, sliding relentlessly in and out of her. 'Look at me fucking you . . .'

Rowena screamed, spasming, and the feeling of her thrashing around him, slippery as an eel, wet and hot and so welcoming, so much his, pushed Krebs right over the edge. He exploded inside her, bursting into an orgasm so intense it made him dizzy, and then he was clutching at her, trying to breathe, taking that second to just remember where the hell he was . . .

'Oh my God. Oh, I love you,' Rowena managed, and Krebs, smiling, panting, flopped backwards on to the soft bed next to his wife.

They kissed; lightly on the lips, then more intimately. Rowena lay next to him, cupping his balls, playing with them the way he loved so much. They were a great fit; even the thought of her body could get him hard, and she lusted after him in such a helpless way: burying her face in his neck to smell his skin, always swallowing him, caressing him even after he'd come in her mouth or deep inside her. He could lie next to her in bed, deliberately ignoring her, and it was a form of foreplay; she would press up against him, her ass would wiggle and move, petitioning for attention. And when he put his hand on top of it, stroking the mounds of her, by that time the train had left the station; there was only one way they were going to end up . . .

'Now,' Krebs said, 'you can tell me everything. Now you're in a calmer frame of mind.'

Rowena laughed. 'So that's what that was, huh? Therapy?'

'If you like. Mindfulness. Assfulness.' He chuckled. 'I should teach some classes. Sex is the most mindful thing you can do.'

'With you it is. Never counted the ceiling cracks once.'

They kissed again.

'So it's been kind of a long day. Thank you for the lovely office, though. That helped. A lot.'

'Tell me everything.'

'I'll give you the condensed version. So, I reckoned it must be a raider buying the company and he must have paid off the board. Then I wonder who'd do such an elaborate thing just to get hold of Musica. And since our business is so horrible right now, who'd be that motivated? Conrad Miles.

'I made the connection to Topaz, too. I called her in New York and warned her what was happening. Turns out that a woman she fired a few months back – Joanna Watson, daughter of a Canadian billionaire – was dating Miles. Topaz then snatches his victory by resigning, so they can't fire her. No revenge for Miles. Win win. I wish I'd done it like that.'

'Me too. But it's not over yet, sweetheart.'

Rowena lay back and exhaled. 'I don't want it to be. I want to fight this bastard, Michael. So goddamned bad. I want to take them all down.'

'Then let's do that,' Krebs said.

'How can we? We're rich, but not like these guys. You have to be the breadwinner now, baby.'

'I'm not a producer any more.'

Rowena sat up. 'What?'

'I quit the day you did. In fact, I have a new career. Developing with somebody who can stand up to Conrad Miles. Nobody he can lean on. You and I have more friends than you think.'

'You shouldn't quit because of me.'

'You are music,' Krebs said. 'You are everything. We do it together or not at all. And anyway, see those?' He pointed to their twin Hall of Fame statues.

'Power couple,' Rowena joked. 'Out on our asses.'

'No. Those are laurels. Crowns. Nowhere else to go. Once you get to that stage, you need to conquer a new world.'

'I love music,' Rowena said stubbornly. 'I always did.'

'Then you need to find some other part of music to own. Because the old style of record company is finished. Let Conrad Miles take the corpse, and you move on to something better. Something that can challenge him. Meanwhile, what I'm doing is out of the whole arena. I dig it, and it'll pay all our bills. A lot more than music used to.'

For the first time in days, Rowena felt a sliver of hope. Her husband sounded so definite. Like he always did. Maybe Conrad Miles was a billionaire, but Michael Krebs was twenty times the man he was.

'Why don't you take a shower, and I'll fix a shrimp curry, and we can go eat in the garden.' It was a balmy evening, and he enjoyed cooking; his wife detested it.

'Sounds wonderful,' Rowena said. She kissed him on the cheek.

'I'll tell you all about my new company. And then we can make plans for you and Topaz. I think you'd better get back to New York.'

Chapter Seventeen

'We expect your resignation,' Jack Travis said.

Joe Goldstein sat at the end of the table in his ten-thousand-dollar bespoke suit and looked at his watch.

'You're not going to get it. Anything else? I have a full schedule.'

'You humiliated this network,' Harvey said. 'You opened us up to legal action from one of our biggest stars.'

'Maria has met with the board and explained her situation,' Emma Sanderson said gravely, as though Maria had announced she had leprosy. 'She feels harassed, badly dealt with and unable to work with you. She wants you fired.'

'We can't always get what we want,' Goldstein said. 'Personally, I'd like a time-travel machine to move me back to a place where I didn't stupidly break up my marriage.'

'This is no time for levity,' Harvey Bostock snapped.

'It's exactly the time for it. You need to start taking this a lot less seriously.' Goldstein threw a neatly typed document on to the desk. 'This is a report by Emmett Fisher, our corporate counsel for human resources. He's reviewed Maria's contract and decided it was fair, without duress. She gets much more consultation and support even though she doesn't get more money. We've followed that through in early development and will continue to do so.'

'And if she sues?'

'She loses. I am quite happy to pick my showrunners and hand over day-to-day to them. Maria never needs to meet with me. If she wants to, my door is open – professionally speaking. Emmett will attend any meeting we have.'

'An unhappy actress isn't going to believe in the work. It will show onscreen,' Lilah stated flatly.

'She's not up for an Emmy. Maria is in the Maria business. What I said to her remains true. As she ages, she needs to find some other schtick than gorgeous actress.' Goldstein refrained from saying 'sex bomb'. 'Despite our mutual mistake, Maria is a smart, witty woman. I would not have behaved quite so foolishly otherwise. She can do comedy – and she can do cult. I'm reimagining her from a prime-time piece of eye candy to a sword-wielding superheroine.'

'Like you say, she can't act.' Harvey shook his head. 'This will be a disaster.'

'No. We will write the script around her. She will be a new generation's Xena or Wonder Woman. It will be a transformative point in her career. And ours, as a network.'

'Not if she quits,' Jack said. 'You've dumped her in public. You messed up. You know you don't shit where you eat.'

'Our break-up is as private as she wants it to be. I can't control her press conferences.' Goldstein pushed the document forward. 'Look, let's cut this off. I've taken legal advice – for NAB and for myself. Maria is bound to a rock-solid contract and she can't go anyplace else. You have given me a year of carte blanche to manage ratings and shows, and that too is rock solid. There is no company policy about dating talent, nor does my contract have a morality clause. You cannot fire me. If you do, I will tie up this network and all of its productions for years in the lawsuit of the century. So let's get this over with. I go back to work, and you remind Maria of the opportunities she has here. Send her to see me. Like I say, a lawyer will be in the room.'

Goldstein nodded at them, ignoring their stares of dislike.

Whatever. This was not his goddamned problem.

'It's in my contract that I do not have to attend excessive board meetings,' he said. 'I now intend to proceed with restructuring our network for the modern day. With or without your support. Frankly, I'm tired of this. Your job isn't to look for ways to get around the legal restrictions and fire me. Your job is to *keep* me here once I've saved this place and my contract runs out.'

He stood up, supremely confident.

'And right now, you're going to have an uphill job.'

Joanna Miles smiled around the room.

The board members, of course, were in her husband's pocket. They smiled back. But not the rest of the staffers. Most looked at her with blank faces or deliberate scowls, or didn't look at her at all. A few of the women studied their fingernails.

'It's great to be back at American Magazines,' Joanna said loudly. She fixed her smile to her face ever more firmly. 'It was such a challenge for me editing *American Girl*, and I'm looking forward to supervising the search for a new editor who can work under me. I know that with Conrad disposing of all our worst-performing titles, we'll really be able to turn both the balance sheet *and* our reputation around.'

Conrad was not here. His limousine had whisked him off to Miles Industries' headquarters. He was preparing a release on the purchase of both groups. Of course the deals hadn't gone through yet, but the boards were backing him.

She was confident. All these people would be working for her man. Yesterday had been a little rough. Conrad had been furious with her.

But I've got the ring on my finger, Joanna thought. *I can turn him around . . .*

Rule number 1: Bust the Topaz Rossi myth. Make it seem like she was as good as fired. Joanna wanted to simply lie, but the lawyers, with much terrified bowing and scraping, said there was no way they could state that she'd been given the can.

'Does anybody want to make a contribution?' Joanna smiled.

Lucy Klein's hand shot up.

'Go ahead, Lucy.'

'Topaz Rossi took our magazine from failing to ground-breaking in just one month. We are at an all-time sales high. Readers are calling us, emailing us . . .'

There was an immediate round of applause. Joanna tensed.

'Topaz achieved a turnaround by using her personal life as a PR hook. That televised tour sold a few extra copies,' she replied dismissively. Her smile thinned.

Lucy spoke up again. 'We've more than doubled our subscriber base and most of those have selected the yearly pay option. That's more than PR.'

Joanna stopped smiling. 'Thank you, Lucy, but that is enough. We can't build a magazine based on stunts, with no industry backing. There's a reason why models and airbrushing are used as standard. The editor I hire will adhere to best practice.'

A young man from the sales team spoke up. 'Best practice nearly cost me my job. It was impossible to sell ads when you were editor. We have to follow Topaz. I've made promises to companies that we'll keep going. That's why they bought from me.'

Joanna cleared her throat. 'Look, I can understand loyalty to a friend, but this is a business. One good month in a blaze of publicity – that's a stunt.'

'Joanna, under you we had *four* months of terrible sales.' The young man was pink in the face. 'I won't lie to my customers. Unless we stick with Topaz Rossi's direction, I quit.'

'You're fired,' Joanna snapped. 'How about that?' Her heart was racing. This was not meant to be a meeting where junior pricks earning thirty thousand a year undermined her. Didn't they know she could buy and sell them?

'Actually, he's not,' said Lucy Klein, also going pink. 'You have no position in this company. It's not even sold yet.'

'Well when it is, you'll be the first to go!' shouted Joanna. 'And he'll be next!'

'Ladies and gentlemen, let's take it easy.' Board member Thomas Watson, fifty and well-to-do, stepped up. 'Topaz Rossi was a very good editor – in her day. But Mrs Miles is *totally* right about the publicity.' He was slick, a lawyer, and could make a great argument before a court, especially with fifty million bucks from Conrad Miles funnelled into one of his shell corporations. 'She leveraged that effectively but it won't last. What we have to deal with is the precipitous decline of American Magazines under Topaz Rossi's leadership. We are looking for a long-term leader, and the success of Miles Industries is not in question here.'

Joanna was seething. They wouldn't dare speak to Conrad like that, none of them would! *I need to be tough, like that bitch Topaz and the Krebs woman.*

'Thank you, Thomas. I warn you all, I won't tolerate cronyism. When the company is sold, I will be on the board and directing new management. And anybody who doesn't want to follow that lead is really very welcome to leave. There are lots of great journalists out in New York City looking for jobs.'

There was a stunned silence. The faces looking at her now reflected shock and dismay. But nobody said anything.

There. That's how to treat them, Joanna thought triumphantly.

'I look forward to working with you, and taking American forward,' she said, her voice high-pitched from the tension. 'Thomas will take over from here.'

'Let's give a big hand to Joanna Miles!' said Watson heartily.

He clapped hard, but barely a handful of people joined in. Across the room, Lucy Klein sat with her arms folded.

Joanna flushed bright red to the roots of her hair. Swallowing tears of anger, she turned on her Chanel heels, and stumbled from the room.

* * *

The plane banked over New York City. Rowena leaned back against the rich hunter-green leather of her armchair seat. Next to her, a small flute of champagne and some hand-crafted chocolates tilted gently on the walnut shelf.

She was flying in Peter Kalow's personal Gulfstream V; absolutely the quickest way to get to New York. They were headed to the private jet airport at Teterboro, where a small limousine was waiting to take her into the city. Rowena had rented, under the radar, a luxury Central Park West apartment from Airbnb; no need to check into a hotel, to draw attention to herself. Topaz was picking up the keys and stocking it with groceries, even now.

'You should stay with us. Why aren't you staying with us?' she'd asked.

'Because you guys need time to settle back together.'

'I'm not going to take him back just like that. You have more right to be with me than he does.'

'I understand. But you do need to be able to do whatever people do when they're glueing back the pieces of their lives. You're a great friend, but this is business. And the worst we've ever had it.'

Topaz was quiet for a few moments. 'OK. I'll get your shopping. And I'll come to your place for dinner. Joe can fix himself ramen noodles for all I care.'

Rowena laughed. 'Great. Let's go with that.'

She looked out of the window now at the city beneath her, that great forest of stone, the skyscrapers jabbing into the sky like fingers. Manhattan always thrilled her. The day she'd first flown here, from England, a young talent scout on a mission to recruit the world's greatest record producer for her unknown band, had changed her life, and the electric excitement had never left her.

'Excuse me, Ms Krebs. If you would fasten your seat belt for landing.' The pilot's voice came over the tannoy, the private announcement just for her. Obediently Rowena tightened her belt. The jet began a smooth, steady dip. Michael's idea was brilliant; she loved that his diggers were already breaking earth, his builders already working. And that there was a separate new company with Kalow on BeachWork; smart thinking there too. Michael was protecting her, and their kids. Rowena felt ashamed of herself for a moment for ever having doubted that. Worse, that she had allowed herself to be scared off by Conrad Miles, even for a day.

He's a bully, she thought. And the only way to beat bullies was to stand up to them. She'd been doing that since before she went to Oxford, since detaching from her abusive, aristocratic Scottish family.

Conrad Miles and his new harpy of a wife thought they could wipe out Topaz and Rowena, just because they had a few billion to throw around.

They were about to find out how wrong they were.

Topaz had made coffee. They sat together in the rental apartment's living room, a typical Midtown park affair, with big pre-war windows letting the light in, overly stylised modern couches and wooden floors stained dark. Rowena was thrilled to see that some of the life had returned to her friend's face.

'How are the kids doing?' Topaz asked.

'Amazingly well. That is, when I see them. The four of them are having a great time, going out to beach bonfires and hiking the canyons and what have you. To be honest, I've been so caught up in work that I don't even ask them what they're doing. I just let them enjoy themselves.'

'You guys are so good to take them. I don't want them to know their dad's home just yet. In case it doesn't work out.'

'Listen, I got fired. I thank God every day your kids are keeping mine occupied. Nothing better than other kids.'

They chinked their coffee mugs together.

'And you and Joe?'

'We went to see a therapist. Dr Glennon. She's very good. I

didn't want to go – that kind of thing seems so fake. But she just let us talk. Joe seems genuinely devastated.' Topaz's anger flashed up. 'He should be. He wanted stroking, see, he wanted me to be a different type of woman. We'll work through it, though. We were two people who loved our careers, who couldn't wait to work harder, and faster, and when something went wrong, Joe didn't handle it well. He projected it on to the kids. It's about control.'

Rowena nodded.

'He had some fucked-up way of trying to make out that he never cheated on me, by pretending the thing with Maria was a real relationship.'

'So why did he dump her? It was pretty quick.'

Topaz shrugged. 'He realised that instead of being in control, he was letting some young chick push him around. And really it's fear, isn't it? For all of us. Even you and me.'

Rowena drank her coffee. 'Am I going to get analysed now?'

'Why waste three hundred dollars an hour?' Topaz laughed. 'You can tell me it's bullshit, but why are we both here? Because of fear. The worst has happened: we're sacked, we're out. But we fear the loss of our reputation. Which is really what Conrad's after.'

'Maybe. But I think it's not just fear. It's anger. And strength. No, I won't be pushed around. I'll quit on my own terms. I'm here now because I want to *kill* that guy and his trophy wife.'

'Attagirl. I hear you.'

'Maybe getting fired is the best thing that's ever happened to us,' Rowena said.

'If it's a blessing, it's got one hell of a disguise.'

'Think about it. We were coasting. We worked our way back. Great. That just repairs the damage. I want to be the greatest record woman my industry has ever seen,' Rowena said. 'No ageing mogul is taking that from me. If he wants a rematch, he can have a rematch. Same bloody result. KO.'

Topaz settled back against the couch. 'You've got spirit, Krebs, I'll say that for you. I was almost enjoying waking up at eight a.m.'

Rowena's eyes rounded in fake horror. 'Eight a.m! The day's half over.'

'Yeah, well. Maybe you're right. I said *almost*. Got bored on day two.' Topaz tossed her long hair. 'Joe telling me to resign gave me that little victory so that I wasn't humiliated. My mistake was thinking that was good enough, when it was just a shitty little consolation prize. *I lost my company.* Joanna Watson went in there today to tell them she's going to undo everything we just sweated blood over.'

'You can't let that happen.'

'I won't. Once we figure out a way. After all, it's only the two of us versus a deca-billionaire, am I right?'

Both women laughed.

'OK,' Rowena said. 'Enough foreplay. Let's get to it. I have a plan . . .'

Chapter Eighteen

Conrad Miles relaxed a little. His wife had just finished giving him head, something she was improving at on a daily basis. She looked beautiful, her body sculpted to perfection by one of the best personal trainers in the city; his money had lifted her looks from ordinary to extraordinary. He'd had two make-up artists and a hairdresser added to their personal staff, and Joanna's routine now included ninety minutes of beautification every morning. He worked out while she was primped and prepared, and when he came back up to the terrace for breakfast, his wife looked like a model – every time.

The weeks since the marriage had been busy. He shuttled between coasts, supervising the buyouts; the stock rose on acquisition rumours, but he played hardball, and the shareholders fell into line. Just as he'd predicted. No future without their starry chief executives. It was all too easy.

Joanna offered a little relief. His wife surprised him with her pettiness, her bitchiness. Miles enjoyed it; proof that something motivated her, other than just money. Joanna did not relax into shopping and manicures. She wanted something more. Revenge.

'Nice,' he said, patting her on the head. 'You do enjoy your work.'

She purred at him, faking it, he had no doubt, but faking it well. His power was a turn-on. He got that.

'Darling, you were thinking of your next move. Taking over another company?'

Miles shrugged. 'Breaking up American Magazines. And Musica Records. You can sit on the magazine board while it happens.'

He'd forgiven her for the Topaz resignation. Maybe it wasn't her. Joanna was playing the game well. Forcing her on to the board was another sign of his muscle, like that emperor who made his horse a senator. Of *course* Joanna Miles wasn't qualified, but they'd just have to sit back and take it, wouldn't they?

'Yes. We need to cut some fat.' Joanna positively beamed. Conrad knew that the thought of firing staffers gave her satisfaction. All those uppity juniors who'd answered her back, didn't clap her. It was vicious, of course, but Miles was untroubled. In defying his wife, they had defied him. Lucy Klein was a dead woman walking.

'Go right ahead. I prefer selling the titles off without fat. But I also want to co-ordinate the break-ups. And you should enjoy this bit, sweetheart,' he said, with a touch of sarcasm. 'Now that I own them both, it's time to dig up the corpses.'

'What do you mean?'

'Krebs and Rossi. People have forgotten about them. I wanted to do it back when we swooped, but Rossi wriggled away. The news conference is a chance to put that right. The entire point of this little exercise was to show that nobody beats me.'

Joanna's eyes widened. 'But she quit – all that good publicity.'

'Yes. Now we get to put it out that she was actually fired. Watch the TV tomorrow, you'll see me at work.'

'Can I help?'

Miles squeezed her ass. 'No. This is big-league stuff. Beyond you.'

'But will it matter? Topaz and Rowena have disappeared. I don't read about them, they've just become housewives. The only interesting thing there is the battle Joe Goldstein's in over at NAB. They say they want to fire him too.' She perked up. 'Maybe you could buy a network, honey? I think I could be a great anchor. Or run a lifestyle channel . . .'

'You just had a new toy last month,' Miles said drily.

'Topaz lives off her husband now. If he gets fired, they're wiped out.'

'You really hate her, don't you?'

Joanna flicked her head. Yes, she hated Rossi. Even fired, her ghost haunted the office. Editors yessed Joanna to death. Nodded and did something different. The acting editor of *American Girl* had put the next issue to bed, exactly the same as the prior one, no airbrushing, controversial news stories, offers and tips. And it was selling. She hated it. Advertising was up, but designer labels were dropping them like a stone. She was *Joanna Miles*; she wanted to be a big shot at New York Fashion Week, not a welcomed customer at Macy's or the goddamned Gap. Maybelline? Screw them! She wanted Crème de la Mer, the hot models, quality, the life of South Beach and the Cap d'Antibes. *American Girl* wouldn't be that. Not until she could wrest control back.

'She deserves it. Look, it's not like I'm putting a horse's head in her bed.' Joanna gave a little laugh, to disguise her cruelty. 'She and her husband have peacocked all over town for years as this power couple. Now he has sex with some slut of an actress and she pretends she quit at the top to repair the marriage. Oh please. She and Joe Goldstein can sell their apartment and live comfortably somewhere quiet for the rest of their lives, can't they? Like *Westchester*.' She spat out the name of the suburb like it was a disease. 'They just won't be in the game any more. I can't stand to think of all this effort and Topaz still being just so smug . . .'

'I'm not making a move on NAB. Tougher to break up. You need to run TV networks, and that's not what we do. All kinds of problems with the FCC. We stay away from broadcast. You'll have to be content with the head of Topaz Rossi on a platter. Let

Maria Gonzales take care of Goldstein.' Conrad snickered. 'Maybe you two should have lunch.'

'Maybe we should.'

'In my world it's about taking your enemies out. Their spouses aren't important.'

Joanna pouted. 'Yes, darling. Whatever you say.'

It was a flawless performance; Miles couldn't fault her. Joanna was going to work hard to keep his approval, now, in the future. He would probably leave her a significant chunk of his fortune, if she didn't embarrass him; what she might do with free rein was deliciously terrifying. He approved.

'So off you go, have a tennis lesson or something.' He'd lost interest. 'Don't go to American Magazines today. You will watch my press conference first.'

'Yes, Conrad.'

She didn't ask him what he was going to say. If he didn't want to tell her, that was an end of it.

Joanna Miles never pushed. She was here for the long haul. 'I can't wait,' she said.

Conrad Miles walked to the podium in his conference room. There were just a few cameras in front of him, but they were the ones that mattered; CNBC, Bloomberg, the *Wall Street Journal*'s internet streams, Fox Business. Hand-picked analysts crammed the rows of seats. They'd just taken notes for the dry presentation by Hank Ivens, Miles Industries' COO, about the asset-rich entertainment sector and 'content stripping' as a strategy. Ivens handed out figures, and nobody really cared. The quants had crunched the numbers weeks ago. Miles Industries stood to make a small score from breaking up American Magazines and Musica Records. It was a nothing deal, really, without some drama.

But the great man was here to provide that.

Conrad Miles rarely spoke directly. This was news. And many of the hacks were primed to hear something even better. A human interest angle that would get their stories out of the back pages and into the news sections. Reporters lived for this.

'Thank you, Hank. Good to be here.' His eyes scanned the room. 'The turnaround we proposed for the assets of these companies depended on price at acquisition. We considered that both target companies would be easier to acquire based on the poverty of the previous management. As most of you know, Rowena Krebs was fired for cause after a disastrous year prior to a final quarter's results delivered by others in the organisation. We felt that under her, Musica Records was being run into the ground. Equally, Topaz Rossi at American Magazines had served the group very poorly of late.'

Behind him, charts and graphs flicked into life on a giant multi-media screen, divided into two. On the top half, Rowena's smiling face was portrayed, like a baseball player at a big match, next to numbers that looked like a downhill ski slope. His analysts could paint a story any way he wanted it delivered. On the bottom half, right below her, was a headshot of Topaz Rossi, with the sales figures for American's last six months. Beautiful women, gazing into the air, next to graphics that called them losers.

Out of their depth. Finished. Dinosaurs.

'Once these two were removed, Miles Industries was confident of releasing value. We will begin break-up of both groups next week. We're talking to multiple suitors. Any questions?'

Back in the apartment, curled up on a nineteenth-century chaise longue while a servile hairdresser combed her tresses, Joanna Watson squealed with delight.

'Bring me a dress!' she snapped at her lady's maid. 'Something amazing! No! Bring me a suit! The pink Chanel tweed! I have to look serious!'

'Yes, ma'am, right away.' The woman had been a senior personal shopper at Henri Bendel. She detested Joanna with all her heart, but Conrad Miles paid her a hundred grand a year. For that Mrs Miles got to be as rude as she liked. Sucker. 'You'll look amazing in that suit,' she lied. *The eighties called; they want their padded shoulders and power dressing back.* Joanna was such a spoiled princess; it was great that she had a horrible sense of what it meant to look like a working woman.

'And hurry up!' Joanna shrieked at her hairdresser. 'I have places to go! I need to be at my magazine group!'

Downtown, off Madison Square Park, at Rowena's rented space, she and Topaz were watching on the tiny wall-mounted TV in the office kitchen. Behind them, coders were working away, debuting their product, testing it, ignoring the TV, the coffee machine and everything else. Rowena and Topaz had hired the best, and they had eyes for nothing but this app. It was falling into place now, better than sex. They all had equity, just a little bit, and they thought it was going to make them rich.

'Look at him,' Rowena said, grinning.

'This is awesome. Freaking hilarious,' Topaz said. 'He's doing it right on cue, exactly as predicted. I love it.'

'It's good to know journalists. Your guys are on the money.'

'Ssshh, let's not miss it,' her best friend said. 'He's hanging himself. It's awesome.'

'I have a question, Mr Miles.' A Bloomberg journalist stuck his hand up. He was in his fifties, and uncowed by billionaires. 'Both managers were credited with turning their companies around. Topaz Rossi quit after producing the best-selling edition of a magazine in group history, and the title has continued to sell.'

'Other titles haven't. I'm glad you bring up Ms Rossi. We think openness is important in corporate communications. She didn't really resign – she was about to be fired by the American Magazines board, after discussions with me. We believe she jumped before she was pushed. She was certainly told of an emergency board meeting the next day, and all of a sudden a resignation email arrived. I call that spin. She was canned. I don't carry passengers.'

'Strong words.'

Conrad shrugged. 'Yes. Next?'

'Doreen Earnshaw, Fox Business. Mr Miles, it seems like you really want to draw attention to the former CEOs.'

'Their dismal record is the reason I bought these companies. We liberate undervalued assets.'

'It seems very personal. Back in the nineties, Rowena Gordon and Topaz Rossi united to defeat a similar move by Miles Industries. In fact their poison-pill approach nearly took over your company at that time.'

Conrad smirked. 'Is that so?' he said, with exaggerated surprise. 'I had forgotten.'

'It doesn't look like you forgot much of it, sir.'

Now there was a forest of hands in the air, reporters shouting out questions. Conrad shivered slightly with pure pleasure. 'Yes, Brent. Go right ahead.'

'Brent Stowcroft, *Financial Times*. So the entire point to this press conference was to drive home the fact you finally took revenge on two prominent businesswomen?'

'I object. They're hardly prominent.' Conrad smiled again, though the English guy was near the knuckle. He narrowed his watery eyes, to make Stowcroft aware that he was watching him. 'Joking aside, Miles Industries trades publicly. We want shareholders and investors to know just what we can do for sloppily run companies . . .'

There was another round of shouting, but Conrad had had enough. He raised one wrinkled hand and walked out of the conference room. Behind him, Hank Ivens stepped smoothly back up to the podium to give them some bullshit about new homes for American Magazines' flagship titles.

'Mr Miles! One last thing!' It was Ulrika Whetstone, the veteran

315

money anchor for Bloomberg. He turned to face her, and the cameras whirred and clicked.

'For you, Ulrika, anything,' he said gallantly.

'Your new wife, Joanna Watson, was briefly the editor of *American Girl* before being fired by Topaz Rossi. Has she got anything to do with this?'

Conrad almost laughed aloud. Clever little Scandinavian, she'd swooped on the last piece of the puzzle. If this didn't get him all the coverage he'd originally wanted, he'd be amazed.

'You know, Joanna did mention American Magazines to me as a purchase opportunity,' he said. 'That business savvy is one reason she's now sitting on the board of the company. So commercial matters aside, in a way I do have to thank Ms Rossi for my marriage. Now, ladies and gentlemen, Hank will be happy to answer the rest of your questions . . .'

In her corner office, Topaz Rossi received a call from Lucy Klein.

'You think we should go now? She's coming into the office today.'

'No. Wait till tomorrow,' Topaz said. 'We've got a plan. Let's stick to it.'

'You got it, boss,' Lucy said. 'Wow. This is really going to be fun.'

Rowena was walking into the Four Seasons for lunch. A few heads turned her way; she saw the business types murmur and shake their heads, and let their eyes slide off her.

She smiled quietly. Let them gossip. She and Topaz were going to give them the kind of show they'd never forget.

She was wearing a simple shirt dress in washed navy silk, with kitten heels and a loose jersey jacket that draped beautifully round her shoulders. She carried a small Hermès bag in black calfskin, and with her blonde hair blown out falling just below her shoulder blades in precision-cut perfection, men twenty years her junior were sighing after her as she walked.

Standing waiting for her was Len Blatinsky, the acerbic CEO of Galaxy Records, the last major label she really had to woo. He smiled as he saw her, his dark eyes taking in her elegance and poise.

'Goddamn, Rowena Krebs. How did that schmucky producer of yours ever get so lucky?'

Waiters pulled out their chairs, and Rowena sat down, feeling confident, powerful, like a woman with something incredibly sexy to sell – and she didn't mean her dress.

'Are you kidding me? I had to hunt him down like a dog.'

Blatinsky laughed. 'Man, I wish my wife would say that about me. Somehow meeting at my cousin's bat mitzvah doesn't have the same ring.'

She smiled back.

'Rowena, you hear that asshole today? All over the news. Screw him. Come and work for me. I can't give you my job, but I'll make you number two and cut you in for so much stock your sexy househusband will never have to work again.'

'Oh Len, Len,' Rowena said. 'Michael always out-earned me ten to one.'

'I can fix that.'

'Not unless you're offering just shy of a hundred million. He's moved into real estate, and it's all going pretty wonderfully.'

The older man's mouth dropped. 'Get out of here. Fucking Krebs. Always three steps ahead of me. I hate that damned guy. Come and work for me anyway, gorgeous. No better record woman than you alive.'

She could have kissed him. 'You're a sweetheart, but no. How about something else? How about I work *with* you, and all your bands?'

Len sighed heavily. 'I might have known there's no such thing as a free lunch with the luscious Rowena Krebs. OK, baby, hit me with it. What you got?'

* * *

Joe Goldstein looked at his schedule, and smiled.

He liked it. Liked every goddamned thing he saw.

The Victrix hotel in LA was crammed with superstars, and right now, Joe was the heaviest hitter of them all. He was camped out in the Roma Victrix suite, their most luxurious of all, with its personal rooftop pool and private garden. NAB had paid up for the week at enormous expense; Goldstein knew it was worth it. No better way to announce to Hollywood that his tired old network was back in business.

Day in, day out, they came up to his suite to hang. The mega-agents, the happening writers, the hottest showrunners. Goldstein had talked to Beth Shacter, the Oscar-winning director, and signed her to run his new prime-time undercover drama, *Witness Protection,* about the men and women who kept America's most secret identities secret.

'You've seen every cop/med/department drama known to man,' Shacter announced. '*NYPD Blue, Summerside, Chicago Fire, ER, The Wire* . . . but this is different. How many families in witness protection have we seen on screen? A million. But what about the guys who keep them there? Who shift them around, who fight detection?'

'I love it,' Goldstein said.

'And I have Roxana Felix lined up to star. As the chief of internal affairs.'

The ex-supermodel?' He was in heaven. 'When can you get me a script?'

'I heard you were clearing house, so . . . Here's the pilot and the first two episodes.'

She dumped the scripts on his table, and left for another meeting. An hour later, Goldstein had his first big signing.

And they kept coming. He poached two *Saturday Night Live* comics to start a US comedy sketch show – no music, just laughs, the way they did it in London. There was the new simple quiz show, rapid-fire and tactical, developed by a young coder and hosted by a muscle-bound hunk from *Game of Thrones*: 'There's zero element of luck,' they told him. 'This is like chess. The guys at home will be trying to follow him across the board.'

Goldstein signed them all. One after the other. Big stars, pop princesses from Nickelodeon who wanted to be edgy and hip, gritty Danish drama where men were the victims and women were the cops, a 7 p.m. light-humour drama based on the Egyptian gods hitting Manhattan, a series adaptation of *Supergirl* for the 6.30 hour – '*Mean Girls* with muscles', as the breathless CAA agent put it. He bought rights to first-run documentaries getting traction online, and added in some new prank-show formats from Japan and Austria. Then there was *Rosewell*, the story of the finest stately home in the American colonies – 'An American Downton Abbey,' said Eli Langton, the best dramatic showrunner of them all, a coveted scalp for Goldstein's team.

He won them all over. Word soon went out that Joe Goldstein was in town to make deals; not bullshit deals, but pay-or-play, hard-money deals. And there was creative control, too. He was letting showrunners cast. The big names that came to him did so with projects of their own. If he hired a smart director, or a great producer, or a writing team – 'You guys cast it. Find an unknown. Pick a great actor. They don't need to be marquee names. We'll trade on the material.'

'You don't need a star?' one agent gasped, sipping his non-alcoholic cocktail next to the pool. Goldstein had just swum twenty fast laps while James Billig studied a series contract. He wasn't leaving the 'office', so he said, until all the gaps were full, until he had the line-up he wanted. And that meant working out right there and then.

'You need half an hour? I can wait. I'll swim,' he'd said, supremely confident.

And the deal-maker watched that tanned, muscled body slice through the azure water and signed his client up, without restrictions. Anybody this determined was going to run a great show.

By midweek, Goldstein had his fall season sorted.

By Thursday, other networks were starting to panic.

And by Friday, as he was getting ready to leave, Joe Goldstein's cover was blown – he was front page of the trades.

GOLDSTEIN GOES BIG, screamed *Variety*. *NETWORK TOPPER HITS TOWN, FILLS FALL SCHEDULE.*

GOLD-STEIN RUSH, yelled the *Hollywood Reporter*. *NAB MOVES IN LIKE A TORNADO – MINES ALL THE TALENT IN TOWN.*

Social networks were buzzing. *Vanity Fair* wanted interviews. And even the regular press were starting to get interested in the new life of TV's toughest executive.

Joe folded up his copy of the *LA Times*, which contained an accurate forecast of his sweeping new slate for the autumn ratings period. He leaned back and smiled. Nothing was secret or sacred in this town – and that was fine. He expected it. In fact, job done.

The board were taken aback by his vigour. He was making up for lost time, completely ignoring them, doing his own thing. It was important to get his dominance of this sector back on track. So he could start crawling back to respectability – look himself in the mirror.

Topaz was allowing him home. After all this time, he could stay, permanently. Their marriage was shaken, but Joe was working on it. Every day. And tonight, he got to go pick up the kids from Michael Krebs and fly them back to their mother. Rowena would be arriving in LA just as he and the kids were leaving. It was a good end to a small slice of hell.

Goldstein's emotions were hard to process right now. The joy of seeing his children, the shame at what he'd done, the terror that maybe he'd thrown it all away, the relief that Topaz had given him a second chance. So he handled it the best way he knew how.

He worked.

* * *

Bright sun streamed down on the Hollywood Hills. The Krebs house was gleaming, its grey marble facade warm, gleaming among the lush landscaping, like some modern version of an Italian palace. Goldstein arrived early, and spent a minute or so exploring the garden, taking in the views and appreciating the design. Krebs had carved out a private place to read, where there was no sense of smog or crowding, just the small green lawn, the fragrant hedge of flowers, the stone-clad house and the sky. Joe loved the pool on top of the house: clever.

He decided on the spot that he and Topaz would move. He couldn't quit New York, but their apartment was tainted. He wanted a house, someplace to call his own. A brownstone. No swimming pool, maybe, but a roof garden, something carefully designed, where they could sit and drink iced tea and look at nothing but sky. And a backyard too, with shade-tolerant roses, all kinds of homey stuff. A fresh start for them all. Whatever happened with her bold new business, or his. He wanted to own something solid, and not worry about maintenance charges or what the neighbours thought.

God almighty, he loved his wife. He couldn't wait to start again. She would never have to earn another cent. NAB was going to be triumphant, and when that was through, he'd go do something different. Develop shows, perhaps, produce something amazing. Something that would pay him royalties till the end of time.

The Krebses' little oasis had a strong pull. Topaz deserved this, for the second half of her life. Joe wanted it to be better. *He* wanted to be better.

He rang the bell.

'Goldstein!'

'Krebs. Good to see you, man. Thanks for having them.'

Michael Krebs slapped him on the shoulder and grinned. They had the easy familiarity of two men whose wives were best friends; who'd heard about each other second hand for years. Krebs was a lot older than Joe, a creator, not an executive – at least up till now. Joe had all his hair still, was lean and strong; Krebs was bald, thicker-bodied, muscular.

'It's been great. We've been careering off every day. Rowena's flown to the East Coast like she's been hailing cabs, and the kids have been oblivious, pretty much. They amuse themselves. Can we book your two again this summer?'

'Joe,' came a voice.

It was Rowena. She stood there in a pair of loose cashmere trousers and a little silk T-shirt, no make-up, looking absolutely stunning, her bare feet in flip-flops. 'Come in, don't just stand outside. Come through and hang out in the living room. I made coffee.'

'Cinnamon coffee, by the smell.' His mouth was watering. 'Just add in some toasted bagels and lox and I'll feel right at home.'

'Can't do it, man. Got some doughnuts, though.'

'Perfect.' He was suddenly starving. 'Wow, your house is amazing. What architecture.'

'Thanks,' said Rowena.

He offered her a hug. 'You look amazing. An angel in cashmere pants. I thought you weren't getting into the city till tomorrow.'

Rowena was leading him through the house slowly, letting him take in the modern art on the walls next to the old Scottish masters, the Afghan rugs, the glass-walled views over LA stretching below them, that fantastic smog-induced sunset streaking gold and peach through the sky.

'I came early. And I brought you a surprise.' She showed him through to the main living room, where coffee, tea, and various cakes were laid out, the glass walls flooding the house with light, looking out on to their green-hedged private garden. And on the sleek Italian couch that filled one corner of it sat his wife, Topaz Rossi.

Joe's mouth opened, then closed again. For a second he could only stare at her.

'I flew down to take the kids back home with you,' Topaz said. 'When they arrive, I want them to find us here together. I love you, Joe. I want to be with you. We'll be a family again.'

His eyes filled with tears. They started to run down his face. Behind him, Rowena quietly disappeared back into the front of the house.

Joe didn't notice. He was already walking across the room, scooping Topaz up into his arms like she was made of thistledown, and kissing her like he would never stop.

Chapter Nineteen

'I do not understand how this can *be*.' Maria Gonzales was full of rage; blind, towering rage. 'Don't they listen to what we are saying?'

Bob Milner, her new agent, cowered in the corner of his office. Maria was so angry you could see it from space.

She flung down a copy of *Variety* on to his desk. 'Another article about Joe Goldstein and his fucking business genius. Not a single one of these shows is even *shooting*. I'm not going to play ball on their little sword-and-sorcery *bullshit* project. I want out of my contract! Yesterday!'

Joe's humiliation of her was complete. He had gone back to his dull little wife in the most public way possible. 'He hasn't even apologised to me!'

'Legal consequences,' Milner told her meekly. 'If Goldstein admits he did wrong to fuck you, you can sue. He has to say you're a couple of legal adults. I'm sorry, Maria, I know it's *insane* he can get away with it . . .'

'I went to dinner at Per Se yesterday,' Maria hissed. 'And some of the tables were *laughing* at me. They were *snickering* . . .'

'Maria.' Bob swallowed. 'Darling, sweetie. I cannot get you out of your contract without taking on a giant lawsuit. It would cost you a lot of money. If the judge went against you it could bankrupt you . . . And then, consider, you couldn't work while this was going on. If you stay away too long . . .'

'I can offer myself to another network.' She tossed her gorgeous black hair. 'Warner would pay for me, or CBS . . . They were always going on bended knee to my agents before . . .'

'That's before you signed. Maria, honey, no network likes working with a TV star who's suing another network. It doesn't matter how big you are. If they get sick of you, they find another girl.'

Maria flopped on to his incredibly expensive couch. 'So you're saying I have to work for them?'

'As your agent, I can only tell you what will keep you a star – and get you the most money. If you deliver a fantastic performance, then . . . At the end of the year, you walk, you blame it on Goldstein, and Warner *will* fall over themselves trying to buy you out.'

Maria fixed him with her dark eyes. 'You don't understand. Joe Goldstein ruined my life. I loved him, I only wanted him to give me a chance . . .' She started to wail, then sob, reminding Bob alarmingly of his boyfriend in a really bad mood. 'He wouldn't even stay a month with me . . .'

'Maria, Maria! Can't you see, dear thing, you made a mistake? Goldstein is nothing! You could marry a billionaire! Or a prince! Somebody English, or . . . or Spanish!' he said, with wild abandon. 'He was lucky you even looked his way! Now you can find yourself a real man. Somebody with money and power.'

Maria Gonzales scowled again and strode to the window of his office. The agency looked down Seventh Avenue towards Times Square, facing the huge billboards and electronic posters that dominated the skyscrapers pointing due north. What was Times Square, really, except advertising? Massive advertising. The centre of the world, because of *selling*. What America did – this country in a nutshell. Under the neon commercials, there was *nothing there*.

Sell the sizzle, not the steak.

She buried her face in her hands. 'What does Topaz Rossi have that I haven't got?'

Bob decided to tell her the truth. Maybe it would make his newest, trickiest client wise up. At this point, he had nothing to lose.

'She loves him,' he said sharply. 'And you don't.'

Maria glared at him. 'Excuse me?'

'Well, ask yourself. Did you really love him? Or was he just a suitable mate? Maria, you are hurt because you are beautiful but have no man you can trust. Do you know the best way to deal with this? Be the one who laughs, and you're *never* laughed at.'

'Very Zen,' she muttered. But she dried her eyes.

'Insist on a big, open meeting. About the new show. Take me along. Arrive looking *amazing*.' Bob waved his hands, excited. 'You should get all dolled up. Smile. Wave at fans, sign autographs. *Pretend it never happened.* My ex-husband . . .' he sighed, remembering, 'he was wonderful at that. It's how the Brits do it. They don't like all the therapy stuff, and emotion, so when two British men want to patch up some big fight, they pretend the fight never happened. Nobody says sorry. Nobody talks about it. It goes down the memory hole and everybody moves the fuck on.'

There was silence. Then she tilted her head, like a little bird, and Bob felt a surge of triumph. Yes! *Sí!* I should become a counsellor! he thought.

'Maria – one thing you are not considering. When you were with Joe, you did a lot of talking about your career; now, you do not want to see him. I suggest the opposite approach. Insist on regular meetings with him and other executives. I will always come.' He shivered with pleasure at the thought of working with Goldstein, who was looking like the hottest executive in TV so far this year. 'After all, the consultation in your contract is there because you took less money.'

'That was so dumb of me.'

'No! See, the papers are – well, they are telling the truth. Goldstein is hiring such smart talent and filling NAB with such hot properties that suddenly for you to be prime-time on the network is a bonus for *you*. Let's see what brilliance he can bring to *our* series.' Bob was getting excited, and he could see Maria sitting a little straighter too. 'You want to get out of this contract, and you cannot. I'm so sorry. But also *he* can't get out of it. You are *locked in*. Darling, stop thinking of this as how he fucked you and start thinking of how you fucked *him*.'

'Fucking him got me into trouble in the first place,' grumbled Maria. But she couldn't help herself. She was defrosting.

'You have the prime slot. Now he is building a platinum network around you. Honey, the neighbourhood just upgraded. Understand?'

Maria clapped her hands. 'Certainly I understand. I like it, Bob. Let's book that meeting.'

'Joe Goldstein can't afford to have a stinker in his best weekly slot. Even if his wife hates your guts, for the next three years he's going to have to work his ass off making you the biggest star in the goddamned world.'

Bob looked up. He'd done it.

Maria Gonzales was finally smiling again.

'This is the absolute latest in private aviation technology.'

They were sitting with the salesman on the wraparound deck of Conrad's oceanfront estate in Southampton. Joanna was wearing an artfully constructed Missoni robe over a tiny gold and brown bikini; endless views of the ocean stretched before them. A white-aproned maid was serving pitchers of iced tea and home-made lemonade. Below them there was the quiet hum of lawnmowers as a dedicated crew mowed the fabulous greenery of his estate. A perfect summer day, and Conrad Miles was really enjoying himself.

He was watching Joanna try not to drool as she pretended to

cast a critical eye over the full-colour brochures for the latest in private jets. Last week he'd allowed her to commence firing some of the staff at American Magazines; Lucy Klein had gone first, and the little sales boy who'd sassed her, and after that Joanna had taken the red pencil to anybody she felt had crossed her. He had his tame board members rein her in now and then; the assets needed good journalism to attract a great sales price, that was clear.

He was quickly disposing of the Musica catalogue, artist by artist. It was a decent firesale, nothing special. Much more importantly, other raiders and investment banks were coming to him with new deals now. Miles Industries was back in business.

He was taking lunches, boasting about his coup to anybody who'd listen. Joanna had arranged for a fawning interview to be done by *Economic Monthly*, their key business magazine. Decades ago, Joe Goldstein had competed with Topaz Rossi to run the title. She'd won.

'But I'm not so easily mastered,' Conrad Miles had puffed. 'She thought she could mess with me and get away with it? No. Not at *all*.'

'The rumours that this was a revenge job are all true, then?'

The writer – what the hell was his name? Leo Rouhani. Some Indian dude. Joanna said he'd begged for the chance – was very eager to please. A new editor, perhaps? If Miles liked his piece enough.

'Absolutely true. Though of course, this is all on background.'

Rouhani smiled and nodded. 'On background! I hear you, sir.'

Conrad Miles was sending out the smoke signals as fast as he could. Mess with me, and you get destroyed. Topaz Rossi and Rowena Krebs were like Mafia informants in witness protection; in the end, they just got hunted down.

It was sexy. There was a certain kind of asshole – Wall Street was full of them – that got off on that. A lot of angry men, screwed for fifty per cent in their divorce settlements, mad at affirmative action programmes and the touchy-feely bullshit that took the fun out of finance. Conrad's holdings were immense, but the Miles Industries stock had stagnated lately. Far beyond the economics of the buyout, he was once again the king. To be feared. A *player*.

The stock was up, and so was his blood. He was making Joanna earn that ring. She had to excite him most nights, and he watched her like a hawk for any hint of distaste.

'There is no better private jet in the world. This is the same model owned by the Sultan of Oman. We customise the interiors to your personal taste. I took the liberty of mocking up a sample for you . . .'

The salesman leaned forward, producing a glossy sheet with a flourish. It showed a pale gold interior, with the letters JM monogrammed on to the back of cavernous armchair-type seats. There were mirrors built into the walnut cabinetry, and the American Magazines corporate dark greens were embedded into the carpet and over the windows, studded with more little JMs.

'It's divine,' Joanna cried. She clutched at her husband. 'But where are Conrad's initials?'

Miles shook his head. It was hideous. But his wife's vanity was afire.

'Oh ma'am, this is the smaller jet, the Gulfstream V. For your personal commuting. Mr Miles would take the larger model. We thought you might be a two-jet family.'

Conrad wanted to laugh aloud. She was wet as the ocean. She looked dizzy. He did enjoy the idea of his wife having her own jet. That was insanity. A victory lap worthy of the glory days of the eighties.

And after all, she'd brought him Topaz Rossi's head on a platter, hadn't she?

'I like it,' he announced. 'But I think Joanna deserves something a little bigger.'

As Joanna and the salesman gasped in pleasure, Miles lay back and focused on his infinity-edge swimming pool, designed deep into a bluff leading directly to the ocean. He kept it heated to the temperature of a warm bath for the entire season. Perhaps later he would go for a swim. Rowena and Topaz had not given him the satisfaction of raising their heads from the dirt, or striking back. But they were women now, not girls, and the courage had probably drained from them. Whatever. Not his problem. He was buying twin private jets, in a way, with their money.

'Contact my office,' he said to the salesman, wrapping it up. 'Joanna. Let's go inside.'

'Yes, sir, Mr Miles,' the man said, bowing and scraping as a butler materialised to escort him off the estate.

Conrad looked at his wife and jerked his head towards their master suite. For a split second, he caught a look of distaste trawling across her face, a small involuntary shudder rippling through her body. Then – as though it had never happened, like a single cloud scudding across the sun – she smiled and jumped to her feet.

'Oh Conrad,' she purred. 'Thank God you got rid of him, sweetie. You read my mind.'

But her billionaire husband was already turning towards the house, his face dark. Joanna had ruined his mood. She could work to get him hard, but no amount of effort would let him un-see that expression.

By the time he had entered his bedroom, three thousand square feet of oceanfront decadence, Conrad Miles once again felt the vile claws of loneliness grip his ageing heart.

Peter Kalow and Michael Krebs stood together on Venice Beach and looked up at their building.

This was the fourth BeachWork to start development. While the Malibu community developed at an unbelievable rate, the building conversions were even faster. Krebs had the perfect ideas for location and design, and Kalow, his junior, came at it from the coder's perspective.

They offered ultra-fast wireless internet, phone banks, meeting rooms, adaptor ports and chargers plugged in to every desk; light, bright kitchens facing the sea; modular configuration; whiteboards, 3D printers, film projectors, and every kind of executive toy. 'What else do they need?' Krebs asked.

Kalow raised an eyebrow. 'What do you mean? Girlfriends, vitamin D, crash pads . . .' He laughed. 'These guys sit at computers all day long, man. They're the elite. They're tough like marines. They're rock stars.'

'Exactly my point.' Michael jabbed a finger at his friend, excited. 'What if we treated them like rock stars? And I mean literally. You know why my studio was the best, why my records were so great? Only fifty per cent of it was the button-sliding – faders and mixers. The other fifty was the musicians themselves.'

Peter stopped smiling.

'OK. Explain.'

Michael repeated what he'd told his builder. 'I set that place up to provide the best environment for a rock group to record. Fitness. Pools. Green spaces. Zen. You could stare at the sea. We brought in great food, healthy food. Lots of rent-a-code spaces have the funky surface stuff, right? Foosball tables and Space Invaders. But we should provide what coders actually *need*, too, in the moment, to make their work better.'

'I think I see where you're going.' Kalow caught the mood. 'Let me list the most common complaints. You fix them.'

'Done.'

'Eye strain, back problems, no exercise, bad sleep, bad diet, stress.'

Michael thought for a second.

'Glare-free monitors, ergonomic chairs, standing and treadmill desks, sleeper couches and a basic shower if they're working late. Soundproofed nap pods. Free healthy snacks. Roof gardens with water features, little solar-powered fountains that make that trickling sound.'

There was a long pause.

'What if we buy in a colder climate?'

'Even more important to have the roof garden, only half of it is inside a heated greenhouse for the winter. We can set that up with tropical plants and flowers, so when they head to the roof, they feel like they're vacationing somewhere hot. We'd get daybeds up there, even a couple of hammocks.'

'God.' Kalow was in awe. 'If I'd had that when I was starting out, I'd have been richer so much goddamned quicker.'

'Would those things solve the problems?'

'I . . . Yes. Most of them. Just installing glare-free monitors would be enough to attract tech firms. And the idea of sleeper couches and a shower room is amazing. When startups are hitting a deadline, they often have to work round the clock. Guys will crash on the floor.'

'So there's one more thing. A laundry room in the basement,' Krebs said. 'We can get a line of unisex pyjamas and robes, something like they give you on airplanes, and buy in the overnight kits – disposable toothbrushes and mini tubes of toothpaste. They can change overnight, and wash and dry what they wore to work. Next morning they dump the sleepwear in our baskets, the caretaker washes it and there you go. Ready for the next round of crisis coders.'

'Wow.' Kalow was stunned. 'Let's do it,' he said. 'Goddamn, Michael. I can't wait.'

Krebs altered the design specifications, and within weeks they were ready to go.

'Now we have to market it,' he said.

They were sitting together in his office, downtown LA, and Michael felt unaccountably nervous.

Marty's treatments were still ongoing. Yes, he seemed to be

recovering, but the docs wouldn't mention remission – not yet. Money was starting to flow from the Malibu development, enough to cover the cancer operations. Yet Michael couldn't sit still. It might dry up, it might end tomorrow, anything could happen.

His kid was sick. He needed more.

The drive he'd had as a young man, even as a master of the universe, obsessed with Rowena, falling out of love with Debbie, the rock world at his feet – it was dwarfed by the feeling he had now.

The company had to work.

'We don't need marketing. It's perfect,' Kalow responded.

Krebs frowned. 'Peter, I know this is just a minor play for you. But it's everything to me.'

'Then listen. Trust *my* end. Marketing in tech is for losers. You want early adopters. We have a great product. All we need to do is get the word out.'

'I'm assuming you have a plan?'

Kalow leaned back in his tilting chair. Michael Krebs was a visionary, and he felt lucky to have fallen into partnership with him. His mistake was assuming he was doing the older man a favour. But Michael didn't just understand music; clearly, he understood *people*. And that was why BeachWork was so great. He had never been more certain of a business in his life.

And finally, it was his turn. Offering Krebs money was nothing – he hardly felt it counted. But now he could give something back.

'I called in a few favours. I had coders come in, engineers from Google, LinkedIn, Twitter, Facebook. And tech reporters. They've each had a desk in the complex for the last day.'

Krebs blinked. 'You let them in?'

'The hardest-working coders in Cali, Michael. Nobody types faster than these guys. They took their laptops, they used our monitors. My phone has been blowing up.'

'They liked it?'

'They loved it. Even the Google employees, and they work in a palace.'

'And the blogs . . . TechCrunch, Wired . . . ?'

Kalow laughed. 'Listen to you. Plugged in. I put them on an embargo till this morning.'

Krebs controlled himself. 'And?'

Peter tapped at his keyboard and turned the monitor towards his friend.

BeachWork Blazes, read the headline across the screen.

There was a huge picture of one of their offices, with the ocean visible through the window, and two coders sitting by their screens, grinning in pleasure.

Temp Offices Are Coder Heaven, said the subtitle.

Krebs blinked at it twice, hardly able to breathe. 'Wow. Holy shit. Were the others the same?'

'No.' Kalow shook his head. 'They were better.'

The first BeachWork rented out in twenty-four hours; the second and third the same. Kalow increased his float, and Krebs extended their plan across California, to every city with a tech hub. Offices were leased at reasonable rates, six months at a clip, with higher rates for three-month leases.

'That's what they want most. Three months. Understand the market,' Kalow said. He was excited in a way Krebs hadn't seen since the kid was listening in behind the mixing desk. 'Most startups in tech program in a scrum. That's what they call it. Three months, all-in, to deliver their minimum viable product.' He scrabbled for something his new partner would understand. 'Like . . . like rough demos, man! Three months to do the rough demos on an album.'

Krebs grinned. 'I love it.'

'We give them everything they need for three months. Quick turnaround, cheap rates.'

'Yeah.' Krebs couldn't believe how well it was going. Money was flowing to him now, money he could hardly believe. He was paying for everything Marty needed, and more. There was enough for everything he could imagine: houses for all three of his elder sons, trusts for grandchildren, you name it.

He hadn't discussed it with Rowena. Not yet. The fact was, he didn't know how to. She had Topaz to worry about, and her own battles. *I have to focus on property, make us secure.* 'California is maxed out for the foreseeable future; our waiting lists are a year long.' He was impatient. 'We need to move into New York. Silicon Alley they call it, downtown around Union Square.'

'No beaches in Manhattan.'

'I know,' Krebs said. 'But we *can* open a BeachWork on Coney Island. Real eatate is cheap as hell there. And we get a new name for city-centre properties. Sister to BeachWork.'

'Coders are going to dig your rock music stuff, man. They all think they're rock stars anyway. Let's get a name that sells. Something to do with your records.'

Krebs thought. 'No. Stick to tech. You said a scrum, right? How about we call our city properties HumScrum. Because we're not. Humdrum, that is.'

Kalow's eyes widened. 'That's freaking genius. HumScrum!' He laughed aloud. 'Let's go buy a building!'

They had insane amounts of fun. And doing it under the radar. No banks, no delays. Kalow funded the purchases at a nominal fee; they supervised the refits, leased them out. Tenants came flooding in through word of mouth. They had more than they could house, every building, every time. The two men started flying around, visiting the California sites, heading back to Malibu daily. That was moving up from nothing almost as fast as if it had been prefabricated. There was a party atmosphere onsite, the builders motivated, joyful, engaged in everything they were doing. And Michael Krebs felt a certain amount of guilt that he was enjoying this second career even better than the first one.

Now here they were back at Venice Beach, nearly ready to open. Kalow had asked Michael to come and check out the kerb appeal.

'This makes me fucking – I don't know what,' Michael Krebs said. He felt an intense satisfaction, the kind of brutal joy he used to feel when hearing a great, rough band for the first time ever.

'Proud,' Kalow said quietly. 'Proud. Right? It's beautiful. It's useful. Kids are going to make things here. You can touch it. Look at it. I can't say that for any company I ever founded, not till now. It was all in cyberspace.'

'We got rumbled by Georgie Eilmann,' Krebs said after a beat. 'She's the best real estate agent in Malibu. She called my office about twelve times yesterday. I showed her the floor plans. Drove her out to the site under promise of secrecy. If I read about it, she gets no exclusives.'

'And?'

'Dude, she nearly had a heart attack. Started hyperventilating. Asked if she could reserve-lease the first twenty apartments for her clients. I told her we need another three months for phase one, but she didn't care. Said she could absolutely rent them all out within the week, move-in date September first. Right after summer. And she can provide two months' deposit and a month in security. We run the credit checks.'

'What's her cut?'

'Nothing for the first twenty apartments, but she gets the exclusive. After that, she charges her regular fee – to the renter. So they need four months in their pocket just to get in the door, and this is not going to be a problem in LA. She thinks we've underpriced.'

Kalow shrugged. 'For year one? It's a high rent.'

'Not high enough. She says filmmakers and executives will slaughter each other for a spot here. It's resort living year-round.'

'I'm not interested in gouging. We'll all make millions. You and I will develop the next residential as soon as phase one of this is done. I'm thinking San Francisco, Paolo Alto. And then we move north and put something in Brooklyn. Then maybe you should consider international development. London. Milan. Rome. Paris.'

Behind them, the ocean crashed on the beach. The promenade was full of people enjoying the sun, living in the moment. Skateboarders whistled in and out of the river of tourists strolling by the water. A group of bodybuilders were laughing and hanging from the bars of the open-air gym. Krebs could hear the sound of a boombox distantly, from somewhere on the sand. It was playing rock music. As he half listened, the notes caught his ear. Atomic Mass. Rowena had signed that band, and he'd produced this record himself. More than twenty years later, some kid was out there with the white California sand under his back, and Krebs's music ringing in his ears.

And his boy, his Marty, a child back then, a child whose family he'd walked out of, was up in New York with cancer growing in his liver.

Finance. Family. He couldn't crumple in the face of Martin's sickness. He needed to run both, to be there for everybody.

It was the answer to all his problems – and it suddenly hit him in the face.

'It's real estate. Headquarters should be in New York,' he said. He was *from* Manhattan, after all, a son of the big city. LA had been fun, too much fun. But something new was happening. Something fresh. It was time to go home.

Chapter Twenty

There is nothing on earth so hot as a New York summer, and Topaz Rossi was right in the middle of it.

The sun beat down between Manhattan's stone canyons, reflecting off the glass walls of the skyscrapers, flashing from the windows of yellow taxis and crawling traffic.

Rowena Krebs was right next to her. The two women were walking down the street towards their new offices. Topaz wore a knee-length silk dress by DKNY, with a dark green Prada jacket, tailored military-style, strikingly gorgeous with her red hair and blue eyes. She was confident in black Dior heels, and carried a mock-croc purse from Kate Spade, dark glasses pushed on top of her head.

Rowena, taller, blonde, green-eyed, wore jeans that hugged her slim ass, high-heeled strappy sandals, and a pale gold satin shirt that accented her rich California tan. Both were lightly made up; Topaz had gone for a palette of rose and amber on her lids, while Rowena had a natural brown blush and matching eyeshadow, a slick of mascara and clear lip gloss. Her briefcase was custom-made; she swung it like a weapon.

Men – even teenagers – turned their heads to look as they passed. The quintessential career women, they could be anyone in this city: models, senators, heiresses, CEOs. They looked gorgeous, but it was the confidence that was so utterly sexy. You couldn't buy that, not in any designer store.

This was a city in a hurry. And they fitted right in.

'Almost showtime,' Topaz said. She looked up across Times Square towards Seventh Avenue, and their new offices, right in the heart of things. 'Think you're ready for it?'

Rowena laughed aloud. 'I was born ready. I can't wait for today to happen.'

Earlier that day, as the sun rose on the city, Michael Krebs shook his head admiringly as Rowena slipped into her jeans.

The kids were at school; they were loving the new city, loving the move. It helped that the Goldstein kids were there too. Ready-baked friends.

Michael went to see Marty and Amelia most nights. The operation had been a success, Dr Rosenthal said. Michael was at the oncology clinic, where he stood with one hand on his son's shoulder, trying not to stare at the walking skeletons and terrified-looking well people wandering around the hallways. He only had to worry about one of them; he had no idea how Rosenthal survived.

She was briskly walking him through an X-ray, but the words washed over him. His eyes were fixed on the little shadows in one frame, gone in the second one.

'Next, we cut out the spotty half,' Rosenthal finally said.

Krebs squeezed Marty's shoulder. 'When?'

'As soon as he's feeling better; once his white cell count is up.'

'Come on, kid. We need to get you something to eat.'

Marty groaned. 'Dad, I can't take any more broccoli quiche. I swear. Svetlana force-feeds me every healthy piece of crap known to man.'

'Forget that. We'll go to Shake Shack. Best burger and fries in the city.'

'Now we're talking,' his son said.

Even when they were living in a hotel, Krebs got to see Marty once or twice a week. Rowena was great about it; she let him go, didn't bug him. That was the support he really needed. And as he reconnected with his boy, Krebs found himself coming back to life.

They settled on a house in the West Village, on West Fourth Street, where Michael used to live.

'Do you think we can afford it?' Rowena clutched her husband's arm. 'Really? This place is huge.'

Krebs kissed her. Now was as good a time as any. 'The real estate is doing better than well. We're pretty rich now, even if you never make another cent.'

Rowena smiled. 'You haven't talked about it much. Want to give me a number?'

He pulled her over and whispered in her ear.

'What? Oh my God. That is a joke, right?'

'No joke, honey.'

'Get out of here.' Rowena shivered with arousal. 'My God, Michael, you made *that* much money? Seriously?'

'Hand of power,' he grinned. Slipping it down to cup her ass.

'You're such a legend. Wow.' She shook her head. 'I guess we can afford it, then.' And she laughed, shaking her head with relief.

'Something funny?'

'Just the way you look after me. I'm so lucky. Now I get to plough everything into Vusical. With no fear, either, because it doesn't matter if I fail. Not any more.'

'You won't fail.' Krebs kissed her. 'You'll smash it. I love you, Rowena. You know that, right?'

Tears filled her eyes. 'And I love you.'

They closed on the house, moved in. Rowena headed downtown to make calls, refinements, working quietly, planning the reveal. And this morning, the big day, she'd melted for him when he touched her, reached to pull him into her, like her life depended on it.

They'd made love like teenagers. He was so into her, so on fire, he couldn't make it to the bed; pulled her clothes off going up the stairs as soon as she waved the kids off on the school bus. Holding her underneath her arms, lifting her lightly as she gasped, teasing her, touching her, thrusting up into her. They wound up tangled on the landing, licking and gasping and writhing around on the soft grey carpet.

Now she was dressing. Going to work. To the fight. The confrontation.

'Are you sure you want to do this today?' Krebs asked.

'One hundred per cent,' Rowena said. And she came back into her husband's arms and kissed him. 'After this, we move on. After this, the future.'

Maria Gonzales looked down at the sheet in front of her and tried to focus. It was the order of episodes, with a list of directors chosen by Petra Lubovnik, her brilliant showrunner on *Moon Stallion*. They'd shot the pilot, and it was like living a dream. The dialogue was so witty, so brilliant. Maria loved herself in a tunic, in chainmail, riding a horse.

'Jason Tuscany? Emile Lazard? Olivia Denman?' She was reading out the names, all of them top-flight dramatic directors, marquee names from the big series at Showtime and HBO. 'You really think we can get these?'

She was sitting at a table in NAB headquarters. Bob Milner was on her left, grinning like a pudgy Buddha. Her new manager, Colleen Litman, was on her right. Across the table were Petra, Joe Goldstein, and a lawyer.

'Maria. The pilot is testing through the roof,' Goldstein said. His eyes met hers, unembarrassed, and he spoke clearly. 'It's a wonderful, humorous, brave character and you're carrying her off perfectly.'

'They are falling over themselves to work with you after just a few minutes of footage,' Lubovnik said. 'I hear directors talk about wanting to release that brain you have under there.'

'*Moon Stallion* is really going to shock them. You're a revelation: Mavia, the Saracen warrior who transcends destiny. To be honest with you, we anticipate a huge series pick-up.'

Goldstein leaned in. Maria raised her eyes. For a second, anger and loss pulsed through her, but then it released its grip and moved on. He was looking at her like it had never happened. But still, he was looking at her with excitement. Maria sensed that. Joe Goldstein was not seeing her as a piece of ass, or even a lawsuit to overcome. He was seeing her as *talent*.

'Test audiences can be wrong. It's possible this won't go as well as we hope,' he said. 'I need to flag that up. But if we get anything like the viewing figures we're projecting, Petra and I are thinking of more than just a TV series.'

Maria Gonzales forgot about Joe, forgot about respectability, forgot about being his wife. That ship had clearly sailed, and she didn't even care. It was *months* ago, right? Ancient history.

'Tell me,' she cried. 'I want to know.'

'I've taken a few meetings with some of Hollywood's best screenwriters. Everybody thinks that *Queen Mavia* would make a blockbuster movie. Maybe even a franchise. We own the character, and we're thinking you can manage the big screen, as well as the small.'

Maria opened her mouth and gasped like a fish. Her heart raced.

'I . . . I don't know what to say,' she managed.

Joe Goldstein smiled warmly. 'Well, why don't you and Bob have a read of this first draft and let us know your feelings?'

He passed two copies of a script over the table. Bob Milner grabbed his eagerly and immediately started to flick through it. Maria reached out, took hers and ran her fingertips lightly over the red cover.

Finally. Recognition – truly. And Joe Goldstein had given that to her. She suddenly understood. He wasn't a user, wasn't a bastard. He'd been true, in his way. To Topaz Rossi – but also to her. No lies, no trampling on her heart.

And in that instant she saw that not every man was out to get her. The world, this world, seemed just a little cleaner.

Maria surrendered. 'I can already tell you my feelings,' she said. 'It's great working with you, Joe. Thank you.'

There was a moment of recognition all around the room. Milner raised his pudgy head, smiling like a priest at the end of a wedding.

'You too, Maria. You know, when we're done here, you should let me introduce you to Jack Travis. He's in today for meetings. Jack sits on our board; you met him once before when we announced the contract signing.'

Maria cast her mind back. 'Jack Travis?'

'He's a big fan of yours. Maybe you guys would get on, have a coffee together, I don't know.'

She felt Milner nudge her leg and give her a discreet thumbs-up sign.

'He's a bit younger than me, a good guy. Anyway, up to you entirely.'

Goldstein looked at his most difficult star and crossed his fingers. God, he hoped this worked. Maria was going to be so huge, Topaz would have to deal with her face every time she turned on the TV or walked past a multiplex. They were OK, now, him and his wife, but it had taken a lot of doing. Now that Joe was rehabbing her 'tired Playboy bunny' brand, Maria Gonzales would be bigger than ever.

At NAB, the board were in awe of him. Joe had scored more in bonus stock than half of them made in ten years. The network turnaround was quite remarkable. He could now do and say whatever the hell he liked. But he figured he could do both Maria and himself a favour and take his network's biggest asset out of his problem list.

Bob scribbled something on a leaf of the script and quietly showed it to Maria. Joe could bet it read something like 'Forty, single, good-looking, megabucks.'

'That sounds great, thank you, Joe. I'd love to make Jack's acquaintance again.' Maria gave a big, open smile, acknowledging her past with her new boss. 'Maybe we will get on. Goodness knows I could use a proper date.'

Everybody round the table exhaled.

'Then let's get back to picking our director choices for the series,' Joe said. 'And we can introduce you two after that's done.'

'Perfect.' Maria smiled warmly back at him. 'Thanks, Joe. You're a good friend.'

And, she realised, he really was.

At lunchtime, Goldstein managed to duck out. He went home, where Topaz was waiting for him. He told her about Maria, and held his breath.

'That's great. That's a brilliant idea. Maria and Jack. It will make a great gossip item in our lifestyle pages.'

'I wish I could break from her completely, but I can't.'

Topaz smiled at him gently. 'It's OK. I know you love me, Joe. I know that now. Besides,' and she gently touched the soft bruise on her neck, the love bite artfully covered with make-up, 'you keep showing me.'

He came over to his wife, stood next to her, kissed her gently on the lips.

'I never knew how much I loved you until I nearly lost you,' he said. 'You're everything to me, Topaz. Everything.'

'It doesn't hurt that you're owning NAB right now.' She kissed him back. Immediately she felt his lean body hard against hers. He put his hands under her dress, moved them upwards to cup her full breasts.

'That's right,' he said. 'They offered me even more stock to stay next year. And residuals as a producer on all the series I'm making.'

His wife lifted one glossy eyebrow. 'Residuals?'

'You heard me correctly.'

He didn't patronise her by explaining. Topaz understood. Joe would get paid, in the future, when any episode of any of this slate got rerun. It would make him tens of millions, and the stock was worth more.

'TV mogul,' she said, chewing her lip. 'Hey, if this is what you get for a mid-life crisis, maybe you should go out and bang actresses more often.'

'Not funny.' He bounced her breasts upwards, teasing her, turning her on.

'It was quite funny,' Topaz gasped, getting wetter. 'Oh Joe, Joe, stop . . . I should get back to the office . . . Not again . . . Oh!'

'Again,' he said, firmly, feeling the slick heat of her, the lust, her curvy, glorious body welcoming him in, loving him, making him feel at home. 'Big day for you today. And you still sneak off to meet me.' He reached down, thrusting into her, and licked inside her ear, making her writhe around him, impaled, arching in ecstasy. 'Do you know how hot that is?'

'Joe . . . Oh my God . . . Joe . . .' Topaz begged. And he moved with her, taking her, kissing her, the two of them absolutely and completely in love.

Topaz and Rowena stood together by a window in the offices of their new companies. They had deliberately located in the same building.

'We should do this together,' Topaz had said, and Rowena had agreed.

The programmers were gathered up front, the journalists, photographers and marketing guys around the corner. There were separate rooms for editorial and commerce, for music and video. All were vital; none could be linked.

'I think we're ready to go,' Topaz said. She was freshly show-ered, quickly blow-dried, make-up repaired. But Joe Goldstein was still lodged in her mind, and echoes of pleasure were still in her body.

Refocus. Showtime.

'This should be fun.' Rowena nodded. 'Launch. Go.'

There was a round of applause, and writers, coders and PR people jumped back to their desks.

'Launch article is up,' Lucy Klein called loudly. A second later, 'Wow – wow, look at that. Going viral already.'

In their newsroom on the main floor, the phones began to ring.

'Mr Miles.' Anna-Maria, his senior assistant, stood framed in the doorway of Conrad's office.

He looked blankly at her. Anna-Maria knew better than to interrupt him. He was talking about the sale of *Economic Monthly* to a couple of investors from Germany. But she just stood there. It must be important.

'Yes, Anna-Maria?'

'I'm terribly sorry to interrupt, sir, but there is something urgent breaking on the wires you may wish to see.'

She walked across the room and discreetly passed him his personalised iPad, concealing it from the view of his guests.

Miles's face went grey. He got to his feet.

'We'll have to rearrange. *Entschuldigen.* My secretary will show you out.'

The Germans looked sour, but got to their feet. There was head-shaking and muttering, but Miles didn't care. He was watching disaster, in living colour.

'Mr Miles. I have the *New York Times* on the phone. Would you like to speak to them?'

The intercom buzzed. It was his second assistant. 'Sir, the *Financial Times* and the *Wall Street Journal* are holding, and Fox

Business would like to know if you want to speak to them?'

He depressed the button. 'No. No goddamned press. Get my advisers in here right now. No fucking comment, got that?'

'Yes, si—'

But he'd already hung up. His withered hands holding the tablet shook. This was an ambush. This was unbelievable.

Topaz and Rowena were back.

PERSONAL, NOT BUSINESS – MILES RUNS PUBLIC COMPANY LIKE TOY.

The headline was four inches high. The strapline below it a little smaller. The piece was by Leo Rouhani. But it wasn't in *Economic Monthly*. It was the lead item on Topaz Rossi's new web magazine, *American Red*. Big photos, breaking news, lifestyle, gossip – she'd put her editor's format to work, hiring the best writers, photo editors, features people, and sales team from her former employers. There was politics, business, life, fashion and make-up – and beautiful, responsive advertising.

She'd opened *big*. Great photos, every department. Before and after. Photoshop vs normal. Make-up vs bare skin. The politics section kicked off with breaking news about a Republican hopeful who was quitting the primaries – *Red* had the scoop on his lung condition first. In beauty, she had supermodel Roxana Felix blogging on age, and how to cope when your face was your fortune. Her sports section was all humour – an ice hockey player live-blogged the figure skating championships, cheerleaders went on the record about their terrible pay. But the lead story was the Miles exposé. And Leo Rouhani was taking no prisoners.

Two weeks after Topaz Rossi quit American Magazines – before she was pushed – I asked to meet her for coffee. The next day I quit my post at Economic Monthly, *saying I preferred to freelance. This interview was set up by Joanna Miles after I carefully cultivated a sycophantic persona towards her. However, I was not contracted to write it for* Economic Monthly. *Everything you read here is on the record – and on tape. And further down this story, you'll find audio files of the most bombshell quotes.*

As a journalist, I believe the shabby vendetta of Miles and his wife needed exposing. And Topaz Rossi agreed.

CLICK TO PLAY.

Conrad Miles's fingers trembled. He pressed the small embedded button on his screen, and heard his own voice, unmistakable, fill the room.

'I'm not so easily mastered. She thought she could mess with me and get away with it? No. Not at all.'

'The rumours that this was a revenge job are all true, then?'

'Absolutely true. Though of course, this is all on background.'

He bent his head, reading again.

I never agreed to place Mr Miles on background, nor did he even request it until after he had admitted his vendetta. No quotes he gave me after the request are used – though plenty he gave me earlier are. His wife, Joanna Miles, was to a great degree even more helpful.

Another button. Now Miles was listening to Joanna. And anger and fear were boiling in his chest.

'I don't know why Topaz thought she could take me on. I mean, just sack me? Before six months were up? This is a woman who can't even keep her husband. Anyway, I believed Conrad would be interested in the opportunity, you know, because of what Topaz and her friend Rowena Krebs did all those years back. He didn't really get to finish them off then. We both liked the idea that he could do this and say it was business. I mean, you know, Leo, the business world always knows the truth . . .'

'Absolutely,' said the little prick.

'And Rowena had done OK in her stupid record company, but that's a dying business. It didn't seem too difficult to get her fired, and then Conrad would just break it up . . .'

'Do you think this contributed to your marriage?'

His wife's voice dropped, theatrically threatening.

'Well, of course I'm not in Conrad's league – yet. But you know what they say, Leo. The couple that preys together, stays together.' She laughed, a brittle, high laugh. *'Get it? Preys – with an e.'*

Rouhani's laugh mixed with hers. The sound file cut out.

Miles was crimson with shame and rage. His heart was thudding, thumping. He felt the tightness in his chest, constricting his breath. *Calm, calm.* Not a heart attack. *You're an old man.* He'd never felt older. Dumber. He walked to the couch in the corner, by the window, and lay down flat on it. Breathing heavily, in and out. Staring up at the blazing blue sky . . .

Rowena stood over her engineer, looking at the monitor with him.

'OK. Here comes the server rush. We're ready, though. Vusical goes live on TechCrunch and Google Play in three, two, one . . .'

The screen flashed. TechCrunch, the biggest tech site in the world, was running its interview. But the photo of Rowena laughing at the camera was small. The main shot was of the homescreen of her new video streaming app, Vusical.

Vusical is MTV meets Amazon – right in your phone. Is this the next Spotify?

Rowena clenched her fist. 'The next Spotify! It's perfect. Could have written it myself.'

She hastily started to read the article.

'Wow – downloads – I can't even count them. We're shooting up the charts. Wow. This is going to number one on the app store,' said her engineer. 'Look at those hits! Look at that number!'

Rowena Krebs is one of the only record execs ever to hit the Rock 'n' Roll Hall of Fame – and one of the only women to top a dying and cut-throat business. Recently terminated for cause by Musica

Records, which she helmed for twenty years, Krebs appeared to have gone silent. But she is still pumping up her jam – and that of millions of others. TC have the exclusive on Vusical, a streaming music video app with an amazing UX that has done licensing deals with all the major labels – except her old employer.

'We hope to add Musica in soon,' Krebs says. 'Perhaps Miles Industries will be ready to talk business.'

Vusical combines instant commerce with video streaming. 'You can buy a record, tour tickets or a T-shirt,' Krebs says. 'We take a small percentage and give the rest back to the artist. We don't charge for data either, and we provide user channels. There's great functionality with Pinterest.'

TC has tested Vusical. It's content-rich and free to users, and we think it rocks. Krebs calls it 'MTV for mobile' and she may well be right. Slideshow of functions below the jump.

'People are buying it. People are streaming,' the young guy said. 'Wow. Look – purchases. So much stuff, man. Oh my God.' He turned away from his monitor and looked up at Rowena. 'I'd say you have a big launch on your hands here. Big.'

'Mr Miles.' Anna-Maria raised her voice.

Conrad was in crisis mode. His personal lawyers flanked him in the boardroom. The company's lawyers, sweating miserably, were on the opposite side of the table. Falling over themselves to pledge how much they hated doing this, how little they wanted to be here.

'You should voluntarily step aside, sir. To clear your name.' Maurice Katz was almost pleading. 'Miles Industries is a public company, and the SEC rules are clear—'

'It's *Miles* Industries. It's mine. This is a set-up,' Conrad barked. His voice was hoarse. Joanna had called him about thirty times, the stupid bitch. She was staying in the apartment. Good. Divorcing her, disassociating himself, that would be step one.

'Better to say I was joking with the reporter and the financials are sound . . .'

'American Magazines is in crisis. Half the reporters quit for Topaz Rossi's venture. The other half are now walking out. The assets there are losing their value . . .'

'So fucking what. Same with Musica. They're just shells. I could write the whole thing off tomorrow. Our assets *dwarf* those two.'

'Stock is sinking, sir. Our stock. Miles Industries stock. The market anticipates lawsuits, anti-trust . . . Sir, your own net worth, your portfolio . . . it's suffering every minute you stay . . .'

'I don't give a damn. This will blow over. You're a goddamned *kid*.' He hated everyone. 'It's *my* company. The little startups—'

'The markets are loving Vusical. That one's a home run already. Venture capitalists are begging to fund a major round. There's chatter all over the wire. And *American Red* is already getting traffic that puts it in the BuzzFeed league. Not quite there yet, but it's day one; she has the magic touch,' said Richard Jackson, his strategic officer. 'Mr Miles, their two companies are going to be bigger than American Magazines or Musica Records. But the difference is, they aren't employees. They *own* these.'

'Mr Miles!' Anna-Maria almost shouted, desperately.

'How much will they make?' Miles demanded.

'In the hundreds of millions is a good possibility, if the content stays strong. With Vusical that's a given; she has licences. With *American Red*, Rossi needs to produce, but the numbers are already big enough for her to do a round and hire the best reporters.' He added lamely, 'I'm sorry.'

'That's enough.' The voice now was male, deep. Miles looked up. Two burly men in cheap suits had shoved their way past his assistant and were showing their IDs.

'Federal agents. Mr Miles, we need you to come with us, please.'

* * *

It was a relatively small media room, but it was absolutely packed. The press conference was announced at three, and by five, there was no room for even one more camera or crouching reporter. Fashion, rock, tech, business, and plain news channels all wanted to cover it.

The meteoric spread of Vusical was headline news in major papers. Magazines' online editions were obsessed with *American Red*. And the mainstream press was desperate to hear about the arrest of Conrad Miles.

Bang on time, the doors opened and Rowena and Topaz walked in, together. They were laughing, like they'd just shared a joke outside. They were beautiful. Confident. Successful. The ultimate career women. And now they were doing it on their own.

Cameras rolled and photographers snapped. There were audible sighs of pleasure from the reporters. This was such a good story.

'Topaz, Rowena – why are you giving this conference together? Was this planned?'

Rowena leaned forward. 'Of course it was planned. What, you think it's a coincidence that Vusical and *American Red* launched on the same day?'

There was laughter, shouting of questions.

'Topaz, Topaz! Did you set Conrad Miles up?'

She shrugged. 'My star reporter, Leo, asked him a few questions on the record and taped his replies. It's pretty old-fashioned. It's called journalism.'

'When did you know that Conrad Miles had been arrested?'

'When I read it on the front page of *American Red* at two thirty-one this afternoon,' Rowena said.

'Did you orchestrate that too?'

'We're not the Federal government.'

'What do you say to Miles Industries' statement that their company is more than one man and that this is a stage-managed soap opera?'

Topaz and Rowena looked at each other and laughed again. Then Topaz leaned back in her chair, and, to a flurry of camera shutters clicking, put one arm around her best friend's shoulder.

'Tune in next week,' Rowena replied. 'We're only just beginning.'

Acknowledgments

To Imogen Taylor, for her deft hand and steady advice – she is a brilliant editor, who allowed me to go out on the same high I came in on. To Rosie De Courcy, who took a chance and made me a Career Girl in the first place. To Georgina Moore, Jane Morpeth, Amy Perkins, and all the staff at Headline Books and Orion for bringing creativity and magic to my books, and to all the titles they work on – stories are collaborations. To all my readers, who have come with me on this incredible roller-coaster ride of strong women and even stronger men, of Cinderellas who wave their own wands, girls for whom ambition will never be a dirty word, women who play to win.

To Barbara Kennedy Brown and Jacob Rees-Mogg, my dearest friends. And to Governor Schwarzenegger, the all-conquering, my inspiration since I was a teenage girl. Your friendship is the greatest honour. Let's not talk about that *Predator* poster.

Most of all to Peter Mensch. Twenty plus years and we're still on the ride. You once taught me to love my work so much I would look forward to Mondays. In your arms I look forward to each fresh sunrise.

'The sun is high in the sky, and God is on our side.'

Onwards and upwards.